138X 3/01 ✓ S/02
156X 1/09 ✓ 1/09

ALSO BY RICHARD NORTH PATTERSON

The Lasko Tangent
The Outside Man
Escape the Night

PRIVATE SCREENING

PRIVATE SCREENING

RICHARD NORTH PATTERSON

VILLARD BOOKS · NEW YORK · 1985

Library of Congress Cataloging in Publication Data
Patterson, Richard North.
  Private screening.
  I. Title.
PS3566.A8242P7 1985   813'.54   85-40185
ISBN 0-394-54275-4

Manufactured in the United States of America
9 8 7 6 5 4 3 2
First Edition

For my mother and father,
Marjorie and Richard Patterson,
and for my daughter and son,
Shannon and Brooke,
with much love, and gratefulness for my luck in having them

PROLOGUE

PHOENIX

THE KIDNAPPING

APRIL 7

From a distance, the players could have been anyone; two figures flailing soundlessly at an invisible ball.

The court was a green rectangle in a crevice of the Napa Valley. For half a mile the terrain swept downhill toward them. A sequence of gullies and rises covered with low green brush, it resembled a sea of heather which swelled to pine-covered ridges miles beyond the court. At odd intervals, oaks cast late-afternoon shadows from the west. Between them, two men with semiautomatic weapons crept toward the tiny figures in white.

They loped, bent to the brush for cover, traversing the gullies and rises in a deadly zigzag forward. As minutes passed, the eye would lose them, find them, lose them again: with each rise they reappeared, but smaller, closer to the court. The only constant was the players, heedless as children.

The men disappeared in a wrinkle thirty feet from courtside. There was a last few seconds' peace. Charging to the net, one player raised his arms in a comic gesture of victory.

The two gunmen burst onto the court.

The players stopped; their masked invaders faced them, a pantomime of indecision.

Suddenly a white van appeared at courtside. Hooded and armed, its driver moved toward the four waiting figures. Without hurry, the new protagonist raised his curious-shaped weapon, and then announced to those who watched him, "I am Phoenix. . . ."

Tony Lord turned up his television, uncertain of what he was seeing.

Deep yet slurred, the taped voice was like a record played too slowly. "For the next eight days, through Satellite News International, you will participate in all I do. . . ."

The picture changed abruptly.

In close-up, Lord recognized the two players as Colby and Alexis Parnell.

He stared at them in disbelief. Instinctively, Parnell moved to shelter his wife from the camera; the gesture was touching and pathetic, a moment from a Chaplin film.

The new angle was that of Phoenix.

"Three days ago, I captured Stacy Tarrant's personal manager, John Damone. Tonight, as you can see, I've taken Alexis Parnell. Tomorrow, I will broadcast my first demand to Stacy Tarrant and Colby Parnell by satellite, for them to answer as you watch on Satellite News International. . . ."

The two armed men moved toward Alexis. Turning to the camera, Parnell mouthed across the tennis net, "Take *me*."

"On television, you will see whether this wealthy newspaper magnate and famous rock star care for the people closest to them as much as for their privilege. And then you will join me as their jurors. . . ."

Lips closing, Parnell watched one gunman bind Alexis's hands as the other held his weapon to her temple. She looked stunned yet perfect, a well-coiffed mannequin; Lord could feel her shock.

"My intentions are unprecedented: a trial for social justice viewed by millions, with Colby Parnell and Stacy Tarrant as defendants, and the lives of those they love at stake.

"No one will stop this electronic trial before its verdict, or rescue my hostages. No one can find the place where I have taken them or track my frequency to its source. No one should try: this place is not only protected by armed guards but by dynamite set to detonate on intrusion, and my pulse is monitored by an electrocardiograph wired to plastic explosives. If my heart stops beating, it will trigger an explosion within fifteen seconds, blowing Damone and Alexis Parnell to pieces. Their lives depend on me alone, and *you*. . . ."

Astonished, Lord watched the two hooded men push Alexis toward the van.

"John Damone will die unless Stacy Tarrant can persuade you to pledge five million dollars, through a unique and public act of selflessness which I will disclose on my first broadcast, tomorrow night. . . ."

The van's rear door opened. Stumbling, Alexis fell beside it, scraping her knee on gravel. Reflexively, she tried to touch the scrape, then remembered that her hands were bound.

"As for Alexis Parnell, in the days that follow you will judge her husband's televised compliance with my demands. Then, on the seventh day of her captivity, you will cast an advisory vote through SNI as to whether she will live or die. . . ."

As the lens moved in, Alexis looked up at it.

"And on the final day you will witness her release or execution—live."

Silver-blonde mane glinting in the sun, Alexis Parnell stared from Lord's television. When the picture froze, there were tears in her eyes. Beneath her face appeared the caption "Courtesy of SNI."

"Mother of God," Lord murmured involuntarily, and then Alexis vanished.

The weekend anchorwoman began speaking in her actress's crisp staccato:

"The shocking film you've just witnessed was found with Colby Parnell early this morning after the terrorists left him, bound but unharmed, in the pasture of a Sonoma County farm. With it was an audiotape in which the so-called Phoenix threatened to execute Parnell's wife, Alexis, if he did not ensure its broadcast over SNI. The terrorists further claimed to be holding John Damone, manager of singer Stacy Tarrant, who was taken late last week from his Los Angeles home. And now the communications magnate and the feminist superstar of rock must wait with millions of others for the broadcasts which 'Phoenix' claims are coming.

"What makes this even more extraordinary is that the Parnells and Stacy Tarrant have suffered prior tragedy. The Parnells' son, Robert, vanished from their Tahoe cabin in a 1968 kidnapping, while Tarrant's close relationship with presidential aspirant James Kilcannon ended in his assassination here last June by Vietnam veteran Harry Carson. . . ."

Her words became the narrative for a clip of Stacy Tarrant. It was a file film, Lord saw at once, taken as she'd left the courthouse. Face drawn as he remembered, she entered the limousine without speaking or looking at anyone.

"Miss Tarrant has not appeared in public since testifying at Carson's highly controversial trial. . . ."

Lord's telephone rang. Hitting the off button, he went quickly to the kitchen and answered.

The downstairs guard sounded harried. "There's a camera crew in the lobby, Mr. Lord—something about 'Phoenix.' "

It took Lord a moment to react. "Put them on."

"Tony? Tom Isaka, Headline News."

"If I'd known you were coming, Tom, I'd have invited you."

"We went by your wife's—she said you'd just left off your son."

Lord could feel Marcia's bitter triumph in passing on what she had come to hate. "Ex-wife. Frankly, I don't like people knowing where I live."

"Why so rigid?"

Lord considered hanging up. "Because I got sick of Tarrant and Kilcannon's admirers calling to say what they'd do to my son *before* they dumped his body in the bay. Look, I just saw your newscast—there's nothing I can add to *that*."

"But UPI quotes the president as saying that defenses like your Carson case encourage 'this unprecedented act of terror.' Considering that Parnell, Damone, *and* Stacy Tarrant all figure in your career—"

"Tell me," Lord cut in, "can this mutant really broadcast?"

"With smarts, and equipment like they used for Carson's trial." The Damone, *and* Stacy Tarrant all figure in your career—"

"He'll threaten to kill both hostages if they don't. And you'll run their film clips, I imagine."

"It's news, Tony."

"Not with my help. Enjoy." Lord hung up.

For a time, his thoughts drove him to the window, staring out at stucco houses colored the pink and white of Portofino; the slim masts of boats in harbor; the azure bay specked with sails and flashes of sunlight through the Golden Gate. But this beauty seemed unreal, a deception.

Turning, Lord saw Christopher's toys still scattered through the apartment. Distractedly, he began to pick up metal cars.

This televised extortion of celebrities—an eight-day race against a public execution to ensure that millions watched—could transmute terrorism by succeeding. And the mind which conceived it had secured the perfect victims: Stacy and Parnell must feel they'd awakened from a recurring nightmare, to find it real.

Putting Christopher's cars away, Lord wandered to the bathroom.

Two razors lay on the sink. Only one had blades. During the Carson trial, when Lord had still been married to Marcia, Christopher had shaved with him to give them time together. It had become a ritual: Christopher had stood next to him in solemn imitation, pushing lather around his face with a bladeless razor. But now he was too old for such pretending, Christopher had announced this weekend—he was a baseball player.

Lord put one razor in a drawer, and closed it.

That left Christopher's cot, and the second mitt which Lord had bought him.

Putting the cot away, Lord contemplated the mitt. Since the divorce, it had been Lord's superstition that to put away Christopher's last toy was to put away Christopher. He left the mitt where it was.

Fuck *her*, he thought.

When the phone rang again, he was walking toward his television.

This time it was Cass, demanding, "Have you seen that film? UPI keeps calling. . . ."

"I've seen it." Lord realized that in her three years as legal assistant and friend, this was only the second time he had heard Cass shaken. "I hope this lunatic won't kill them. . . ."

"You *do* know what the president said."

"Yes. Has he brought on the usual death threats?"

"No—not that."

"What is it?"

He heard her exhale. "Stacy Tarrant left her number with the service."

Lord looked out the window. Finally, he answered, "It's a joke, Cass."

"I called information. She's not listed, naturally, but it's a Malibu exchange. That's where she's been holed up since you and Harry drove her into exile, as *People* magazine would have it."

Lord was silent.

"Tony? Let me give you the number, just in case."

Lord wrote it down. "Anything else?"

"Only one." Her tone was flat. "Larry Parris called from Hollywood. He says you'd better sell film rights to the Carson case before 'Phoenix' makes him passé. He's quite concerned that what with your divorce, Harry's been 'bad luck' for you, moneywise."

"Tell him luck is a talent."

"He also thinks he can get Jaclyn Smith as Stacy Tarrant."

Lord now remembered Stacy as he had asked his final question at the trial. "She doesn't look like Tarrant."

"Nobody looks like Tarrant."

"Then maybe he should try Jodie Foster."

She spoke more gently. "Feeling lousy, aren't you?"

Lord could hear her concern. "You're a nice person, Cassie. I love you, in my funny way."

"Ah, honey, if only you weren't a boy. . . ." She waited a moment. "I can't help feeling sorry for her, now."

Through the window, dusk fell like pink powder on a gray-blue bay. Closer, in the attic of a brown Victorian, Lord saw the sudden glow of someone switching on a television; he imagined this repeating in homes across the country. Finally, he said, "And I can't sell those film rights."

"I know."

Cass rang off.

Disconnecting the telephone, Lord walked to the living room and turned on SNI.

They were running the other film of Stacy, as he had known they would.

Preparing for the trial, Lord had studied it perhaps twenty times. But cross-examination, when he had forced her to watch with him, was the last time he had seen it. Kilcannon lay wounded on the stage; as the lens closed in, Stacy bent her face to his. Her lips moved, and then Kilcannon's. She looked up, beseeching help, into the eye of the camera.

With Carson's life at stake, Lord had asked her if his act seemed rational. But neither of them, he understood now, had truly known the answer.

Once more, SNI began to run the kidnapping.

Lord returned to the kitchen. The terrorist's words pursued him like the voice of a fun-house monster: "I am Phoenix. . . ."

It troubled Lord that he was already used to the name.

"John Damone will die unless Stacy Tarrant can persuade you to pledge five million dollars, through a unique and public act of selflessness which I will disclose on my first live broadcast, tomorrow night. . . ."

At that moment, Lord was certain that the hostages would not be rescued.

Reconnecting the phone, he dialed the number Cass had given him.

"Hello." A woman, answering on the second ring.

"Stacy?"

"Yes?"

"This is Tony Lord."

Silence. "I wasn't sure you'd call."

Lord recognized the voice now, smoky and a little low. It was so bizarre that, in his discomfort, he almost laughed. "It really *is* you."

"It's really me."

Her tone was cool. "About Damone," he said. "I'm sorry."

"I suppose you are." That was meaningless, and meant to be. "I want to see you."

Lord paused. "Are you sure it's really me you want?"

She ignored that. "He's televising tomorrow night. Can you come?"

The tape of Phoenix echoed from Lord's living room: "And on the final day you will witness her release or execution—live. . . ."

"I'll come," Lord answered. "You knew that."

PART 1

STACY TARRANT

THE CONCERT

JUNE 2, THE PREVIOUS YEAR

1

Lying in bed, Stacy Tarrant felt a stranger in her own city.

Jamie dressed in silent concentration. With the drapes closed, their suite was a collage of all her other mornings on the road. Running for president had begun to seem so much like rock 'n' roll that she was living in a time warp; in fifteen hours, for the first time in a year, she would face twenty thousand people she already feared.

"Fuck this," she announced, put on her glasses, stalked naked to the window, and jerked open the drapes.

It was 6:00 A.M.

A dawn-lit haze made the tangled freeways look like the map of a mirage. Turning from the mirror, Jamie bantered, "It's Los Angeles, all right. But what does it mean?"

Stacy smiled. "I'm more curious about where we're going."

Behind her, she felt him summoning Senator James Kilcannon, slim and tailored and quick. "On a magical mystery tour of Los Angeles, San Diego, San Francisco, Sacramento, and San Francisco again, for Alexis Parnell's cocktail party and the rock 'n' roll spectacular which will finance next Tuesday's triumph. I hope." The last words, closer and softer, were followed by a kiss on her neck. "As if my boyish charm weren't sufficient, you're about to make me the Democratic nominee for president."

He sounded rueful, Stacy thought. Half-teasing, she answered, "Isn't that what you expected when we met?"

"You told me you wouldn't sing then," he parried gently. "And the circumstances were distracting."

Turning, she touched his face. "Why the Mona Lisa smile?" he asked.

She hesitated. "I guess I was thinking that people like us get the lives we ask for."

His eyes were bright with irony and understanding. "But then nothing's perfect," he said lightly. "Nothing, and no one." Kissing her, he went to meet the aides already waiting in the next room, to plan his day.

Suspended between present and past, Stacy stared out at Los Angeles.

She had loved it since she had driven there with John Damone—a kid singer, her first single just released, who had never heard of James Kilcannon. "The freeway is forever," a disc jockey had proclaimed as her beat-up Volvo joined a river of people on the move. She had begun tailgating and braking, shifting and accelerating, and as she'd hit Beverly Hills still high on the challenge, rows of palm trees seemed to float and vanish in the shimmering subtropic light. The image of a mirage had come to her then, and over time she had seen Los Angeles as a deceptive Oriental city and its absence of center as a metaphor: you could drive the maze for years, searching for the place where you could make things happen, but it kept moving behind some palm tree in a canyon you couldn't find. Yet, that first day, she had felt that *they* would find it, she and Damone— passing a convertible at the West Hollywood line, her voice had come from someone else's radio.

It had been the first time. Stacy had pulled over to the side, and realized she was close to crying.

She had been twenty-five then, and had written the song when she was seventeen, a thousand crummy clubs ago. "We've worked so hard," she'd murmured.

And one year later, when she had come back from her first exhausting concert tour to realize that she was making more money than God, she'd found a Spanishy-looking house in the West Hollywood hills so outrageous in its campiness that she'd grinned just walking through it: a bar modeled as an English pub with slot machines; a sunken bathtub with a bidet next to the sauna; Greek columns surrounding the pool. By the time she and Damone had found the black bedroom with mirrors she had been laughing out loud. "Looks like a wet dream from Walt Disney," he'd remarked, and Stacy had decided to buy it on the spot. She'd moved her piano and all her sound equipment into the mirrored bedroom and stuck two palm trees by the pool so she could write songs under them. And now her face was as famous as her voice, and the city of mirages was her home. It disoriented her to stare at it from Jamie's suite.

She had met him four years later, with her third album number one, and her time so consumed by writing and touring that Stacy had wondered if she'd killed the rest of her. And then Damone had called to announce with exaggerated reverence, "Senator James Kilcannon wants to meet you."

That strangers called because they both were famous had no longer startled or impressed her. "He wants money, right?"

"He wants you to sing—the way the law works *you* can only give a thousand bucks, but by packing an arena you can raise four hundred thousand more."

"But why would I *want* to?"

"Shall I tell him that?"

She thought a moment. "I will."

But James Kilcannon had surprised her.

Stacy had been used to meeting politicians so determined to project warmth that it felt like she'd been mugged. But an air of amusement about Kilcannon suggested that he held part of himself back; this hint of complexity had appealed to her. His hazel eyes had an iris so much wider than the normal that they seemed to absorb everything around him, yet his fine sculpted face made him look impossibly young to be president. "You're wondering what I want from you," he'd said. "Besides thirty seconds as a gossip item."

They were having lunch at Harry's Bar. Like other things in Los Angeles, its original was elsewhere; one difference from Hemingway's Florence haunt was the faces turned to watch them. Smiling, Stacy answered, "I'm just curious how you'll rationalize it."

"Simply. I want to be president and I think I need you to do that."

"I don't believe that. And I don't believe you do."

"I'm afraid I do, though. Six months ago, I came to see you in Washington. People who waited for hours to hear you sing wouldn't cross the street to vote for me or anyone."

"It's because they can feel things without being used."

"Stacy, it's because there are two Americas now, and the one you reach doesn't respond to words or ideas, but to sound and pictures—film, TV, video games, music. I don't like this, but I'm not responsible for them— you are." His face was keen with challenge. "I wonder if it's enough to let them make you famous because you're a beautiful woman who can sing."

She tilted her head. "If you're trying to make me feel guilty, skip it. I've worked too hard."

"Then you've achieved something," he answered crisply, "for yourself. But if people like you don't ask their fans to commit to the world they live in, we'll end up with a generation so passive and easily manipulated that the next Hitler could stage the Holocaust as a miniseries."

She gave him a comic look of skepticism. "You're running to keep Hitler off of MTV?"

"I'm running for things *you've* said you care about—like women's rights, for openers." Shrugging, he finished in a throwaway tone. "And because I can't imagine being dead unless I'm president first."

Suddenly, she wanted to communicate with him, not just fence. "Does needing it that much ever scare you?"

For an instant he looked so vulnerable that Stacy knew she'd caught him by surprise. "Does it you?" he asked.

"It sets you apart," she answered softly, "to try and do what other people can't. It doesn't help that you never quite know why they want to be with you."

As Kilcannon glanced down, she noticed his lashes were unusually long. "Stacy, I'm not asking you to sing, all right?"

"Then what do you want?"

"Something more, I think." Looking up again, he asked quietly, "Are you free?"

There was no missing it. After a time, she said, "I can be."

As they left, Stacy realized they made a striking couple.

Later, as he held her in the dark, she wondered why it had happened. "Stacy?" he murmured.

"Yes?"

"I really *did* like your concert."

Stacy laughed aloud. "So you *are* going to ask me to sing."

"Not after this." His voice softened. "What I want now, is to see you."

For two years he had done that, in fragments stolen from his race for president or jammed between her tours. For weeks he'd be a face on her television; then they would be lovers on the Baja. They'd rented a house there. Mornings they would swim, or run the beach. In the afternoon, hiding from the savage brightness, they would make love. He read poetry to her, Yeats and Dylan Thomas. Sometimes Stacy sang new songs she'd written as he listened, thoughtful. Her reasons for performing seemed to fascinate him—as if, perhaps, he saw himself reflected. Besides Damone, he was the man with whom she talked most easily.

"How is it for you?" Jamie asked her. "Onstage."

They were sitting at a white wooden table overlooking the ocean; their bottle of Chardonnay was half empty.

"It's getting harder," she said finally. "They expect so much now."

"You never use drugs?"

"It's safer to depend on myself." Stacy shrugged. "Sometimes, before a show, I don't feel too great."

Jamie gazed out at the ocean. "Do you know why you keep doing it?"

Stacy wondered how to explain this. "When I write a song," she said, "it's still not finished. It's only when I can take something that doesn't exist outside me, and put myself out there to give it to other people, that I feel complete. There's nothing I've ever felt as strong as that." Speaking this, she realized how much it scared her. "Sometime, I won't have that anymore. Maybe they'll stop coming. Maybe, some night, I won't step through the curtain."

"And if you can't, then who will you be?"

She turned to him. "I've never really known."

Jamie reached out, brushing the hair back from her face.

Afterward she lay on his shoulder. When he spoke, it was almost to himself. "All that effort, Stacy. But what does it mean?"

She did not answer. He never asked this again—not of what she did.

This silence embraced his campaign. Away from him, she followed it, until at times she could not help but wish to be part of what he did. But he seldom spoke to her of his ambitions; she began sensing that he wished to hold them separate. The campaign was a void between them. She did not know what happened to him there. He never asked for help.

But she could tell that it consumed him. He would loll in an armchair, looking at the Baja sea; suddenly the look would grow hooded. Then, as if feeling her thoughts, he would laugh at himself. "AWOL again," he would say, and take her hand.

They kept the press away. It did not matter if his reason for this reticence was politics; she did not wish to speak of him to others, even to Damone. He learned to ask when Jamie was coming, and never call. His only comment was a question, "Has he asked you to sing yet?"

"He never will."

"No? That's good, then. If that's what you want."

"What do you mean?"

Damone's smile was no smile at all. "I just wonder if he isn't teasing you a little."

Jamie won in New Hampshire, and then Florida and Massachusetts, and did not ask. For those three months she did not see him. In mid-May, when his campaign came to California, only one man stood between him and the Democratic nomination, and his life seemed more vivid than her own.

Ten days before the primary, after a day campaigning in five different cities, Jamie spent the night with her.

She was shocked by the change in him. On television, he seemed vital and triumphant. Now it was as if the cameras had bled him. He was pale and too thin; there were new crow's-feet at the corner of each eye, the first flecks of gray at his temples.

"You look like hell," she said.

He stretched out on her sofa, watching the eleven o'clock news like a tired husband about to fall asleep. "They say people over forty earn their own faces. Today's my forty-third birthday."

Not to have known this troubled Stacy. She went to the kitchen, popped a bottle of French champagne, and brought it back on a tray with two glasses. Jamie had leaned forward. A film clip of his opponent was on television, reading a speech to a group of Jaycees; woodenly, he muffed the opening joke his gag writer had inserted. Jamie watched with something close to sympathy. "Never violate your own nature," he murmured.

"Happy birthday."

Turning, he saw the champagne, and smiled wryly. "At my age, that'll put me to sleep."

"You're allowed."

They sat at opposite ends of the sofa, feet touching. Jamie stared into the glass.

"What's wrong?"

He did not look up. Finally, he said, "I'm going to lose, Stacy."

"How can you know that?"

He angled his head toward the screen. "That's going to kill me. Right at the end."

"You're being awfully Delphic." As he hesitated, Stacy saw that his fingers were swollen from shaking hands. "Tell me about it—all right? I'm tired of not knowing."

Jamie sipped champagne. "All right," he said at length. "The simple truth is that I'm ten days short of money." The bitterness in his voice surprised her. "In 1980 no one west of New Jersey had ever heard of me. For four straight years I've flown coast to coast shaking hands and begging money until sometimes I didn't know where or who I was. Now all that work has come down to California—whoever wins here wins the nomination. Three weeks ago I was ten points behind in a state so large and complex that I'll live or die on television. Since then I've spent four hours daily on the phone extracting checks from the last contributors in America to pledge the thousand-dollar max, pumped it all into TV spots, and cut his lead to five percent with seven undecided." For the first time, he looked directly at her. "That finished me, Stacy. I'm broke."

Stacy tasted her champagne. "How much do you need?"

"Do you mean, Is that why you came?"

"That's not what I asked."

He closed his eyes. "Four hundred thousand," he answered. "The exact amount Damone told me you could raise by singing, two years ago."

Stacy studied the lines of his face. "Well," she said, "next time you can pay for dinner."

When his eyes opened, she was smiling at him. "I can't let you lose. Not if I can help it."

Jamie could not smile. Taking his hand, Stacy realized the palm was damp.

"I'd love to have seen *that* performance," Damone said when Stacy phoned him the next morning. "Did he suffer a little?"

"Look, John, I called to ask how long it'll take to put together a show."

"Hasn't he noticed you haven't sung lately?"

"He's running for president, dammit."

"So you didn't bother telling him that you came back from the European tour ten pounds lighter, 'cause you started getting sick."

"No," she shot back, "because I want to do this."

There was silence. "He'll need it by next Friday to do him any good."

"Can you set it up?"

"At the Arena, in San Francisco." Damone laughed without humor. "I reserved the date three months ago."

Stacy hung up.

That night, Jamie telephoned from Sacramento; in the background, a PA system called out flights. "Come out with me," he said.

"Campaigning?"

"Uh-huh." He sounded fresh and cheerful. "It'll set you apart from the rest of my contributors."

"I don't know, Jamie. The press . . ."

"If you're going to do this for me, I want you to be a part of it."

Stacy realized that this was what she wished to hear. "Okay," she said. "Where do I meet you?"

Two days later, their picture was on the front page of the L.A. *Times*.

It had happened so quickly that she still hadn't absorbed it. The first day out, when the secretary of the interior had remarked that "if you've seen one redwood, you've seen them all," some reporter asked her opinion. "If he'd seen even *one*," she'd snapped, "he'd know how small he is." It was instinct; she had answered because it felt good. But the media had loved it—she gave them glamour and a fresh angle, and Jamie had not seemed to mind.

Now, in their suite forty-five stories above Los Angeles, Stacy tried to analyze how she felt about it.

The day before they'd swooped down from the Central Valley on a campaign high, with the press pool drinking and laughing and each crowd bigger than the one before. Jamie started throwing away his speeches; surrounded by migrant workers, he joked and quoted Yeats and Robert Kennedy, and they cheered with an intensity which surprised her. By the time the plane reached Los Angeles and they scrambled to the limousine, she sensed that Jamie really could be president. And the crowds were there for him again, packed between the stucco apartments and corner groceries and whiskey signs in English and Spanish, slowing the limo to a walk. "They can't *see* me," Jamie had murmured. Oblivious to danger, he opened the door and got up on its hood as the crowd reached out to him. The moment had a terrible beauty; Stacy wished to turn from it, but could not. Above the bobbing, shouting heads, someone raised a "Stacy for Veep" sign. Grinning, Jamie pointed to it, and then the driver opened the sunroof. She stood without thinking, waving with the sun in her eyes as the crowd cried out, "Stacy . . ." She could no more see faces than in the darkness of a coliseum.

But she stood all the way to the hotel where Jamie was to speak. She was part of it now.

There were more signs for her. She was sitting at the head table when Jamie rose.

"You may remember me," he opened. "I'm Stacy Tarrant's warm-up act."

Stacy looked up in surprise.

In their cheers and laughter, Jamie smiled at her. Stacy thought he'd never looked younger.

Two hours later, in their hotel suite, his face looked slate-gray. His hand was swollen again.

"Stacy," one of his aides said, "your fans outside will keep him up all night."

"I can talk to them. . . ."

"Probably better to cool it. The security people will chase them off."

She glanced at Jamie.

Aides surrounded him. Someone had scrounged cold sandwiches; another had paid the hotel to keep its laundry going all night; on the television news, their motorcade looked like jump cuts from an action film. Jamie pointed at the screen. "A sixteen-hour day, and all that counts is thirty seconds."

"Looks good," someone told him. "A campaign on the move."

A red-haired aide shook his head. "It's too 'hot'—all those Latinos screaming at two celebrities. Joe Six-pack's not gonna get that at all."

"Screw him," Jamie murmured.

"It's okay," the first man assured him. "The last ads are all green lawns and shade trees. No music even, just actors and a voice. Lauersdorf's bringing one by in the morning for us to look at, so we can run 'em statewide after Stacy's concert."

Jamie's sad-faced California manager, Tim Sherman, came in with statistics from the nightly tracking. "Two hundred calls," he told Jamie. "Mostly to San Diego. The seniors are worried about Social Security, the women about war, and the under-twenty-ones about employment—they're getting close to graduation. Hit those in tomorrow's speeches, and I'll tell the TV people to look for that."

Jamie nodded.

Sherman stuffed the figures in his pocket. "About the cartop routine, you're not a bullfighter. I get sick thinking what could happen."

Jamie looked up. "No help for it, Tim."

His voice conveyed a second message. "Let's let the candidate get some sleep," Sherman announced, and suddenly they were alone.

"What do you make of all this?" Jamie asked.

"You're good." She hesitated. "Cynical, isn't it?"

"Practical," he amended. "Politics is the business of getting people to let you do a little of what you want. Even your songs are written for an audience, remember?"

"It's different, though."

"Is it?" He smiled quizzically. "Would they let you sing if no one came to see you? Would you still write?"

Stacy flicked the hair back from her forehead. "Maybe I just don't belong here. Some of your staff doesn't think so."

"They will tomorrow night." His tone lightened. "You're not worried about old Charlie McCarthy's 'Jamie Jagger' lines, I hope."

She smiled at Jamie's nickname for his rival, a former vice-president so mortgaged to his contributors that when he'd spoken at a candidates' dinner Jamie had whispered, "Watch closely—when they pull the strings, his lips move." But still she asked, "You don't think that hurts you?"

"Not in this state. In addition to the minorities and jobless, who wouldn't care if I were a hermaphrodite, I need young singles, single mothers, and white liberals—the ones who buy your albums in the millions. For those people, we belong together, and every time old Charlie appoints you 'secretary of stereo' you can hear them yawn from Berkeley to the Baja. He's guaranteed you'll pack them in, even on short notice." He examined his swollen hand. "Once you sing, we can buy the airtime to run my final spots statewide, and just maybe I'll get the thing I've wanted ever since I went to Congress."

Stacy studied him. "My being here—you've thought it all out."

He looked up with the tactile gaze which was part of his appeal. "Stacy," he said coolly, "I've thought everything out."

She waited a moment. "Even what might happen to you?"

His expression grew curious and a little distant. "Spiritually, or physically?"

"The motorcade. I agree with Tim—it scares me."

He shrugged. "It's the only time anyone really sees me."

"Instead of an image?"

"I like to feel there's a difference." He rose, heading for the bedroom. "Although at the moment . . ."

"There's a difference, Jamie. I saw it in the Baja."

"Quiet, wasn't it?" He turned in the doorway. "It got lonely without you. I thought that out, too."

Stacy smiled. "But what does it mean?"

He smiled back, and then his look grew serious. "That I'd have to start living with mixed motives, and that you've lived enough in public to accept them—and your own." He disappeared inside.

Stacy was not tired. But the day remained a jumble. When she went to the bedroom, Jamie was sleeping.

His hair was rumpled as a teenager's. Kissing his forehead, Stacy turned out the light.

When she woke again, it was not yet morning.

It took her a moment to realize where she was. Beside her, Jamie breathed evenly. She could not see his face.

In the darkness, Stacy began to search her memory for a song.

It was a trick she had learned on the road: when she was frightened of performing, or afterward, when she was strung out on her own adrenaline, she wrote to remember who she was and how she'd gotten there.

Lying next to Jamie, she remembered the first time she'd made love.

The boy had parked in the Berkeley hills; they'd looked across the bay toward San Francisco from his car. The city's luminescent patterns glinted as if refracted by a diamond; the Golden Gate was an arch of lights, its traffic two opposing streams of yellow. When she had been small, wrapped in a blanket between her parents, she would invent lives and destinations for the people on the bridge. At fifteen, the memory made her squeamish.

"I love you, Stacy." He moved closer. "I can make it good."

His eyes were wide as a rabbit's, so innocent that he might almost believe it. She took his face in her hands. "All I want is for you to be scared with me. It's okay if you are. I just don't want you pretending not to be. . . ."

Awakening, James Kilcannon had touched her.

Now, meeting with his aides, Jamie's voice came from the next room. Stacy stood in front of the window, alone.

That she could never quite lose herself with him, she thought, must be as much her fault as his.

For another moment, she was pensive. Then she turned from the morning light, and opened the notebook she wrote songs in.

"Scared with Me," Stacy scribbled for its title, and smiled at herself. Thirty-one, and still ripping off your life for lyrics.

Pausing, she wondered if *that* hadn't begun scaring her a little. Perhaps what had made her want to campaign, even more than Jamie's need, was that she needed to care for someone or something too much to sing it away. Too soon, and by surprise, her songs would be someone else's trivia question, and then she'd face Jamie's ironic catch-question, "But what does it mean?"

Beneath the title, she wrote its first lines:

> Please don't deceive me
> That the morning will show
> What it means to be lovers
> When our hearts cannot know . . .

Suddenly she recalled the morning after she'd made love to the boy.

She'd awakened to silence; somehow, she had felt her parents knew. Guiltily, she tiptoed from her room. In place of breakfast talk and clattering dishes, she heard their television.

Her parents were in front of it. She knelt beside them. "Robert Kennedy's been shot," her father said.

For a crazy instant, Stacy wanted to confess to him, so that Kennedy might live. "I'm sorry," she remembered blurting.

Stacy closed the notebook.

Nerves, she thought—less than twelve hours now. Stacy walked into the bathroom, glancing wryly at the thick glasses, the first hint of lines they magnified.

She showered, put in her contact lenses, and joined Jamie.

He was picking up the telephone as Sherman held an index card in front of him. "Why am I doing this?" he asked.

"A morale-boosting call from the candidate. Old man Parnell is an absolute reactionary and she's having this party anyway. Plus, she's a pipeline to new contributors."

The red-haired aide stepped forward. "I called one of our Bay Area people this morning. Some hotshot young lawyer has hold of a gay rights suit against Parnell and his paper."

Kilcannon glanced at Sherman. "Why didn't I know that?"

"*I* didn't know—anyway, we need the money and it's too late to change." Sherman gave the aide a pointed stare. "Maybe you can set up a meeting with some presentable gay leaders. *After* Stacy's concert."

Jamie looked from one to the other. Then he dialed, peering at the card. "I don't see any children."

Sherman nodded. "The son got kidnapped, remember?"

"Vaguely." His tone changed abruptly. "Alexis? This is James Kilcannon." Listening, Jamie laughed. "I'm just calling to thank you in advance. I know you're Colby's liberal conscience, and that's not easy work."

Catching Stacy's eye, Jamie made a grimace of self-dislike, then smiled into the phone. "Yes, I'm bringing her—she's *my* liberal conscience. . . ."

"Black coffee, Stace?"

She smiled up; Nat Schlesinger, Jamie's press secretary, had already learned what she liked. Of the people who surrounded them, she felt most affection for this rumpled, homely man who lived his life through Jamie. "Nat," she told him, "you're my home away from home."

As Nat beamed with pleasure, Jamie hung up. "What's in San Diego?" he asked Sherman.

"An old-folks hit. Sacramento's the day-care hit."

"What's this about?" Stacy murmured to Nat.

Nat bent closer. "What Tim calls a 'hit' is to go somewhere that makes a point in thirty seconds of airtime. If Jamie goes to a day-care center, people know by watching the news that he's for working parents." As the door opened, Nat looked up. "Here's one of the TV spots you're buying."

A man whose pin-striped suit cloaked too much bulk hustled in with a cassette. "Who's he?" she asked.

"The media buyer, Bob Lauersdorf. He negotiates for airtime in the media markets statewide—represents big private accounts like Procter & Gamble that pay top dollar year-round. With that kind of clout and a little of our money, he can stick Jamie's final spots right in the middle of 'Dallas.' " Nat's face clouded. "Your guy Damone—he's got things all put together, even security?"

He fidgeted with his navy-blue bow tie; Stacy remembered that he wore it whenever Jamie needed luck. "John can do anything," she assured him.

Lauersdorf stuck the cassette into the video player.

Jamie stood to one side of the screen, hands in his coat pockets. Stacy leaned forward.

On the screen, an older man lovingly painted the door to his white-frame house a sylvan green. As he added the final touch, a grandmotherly woman finished polishing the brass door knocker. Turning, their eyes met; in a husky voice, she said, "We brought five children through this door."

The man nodded sadly.

With agonizing slowness, the camera pulled back from them across a neatly tended lawn. As the old couple's hands linked, a "For Sale" sign appeared in front of them. Through this silent image, an actor's voice intoned, "Don't let them tarnish *your* golden years. Vote for James Kilcannon, for a safer tomorrow."

"Dynamite," the buyer enthused.

Jamie ruffled his hair. "Who was 'them'?" he asked bemusedly. "Termites?"

"Inflation; cutbacks in old age benefits; the opposition—"

"We have met the enemy . . ."

"And *them* ain't us." The buyer smiled. "When we pretested this, one old lady cried."

"But what does it mean?" Stacy murmured.

As Jamie turned to her, the buyer's smile looked pained. "Have you seen *his* ads?" he asked rhetorically. "The one where he takes his mongoloid granddaughter fishing and tells her about Medicare?"

Jamie was silent. "We'd better go," Sherman told him. "You're running for president, remember?"

For another moment, Jamie looked at her. "I'll call John," she told him softly. "He can pick me up in San Francisco for the sound check."

She did that. And then they were off, sweeping through a hotel lobby filled with cameras, smiling for the midday news.

2

Reaching into his duffel bag, Harry Carson felt the snub nose of the Mauser.

In his mind, Stacy finished singing "Love Me Now." From the darkness, the crowd screamed for more, until she beckoned to Kilcannon. As he stepped into the light, Carson raised his arm. But the revolver would not fire. He was paralyzed.

"Harry?"

Carson flinched. Moving his hand, he found the pack of cigarettes beneath his journal of poetry, and flipped it to Damone. Damone tapped the bottom, pulling out a cigarette with his lips. Even with the beard, Damone's face looked like hammered bronze.

"You all right?" Damone asked.

Carson realized he was sweating. "Just bored."

"That's why I hired you—to be chairman of the bored." Taking a drag, Damone watched the television he'd set down on the stage.

"There's too many amplifiers," Carson told him.

Damone didn't turn. "Leave the extras out till after the sound check. If we don't need 'em, I'll load the boxes back on the truck."

On the screen, Stacy was moving with Kilcannon through the lobby of some hotel. Beneath the blonde-brown curls, her green eyes seemed wary, reminding Carson of Beth. When her smile flashed, guileless and surprising, he looked away.

"Satellite News International will continue its live coverage of the Kilcannon campaign with a rally in San Francisco's Chinatown. . . ."

Switching it off, Damone turned to the crew. "Make sure the monitor's set up and working. I'm picking Stacy up at noon."

Carson lit a cigarette for his nerves.

Empty, the stage was an enormous concrete bunker. Four levels of catwalk rose from each side; banks of lights and colored cloth backdrops hung from the ceiling; the crew hauled beat-up metal boxes from the loading dock, footsteps echoing on the dirty wooden floor. They worked steadily, laconically. When they were finished, the lights would be lowered and angled to make the backdrops look like multicolored silk and the stage a bubble suspended in the dark, and then Stacy would appear in a blaze of spotlights.

"Golden Anniversary" Carson decided he would call the poem.

This morning, he'd read the lines he could not finish:

> Each year I remember you
> Hair golden, free to live
> Waiting for the camera
> His golden life to give. . . .

Carson closed his eyes.

Capwell's blood spurted into his hands, and then he was landing in Oakland. A newspaper said that it was June 2, 1970; Carson still could not remember the thirty-six hours before Capwell had died in his arms. He stared at his hands for blood.

The cigarette had burned to a nub. Carson looked up, and saw that Jesus, one of the sound men, watched him.

"You have some kind of problem, man?"

Jesus shrugged. "I was needing help with the sound."

Carson stubbed out the cigarette. "You want me to read your mind, Jesus, try moving your lips."

Sharp-eyed fucker. Opening a box, Carson stepped over the cords of the sound system as if they were trip wires and the amps could blow him to pieces. That the past bled into his present didn't scare him so much as that he couldn't control when it happened or remember why. And the part still missing in 'Nam had already cost him his kid.

He began unloading the box.

Beth's two-month-old postcard was in the duffel bag next to the Mauser, addressed to him care of Damone. Cathy was all right, she had written, and she'd found work as a cashier. It was postmarked Columbia, South Carolina, but Beth gave him no return address. She didn't want to see him again, she finished, and knew he had no money to help care for their daughter. That night Damone had slipped him ten bucks for a fifth of tequila.

Patching in the amp, Carson felt its sudden electronic current as a revolver in his hand. It surprised him; for a moment he did not know whether to associate this with past or future. Then he thought of the postcard.

Rising by instinct, he walked to the center of the stage.

The body lay behind him on the floor. Calmly, he began to follow the plan.

"Where you going, Harry?"

There was screaming; he did not even turn. "To pull more boxes off the truck."

They would catch him if he took the elevator. Moving toward the catwalk, he counted fifty feet.

Three flights of metal stairs down, ten steps each, and Carson reached the entrance to the loading dock. His motorcycle was there. Less than thirty seconds' time, he guessed. The adrenaline felt like a Dexedrine rush.

Mentally, he jumped onto the motorcycle and escaped into the darkness.

Hoisting another box, Carson took the elevator.

Once onstage, he walked to his duffel bag. Next to it lay the newspaper Damone had lent him, open to an inside page. It was dated June second; like someone memorizing words, Carson scanned the headline "Lord to Question Parnell in Gay Rights Suit" as he lit his cigarette.

3

Tony Lord felt the jury moving with him toward Colby Parnell.

He stopped for an instant, the way an actor uses stillness to dramatize what will come. In that moment, he was conscious of the judge's stare; the court reporter bent to his machine; his client's tautness; the heightened interest of the press; the jury poised to make its judgment. Then he stepped forward.

Parnell's wool suit, club tie, and neatly shined shoes seemed intended to remind himself of who he was. He touched two fingers to the handkerchief in his breast pocket.

"Good morning, Mr. Parnell."

Almost imperceptibly, Parnell leaned back. "Good morning."

"You've testified that my client's sexual preference did not influence your decision to approve his firing. Is that correct?"

"Yes. It is."

"My client was terminated last November, was he not?"

"Yes."

Lord moved to Parnell's left, so that the jury to the right of him could see the witness's expression and the movements of his body. "And you have also said that the specific grounds were his refusal to accept reassignment to a less important area than city politics."

Parnell folded his hands. "As presented to me by Mr. Halliburton, his editor."

"Did you ever discuss this situation directly with Mr. Cole?"

"I did not." Parnell touched one stem of his thick, horn-rimmed glasses. "I make it a point not to interfere in personnel judgments."

"You *are* the newspaper's publisher, aren't you?"

"Of course."

"And Mr. Cole asked to meet with you?"

"Yes." Parnell stopped, as if hoping for another question, and saw that Lord waited. "I didn't feel it would be a comfortable situation."

"Uncomfortable for whom? Mr. Cole?"

"For both of us." Parnell searched for a better answer. "And for me as an administrator."

"At the point that you declined to meet him, were you aware that Mr. Cole was homosexual?"

"Yes."

"How did you learn that?"

"Through a combination of circumstances." Parnell considered his fingernails. "I suppose the fact that his divorce involved allegations of homosexuality confirmed certain tendencies in his writing."

Lord cocked his head. "Define *tendency*, if you would."

Parnell tented his fingers to his lips, a new, unhappy expression making the gesture vaguely like prayer. Lord made his first instinctive judgment: Parnell disliked some aspect of the position he was in, but did not yet hold this against him. He decided not to raise his voice. "Was my question unclear?"

Parnell removed his glasses, cleaning them as he spoke. "What I detected was a concentration on so-called gay issues."

"Such as?"

"AIDS disease, the relative lack of gays on the police force or in city government, violent crime against homosexual men. One of Mr. Halliburton's complaints was that Mr. Cole had lost interest in other facets of his beat, as it were."

"Mr. Parnell, if I suggested that the gay population here in San Francisco is close to twenty percent, would you dispute that?"

Finishing his glasses, Parnell looked up. "No, sir."

"Larger than our Japanese community?"

"I suppose so."

"And yet two years ago a Japanese-American reporter on your newspaper ran a series of articles on the Japanese sent to internment camps during World War II. Did you fire him for lack of objectivity?"

"No, sir." Parnell sat straighter. "We initiated that series of articles."

"But not Mr. Cole's articles on the problems of gays?"

"That was his own initiative."

Lord paused as if something had just occurred to him. "Has it ever struck you, Mr. Parnell, that some nonobjective reporter should have worried about the Japanese a little sooner?"

"Objection." As three associates mimed rapt attention, John Danziger stood, white-haired and imposing. "Mr. Lord's so-called question is a spurious attempt to draw parallels that don't exist."

Watching Parnell, Lord saw that his pensive look had reappeared. Before Judge McIlvaine could do so for him, Lord responded carelessly, "I'll withdraw the question," then asked, "Mr. Halliburton had other complaints, did he not?"

"Yes, he did." Parnell became more forceful. "Inattention, and irregular hours."

"For how long?"

"The two or three months before his termination."

Lord paused, phrasing his next question with care. "Based on your own experience, would you consider such behavior as typical of someone facing a crisis within his family?"

Parnell blinked. "Objection," Danziger snapped.

"I'll rephrase it. Specifically, Mr. Parnell, would you consider such behavior typical of someone going through a crisis which had alienated him from his wife and threatened to deprive him of his only child?"

Parnell sat back, staring.

"The same objection." Danziger's voice rose. "My client is *not* a psychiatrist."

"Sustained."

"You never tried to determine the basis for Mr. Cole's alleged erratic behavior?"

Parnell shook his head. "As a publisher, I don't consider that my province."

The response was less stubborn than wounded. "And as a man?" Lord asked.

"Objection!" Danziger stepped forward. "I ask the court to forbid this subjective and thinly disguised harassment of my client."

Lord had never raised his voice.

Addressing McIlvaine, Lord underscored this for the jury. "My effort was not to distress Mr. Danziger," he said mildly. "But to move Mr. Parnell to reflect on whether there might be some reason he did not accord my client the understanding that he otherwise might be predisposed to give."

Leaning over the bench, McIlvaine raised an eyebrow. "Then you should ask him that straight out."

Moron, Lord thought. Smoothly, he answered, "Thank you, Your Honor." He knew that no one on the jury with a memory could have missed the tacit thrust of his last questions; when he looked back, Parnell was cleaning his glasses again, and there was dampness on his forehead. "Tell me, Mr. Parnell, has your newspaper ever knowingly hired a homosexual?"

Parnell put away the glasses. "We don't ask the sexual preference of our employees."

Lord moved closer. "Do you know if there are currently any homosexuals on your staff?"

"No, I don't."

"So if there *are* any, they've not told you?"

"I suppose not." Defiantly, Parnell added, "And I don't ask them, either."

"And they don't bring gay friends or partners to social functions at the newspaper?"

For the first time, Parnell looked angry. "I don't see why anyone should publicize what are private sexual matters."

"But don't you find it remarkable that in a city with a substantial and open gay community you don't know a single homosexual at *your* newspaper?"

"Remarkable? I don't know."

"Isn't the only fair conclusion that no homosexuals are hired, or that they're afraid to acknowledge it once they are?"

"That's an assumption I can't make—at least not that my newspaper's the reason."

"But the assumption you made on meeting Mr. Cole was that he was heterosexual."

Parnell hesitated. "He mentioned a wife and child. . . ."

"And when Mr. Cole's wife asserted his homosexual orientation in her efforts to gain exclusive custody of their daughter, your impression changed?"

"Yes."

"That was approximately June of last year."

"Yes."

"Before that Mr. Halliburton had promoted him several times."

"Yes."

"And you approved those promotions."

"On Mr. Halliburton's recommendation."

"When did you first notice Mr. Cole's 'lack of objectivity' concerning gay issues?"

"I don't recall. I remember discussing it with Mr. Halliburton."

"Before or after Mr. Cole's wife asserted that he was homosexual?"

"Afterwards, I believe."

"And then you noticed his so-called bias."

"Yes."

"When you hadn't noticed it before."

Once more Parnell removed his glasses, and wiped a smudge. "I suppose, Mr. Lord, that it simply hadn't crystallized."

"And what crystallized it was that Mr. Halliburton now wished to fire him."

Parnell nodded.

"I'm sorry, Mr. Parnell. We need an audible answer."

"Yes."

"And when you approved his dismissal, Mr. Cole asked to see you?"

"Yes."

"To discuss the problems he'd been having, and ask to keep his job."

"Yes."

"But you refused."

Putting on his glasses, Parnell looked away. "Yes."

Lord waited until Parnell glanced back at him. Quietly, he asked, "Because to meet with a homosexual would not have been 'comfortable' for you?"

Parnell's mouth opened slightly. "Objection," Danziger interrupted. "Asked and answered—Mr. Parnell has already testified that any discomfort on his part was administrative."

"Sustained."

But Parnell was watching Lord. With the intimacy he knew to be his gift, Lord walked slowly to the right-hand side of the witness box, so that the jury saw both his face and Parnell's. "Examining your conscience, Mr. Parnell, and understanding that what's at stake here is the career of a man who's already paid a great deal for being homosexual, can you swear to the jury that Mr. Cole's sexual preference played no role in the way you authorized his firing?"

Lord felt the jury leaning forward. Patting his handkerchief, Parnell murmured, "Yes."

Lord slowly extended one hand. "The jury, Mr. Parnell, is over there."

Parnell stared at his pointed finger. "Asked and answered," Danziger called out. "I object to these theatrics at my client's expense."

His associates nodded. But Lord did not bother to respond. Instead, he watched Parnell with a quizzical smile, silently asking that he face the jury.

"Mr. Lord?"

Lord let the silence hang a moment longer. Still facing Parnell, he responded, "I'll withdraw it, Your Honor. I think Mr. Parnell will be asking it of himself."

Parnell did not look at the jury, but at Lord.

"I think it's time for a recess," McIlvaine said hastily. "You're excused for now, Mr. Parnell." There was muffled sound from the press, and then Parnell left the courtroom.

As they filed out, several jurors looked quickly at Lord. But he walked back toward his client with the nonchalance of a professional.

Cole's smile was one of pained gratitude; that the formerly secret half of his life had made him see the underside of things was a reason Lord liked him. "Nice job," Cole murmured.

Lord shrugged. "Parnell's a decent man, in his way—at some point he realized that he didn't want to hang you. I just helped him to remember why."

"I doubt he enjoyed the reminder."

Cole's tone was dry. Despite the contrast between his slight jockey's body and Parnell's paunchy awkwardness, the degree to which his client's spruceness mirrored his antagonist's—even Cole's mustache seemed dry-cleaned—had moved Lord to ponder the relationship between obsessive neatness and inner turmoil. He put a hand on Cole's shoulder. "I also doubt Parnell will want to put either of you through any more."

"Settlement?"

"Possibly. And if we get your job and back pay then maybe you can win joint custody of your daughter." To lighten things up, Lord added, "You might even pay me—which is why I'm buying you lunch."

Cole flipped on his panama hat; it was the first careless gesture Lord had seen him make. "In that case," Cole answered, "I'll let you."

"Tony?" It was the bailiff. "Judge McIlvaine wants you in chambers."

"Is Danziger there?"

When the bailiff nodded, Lord turned to Cole. "Sorry, Jack. Think you can bring back a sandwich?"

"Nothing wrong, is there?"

"Doubt it—Danziger probably wants a recess to reassemble Parnell." Lord gave Cole some money, and went to the judge's door.

McIlvaine and Danziger looked up as if interrupted; Danziger's three acolytes had retreated to his limousine, the better, Lord assumed, to bill Parnell in comfort. "Come in, Tony," the judge boomed.

Noting Danziger's proprietary elbows on McIlvaine's desk, Lord sat so that the older man could speak to him only by turning from the judge. McIlvaine leaned forward. "John's requested a recess till Monday morning. I'm listening to any objections."

Lord feigned surprise. "On what grounds, John?"

Danziger had a heavy way of sitting which suggested that he ennobled a chair by settling his bottom into it, and to turn at all clearly annoyed him. "Mr. Parnell wishes to consider settlement."

"No point in that—unless he throws in my client's back pay. In addition to his job, of course."

Red mottling appeared on Danziger's face. Quickly, McIlvaine put in, "I'm sure John will convey your terms to Mr. Parnell," and looked to Danziger for approval.

"As an attorney"—Danziger spoke the word as if describing a separate race—"it's my ethical obligation to report any and all demands to my client."

"In that case," Lord said agreeably, "take all the time you need."

"Thank you," Danziger said to the judge. He rose from the chair in stages, nodded in Lord's proximate direction, and left.

McIlvaine motioned Lord to stay. "I don't think John cares for you," he said approvingly.

Lord looked grave. "You're a sensitive observer of human nature, Your Honor. I hope it's just that I'm kicking his ass."

McIlvaine raised one eyebrow, and then screwed his mouth into a bark of laughter. Lord thought it remarkable that any one man could look pious, cynical, good-humored, and corrupt all at once, when in fact he was only the last. Each part of McIlvaine's politician's face seemed dedicated to a separate function: the raised eyebrows signaling worldliness; the eyes wide with an acolyte's sincerity; the nose a red beacon of sociability; and a rubbery mouth that could stretch to cover all the emotional territory in between. When the mouth finished laughing, its owner said, "It *can* make cases harder to settle."

"Harder than losing?"

"No matter," McIlvaine said amiably. "But I do have a modest suggestion which may smooth the way to settlement, particularly where your client's future plans seem to rest on securing back pay."

Lord sensed that he would not like what was coming. "I can always use advice."

"Fine. Now, you embarrassed Colby Parnell this morning." McIlvaine raised a mollifying hand. "Perhaps unavoidably. But some gesture of respect between gentlemen . . ."

"A trial is mental combat, Your Honor. It's hard to strike too many grace notes."

"There are other places." McIlvaine cleared his throat. "Mrs. Parnell is hosting a party this evening."

Something, Lord knew, made this incredible suggestion in McIlvaine's interest. "A party?"

"Yes. For Senator Kilcannon."

All at once, Lord saw where this was heading. "A fund-raiser," he said in his flattest tone.

McIlvaine nodded. "She's quite an admirer of his, as are many of my classmates from USF. . . ."

You crafty buffoon, Lord thought: you want that charlatan to make you a federal judge.

"In fact, *they* seem to feel that James Kilcannon's extraordinarily capable. . . ."

Life tenure and a pension. All you have to do is help your friends raise money.

"And I'm sure you'd enjoy meeting him." The judge summoned a lascivious smile. "Not to mention his girlfriend, what's-her-name."

"Stacy Tarrant." The morning had turned ugly; only the remembered careless flip of Jack Cole's panama hat kept Lord from walking out. "Frankly, these affairs are a little much for me."

"Much?"

"Expensive." It was the truth, as far as it went: the money he had given Cole for lunch, borrowed from petty cash, left him five dollars pocket money for Christopher. "I've also promised my son I'd take him to the baseball game tonight. It's his first."

"There'll be others." McIlvaine rested both hands on his stomach. "How old are you, Tony?"

"Thirty-three."

"Your career in private practice is just beginning, and you're doing it the hard way—a one-man office. Don't you think you need help?"

Lord tried to deflect the question. "I like working for myself," he said easily. "It lets me define who and what I care about."

McIlvaine looked nettled. "Still, there are men in the city associated with Kilcannon whom it would do you good to know. I'll be there to make sure you meet them." McIlvaine smiled. "After all, a settlement or verdict which includes back pay should make the investment in a grace note easier to swallow. The way this trial's gone thus far, you've got every reason to hope."

Lord realized that he could have choreographed it, right down to the unspoken reminder that McIlvaine could screw up his case by not approving a settlement, prejudicing the jury against him, or giving them instructions so adverse that they would never award Jack Cole's back pay. If he could help it, Lord promised himself, McIlvaine would also never become a federal judge. "What's the tariff?" he asked coolly.

"Two hundred fifty," McIlvaine said in his most depreciating voice. "A small price, as I say, for improving the prospects of settlement." He smiled with conspiratorial male bonhomie. "Frankly, I wouldn't mind getting that fairy off my docket."

Bias and misuse of office, Lord thought, and McIlvaine could get away with it. "Frankly," he responded blandly, "*I* wouldn't mind getting 'that fairy' off your docket."

In his annoyance, McIlvaine's smile strained so wide that his gums showed. It gave Lord time to do some column addition: $1,700 a month for their two-bedroom house, $173 for the car, $200 for Christopher's school. Which reminded him of the daughter Jack Cole couldn't see.

Lord stood without amenities. "I'll try to make it," he said, and headed for the door. He had mentally taken the last $500 out of savings even before the judge called after him, "And bring your wife."

4

Jamie climbed onto the black limousine.

They had stopped in the middle of San Francisco's Chinatown. Stacy stood by the passenger door. Surrounded by aides, reporters, and a cordon of police and Secret Service, she could see but a few faces. In the swelling roar, Chinatown came to her only as the smell of pork or fish or vegetables cooking, Chinese characters in neon, the face of a woman in a second-floor window, holding a baby with fine black hair.

Between the shoulders of police, a young voice called to her, "See you tonight." Nine hours to go, she thought, and smiled in no particular direction.

Jamie stood above the noise, shoulder-held cameras seeking his face.

"The Second Coming," a familiar voice said.

The Bronx accent was unmistakable; Stacy turned to John Damone's sardonic half-smile. "Just get here?" she asked.

"Uh-huh—your boyfriend's packed the streets. Lots of white folks out for dim sum."

After close to ten years, Stacy could still be annoyed by his gift for speaking her least comfortable thoughts. "I saw some Chinese."

"Not many. But then what does all this have to do with them?"

She didn't answer. Damone kept looking from Kilcannon to the cameras to the crowd: he had a hyperalertness to new situations, an edge to the way he looked and moved, and there was nothing soft left in his face. The black beard accented the skin stretched across his cheekbones, the aggressive prow of a nose, the lines etched at the corner of his eyes. Gazing at the rooftops, he murmured, "What idiot told Kilcannon he was bulletproof?"

She began looking from the buildings to the limousine and back. Above them, Jamie raised one hand; the roar subsided to scattered cries. "*Jamie,*" a woman screamed.

He grinned. "Well"—his voice resonated through the microphone—"it's nice to be wanted. But will you respect me in the morning?"

Laughter. Stacy saw the press corps smiling with Nat Schlesinger: they loved Jamie best when he was playing off his crowds.

"*Yes,*" more voices called back.

"And on Tuesday?"

"*Yes. . . .*"

"Good. Because I mean to make a difference and I need your help to do that."

In the cheers and applause, Jamie let his smile linger. "I've come here to the Chinese community, where unemployment stands so high, because the man I mean to replace as president thinks this is a place to eat. When he thinks of it at all."

An approving burst of laughter. As it died, Stacy heard the whine of news cameras. Damone's gaze flickered to the rooftops.

"The president says that he's color-blind. I think that's true. . . ."

"*No,*" someone shouted.

"Really, I believe that. Remember when he appointed a black man to his cabinet, then met him at the inaugural and called him 'Mr. Mayor'?"

A ripple of laughter, cameras jostling.

"That's when I realized that the president not only thinks that all minority citizens are equal, he thinks they're interchangeable. . . ."

As the laughter rose, Jamie's voice rang out, "When he thinks of them at all."

Leaning back, he let the applause widen until it came back to him again. Stacy felt the same disturbing excitement—she could help him become president.

Damone edged close to her. "Good at this, isn't he?"

"It's easy for him."

A reporter in the press pool called out, "Forty seconds," and resumed timing the applause on his wristwatch. Stacy saw a camera aiming toward her, and smiled up at Jamie. A part of her began wanting to escape.

Damone stared at something. She followed his gaze to a lone man, crouched on the roof of a trading company. "You're making me nervous," she told him.

"I don't like this. Especially for you."

Jamie raised the microphone again.

"But the unemployed in this community are forced to think of *him*. For they've been forced to serve as extras in the Grade B script he calls an economic program. . . ."

There were three sharp cracks.

Jamie recoiled, mouth falling open.

"*No . . .*" someone screamed.

Damone hurtled onto the car and hit Jamie at the knees; as they fell together, the crowd released a keen of agony.

"*Jamie!*" she cried out.

In the chaos, police covered Damone. As Stacy tried to reach them, a cameraman pushed her aside. All she could see were Jamie's legs; the camera was in his face.

"Stop!" a policeman shouted at her. Two Secret Service agents wrenched Damone to his knees.

Slowly, Jamie raised his head.

The two men stared at each other. "You all right?" Damone managed.

Cameras whirred; the crowd pressed against a barrier of police. Looking to the men who held Damone, Jamie's face was white.

"Let him go," he said. "What was it?"

"Probably firecrackers, Senator."

There was sourness in Stacy's throat. Jamie mumbled to Damone, "Thanks, anyhow," but did not look at her.

As Damone crawled off the hood, she saw his lip was split.

"Oh, John. . . ."

"Reflexes," he muttered. She touched his lip, and then his forehead bent to her shoulder.

She looked back up at Jamie. Please, she thought, you have to stop this.

He stood on the cartop as if nothing had happened.

Cameras followed him. As the tumult died, Damone turned back to watch.

Jamie spoke. "It was only *firecrackers.* . . ."

A deep groan.

"Still, I have to worry. At Princeton, no one ever tackled me from behind."

The nervous laughter became applause, swelling with gratitude. For the first time, Jamie turned to her.

She grinned at him, words stuck in her throat.

5

Arranging to meet Danziger, Parnell had suggested the Pacific Union Club.

They'd needed lunch and a quiet place to talk. It was only as he waited, examining how deftly Lord had questioned him, that he fully understood his choice: the trauma Lord touched on had begun there, sixteen years before.

Parnell sat back, remembering.

He had been playing bridge when the phone was brought to his table; in these decorous surroundings—oak and leather and soft-spoken waiters—the caller had sounded like an applicant for membership. With the gentle wheeze of an asthmatic, he asked when Parnell had last heard from his son. The question was so polite, and its setting so incongruous, that for a moment Parnell was merely confused.

"Who is this?" he asked.

The caller hung up. After a moment's thought, Parnell excused himself, and went to phone his lawyer.

"What *have* you heard from Robert?" John Danziger asked.

"Very little." Parnell's mouth felt dry. "He's been living at the Tahoe place. There's been somewhat of a rupture."

"Occasioned by . . . ?"

"Cumulative disagreements. At seventeen, he no longer fit comfortably at home."

"I see. And have you tried to reach him?"

"Not yet." Parnell adjusted the rim of his glasses. "As I said, we don't really speak."

"If you're determined to stand on ceremony," Danziger responded dryly, "you might have Alexis call. And let me know what happens."

Hanging up, Parnell dabbed his forehead with a handkerchief. Without calling Alexis, he phoned Lake Tahoe.

There was no answer.

At dinner, Alexis was full of high-strung humor. That afternoon they'd shown one of her old films on television, the swimsuit walk-on scene with Cary Grant. It reminded her, she told her husband, that Dorian Gray had also had a body.

Parnell excused himself, went to the library, and placed a second unanswered call. The next morning, after his third call, he invented an excursion to Bohemian Grove and drove to Tahoe without stopping.

On the piny, sunlit hill, the door of their ski home was ajar. As he approached, Parnell saw that the lock was broken; the subliminal wish to have no son became chill on his flesh.

Entering, he saw a captain's chair toppled, a beer and half-sandwich on the coffee table, the corner of a throw rug kicked up. On the floor behind that was Robert's typewriter with one sheet curling from it.

The note read simply: "Is your son worth one million dollars? Details to follow." Without touching the telephone, Parnell drove to a gas station and called the FBI. He did not call Alexis.

For two hours he waited on the front steps, fearing their inevitable question, Why was he here?

Parnell could never tell them.

Part of it he did not know. The seeds of that last incident, he understood, lay somewhere between Alexis and himself. But by the time Robert had been forced to leave, his causes and effects were so entangled with their lives that to think of them did not illuminate, only wounded.

The tangle began with Alexis herself.

He had met her at his roommate's wedding in Newport, the same June that he had finished Yale. Daydreaming through a prewedding party, he had quite literally bumped into Alexis.

As she caught her balance, Colby saw that she was more than pretty. "I'm sorry," he managed. "I was on a mental trip to San Francisco."

The laughter in her cool gray eyes seemed friendly. "Then I should go with you," she said. "To see you don't bump into things."

Relieved at her good humor, he began to think he'd like that before he'd even asked her name.

She was Lexie Fitzgerald, she answered, and an actress. "And I'll be working in Hollywood, so perhaps some weekend I *will* visit San Francisco."

But three months later, when he took Alexis home, his father did not warm to her. "She's an actress without money," John Joseph told his son. "And that makes her an adventuress. If her first ambition fails, then you're her consolation prize."

It did not matter to his father that Lexie had found acting while on scholarship at Smith, and Colby was too proud of her to yield. Instead, he financed her weekend visits between bit parts as a contract player at Fox, until he wanted her more fiercely than he'd ever wanted anything. She was small and poised and lively, with features so precisely cut that he found the subtle overbite when she smiled at him a charming flaw. Her lack of wealth helped him feel more assured: seeing her delight in the sailing trips and polo games and parties, he began to hope that shared enjoyment might replace the male magnetism he knew he did not have. Yet she seemed so adaptable to the life he led that it bothered Colby to imagine the unspoken side of her which San Francisco did not satisfy. As Lexie drew oblique, admiring glances over dinner at the Blue Fox or dances at the Fairmont or the Mark Hopkins, he began floridly envisioning Hollywood as the palm-laden Byzantium of suntanned men who wished to trade its secrets for her own. A year after his roommate's wedding, Colby was still a virgin.

He felt Lexie responding when he kissed her, but their kisses gave no hint of whether more was wanted, or whether she remembered them as he did. Lacking his father's hearty maleness, and fearful of his own, it felt safer to be the gentleman whose code respected virtue.

One night, parked in front of the Parnells' brick Georgian home, Colby tried to broach this as protection for them both. "You may not always live in Hollywood," he told her. "I don't want them to change you."

She smiled. "It's not what you're imagining."

"Then why don't you want me to visit?"

Her gaze was so self-contained that Colby felt uneasy. "Because you're something separate and apart from that. I want to keep you both clear in my mind."

"But what is it you need there?"

"I want the chance to be more than just one person, at least for a little while. Perhaps I need the attention." She kissed his cheek. "But nothing I ever do there will make a life with you impossible."

The promise reassured him; only later did he hear a second meaning.

In the months that followed, Colby strained to personify his city, all safety and security and regard for her best side. His guilty hope was that her roles seemed fewer; she spent more time in San Francisco. Waiting, he did not speak of marriage.

That September his watchful tension ended.

They had eaten at Orsi's: walking her to the Mark on a crisp, clear evening, Colby pondered her lack of appetite. Near the Fairmont, she asked to stop. As Colby sheltered her from the breeze, she gazed down at the lights of boats inching across the bay. A cable car of tourists, crossing in front of them, vanished down a precipitous grade with its bell still clanging. Leaning on his shoulder, Lexie murmured, "I love this city."

Colby fought against his impulse and lost. Pulling her to him, he said, "Marry me, Lexie—please."

She looked at him so intently that for a moment he felt his chance collapsing. Her voice was husky. "Yes, Colby. I will."

Awkwardly, he kissed her. "Come back with me," she whispered.

The bedside lamp was on. As they embraced, her hips pressed into his. Elated and confused, Colby slid down the spaghetti straps of her dress: suddenly he did not know whether her shudder was desire or distaste. Then Alexis cupped his chin and murmured, "Help me."

It was done so quickly that he felt embarrassed. He could not see her face.

"Did it hurt too much?" he asked.

"No—not too much."

"I wasn't sure." The act made him confiding. "This was new to me too."

As she moved closer, he could smell the perfume on her skin. "Once we're married," she said, "we'll have many years and many times."

The thought made things much easier. "When shall we?"

"Soon." Her urgency surprised him. "Now that I've decided, I want to be in San Francisco with everything else behind me."

Colby realized that in some parallel conversation he had been broaching this to John Joseph. "What about your contract?"

For a moment she grew quiet. "I think they'll let me go."

The next morning Colby told his father. "So she failed there," John Joseph replied.

Colby flushed. "I've learned not to expect too much approval. So I came here ready with an answer."

"Yes?"

"Fuck you, Dad."

Colby walked out. Six weeks later, Lexie told him she was carrying his baby.

In the excitement of their hasty wedding, Colby savored the toasts and knowing backslaps which signaled that he was quite a fellow, and lucky in Alexis. But the part of him which felt his father's silence began counting months.

He did not do this often. Once married, Lexie seemed so delighted to be pregnant that he could not help but join her. He felt them becoming a couple without the anxiety of sex. The baby sealed their marriage: once they could make love again, time would lay his doubts to rest.

Eight months after they had first made love, Lexie bore him a son of normal size, with black hair like his own. John Joseph did not come to see him. When Colby could not choose a name, Alexis called him Robert. On the first night she could make love again, he reached for her.

As more nights followed, and she began crying out beneath him, he recalled she was an actress. But the pregnancy which followed shamed him: Lexie seemed more pleased than before. When sharp, sudden pains signaled a miscarriage—ending her childbearing and quite nearly her life—they agreed to dedicate themselves to Robert.

Determined to give the affection he himself had lacked, Parnell emulated Alexis, playing or talking or smelling the newness of Robert's skin. But at night he found himself staring into the crib. Robert would look back at him; Parnell had the odd sensation that the baby knew his doubts.

It did not help that as a lover he felt awkward and too quickly spent. As worry that Lexie's cries of pleasure were a pretense became fear that she feigned pleasure in their life, he became obsessively thoughtful, filling his appointment book with dates he should remember or gifts that had pleased her. And always, he tried to share with her the flow of a life he felt them part of: the charities and social seasons; the largesse through which they graced some corner of their city with an artifact or cherry tree or perform-ance by a new soprano; the pleasant backdrop of familiar faces who shared this same communal purpose, to make the place where their parents and children alike were rooted something finer than it was. Their house on Broadway overlooked the soothing sameness of the water, and the window where they took their drinks filtered sunset into shafts, casting the spell of the only time and place Colby ever wished to know. But in the calm with which Alexis looked through this same window, Parnell sensed that part of her was still in Hollywood, or somewhere else beyond his reach, with Robert.

As soon as he could speak she began inventing plays for him, acting out each role in turn as Robert clapped in pleasure or watched her with bright black eyes. By four he too was wildly inventive, ascribing each trampled flower or broken dish to some imagined friend so sharply realized that it struck Parnell as eerie. When Alexis bought him a television, he began appearing at the dinner table as whatever singer or actress he had seen, de-manding to be called by her name. Parnell said little; Alexis was delighted.

As if excited by this dual response, Robert began smearing on his mother's lipstick. "We've got to stop this," Parnell suggested over cocktails, "before he finds your sanitary napkins."

She smiled at the window. "He's imaginative. I of all people should understand the impulse."

"This is no impulse. It isn't normal."

"Does that mean I'm not either?" She turned on him. "He's your son too, Colby."

Parnell sipped his manhattan. "That's why I'm concerned about him."

"I understand. Just please try to be that without becoming *your* father." When Parnell looked up again, she had turned back to the window.

His puzzlement seemed to make her smile more at Robert. The five-year-old would follow her even when she undressed: she would hold him close and murmur, "Lexie-love," until he would repeat it as his name. Parnell grew more detached.

One evening, leaving the paper, it struck Parnell that, like his father, he did not play with his son. On the way home, he bought a baseball bat, and took it up to Robert. "Here," he said.

For an instant, Robert's wish to grasp the hand-tooled bat was palpable. Then he looked up at his father. With a bright, peculiar smile, Robert ran away.

That night, the pattern of his bedtime started.

Still hurt, Parnell wandered into the darkened room. But as he bent to kiss his son, Robert drew one hand across his eyes. The boy's face and body were quite stiff; Parnell did not know if this was fear or theater or dislike. Shaken, he rose to leave. In the several years of nights to come, as Robert would cover his face, Parnell would recall the child's voice behind him saying, "Lexie-love . . ."

As Robert grew, Alexis listened to fantasies which ranged from being Laurence Olivier to president of his own republic. The music room became his province.

Accomplished at classical pieces, Alexis played piano for him. Robert's favorite was the Paganini Variations; again and again, he asked for it, watching until Alexis placed his chair nearer the keyboard. But for reasons he could not define, Parnell avoided joining them, until he told himself there was no reason he should not. Returning from work, he heard Alexis playing the variations. He entered the music room, standing behind his son until his wife had finished. As she gazed down at the keys, lost in what she had played, the ten-year-old Robert stood, and touched her face.

Alexis smiled to herself, then saw her husband. Following her embarrassed glance to the father at his back, Robert bolted from the room. The two parents looked at each other. Murmuring, "I'm sorry," Alexis went to find their son.

In the silent language of their marriage, Parnell began to read her guilt at Robert's preference. But his sense that part of her was absent persisted when he touched her. Without clear reason to be jealous, he felt her waiting for some nameless lover. And as she dressed in the window above their courtyard, he realized with an anguish which bordered on self-loathing how much he feared that someone else might see or have her.

He struggled not to punish her for this. It helped that John Joseph's sudden death had freed him to run the paper, and that it seemed to prosper from his air of calm and sense of whom to trust. He was not a founder, Parnell reasoned, but a preserver. Few events of substance in the city occurred without his knowledge; he and Alexis led a pleasant public-private life in a circle where they both were liked—all this distracted him from doubts about her happiness, and the unseen something he felt between himself and Robert.

As Robert moved into his teens, their relationship assumed the classic forms of parent-child conflict, in a way Parnell distrusted. With Alexis, Robert would take pleasure in the staging of an opera or ballet, but the boy scorned his father's world or any plans he made for him. Though Parnell selected the finest schools in San Francisco, Robert's grades were poor. Even his schoolboy talent for acting suffered from eccentricity of interpretation and penchant for inventing his own lines, and though such marked singularity seemed to fascinate his peers, he had no real friends. Tall and rangy, Robert took on a posture of masculine protectiveness toward the smaller Alexis; in his son's gaze, Parnell felt a first hint of violence. His son would not talk to a psychiatrist; he wished only to hear his mother play piano. The maid found marijuana in his dresser.

Parnell resolved to send his son to a boarding school in Maine.

The idea seemed to frighten Alexis. "He's just fifteen—it's obvious that Robert needs us."

"At his age, my father shipped me off to Groton. We have to face that there's something wrong here—at least wrong for him. It's selfish to go on saying 'one more year' when every day now he gets stranger."

She turned on him. "You *want* him gone. That's what this is."

For once he did not look away. "I don't love Robert the way you do," Parnell said softly. "And I never will."

Her face contorted. "You're blaming me."

"No, Alexis. I'm just not blaming lack of love."

At dinner, Parnell told Robert of his decision.

Standing, Robert leaned across the table toward his father, face distorted. Parnell stood. "Robert!" Alexis cried out.

Her eyes were wet. Robert turned to his mother and, quite softly, said, "You bitch."

Tears ran down her face. Slowly Robert walked to his mother, resting his forehead against hers.

"I'm sorry," she whispered.

In the candlelight, Parnell saw his son's throat working. He closed his eyes.

A week later Robert left for Maine.

But things went no better there or at the next three schools. Robert started fights and would not stop until he'd broken someone's nose or teeth. He was a loner who found drugs and lived at the edge of rules. There was to him, one poetic headmaster wrote Parnell, bright anger and a ruined sensitivity. At seventeen, the last expulsion brought him home.

His rhythms changed abruptly. Robert showed no inclination to bait his father or do anything but watch him. Though his mother saw this as a sign of progress, Parnell felt his son taking stock of him: recalling that Robert's bedroom window had an angle on their own, he began to draw their curtains. He sent Robert to a psychiatrist. Returning, Robert would closet himself with a film projector, studying old John Garfield movies as if his life depended on it. He made calls late at night, followed by strange absences. Parnell began waiting for something to happen.

But Alexis seemed certain that she could make Robert whole. At first, he spurned her impulsive hugs and invitations to some film or play. Then, as though seized by childhood cravings or sure that he had punished her enough, Robert began to ask that she play sonatas for him, or come to his room to watch a musical they had enjoyed when he was younger. Encouraged, Alexis asked him to the opera. He spent more time with her, and showed no sign of leaving.

"What's he planning?" Parnell asked her.

"In what sense?"

"In the sense that he never finished prep school."

"Please, Colby—don't push him away yet. We're so close to where we were."

The following afternoon, for the first time since his son's return, Parnell heard Paganini coming from the music room. That night, leaving with Alexis for the opera, Robert smiled at his father. The smile struck Parnell as so triumphant that he could not sleep.

The next morning, as Alexis dressed, Parnell put on a robe and went to Robert's room. Within an hour, Robert was gone.

Six months later, Parnell shook hands with the FBI agent who met him at the cabin.

Special Agent McCarry brought two others with him. They searched the area as he questioned Parnell, his red-veined face expressionless.

"Do you know who'd want to do this?"

Parnell shook his head. "No. But that my family owns a newspaper is no secret. Or that we own this cabin."

"Why was he living here?"

"His school performance has been disappointing." Parnell had rehearsed his answer carefully. "This cabin was a kind of retreat. To reflect."

"Who else knew he was here?"

"His mother—perhaps a few of our friends. I don't know Robert's friends. He's been East until recently."

"Any involvement with drugs, or sudden need for money?"

"He's smoked marijuana. About the other, his mother gave him money whenever he needed it."

"How about problems over girlfriends."

"No—nothing like that." Parnell hesitated. "What are you after?"

"Several things." The agent's gaze was steady. "Any unusual conflict, for one."

Parnell waited.

"Was there?"

"My son and I had the usual conflicts—lifestyle, and grades."

"Nothing deeper?"

"He seemed troubled. . . ." Stopping, Parnell took off his glasses, and began to clean them.

"How well did Robert get on with his mother?"

Parnell looked away. "Quite well."

"Better than with you?"

Parnell put on his glasses. "She was his mother."

Hands in his pocket, McCarry watched him. "You said he fought. Was there ever violence between you and Robert?"

"It—it didn't come to that."

"What about toward his mother?"

Slowly, Parnell shook his head.

"When was the last time you saw him?"

"Six months ago."

"Or spoke to him?"

"Then."

McCarry looked up sharply. "Was there some specific incident?"

"You keep harping on that. Am I a suspect?"

"Should you be?"

Parnell felt tired. "No—of course not. I'm sorry."

"What about Robert?"

"How do you mean?"

McCarry seemed to choose his words.

"When a teenaged child disappears, the reason often has less to do with money than with hatred—something within the family that makes the child want revenge."

Parnell turned to the cabin. A second agent walked toward them, holding a pair of hiking boots. "Are these your son's?"

Parnell nodded. "I believe so. Yes."

The man spoke to McCarry. "We're lifting a boot print from near the window—a size and a half larger."

"Worn or new?"

"We think worn. Also the typist wore gloves, and there don't even seem to be prints for the boy. Of course, at his age he's probably never been printed anyway."

Parnell looked back to McCarry. "If I follow that, there's no doubt someone took him."

"Perhaps." Parnell wondered if the agent's voice seemed cooler. "Just how clever is he, Mr. Parnell?"

"He's an imaginative boy—I really don't know how clever."

"You don't seem to know Robert all that well."

"I wonder, Mr. McCarry, how many fathers really understand their sons?"

McCarry did not seem to like the question. "Sooner or later, someone's going to ask you for a million dollars. If it looks legitimate, you'll have to decide whether to pay it."

"What should I be thinking about?"

"Besides your son? Several things. A ransom drop's usually our first clear shot at the kidnapper. But we can't guarantee we'll catch him or get back your million dollars. What would that kind of loss mean to you?"

"I'd probably have to sell the newspaper. Do you ever use fake ransom?"

"At times. But the danger is that the kidnapper will stay pissed off and free long enough to take revenge on the victim."

"What other choices do I have?"

"If you announce up front you're not going to pay it, at least they'll have time to think about it rationally and release him. They also might have time to dispose of Robert where no one will ever find him."

Parnell rubbed his eyes. "I see."

McCarry's tone softened. "Do you have other children?"

"No—only Alexis."

"Still, there's one more thing I should say. You're a wealthy man, Mr. Parnell—a mark. Once you pay ransom for your son, there's no guarantee that this kidnapper or another won't want more money for him next year."

"Or for Alexis?"

"Her, too."

Parnell touched his ear. "I should call her. She doesn't know yet."

"Say we'll want to talk to her."

"Is that necessary? She doesn't know anything more than I do."

"You understand that we can't be sure."

"I'll tell her, then." Parnell began trudging toward the car.

"Mr. Parnell."

"Yes?"

"We'll be receiving crank calls in the next few days. We'll need a question that can only be answered by Robert, if he's still alive. Then you can decide."

Parnell felt sick to his stomach. "Ask him—ask them what his mother called him when Robert was a little boy."

On the telephone, Alexis seemed unready to accept it. But he returned home to find her in the music room, strangely calm. "They've already been here," she told him. "Two agents. I couldn't tell them what happened."

"It doesn't matter. Unless *he's* done this."

She began crying. As he knelt beside her, she shook her head, almost angrily. "He loved me. . . ."

Alexis ran upstairs, near hysteria. The doctor gave her sedatives.

Parnell called Danziger to ask advice. But he did not explain to the lawyer the reason that Alexis would not speak to him.

For the next five days, their life became the focus of a drama, from which Alexis withdrew. Their front grounds were the scene of press conferences; strangers tapped their phones to screen the flood of hoax calls; Parnell and Danziger made contingency plans to borrow cash in large denominations. But until the evening of the fifth day, Parnell did not know if Robert lived, or what he would decide when the demands were made.

He was in the library when McCarry phoned. "The kidnapper called *me*, by surprise—he must have caught my name on television. They want a light airplane to drop the parcel at 11:30 tomorrow evening in a meadow near your cabin. It was too short to trace the call, but the voice was like you described—a wheeze."

Parnell hesitated. "Did you ask the question?"

"Yes. He said he'd call your house in half an hour. I'm on my way."

Hanging up, Parnell turned to watch Alexis.

She sat in the music room; Parnell could not bring himself to enter.

Through the window of the library, he saw two headlights. A moment later, a policeman let McCarry in.

Shaking his hand, Parnell asked, "What if they know the answer?"

"Then he's alive."

The telephone rang.

McCarry went to answer it. As Parnell turned, he saw that Alexis had looked up at the sound.

Putting down the telephone, McCarry gazed at Alexis, and then Parnell. In the semidark, his eyes seemed clear and comprehending.

"Lexie-love," he said.

For a last moment, Parnell looked back at his wife. Sitting at the piano, her profile seemed like china.

"I'll pay no ransom," he answered softly.

"Colby?"

Parnell realized that he had closed his eyes. Standing, he shook hands with Danziger, somewhat formally.

"Sorry to be late," the lawyer said. "Quite a crowd coming out of China-town. Are you in a rush?"

"A bit. Alexis is rather nervous over this Kilcannon party, and I feel I should be there. Personally, I don't like his politics but . . ." He shrugged, helpless. "The man taps something in her."

Danziger smiled in sympathy. "Charisma."

They ordered drinks. Sipping his manhattan, Parnell mused, "I suppose it's good for her, in a sense. An emergence . . ."

"Of course."

Parnell snapped from his reverie. "Now," he said. "Young Mr. Lord."

"I spoke to him." Danziger's tone was one of distaste. "He asks too much."

Their eyes met. "He did well this morning," Parnell answered quietly.

"It was cheap. Lord's a hired gun looking for headlines."

"What does he want, John? Cole's job back?"

"*And* retroactive pay. There's some complex custody matter involving Cole's daughter, and I'm sure Lord means to use you to finance his client's efforts."

"I see."

"You don't have to pay it." Danziger's voice sharpened. "There's no justification for that."

Parnell finished his drink. "Settle with him."

"Don't be a fool, Colby. The jury won't . . ."

"Pay him, dammit. Just pay Lord the money." Standing, Parnell excused himself without ordering lunch.

6

Damone had moved so quickly, Stacy remembered, that nine years later it still scared her.

She'd been singing at a crummy club in Oakland; the floor smelled like stale beer, and the bathroom had an acrid stench from kids throwing up drugs—Stacy could hear them vomit during breaks. Damone stuck with her, hustling deejays and club owners in to hear her sing. But the last night her only audience was some lesbian bikers; Stacy won them over with "My Funny Valentine."

Afterward she waited in the back room for Damone to settle with the owner. Then Damone rushed in, taking her arm.

"Did we get paid?"

"That's next. Something's funny—I don't want you in here any longer."

The owner lived in a trailer behind the club. A light was on; the bouncer who should have been guarding Stacy stood at the door. In the dark, she saw his shadow shift slightly, arms loose at his side. He was taller than Damone.

"Where's Naxos?" Damone asked.

"Sleeping."

"Wake him up. We haven't been paid yet."

"Then chalk it up to experience, asshole."

As Damone moved past him, the man pulled a revolver and swung at his head. Stacy started to scream; suddenly the bouncer lay at Damone's feet, hand clapped over his ruined mouth. Damone picked up the revolver, took three long strides, and kicked in the door to the trailer. Her scream died.

A soft voice came from the trailer, Damone's. The bouncer moaned in the dirt.

Damone came through the door clutching a wad of money. Reaching the bouncer, he murmured, "Chalk it up to experience, asshole," and stuffed one bill in his mouth. Then he put an arm around Stacy and walked her to his rusted-out Ford.

They were on the freeway before either spoke. "I scared you," he said.

"It's just that it happened so fast."

Damone lit a cigarette. "Vietnam."

"You never talk about that."

The tip of his cigarette had glowed orange. "I never will," he said at last.

Now, reflecting on their silent ride from Chinatown, the memory made her hesitate. "You could have been saving Jamie's life," she finally told him.

They were in the tuning room, following Stacy's sound check. The band's guitars were in metal racks; Damone had dragged in a garbage can filled with ice and beer. They sat on the rug, backs against the wall, drinking beer from cans. The ritual reminded them of how far they'd come; the others left them alone.

"I embarrassed him," Damone replied. "He was afraid of how he'd look on television."

Stacy felt his chagrin. "It wasn't that. Really."

"Whatever, tell him to be careful."

"I have." Stacy turned to him. "It's like he's trying to prove he's real, John. It scares me."

Damone nodded. After a time, he asked, "Is that what was wrong just now?"

"It was a rehearsal. I'll be okay tonight."

Shrugging, Damone let it drop. "What will you wear?" he asked.

"Don't know." Stacy sipped her beer. "When I opened the suitcase, my silk blouse looked like the Elephant Man."

"The romance of the road." Damone gave a one-sided smile. "You didn't have to do this, Stacy."

"Just like you didn't have to play road manager."

"And miss your first case of stage fright in a year? Besides, driving the truck's nostalgic."

She touched his hand.

The roadie, Carson, drifted in. Quickly, Stacy smiled at him. "Thanks, Harry—the sound's great."

"No problem," Carson answered in a monotone, and continued his trancelike amble toward the garbage can. To Stacy, Carson had the inbred look of a typical roadie: lean-muscled, with spectral eyes, sharp features, a wispy blond mustache. But there was something else inside him, remote and a little scary. Reaching into the ice, he pulled out a chilled fifth of tequila, took one long swallow, and wiped his mouth.

"Find your kid?" Damone asked him.

Carson's gaze was glassy, as if the question was taking detours in his brain. "Not yet," he finally answered, and walked off with the bottle.

"Is he all right, John?"

Damone pulled his knees up to prop both elbows, and stared at the beer. "Harry does his work, and he hasn't crashed his cycle lately." He took another sip. "He drinks sometimes."

"He was in Vietnam with you, wasn't he?"

Damone gave her a sideways look. "Harry didn't quite get back," he said, and resumed drinking the beer.

Stacy finished hers. "Off to the hotel," she said. "I'm writing a new song."

"You *are* jumpy."

"It's good, I think." She stood. "Coming to the Parnells'?"

"Swine city?" Damone tossed his can in a wastebasket. "I'd better count the gate. Rock 'n' roll's a cash business, remember—like politics." Turning, he gave her a keen, upward glance. "Isn't Kilcannon worried that being with Parnell will piss off gays?"

Stacy felt defensive. "He'll be all right."

"The idea is to win." His half-smile returned. "If he does, I guess you'll keep on doing this."

"He hasn't asked."

"Does he have to?" Damone still smiled, but not with his eyes. "You've finally met temptation, Stacy. Whatever it is Kilcannon gives you, you can't refuse."

Kneeling, Stacy kissed his face. "See you tonight," she said, and left.

7

Dead time.

Six o'clock, three hours before the concert, and Damone was already checking receipts. The crew was shooting the shit and smoking dope in the tuning room; Jesus had put together a cocaine run; someone had found Curtis fucking his cross-eyed girlfriend; a woman in a beret and purple stockings was hanging out by the loading dock. The place felt hollow. There was so little happening that it made Carson jumpy.

Picking up the duffel bag, he took the fifth of tequila upstairs, to shower and work on his poem. The bottle was cool in his hand.

Curtis's girlfriend was in the shower, looking wasted. Drugged-out sexual apparatus, Carson thought—no muscle tone and dull bruises on her legs. It was easy to imagine her dead.

Dead as Capwell, twitching in his arms like a shot dog. Fourteen years ago, and the poem wasn't finished.

Duffel bag at his feet, Carson took hits of the tequila, waiting for the shower. The girl drifted out, picked up her clothes from a pile, and left.

The hot water felt like 'Nam on his skin.

Sometimes it's beautiful. The sun comes out of the delta like an enormous orange ball, and at the ocean a sea of rice flows into a sea of water. The flowers are so bright it almost hurts to look at them; there are pineapples, bananas almost dropping off the tree, monkeys lobbing coconuts for the hell of it. In the dry season he can whack the trunk of a bamboo tree with a machete, and cool water pours into his throat.

Leaning against the shower stall, Carson took a burning swallow of tequila.

A headless monkey, falling; water to their necks.

Carson stared at his hands.

It kept surprising him to see no blood. He couldn't remember landing in Oakland or what he'd done. Water and sweat ran down his face.

They were following—he had to lose them.

Stepping out of the shower, Carson's footprints smudged one of the girl's. Erasing them, he though of Cathy.

When she was born, her skin and hair had smelled new. I'll take care of you, he'd thought.

Water flooded his open lungs.

Carson dropped the tequila.

The bottle shattered; Carson dove for cover, saw the half-footprints, broke his fall with both palms. They began stinging. There was blood on his hands.

He walked to the urinal and vomited.

Sticking his face in cold water, he remembered the telephone.

Slowly, he began to dress, keeping the blood off his T-shirt. His limbs felt poisoned.

He covered the Mauser with his wet towel, and took the catwalk to the stage, bag swinging in one hand.

Curtis sat on a box next to the telephone. "Seen Joan?" he asked Carson.

"Yeah—in the shower. I think she was naked."

Behind them, Jesus laughed.

Carson remembered holding his daughter. Putting the bag between his feet, he said, "I need room."

"What the fuck you do to your hands?"

"Your girl thought my thumb was your prick." Carson reached for the telephone, snapped, "Take off, man," and dialed.

Just let me find them, he thought. Jesus and Curtis left.

"Operator 270."

It surprised him. "Uh—Columbia, South Carolina."

"Yes?"

"Mrs. Harry Carson. Or maybe Beth Carson."

"Any address, sir?"

"No—just Columbia."

He imagined pages flipping. "I'm sorry, sir. Could that be a new listing?"

"Yeah—I forgot."

Oakland, and he couldn't remember. The poem wouldn't come.

"I'm sorry, sir . . ."

"Winship," he said. "Beth was called that before we got married."

"How do you spell that, sir?"

"W-I-N-S-H-I-P."

"I'm sorry, sir. There's nothing."

Carson's voice rose. "You didn't have time to look. . . ."

"I'm *sorry*, sir. . . ."

Carson hung up and dialed again.

"Operator 270. . . ."

Putting down the telephone, he saw a red-orange palm print on the wall. His head pounded.

"No luck?"

"She's scared of me," Carson said automatically, then realized Damone was behind him. As he turned, Damone reached into his bag.

"Cigarettes still here?"

Carson's throat was tight. "Yeah."

Damone took out the pack, standing with a cigarette between his lips. "Stacy asked if you're all right."

Carson shrugged.

"Want to go home?"

"Where's home?"

Damone stared past him at the palm print. "I cleaned up the glass," he said softly.

Carson shifted his weight. "I'll take it easy, John. No sweat."

Damone examined his face. Looking down, Carson saw the box he'd been carrying. "Want me to load the extra amps?" he asked.

Damone picked up the box. "I'll take care of it," he answered, and walked slowly to the truck.

Carson waited until he was gone.

The stage was dark, empty, just him and the amps and the platform. Picking up the bag, Carson walked to where they would stand.

Suddenly it came to him, the second verse, fragments linking to fragments:

> A soul in sunglasses
> Hair golden, many plans
> His life your stepping-stone
> His blood upon my hands. . . .

Alone, Carson took out the revolver.

8

In her next life, Stacy would outlaw air conditioning.

The limo taking her to the Parnells' was the temperature of Greenland. In the hotel suite, she hadn't been able to find lyrics for her song; it had made her so superstitious that she'd commandeered the limo as diversion, to detour through North Beach. But the whine of its air conditioner unnerved her; like a postcard, the restaurants and delis and people she saw had no sound or smell or feel.

"Could you roll down the windows?" she asked.

The driver stopped by Washington Square. As the electric windows slid down, it came to life.

On the grass, a dog chased a Frisbee, two couples drank wine, a panhandler bummed change and cigarettes. People on benches talked or read books; a saxophonist with his case open for donations played mellow jazz. Beyond them was the Church of St. Peter and Paul, a white mass of marble topped by spires. Though Stacy was not Catholic, she imagined generations of Italians passing in and out, drawn by its mystery and space. A light breeze rippled her hair.

The driver watched her in the rearview. "Know the neighborhood?" he asked.

"I used to come here—in college."

On Sundays she would drive from Berkeley, sometimes with Damone. He had found North Beach before she did—Italian genes, he had explained—and knew where to find the best cheese or salami or Chianti classico, the coffeehouses and family restaurants. Once, heading into a bakery with a window full of fresh-baked bread, she had stopped to count the loaves. "Go ahead," Damone had told her. "North Beach won't always be like this for you."

She could see that now. The restaurants looked more glittery and pricy; there were fewer old men in sweaters or European hats. On a bench near the car, two women turned to stare at her.

"There was a bakery," she told the driver. "On Green Street. I want to see if it's still there."

This, at least, was the same. Stacy checked her watch. "I'll be right back."

The bakery smelled like fresh dough, twisted into various shapes and sizes. From behind the counter, an old Italian woman peered at her in such obvious unrecognition that Stacy grinned. "You had something called panettone," she said. "Sweet tasting, in kind of a round loaf."

"Still." The woman's accent was sibilant; she pointed in triumph to a shelf behind Stacy. "Over there."

The yeasty loaf was filled with fruit. Placing it on the counter, Stacy fished in her purse. "I used to eat this all the time," she explained. "It tasted too good to put anything on."

The woman smiled. "Still," she said, and slipped a cookie in the bag.

Leaving, Stacy waved. "It's the same," she told the driver.

He raised the windows and left North Beach.

Stacy checked her watch; it was less than three hours until she sang. For a moment, she wished that she could share the bread with Jamie, and not worry about keeping it down. She ate the cookie on the way to the Parnells'.

Overlooking the bay, their home on Broadway was three stories, with a circular drive and sculptured Mediterranean garden that stirred vague memories.

Colby Parnell had stood on his front grounds, she realized, answering reporters' questions. She and her parents had watched the news. His son had been kidnapped; Parnell had looked like he'd lost his power of movement, but not of speech. Silent, her mother had placed a hand on Stacy's shoulder. Her light remembered touch triggered a second association: the Parnells' son had disappeared the spring that Robert Kennedy was shot.

"Can you turn on the news?" she asked.

The driver found a soothing voice on an FM station.

"Following today's frightening incident in Chinatown, presidential contender James Kilcannon is returning from an enthusiastic rally on the steps of the Capitol to appear with rock star Stacy Tarrant. . . ."

"Thank you," she told the driver. When he circled to let her out, she took the loaf of bread.

The door was answered by a bodyguard. As she stood there, feeling foolish, Colby Parnell emerged from behind him.

"Hello." She felt as if she were extending her hand across an enormous gulf. "I'm Stacy Tarrant."

Hesitant, Parnell took her hand. Stacy realized that meeting her must seem like encountering a Martian; he wasn't sure his manners still applied. "It's nice of you to do this," she added. "I've looked forward to coming."

His face relaxed; though he was a large man, the soft returning pressure of his hand gave the impression of a gentle mastiff. "We're delighted to have you," he answered, and led her inside.

The alcove opened to a spacious first floor. From the dining room, Stacy heard the sound of caterers preparing for a party. But the quiet room they entered was sparely appointed with antiques and a hand-loomed Chinese rug, placed in perfect relation to one another. This symmetry reminded Stacy of a museum which had been cordoned off from trespassers; she had no sense of people moving through it, bringing the outdoors with them. At the end of the room, a slender woman turned from one of several windows which arched to a fifteen-foot ceiling. "Alexis," Parnell said, "this is Stacy Tarrant."

The woman stared; the quick smile that followed seemed to cover nervousness. "In my day," Alexis told Stacy, "girls as beautiful as you were film stars."

"Thank you."

"I mean it." Parnell watched his wife protectively; Stacy sensed tension in her Katharine Hepburn voice. "Is Senator Kilcannon with you?"

"He's flying back from Sacramento." Stacy held out the bag of panettone. "But I brought you something. From North Beach."

"For me?" Alexis's smile brightened; Stacy saw her husband smiling next to them. "What do they call it?"

"Panettone. It's my favorite."

"Are you from here?" Parnell asked.

"My dad used to teach at Berkeley, and that's where I went to school. On weekends, a friend and I would eat our way through North Beach."

"Colby and I used to go there too, though not for years." Alexis took the bread. "This is charming of you."

"Wait till you taste it."

The Parnells laughed. Alexis handed the bread to her husband, asking, "Can you hide this somewhere?" He gave her a quick look, as though afraid to leave, then excused himself.

As she took Stacy's arm, Alexis's touch was feathery and tentative. "You're our first guest this evening—we wanted to visit with the senator and you. May I show you our home?"

"I hoped you would." Through the window, Stacy saw a formal garden surrounded by wings of the house, above a panorama of the bay. "This view—it's what I used to imagine if I could get my dad to work harder."

"It still mesmerizes Colby." They began walking along the windows. "It must be exciting—being part of this campaign."

Stacy heard a note of wistfulness. "It is," she answered, then saw that one side opened to a music room with a piano. "Do you play?"

"Since I was a girl." At the threshold of the music room, Alexis seemed to speak more softly. "It's a wonderful interest, don't you think?"

"And a beautiful instrument." Stacy walked to the piano, touching its smooth finish. "May I hear you?"

Alexis tossed her head back, the surprised, flattered gesture of a younger woman. "Are you certain?"

"You'd be doing me a favor—I'm a little edgy about the concert, I guess. It's relaxing just to listen."

"Then of course." Alexis sat at the piano, arranging her dress. "You must work quite hard at what you do."

Stacy smiled. "Sometimes, on the road, I think that life is the search for a good night's sleep."

"It's performing for an audience, with all that tension. Much more difficult than film." Alexis set a piece of music in front of them. "I was at Fox, a million years ago. But I really never got past the stage of wanting."

Stacy nodded. "I think that was the least complicated time for me, in a way. When I knew what I wanted, and didn't have it yet."

"And look where you are now." Alexis composed herself at the keyboard. "I forgot to ask if you'd like a chair."

Sensing that this would please her, Stacy took a Chippendale chair from behind her, sitting where she could see Alexis's hands. "I'd like to hear your favorite," she said.

Alexis studied the keys. "Do you know the Paganini Variations?"

"The third movement's beautiful."

"As written," Alexis said lightly, and began.

She played deftly and well. As moments passed, her eyes seemed to close, as if she were playing from memory. Yet she sat erect, conscious of being watched. Her silvery ash-blonde hair was cut above her shoulders, and the network of lines on her face was so fine that from a little distance she looked much younger than she was. She was not of the generation that exercised; her willowy slimness had come from dieting. Yet this pride in appearance accented Stacy's sense of her frailty, and something else she could not quite define—a kind of widowed sexuality.

"Beautiful," Stacy said when she had finished. "As played."

Alexis's eyes opened. "That's very kind. How did you become interested in classical music?"

"I wasn't given a choice. When I was four, my dad found out I had perfect pitch. He hit a note, tuning the piano, and I told him what it was."

"What did he do?"

"He was so excited that he got on the telephone and called every relative we had, trying to figure out where it came from."

"Did he find out?"

"My great-aunt Dorothy has it. She's a teetotaler who belongs to the John Birch Society. Dad couldn't stand her."

For the first time, Alexis laughed. She touched a key and looked up at Stacy, querying.

"A-flat," Stacy said.

Alexis played another.

Stacy grinned. "F-sharp."

"Damn," Alexis said. "You really do."

They laughed together.

"What's *this* performance?"

From the doorway, Stacy caught Parnell's complex look of worry and relief. Next to him was Jamie.

As Alexis rose, flushed with excitement, Stacy could see the girl she had been. Extending her hand, she said, "Senator, Stacy is an absolute treasure."

His eyes crinkled. "And to think that when I rescued her she was a hopeless addict."

"And to think," Stacy told Alexis, "that you ever took him seriously."

"An obvious mistake." Alexis went to Stacy, kissing her on the cheek, and then took Jamie's arm. "Come, Senator—we'd better see to you."

Parnell's eyes flickered to the piano, and then toward Jamie and his wife. Laughter trailed behind her.

Carefully, Parnell replaced the chair. "Thank you," he said to Stacy. "Alexis seldom plays."

"It was fun."

As he led her from the music room, Stacy realized that her concert was less than two hours away.

9

"Five hundred dollars," Marcia said.

Lord sat in the wicker chair. "He had me."

She tossed her bra on the bed. "He had Jack Cole."

"Same difference."

She turned, interrupting her march to the shower. "Then you can't afford to be in private practice. Not this way."

Silent, Lord found himself studying her slim body and fox-pretty face, with its light dash of freckles and brown hair and eyes. In seven years, he thought, nothing about her looks had really changed, except the way he saw her.

"What's wrong, Tony?"

"Nothing."

"You're giving me that look."

"It's not a conscious thing, Marsh. Whatever it is."

She walked into the bathroom. She would weigh herself, Lord knew, and pinch her stomach for extra skin that wasn't there, as she had done since Christopher was born. When she leaned out again, he asked, "How much do you weigh?"

She smiled fractionally. "One-o-eight. Really, is it even a good idea for Jack Cole to have joint custody of his girl?"

"I think he's a good father. By the way, did you tell Christopher we'll have to skip the game?"

"I thought that was your responsibility."

Her tone annoyed him. "Like making money?"

"You have a law degree, I had Christopher. I didn't have the opportunity. . . ."

"Sorry." Lord held up one hand. "By now we could have this conversation in Swahili."

More softly, Marcia said, "If you went back to the district attorney's, at least you'd be on salary."

"I'd also be working for Ralph DiPalma."

"He can't be *that* bad."

"He's a psychopath in pinstripes. Besides, I've done that job."

She frowned. "Well, you wouldn't go to a firm. With your record you could have doubled what you were making. . . ."

"I can't see working for someone like Danziger, either."

Marcia watched him. "Or anyone else?"

Lord leaned against one armrest. "All right," he said wearily. "Or anyone else."

"But why are you *like* that?"

"My dad, I guess." Lord inspected the label on his tie. "Each morning he put on his hat—and his work face with it—and rode in a carpool of other men in hats to an insurance department jammed with metal desks. The man he worked for was a bully. Every so often he'd raise Dad's salary a pittance and Dad thanked him, for my mother and for me." Lord looked up at her. "Because he did, *I* went to an expensive college, when he never went at all. I love him for it, and he knows that. But what he'll never know if I can help it is that I hate what he had to do."

"That was years ago," she sighed. "Tony, why can't you join the human race?"

"I have a talent." Saying it, Lord knew this must sound like a catechism. "I need one big case, that's all."

Marcia paused. "You're afraid of being ordinary," she said finally.

It was so right that it scared him. "Yes."

She let her body slump in resignation. "I wonder if Captain Ahab had a mortgage."

"Not in California." Lord smiled faintly. "But then he didn't have Christopher, either."

Marcia did not smile back. "He's downstairs," she said, and stepped into the shower.

"Hi, Daddy."

Taking the last steps to the basement, Lord smiled. "Is that *all*, Christopher?"

His son dropped the rubber ball to start a running leap which ended in Lord's arms. He kissed his father on the cheek. "Boys don't kiss other boys on the lips," he explained. "Not when they're six."

"*I'm* not six. Besides, I still kiss Grandpa."

"*And* Mom. Right?"

"Right."

Face to face, they smiled at each other. But for a dash of freckles, Christopher was a six-year-old version of Lord—blond hair, blue eyes, confident smile, even the cleft in his chin. The resemblance was so marked that strangers laughed out loud; Christopher would laugh too, enjoying the effect they made. "I told the whole class we're going to see baseball," he said.

"You did?"

"Uh-huh." Christopher wriggled to the floor. "Clifton got mad. He's Chinese."

"Did he stay mad?"

"A little. Afterwards, we were friends again. Sometimes we are, and sometimes we're not. When I play with Mikie."

He headed for his toy shelf; a six-year-old's swayback made the purposeful stride a slightly comic swagger. Turning with a baseball cap on his head, he asked, "Are you wearing *that*?"

Lord mentally cursed Marcia. "I'm afraid we'll have to go tomorrow."

His son's shoulders drooped; it was when Christopher was sleepy or disappointed that Lord noticed how small he was. "You said tonight, Daddy."

"I know, mugwump. Something happened."

"What was it?"

"It's kind of complicated." Lord sat, patting the floor beside him. "I'm trying to help a man who has troubles."

Christopher sat an inch or two from Lord. "What kind?"

"Lots, really. He got divorced, and then he lost his job and the money he was making."

"And you're giving him more money?"

"I'm trying to help him get it back. You see, he has a little girl about your age, and since the divorce the girl's mommy won't let my friend see her."

"Why not?"

"She's mad—her feelings were hurt. But I think my friend should get to be with his girl, and if he has money and a job, maybe the people who decide these things will let him."

Christopher was quiet. Lord felt his shoulder against him.

"What do you think, Christopher?"

"I think daddies should be with their kids."

Lord put one arm around his son, and then the telephone rang.

He listened until he was sure that Marcia wouldn't answer, and went to the phone near the stairs.

It was Cass. "Danziger called," she told him. "He wants to meet with you tomorrow to discuss settlement."

Lord glanced at Christopher. He had picked up the ball and begun bouncing it. "Did he mention a time?"

"Noonish."

"Try to make it morning, all right? I'd like to keep the afternoon free."

"I'll try."

"Be firm with him," he smiled. "Just leave a message with the sitter."

"Enjoy the party," she said dryly, and hung up.

Christopher was throwing the ball at an angle, trying to make it ricochet off the wall up into the Chinese lantern that Lord had hung for him. "What happens if you get it in?" Lord asked. "It'll be stuck there."

Christopher's eyes danced. "That'd be delightful."

"Delightful?" Lord grinned now. "Where'd you hear that?"

"That's what *you* said when the toilet stuck." Turning, Christopher got ready to throw. "Let's make a rule—you have to stay here till I get the ball in."

Lord leaned against the wall, smiling. "But by then I might be very old."

"Not *too* old. . . ."

"Tony?" Marcia called. "The sitter's here."

"Just one sec." He scooped up Christopher and kissed him. "Got to run now."

"But we didn't get to play."

"You're going to need your rest. We've got a big day tomorrow."

As they left, Lord watched him in the rearview, waving through the screen door. Their home was tucked into a hillside, with trees surrounding it and a deck overlooking the Noe Valley district; idly, Lord reflected that this was the only house his son had ever lived in. "You look nice," he said to Marcia.

"I try to. Actually, I'm looking forward to meeting James Kilcannon. He certainly comes across on television."

Lord adjusted the rearview. "With or without makeup?"

"That's mean, Tony. I really do like what he stands for."

When Lord did not answer, Marcia turned on the radio.

10

Spotting faces at the party, Stacy guessed the lives they led.

She and Jamie stood in the living room, chatting with guests brought over by Alexis or Jamie's aides. Around them, people drank and talked until their turn arrived. Nat Schlesinger hovered on Jamie's left, murmuring the names of those with money to give, then easing them to Stacy before they used up too much time. Like the lead in a drawing-room comedy, Jamie made his role look effortless; no one but Stacy knew that he was working hard at something he disliked. But for her, watching people was a distraction from twenty thousand other people, waiting. Her stomach was empty.

"This must be so *different* for you," the overdone blonde in front of her condescended.

Smiling, Stacy answered, "That's what makes it interesting," and then the aging coquette stared up at Jamie.

"Oh, Senator," she trilled, "I must think of something clever to say to *you*."

Jamie laughed, taking her hand. "Just be nice to me."

Amused despite her edginess, Stacy looked around the room.

Teeth flashed; heads bobbed; mouths moved that made no sound; waiters served champagne and drinks from silver trays. No one really stood out. For sport, Stacy guessed that the pinstripes and alert, attentive looks belonged to lawyers or investment bankers; the continental suits, affected languor, or young faces without character to real estate speculators, and those with an inheritance; the silk handkerchiefs and bright-eyed animation to restaurateurs and decorators and younger entrepreneurs; the blue or gray suits and added bulk to older self-employed businessmen or local politicians. One of these, a man whose red hair was cropped to bristles on a pink fleshy neck, talked to a blond man in a tan linen suit who studied him with keenness but without respect.

This man, Stacy decided, didn't look like the others.

He was in his early thirties, she thought, and the slimness and clean angles of his face suggested exercise. His ridged nose and ice-blue eyes were those of a model in a cigarette ad, but their effect was more arresting. Part of it, she realized, was the stillness of someone in perfect control of his own thoughts.

"It's been *so* nice to meet you, Miss Tarrant."

Nat had steered the woman back. "Thank you," Stacy replied.

As the woman paused, Stacy sensed that her face was being checked for lines. "You're in such an *odd* business, after all. Aren't there a lot of drugs?"

Stacy smiled cheerfully. "*And* sex."

The woman looked startled; Stacy felt Jamie's elbow nudge her own. "But it's normal sex," she added. "Mostly."

"Oh—I see."

Stacy's smile widened. "It's been nice to meet you, too."

As the woman retreated, staring, Jamie murmured, "I really never wanted to be president." He did not sound amused.

Wondering if she should try to eat an hors d'oeuvre, Stacy glanced back at the room.

The women, she reflected, pretty well matched the men. Some had the tailored clothes and confident air that went with having jobs. Others were so perfectly coiffed and dressed that they spent too much time at it to work. Stacy reflected that these last ruffled both the middle-class girl and feminist in her; she thought it bad taste and unliberated to dress like an ornament from *Vogue*. But the small brunette with the blond-haired man merely puzzled her.

She had a thin, pretty face, slim figure, and a quick, high-strung smile. Like the blond man, she dressed simply and well, but they were quite different in manner. Listening to the red-haired politician—that was how Stacy had pegged him—she flashed all the nervous party animation her companion would not. She leaned slightly away from him. He did not look at her.

What set him apart was his manner of watching.

Flickering across the party and back to the politician, his gaze seemed meant not to ingratiate but to dissect. She wondered what he was doing here; if he had ever been anyone's fan, it was probably so long ago that he couldn't remember. Then it struck her that he might be some relative of Alexis's.

"What on earth did you say to Nancy Pickering?"

Alexis had come to her side, whispering avidly. "I just put her on a little," Stacy confided. "She was about to check my arm for puncture marks."

Alexis laughed. "Don't I know *that* one. I think Colby half-believed I went to Hollywood to become Sam Goldwyn's mistress." Patting Stacy's wrist, she moved into the crush again, high-spirited and alert. For an instant, Stacy saw Parnell's eyes following her from a circle of older friends, as though she were some exotic bird who might take off into flight, or else be trampled by the crowd.

"Stacy." Jamie was breaking away from a florid, friendly man. "Have you met George Carroll?"

He managed to make this sound as stimulating as a trip to Marrakesh. The thought made Stacy smile again. "Hello," she said, and the party went on around her.

Its rhythm seemed to quicken; Stacy sensed Jamie's aides ensuring that everyone saw the candidate before he had to leave. Faces passed so rapidly that her smile felt like a reflex.

A woman in a silk dress put a pen and album in her hand. "I promised my son I'd ask you to sign this."

"What's his name?"

"Charles."

"For Charles," she wrote, then asked, "How old is he?"

"Eighteen."

"Please vote," she finished writing. "Love, Stacy."

Smiles all around; more faces and hands to grasp.

"I never realized that Senator Kilcannon was so handsome."

Stacy put a finger to her lips. "Don't let him hear you."

Laughter. Watching, Nat Schlesinger smiled. Stacy began to like the people she was hardly meeting better than she liked her role. Preconcert nerves, she thought; it was better to be alone. Checking her watch, she saw that it was 8:15, and decided not to eat.

"But what about the balance of payments?" a man was asking Jamie.

"It's a ten-year problem." Jamie's smile flashed. "Unless Stacy sells more records to the Japanese. By the way, have you two met?"

As the man went by, Stacy sneaked a quick glance at the Parnells.

Head held high, Alexis searched for couples to meet Jamie. But Parnell, encountering the blond man, nodded and edged away. Stacy was trying to guess the meaning of that when the blond man's gaze met hers. Though she was used to men acting afraid of her, this one did not turn away. Just the faintest amusement suggested that he saw through the veneer of charm and glamour to the heart of Jamie's business.

"We hope to see you again, Senator."

She could hear the smile in Jamie's response. "You're coming to the inaugural, aren't you—that's why I'm working so hard." Then he added,

"Stacy, this is Alexis's good friend Carla Curran," and she turned from the blond man to the pixie grin of a department store heir's second wife.

More faces. By now, Stacy should be pacing backstage; she'd been standing still for close to two hours. The next time she glanced around her, restless, the blond man had disappeared. The party was louder now; the cigarette haze had lowered, and guests drank and smoked in the loose-jointed rhythm that comes with the second cocktail. Spotting her, Alexis waved and then came over, murmuring, "It's going very well, don't you think?"

"Beautifully," Stacy answered. She'd begun to swallow as she did when feeling sick; for a moment she debated asking for a quiet place to sit. But Alexis was already gone.

When Stacy turned, the blond man was talking with Jamie.

Angular and unlined, his look of boyish alertness would have stamped him as an American if this were the middle of Paris. The brunette stood next to him—his wife, Stacy saw from their rings.

"So you're a friend of Colby's," Jamie was saying.

"An acquaintance." His answer was quiet so that only those closest could hear. "Our relationship's a little more complex."

Jamie's face grew wary. "Oh?" he said easily. "How so?"

"I cross-examined him this morning in a lawsuit."

Nat Schlesinger edged nearer; as Jamie hesitated, Stacy saw the mental connection moving through his eyes. He covered in a joking voice. "So my campaign has brought you together."

"The judge is a supporter of yours." The muted response suggested someone too polite to spoil a party. "I was impressed by the depth of his commitment."

Jamie glanced past him, but the other guests seemed not to have heard. "What do you mean?"

"Exactly what you suspect."

The brunette looked stricken. Jamie seemed to be gauging how serious the stranger was when she spun and left him there.

"We'll return your contribution," Jamie said.

"Please don't." The man smiled a little. "Nice to have met you, Senator."

He began turning.

"But you're not exactly an admirer, are you?"

The man looked back at Jamie, as if considering whether to speak. "Not exactly," he answered softly. "But what scares me is how smart you are."

As Jamie bit back an answer, the man stopped in front of Stacy. "Sorry," he murmured, and turned to leave.

Stacy watched him.

"Jesus," Nat Schlesinger muttered.

"Stacy," Jamie asked. "Have you met Nancy Stewart?"

11

"Damn you," she said.

Her angry profile faced the windshield. Quietly, Lord answered, "They'll take care of McIlvaine."

"*That* was done." Marcia's voice grew level. "I must say that Senator Kilcannon handled it very well."

Lord watched their headlights cut the dusk. "Reagan's not the only actor in politics. Just the only one with screen credits."

"You insulted him, Tony. And humiliated me."

"You weren't humiliated by being there?"

"It's a lot more practical than hoping for 'the big case.' " Marcia leaned closer to the dashboard. "What's that sound?"

"The gears are worn."

Marcia let that hang for a while. "But you had too much pride to help your practice."

"It's just that I'm not a courtier."

"And you couldn't stand to have anyone think that, either." She turned. "I saw you look at Stacy Tarrant."

For the first time, Lord smiled. "Where did that come from?"

"You *were*." Marcia frowned. "I know you like that type."

"What type is that?"

"The tall, model type. You buy her records, don't you?"

Lord smiled again. "That hardly rises to adultery, Marsh."

She fell silent. Crossing Market Street, they headed for Noe Valley on the main drag of the city's gay nightlife. Lone men and men in twos or threes cruised the sidewalk of shops and cafés packed into a two-block area. Faint colored lights and bits of rock and folk music rose and fell with the traffic through the doors of the clubs; Lord was depressed by the feral, rootless rhythm of seeking.

He touched Marcia's hand. "This whole conversation is silly. We have a marriage, a home, and a child."

Softly, she asked, "Is there someone else?"

"Of course not."

Waiting for the babysitter, he wondered why she'd asked that. When he returned, she was staring into the mirror, face stripped of makeup. He went to Christopher's room.

His son slept with the batting helmet next to his hand.

Lord felt a kind of sadness; the day seemed so long that cross-examining Parnell must have happened the day before. Which day, he tried remembering, had he last made love to Marcia?

Perhaps that would help things.

The next morning would be filled, he recalled, by Danziger. Watching

Christopher's dreamless face, for the first time Lord let himself think about giving it up.

"Tomorrow," he promised his son. "I'll spend time with you tomorrow." He went to find Marcia.

As they left, Alexis hugged Stacy. "We'll watch for you on television."

Stacy kissed her. "We'll be back. Really."

Alexis looked pleased. "I hope so."

From behind her, Parnell nodded, then said, "We'd better let them go, Alexis."

Jamie shook his hand, then began walking Stacy toward the limousine. When she turned to wave, Alexis was halfway down the steps.

The limousine was ringed by shadows, reporters, and Secret Service. Another shadow stepped from the darkness—Nat Schlesinger. Jamie bent close to him. "Put someone in touch with whoever that judge is," he said quietly. "I don't want problems from this."

"Senator!"

Jamie's head snapped up. "We're running late," he called. As he and Stacy hurried to the limousine, Nat opened the door.

Stacy slid in. A lone man caught Jamie. "Just one, Senator. Do you think your opponent's slip on nuclear weapons is like Romney's admission that he was 'brainwashed' on Vietnam?"

Jamie turned. "Oh, I don't know," he said carelessly. "In this case, I think a light rinsing would be sufficient."

The reporter laughed. Hastily, Nat stepped in. "Jamie's tired—for God sakes, don't print that."

Smiling, the reporter turned to Jamie. "You owe me."

"Always."

Jamie got in the car.

Nat closed the door behind him. Jamie propped his elbow against it, staring out. As they pulled from the driveway, Stacy saw Alexis waving in the faint glow of a porch light. Arm around her shoulder, Parnell looked not at the limousine, but at his wife.

"Well," Jamie said. "That's done."

Stacy gazed past him. "She looks so fragile. Like a butterfly in a box."

"Does she?" He glanced at his watch.

Stacy felt her stomach tightening. "Don't worry," she said. "John's on top of it."

They passed from streetlight to streetlight, accenting the hollows of his face. "God save me," he murmured, "from frustrated, ambitious men."

"John?"

"This man Lord." Jamie kept watching the dark. "Norman Mailer once told me that everyone thinks they can write. The truth is that everyone thinks they should be president. But what does someone like that lawyer know about living in the media?"

"It could have been worse, Jamie. At least he was quiet."

"*You* heard it, didn't you?"

"It doesn't matter." She breathed in. "The thing that bothered me was Chinatown."

He lapsed into silence. When he spoke again, it was in the tone of a man remembering something he once had heard. "The definition of a fanatic," he said to the window, "is someone who goes on when he can't remember why."

Fretting with her bangs, Stacy let this pass. It was 9:15; she was late.

"What *did* Romney say about Vietnam?" she finally asked.

"That he'd been brainwashed into supporting the war." Facing her, Jamie's eyes glinted. "It was probably the most honest thing he said. Nixon killed him with it."

Stacy tried to picture the concert. "There's a guy on the crew," she said at length. "John doesn't say much about it, but he thinks Vietnam fucked him up."

"He's probably right." Jamie's gaze returned to the window. "I've met with some veterans. But they're not organized enough to have any impact. What can *I* do if nobody gives a damn?" He stared moodily into the darkness, his question foreclosing all others.

Stacy turned from him.

In her mind, she could hear them yelling "Sta-cee." But she saw no image of stepping through the curtain; it still bothered her that she could not write the song.

12

Behind the curtain, Carson felt like a pair of ears and eyeballs.

On the other side Secret Service ringed the stage; feet stomped the concrete floor; fans snaked to the toilets for a last snort of coke; deejays and distributors clustered by the ramps. Carson heard and saw them on his nerve ends.

"Sta-cee. . . ."

The luminous dial of his wristwatch read 9:25.

It was 12:25 in Columbia; Cathy was sleeping.

"Sta-cee. . . ."

Daylight.

A suicide mission so golden boy can look good. Damone isn't there; in the sun he and Capwell won't pass for Vietnamese; they've napalmed the trees so there's no cover now.

"Sta-*cee*. . . ."

Leeches stick to his feet.

"She's giving me good vi-brations. . . ."

They've changed the tape.

The sonofabitch is listening to his Beach Boys albums.

"Sta-*cee*. . . ."

Fucking parasite; thank God she was sleeping.

"She's giving me ex-ci-tations. . . ."

Capwell's blood on his hands. Palsied fingers.

"*Sta-cee*. . . ."

Fumblingly, Carson opened the journal and read the poem he had finished:

> Feeding the camera
> Hair golden, spirit dead
> Time circles back to you
> A bullet through the head.

Hands trembling, he put a bullet in the Mauser.

The limousine stopped at the rear of the Arena.

The loading dock seemed pale yellow, dim light coming from inside. The Secret Service men waited. When one of them opened the door, Stacy heard the cry echo from above.

"Sta-cee. . . ."

Jamie stepped with her up the ramp, into the bowels of the Arena. In a cocoon of Secret Service they waited for the freight elevator. Metal boxes were stacked crookedly around them; Stacy saw a motorcycle by the catwalk.

"Sta-*cee*. . . ."

They crowded into the iron cage. As it groaned upward, past two levels of cement walls and catwalk, their call for her grew louder. She noticed Jamie's faint, ironic smile.

The elevator lurched, stopping at one side of the darkened stage. Their sound came through the curtains.

She was not ready.

Curtis waited with a flashlight. Waving them forward, he shined it at their feet. "Band's in the tuning room," he murmured.

"Sta-cee. . . ."

They followed the beam of light. At its edge, she noticed a form slumped beneath the telephone. Was somebody else sick, she wondered, but had no time to ask. As they reached the dressing rooms a door closed behind them, muffling the sound.

In the tuning room, Greg Loughery, her bass guitarist, was squinting at his instrument. The keyboard player, Leon Brennis, grinned at them. "I was getting ready to stand in for the senator," he told her. "John's in your dressing room."

Jamie shook his hand; Stacy thought he had the bemused air of a grown-up playing with kids. She hurried to the next room.

"Sta-*cee*. . . ."

She closed the door behind her.

Damone turned from the mirror. "Trying to remember how I looked without a beard," he said dryly. "How're you feeling?"

"I can feel them in my stomach."

"At least they're out there." His smile was teasing. "Remember that club you played in Oakland?"

"Sure."

"You've put more than years between then and now." He pointed to the adjoining bathroom; a blue silk blouse hung from the door. "I figured no tank top tonight. So I ran the shower till the wrinkles steamed out."

For all of his sardonic toughness, Stacy thought, the almost feminine sensitivity was more remarkable. "What would I do without you, John?"

"Your own blouses." Walking over, he touched two fingers to her face. "Do good, Stacy."

As the door closed, she saw that he had opened her suitcase and makeup kit and placed them on her dressing table.

She'd be all right—she wouldn't think about it.

Hastily, she undressed; standing naked in front of the mirror, she wondered if she looked too thin. She felt the crowd on her skin now, their vibration through the floor and walls, like the tremor of a distant earthquake.

"Sta-cee. . . ."

She could hear it again, faint but clear. She forced herself to sit. Carefully, ritualistically, she touched her lips with Vaseline so that they glistened and then traced the outline of both eyes with kohl, until the young boy she imagined sitting in the most distant row could see them.

"Sta-cee. . . ."

Standing, she slid her jeans on. They were tight; the blouse was satin cool on her skin. She had the taut, explosive feeling of facing a new lover.

Opening the door, she beckoned to Jamie.

He looked tired. "What's up?"

"Forgot to tell you which song's your cue. Do you know 'Love Me Now'?"

"Uh-huh." For the first time in hours, he grinned at her. "It's time for a confession—I've got the tape. See, I really *did* like your concert."

She kissed him.

" 'Miles to go,' " he murmured, " 'before we sleep.' "

Turning to the band, Stacy said, "Let's do it." They ambled toward the stage.

Stacy turned in the door of the tuning room, quickly smiling at him. Then she was moving back down the corridor, between the guards who lined each wall.

"Sta-cee. . . ."

The stage was dark. Seeing her, Jesus pulled some light switches on the wall.

On the other side of the curtain there was a hush, as if the crowd had swallowed its own sound.

Curtis appeared with the flashlight. Single file, the band moved ahead of her to the platforms for their keyboard, drums, the two guitars. They stood behind their instruments like figures in a wax museum.

"Okay," Curtis whispered.

Stacy noticed the same slumped figure standing, as if she had awakened him. Then Curtis was leading her forward, flashlight moving across the wires and wooden floor to the curtain, until she stood behind it. Handing her the microphone, he whispered again, "Good luck."

She heard his footsteps retreating across the stage. Then the only sound came from the other side of the curtain, low and expectant and immense.

Together, Stacy thought, they might make a president.

She closed her eyes, breathing in. For a moment, familiar yet more frightening, she wished she did not do this. Then she burst onto the stage.

Spotlights cut into her eyes. She froze, stunned and almost blinded, engulfed in their animal roar. Arms raised like pistons from the crowd; mouths screamed for her; streams of colored light darted through the smoke and haze and black, intersecting in split-second rainbows, then flashing to the far corners of the arena where more people stood, caught in their beam. It was dark and vast. The crowd on the floor, oozing and colloidal, stretched until she could not see it; a two-tiered oval of seats surrounded her, more people standing, shouting, screaming so the rafters echoed. Projecting downward, suspended above the crowd on a four-sided screen, was the giant image of her face. Her lips glistened; her eyes were large and round. Stacy saw that she was smiling.

"Sta-*cee*. . . ."

The curtain split behind her.

The stage was a sudden blaze of light. The band tore into the metallic opening snarl of "Equal Nights"; the crowd screamed its recognition; Stacy sucked air deep into her lungs.

She began singing:

> "I'll take freedom
> You take my nights
> Long as you can face me
> When I turn out the lights. . . ."

The answering cry, frenzied and primal, drew her to the front, whipping the cord of the microphone as hands reached out for her. She felt the power of the music in her lungs, felt it course through the sound system and echo back to her until she was part of it, changing her nervousness to a surge of crazy energy she loved them for. As if drawn by some magnet, she began to stalk back and forth across the stage. It vibrated with the crowd and amplifiers, like a current running through her. At the corner of her vision, she saw the TV cameras, Jamie's cameras, following her as she moved. High above the outstretched hands, her four-sided image moved with her. Her song cut the dark like a laser.

She stopped moving.

Utterly still, voice now pure and high and solitary, she slid into the plaintive beginning of "Reruns at Midnight."

> "Slivers of fantasy
> On childhood's screen
> Scared for believing
> What I've already seen. . . ."

The crowd was hushed.

She felt close to them now; their faces, upturned and silent, watched hers. Her eyes shut.

In the song, a city-worn woman watches television with a man who once had left her. It is night; the screen is silver; the man asks to be her lover again. She does not trust him, or wish to be alone. At last, as a romantic TV series from her childhood flickers on the television, she gives in to promises she's heard before. Stacy could see and feel it.

She finished.

In their silence, caught like a breath, she eased into the opening of "Love Me Right." Her eyes were still closed.

The only instrument was the keyboard, a soft, hesitant few notes. Slowly, in the crystalline voice of a girl, Stacy began:

> "Darling, love me, if you can
> I can't wait, can you understand
> Ash is the fire of yesterdays
> You've got to play me as it lays. . . ."

The band broke loose.

There was a trip-hammer drumbeat; then Stacy's voice took off with the pounding rhythm of both guitars:

> "Learn that the fire
> Lives through lovers
> Before the fire
> Turns to dust.
> Don't make the fire
> Give me others.
> We'll make the fire
> Burn for *us*. . . ."

They screamed for her.

Now they were undulating, needful, pushing toward the stage. Stacy paced, wheeling, shouting into their faces, then imploring them closer, barely conscious of being just beyond their reach. The crowd was clapping, dancing, transported. From the rear, it thrust a dark young man on its shoulders, ever closer to the stage, as if as a sacrifice to Stacy. The fetor of sweat and dope and bodies mingled; the arena smelled like sex.

> "Learn that the fire
> Lives through lovers. . . .
> We'll make the fire
> Burn for *us*. . . ."

Her blouse was soaked through. The dark-haired boy was thrown shoulder to shoulder, reaching toward her, crying out until she heard him, "*Fuck me, Stacy. . . .*"

Stacy grinned at him.

He threw up his arms, laughing and ecstatic, and fell into the crowd. Waving, jumping, screaming, they seemed to pass beyond control. For a moment Stacy wanted to be part of them.

Then, as suddenly as the muted opening had become a shouted cry for love, her voice fell. Only the keyboard stayed with her. In a smoky, soft near-whisper, she finished:

> "You know the fire
> Lives through lovers.
> This night the fire
> Burns in *us*."

There was silence, a hush. They were hers.

"Sta-cee. . . ." A lone voice, calling from the rafters.

Stacy shaded her eyes. "Hi," she said.

Laughter, then cheers.

"Sta-*cee*. . . ." More voices shouting now, until they came together.

"Sta-*cee-e-e*. . . ."

She stood, still and alone, the focus of their energies. Her heart pounded. Behind her, Damone darkened the stage.

In the circle of light, she held up one hand.

"Kilcannon," she said softly.

There were scattered murmurs of his name.

"Kilcannon," she repeated.

They picked up the cry. "Kilcannon. . . ."

Her voice grew louder, more insistent. "Kilcannon."

"Kill-cannon. . . ."

Stacy looked up at the screen. On the stage behind her, walking from a cluster of bodyguards, was Jamie.

"Kill-*cannon.* . . ."

Jamie moved forward. Their cry rose to greet him.

"*Kill-cannon.* . . ."

As Jamie reached her side, she raised her hand again. In a soft, clear voice, she said, "United States Senator James Kilcannon."

Their fingers touched.

From the curtain's shadow, Carson watched them.

With a dazzling smile, Stacy turned to Kilcannon. They stood in an intersection of two spotlights, as if suspended above the dark. The crowd blessed them with its cheers.

Carson's hand tremored.

The bodyguards could not see him; he could not see Damone.

"Kill-can-non. . . ."

As Kilcannon stepped forward, Carson closed his eyes. In her bed, in a house that he would never see, Cathy was sleeping. The stage shook beneath his feet.

"Kill-can-non. . . ."

On the other side, Carson heard the whine of a cameraman filming.

"Kill-can-non. . . ."

There was blood on his hands; the camera kept whining. Over and over, they repeated it, banks of sound rolling over him, echoing, merging into each other: "Kill-cannon. . . . Kill-cannon. . . . Kill-cannon. . . ."

Carson's eyes opened.

Kilcannon raised his head, smiling as they called for him. His hair seemed golden.

Stacy stepped aside, giving him the crowd. Beneath their roar, Carson heard more cameras.

"*Kill-cannon.* . . ."

He took one step forward, the Mauser slack at his side.

The cheers became a shriek.

He did not hear them; his eyes fixed on the target, twenty feet away. Like an automaton, he moved forward to complete his mission.

One clear shot.

Fifteen feet now. The escape route opened in his mind: thirty seconds down the catwalk to the motorcycle, into the night. He raised the Mauser, bracing his wrist with the other arm.

His target turned, mouth falling open.

Carson froze.

In the periphery of his vision, Secret Service leapt onto the stage. Five more seconds. He stared into Kilcannon's face.

Three seconds.

A flashbulb exploded. Kilcannon's face became a faceless head, crowned by a blond nimbus.

> Time circles back to you
> A bullet through the head. . . .

Carson took one last step forward, and fired.

The gun recoiled in his hand. The head snapped back; the screams that followed were white noise to him.

He turned to the catwalk, guards running behind him. His route was still open.

He started toward it.

Sliding onto the stage, a cameraman aimed at Carson.

As if from muscle memory, Carson knelt and pumped three bullets into the camera.

The cameraman fell sideways, unhurt. Carson could not recognize him.

He could not remember his escape route.

Turning, he stared back at the stage.

The guards were about to reach him; Stacy Tarrant knelt over his target.

Kilcannon, he thought dazedly, and heard the shrieks.

As Carson dropped the Mauser, they hit him from both sides.

It had happened so fast.

The touch of Jamie's fingers was cool, electric. He stepped forward; she gave him her microphone; cheers washed over him.

She looked up at the screen.

Head cocked back, Jamie smiled as if at her. As the picture widened to show her answering smile, she saw the man behind them.

He raised his gun.

The crowd shrieked. It was as if she were watching a movie; she could not turn, and make him real.

Jamie spun.

As she cried out to him, the hair on his crown seemed to rise.

He crumbled, falling on his side, then his back.

Stacy dived to shield his body.

Skidding on the stage, she sprawled across him. Cries split the air; she closed her eyes, waiting to be shot. Beneath her, his chest rose and fell. As she touched his head, she felt warm dampness on her fingers, his breath against her cheek. There was no second shot.

She looked at him.

His face was unmarked. His eyes fluttered, then opened.

With her fingertips, she brushed the forelock of hair away from his eyes.

His lips parted. Weakly, he murmured, "Is everyone all right?"

Oh, God, Jamie, she thought. But she nodded for him. "I think so."

His eyes moved toward the top of his head; Stacy could not be sure whether he had seen or heard her.

"Such a joke," he whispered. "But what does it mean?"

There were tears on her face. Stunned, she looked for help.

Security men pushed back the crowd. Between their legs, a camera pointed its lens at Jamie.

"Clear the way," Damone was screaming.

She turned to his voice; Damone and two cops reached her. Paramedics ran behind them with a stretcher.

Kneeling on the other side, Damone looked down at Jamie. There was a pool of blood beneath his head.

Their eyes met above his face. Damone was pale. "Harry," he said.

"Tony!"

Lord ran from the shower.

Naked from their lovemaking, Marcia sat upright in bed, pointing at the television. "*Look*," she demanded shrilly. "*Look* at what they've done."

Lord turned to the screen.

Kilcannon lay on the stage, blood glistening beneath his head. Stacy Tarrant touched his forehead; her lips moved, then his. Their words were lost in chaos.

"Oh no," Lord groaned. "That can't be."

Marcia turned, as if he were not entitled to speak.

Silent, Lord sat on the edge of the bed.

The film zigzagged wildly.

In the background, a T-shirted man stared at Kilcannon as if appalled at what he saw. A gun fell from his hand; he did not struggle.

"I hope they kill him," Marcia hissed.

They let her in the ambulance. She huddled in one corner as paramedics bent over Jamie. They did not speak; their eyes spoke for them. The siren's shriek reverberated.

Vaguely, she remembered riding down the freight elevator; somewhere she had lost Damone. Her ribs and elbows felt raw.

She shivered.

They stopped; the door burst open. As they unloaded the stretcher, she saw Jamie's hair falling back across his forehead. Someone had opened his shirt.

"He's still alive," a paramedic called.

Cops flanked the path to a double door. Its neon sign read "Emergency."

They rushed the stretcher toward it. From behind the police, flashbulbs spat, and then Jamie disappeared inside.

"Miss Tarrant!"

Two police reached toward her; she let them lift her down. At the edge of her consciousness, she heard the persistent whir of cameras. More flash-bulbs burst in her face.

"Stacy," someone shouted. "How is he?"

Covering her eyes, she found herself in a bleak tile corridor. Someone touched her, Nat Schlesinger.

"He's upstairs," he said. "They'll operate."

His eyes were red and pouchy. Dazed, she stared at his good-luck bow tie. As if answering, he said, "Maybe he has a chance, Stacy."

She leaned against him. "To be what?"

Nat took her to the elevator. Watching its numbers, they rode to the fourth floor.

A wing was cordoned by police. Passing through them, Nat led her down more tile to a green chair, next to an ashtray she didn't need.

"I'll be back," he said. "As soon as there's news."

Stacy watched him disappear. The overhead lights seemed pitiless; there was blood on her fingers and sleeve.

Jamie's aides appeared, lost young men speaking in low voices. Their footsteps clicked on the tile, aimless and hollow. Stacy could not look at them.

"Stacy?" a soft voice asked.

It was Damone, next to her.

"How did you get here?"

"No matter. I wanted to be with you."

She leaned closer. "Why did he do it, John?"

"I don't know." Damone looked away. "Stacy, someone stole the concert money. It's gone."

It did not truly register. Staring, Stacy saw the distant figure of Nat Schlesinger at the end of the corridor, coming toward them. His steps were an old man's.

"That's all right." She said this gently, foolishly, to Damone. "Jamie won't be needing it."

It was 3:00 A.M.

Unable to sleep, Lord and Marcia watched television.

In the hospital press room, a weary-faced man in a bow tie began reading from a piece of paper.

"At 2:17 this morning, June third, United States Senator James J. Kil-cannon died from an assassin's bullet. . . ."

Marcia turned to Lord; the man's voice quavered.

"The cause of death was a single shot, entering the rear portion of the senator's skull and passing through the cerebral cortex. . . ."

The telephone rang.

Mechanically, Lord picked it up. "Yes."

"Tony, this is Ralph DiPalma."

DiPalma's voice was taut. "Yes," Lord repeated.

"I'm at the Hall of Justice. You'd better come down."

"For what?"

"Harry Carson—the guy who shot Kilcannon." DiPalma paused, expelling one short breath. "He just asked for you."

For a moment, Lord was silent. "I'll be there," he answered. He was a long time putting down the telephone.

On their television, Stacy Tarrant left the hospital, circled by cameras. Marcia turned, crying. "What is it?" she asked.

But Lord did not truly hear her.

"Psych defense," he murmured. "It's the only way."

PART 2

TONY LORD

THE TRIAL: HARRY CARSON

JUNE–SEPTEMBER, THE SAME YEAR

1

What Lord remembered was the sirens.

They started as a thin cry in his wind-wing. Block by block, the cry rose in the empty streets, more sirens joining at higher pitches. By the time he reached the Hall of Justice, their shrieks clashed around him.

A silent crowd covered the lawn and sidewalk as if watching the reflected swirl of squad car lights, red shimmering on black windows. Parking in an alley, Lord saw a Chicano with a tire iron smash the windshield of a TV truck. But the others seemed near shock.

Reporters waited at the entrance, cordoned from the rest by police. When Lord reached one, angling between a vagrant and a young woman crying, the cop pressed a palm to his chest.

"*Jamie . . .*" the woman sobbed.

Lord spoke under his breath. "I'm Carson's lawyer."

The cop took Lord's briefcase and half-dragged him forward. Reporters stirred. "Hey, Tony," one called. "You defending this guy?"

Lord kept moving. To the police guarding the entrance, his escort murmured, "He says he's the shooter's attorney."

A guard signaled another inside the glass doors. Opening them, a black deputy sheriff took Lord's wallet. Then the doors closed behind him.

The lobby was a dim, echoing capsule. Checking Lord's briefcase for weapons, the deputy telephoned DiPalma, then led him to the elevator. As it rose, Lord tried to absorb that Kilcannon was dead.

On the seventh floor, the deputy unlocked a barred door, the first of several. Lord heard ringing telephones, voices.

They came from a squad room filled with cops and plainclothesmen. At its center, three homicide detectives briefed the district attorney. DiPalma's too-bright eyes flickered from one to the other, then stopped at Lord.

The detectives left.

DiPalma began tapping a pencil against his teeth. "How does Carson know *you*?"

"He doesn't."

DiPalma's eyes shone. "I hear you had words with Kilcannon. . . ."

"Cut the crap. I want to know what he's said."

"Nothing." Pressure seemed to make DiPalma speak too quickly or not quickly enough. "Kept repeating his name and address."

"What was the weapon?"

"Mauser. A perfect assassin's gun."

Lord felt himself squint. "On television, it looked like he came from backstage."

"He'd hired on with Tarrant." DiPalma glanced at the room, then sharply at Lord. "His motorcycle was at the loading dock. It's a rational, premeditated hit."

"In front of twenty thousand witnesses? What's his motive?"

DiPalma's smile was a tic. "While *he* shot Kilcannon, someone robbed the concert money. Over four hundred thousand, her manager says."

In his surprise, Lord realized that his skewed mental reflexes mirrored DiPalma's. "Are you charging conspiracy?"

"As soon as we find the money—*or* his friends."

"Assuming there are any. And assuming he lives."

DiPalma's eyes became slits. "He's in the Dan White cell—no cellmates, no sheets or belt to hang himself. I'm not going to lose him."

Lord nodded. "What did you find besides the Mauser?"

"A duffel bag—cigarettes, newspaper, a diary."

"I'll need to see those."

"I'll consider it." DiPalma jammed the pencil in his coat pocket. "*If* you defend him."

"Maybe," Lord responded, "I should talk to him first."

DiPalma stared at him. "When you do, ask about his friends. His best hope of living is to trade someone."

Lord's eyes met his. "I'll consider it," he answered softly.

But DiPalma's stare had moved past him. Turning, Lord saw the mayor, the police chief, the United States attorney. It struck him that DiPalma, cursed with a heavy beard, had shaved before arriving. "If Carson has co-conspirators," DiPalma said in a lower voice, "he's headed for the gas chamber. You could look like an asshole in front of God and everyone." He hurried toward the others, glancing to each side.

Lord bought cigarettes from a machine. Then he followed the deputy through more locked doors, to a bare white cubicle.

Carson wore a prisoner's orange jumpsuit. When the door closed, sealing Lord inside, he did not look up from the table.

Sitting, Lord saw a ropy-looking man with a blond mustache and greyhound eyes.

"I'm Tony Lord."

Carson half-nodded.

"Cigarette?"

The eyes flickered. Carson took one, twisting off the filter and tapping one end on the table. As if in disbelief, Lord said, "They tell me you shot Kilcannon."

There was a slight, second nod.

The meaningless confirmation jarred Lord; Carson had murdered someone he had faced nine hours before, ironic and alive. Lord lit his first cigarette in years, then Carson's.

"Why did you ask for me?"

"Today . . ." Carson took a puff. "I read your name in the paper."

His tone of voice made this seem a distant memory. "Did you think you'd need a lawyer?"

There was no answer, nothing in the eyes. Lord wondered if this were selective.

"When did you first decide to shoot Kilcannon?"

Dully, Carson shook his head. "I don't know."

"Then what do you remember about the shooting?"

"Screaming." Carson sounded oddly detached. "I looked down, and saw his face."

"Do you recall firing at the camera?"

A slight flush. "Uh-huh."

"Why didn't you try to get away?"

Carson's stare became fixed. "He was filming us."

"Us?"

"All of us . . . there—"

"How did *you* get there?"

Carson gazed at the ceiling. "John Damone."

Lord tried to sound casual. "Who's John Damone?"

"Her manager." Bending forward, Carson twisted the broken end of his cigarette like a joint. "He hired me."

"How did you know him?"

Carson returned the butt to his mouth. "The Army."

"In Vietnam?"

Surprise appeared on Carson's face. He nodded.

Lord spoke softly now. "Did he know you'd shoot Kilcannon?"

Carson's eyes went lifeless as nail heads.

"Damone or anyone?" Lord snapped.

No expression; it was as if each question pushed Carson further beneath the skin. Then, quite slowly, he shook his head.

Lord stubbed out his unsmoked cigarette, still watching him. "Did Damone steal the concert money?"

Carson blinked.

Lord leaned forward. "The money's gone—they think that's your motive. If DiPalma finds it on anyone you know, he'll use it to get the death penalty."

Carson ground his cigarette to a nub. Softly, he said, "I don't know about any money."

"Did someone pay you?"

Carson stared at the ashtray. "No."

"Then why in hell did you shoot him?"

Carson seemed to steel himself. "He sold out veterans."

"In what way?"

"He wouldn't help us. During the war—he led demonstrations. . . ."

Lord tilted his head. "You must have been in high school."

Carson nodded, as if this ancient anger were fresh and reasonable. "Where did you live?" Lord asked.

"New Jersey."

"Did you ever meet him?"

Carson's mouth twitched. "Just tonight."

Lord gave himself a moment. "Where in New Jersey?"

"Monmouth County." It seemed to require thought. "Near Clarksburg."

"Is there someone I should call? A wife?"

A moment's feeling in the eyes. "It doesn't matter."

The answer sounded more human, even lonely. "She'll need to know, Harry."

Folding his arms, Carson stared past him.

"I've got some advice," Lord said at length. "You'd better listen."

Carson broke the filter off a second cigarette.

"DiPalma," Lord began with emphatic clarity, "needs to convict you worse than you can ever know. He's not above taping you, even though it's illegal. Don't say or do anything. Don't show emotion, don't trust any other prisoner, because they might slip a spy in on you. Go on like you're a POW —name, rank, and serial number. And if this is an act, keep it up." Behind the hand which held the cigarette, Lord thought he saw the shadow of a smile. Softly, he finished, "Except with me."

Carson looked away. Lord wondered if he'd imagined the smile because he remembered Kilcannon's.

Turning, he waved to the deputy.

When he glanced back, Carson was holding out the pack of cigarettes.

"Nonfilter," Lord said. "I'll remember."

The deputy stepped between them, clapped Carson in handcuffs, and led him away. He did not look back.

DiPalma was waiting. "Got anything?" he asked harshly. "Or any*one*?"

"Not yet." Lord hesitated. "Where do I find Damone?"

DiPalma's chin raised. "At the Fairmont."

"Thanks."

DiPalma stepped in front of him. "If I get no help from Carson, it's a death penalty case."

"I'll hold the thought." Lord brushed past him, headed for the elevator.

When he reached the entrance, the crowd remained, though it was nearly light.

Reporters surrounded him, cameras, flashbulbs. It had happened too quickly, Lord thought, and in the wrong way.

"Is there a conspiracy . . . ?"

The question was lost in others. Into the nearest microphone, Lord said slowly and distinctly, "Mr. Carson has asked me to defend him. I intend to."

"Fucker," someone shouted from the sidewalk. "You'll get it in the back."

Scattered cheers arose. Three police formed a wedge, breaking Lord through to the alley where he had parked.

His windshield was shattered.

"Thanks anyhow," Lord murmured. Then he started along the sidewalk, past TV trucks and away from the crowd and cops, rushing toward his office, a mile away.

Cass was sitting with a newspaper folded in her lap. It was seven o'clock.

"Sorry," Lord said. "It took longer than I thought."

Cass brushed a hand through short red-brown hair. She looked tired, subdued. "What's he like?"

"Semidissociative or a brilliant actor." Lord sprawled in his chair. "He's also a Vietnam vet."

"*That's* his reason?"

The phone began ringing. "The reason he gave was politics."

"Not money? Do you believe that?"

"Clients lie to you all the time." Lord paused. "The stuff about politics sounded like a recorded message. So did everything else."

"Maybe he eats junk food."

Lord stared at her. "I know you liked Kilcannon," he said at last. "But I can't turn this down."

Cass smiled bleakly. "What does Marcia say?"

"What you'd expect. She liked Kilcannon too."

The telephone kept ringing. After a time, Cass said, "I'll try to help keep things going. You won't have much time."

Lord imagined trying to build a defense while it was examined by the media and second-guessed in bars. "I'll need help with Carson too. Right away."

With exaggerated care, Cass picked up the telephone, depressed the receiver, and left it off the hook.

"Carson answered DiPalma with a formula," Lord said, "right out of the manual for combat soldiers. It's interesting in light of how he acted." Cass picked up a pad and pencil. "Call the VA and veterans' groups. Find out who I can talk to about Vietnam stress syndrome, especially psychiatrists."

"Aren't you jumping to conclusions?"

"I have to jump somewhere. But I also want school, service and employment records, any priors, psychiatric treatment, et cetera, et cetera. Go heavy on political involvement—see if it's real. After that we'll talk to friends and relatives. I think he's got some in New Jersey—Monmouth County."

Cass wrote this down. "Unless Carson gives me some basis for a deal," Lord went on, "I'll have to plead him guilty or insane. DiPalma knows that. He'll try to connect Carson with co-conspirators, radical politics, or the robbery—any form of rational motive—and send him to the gas chamber. To prove him legally insane, we've got to show that he didn't understand what he was doing and that it was wrong." Lord paused, searching for a rationale. "A jury might believe that shooting Kilcannon was a crazy thing to do. . . ."

As he paused, Cass glanced at the folded newspaper.

"What is it?" Lord asked.

She placed it on his desk, open to the front page. The headline was "Kilcannon Slain." Beneath it, Stacy Tarrant bent over him, lips parted.

Lord stared at the photograph. "We met last night," he murmured finally. "DiPalma's going to kill me with her."

Cass turned away.

The telephone started buzzing, interrupting their silence. "The receptionist will need a standard speech," Lord said, crisp again. "No interviews or statements until I decide otherwise. Meanwhile, I'm going to the Fairmont."

She seemed to color. "You're trying to see Stacy Tarrant?"

"Her manager—a man named Damone. He reported the robbery. He also hired Carson, which bothers me. I'd like to get to him before he has time to think."

"Isn't he the one in Chinatown who tried to save Kilcannon?"

"Was he?" Lord rubbed the bridge of his nose. "I guess that slipped my mind. Anyhow, I've got to see if he'll tell me what he told the police."

He stood to leave, then turned back, angling his head toward the newspaper. "Read that for me," he asked softly, "then throw it out, okay?"

"Okay."

"Thanks."

Lord headed out the door.

* * *

The trip was uneventful. The passengers on the bus seemed drained; the reporters watching the ornate lobby of the Fairmont did not yet know his face. When he picked up the house phone, asking Damone's room number, no one heard him.

He took the elevator to the sixth floor, to evade the guard who would be waiting on the eighth. But the second guard he'd half-expected patrolled the stairwell.

"Are you a guest, sir?"

"A vistor—to room 803."

The guard shook his head. "That's Mr. Damone's."

Lord took a card from his wallet, wrote "Harry Carson" above his name, then added, "Vietnam?" "Give him this."

The guard stepped into the hallway, calling someone.

As moments passed, Lord had the sense of acting out a tasteless dream, certain that Damone would not see him. When a cop appeared to shepherd him upstairs, he was startled.

Two uniformed police watched the suite next to Damone's.

The guard followed Lord's gaze. Pointing to 803, he said, "It's *this* one."

The door was cracked open. Hesitant, Lord knocked, then stepped inside.

The drapes were drawn. Sitting cross-legged on the floor was a barrel-chested man with olive skin, black eyes, and a black beard. He stared with such fixity that Lord simply murmured, "I'm Carson's lawyer."

Damone's head tilted toward the next suite. The gesture said that Lord had so little excuse for coming that it did not require comment.

"Sorry," Lord said. "But I'm trying to find out why."

With the fluid menace of a boxer, Damone rose and pulled the drapes open. Turning, he asked, "What makes you think I know!"

Like the guarded suite, the sense of Damone's latent anger unsettled Lord. The sunlight hurt his eyes.

He turned from it, walking to the center of the room. "You never discussed Kilcannon?"

"No." In the light, Damone's face was blunt-featured and hard. Only his voice became softer. "Doesn't he say why?"

"Not yet." Lord saw that there were circles beneath Damone's eyes. "Before the concert, how did Carson act?"

"Edgy. But he did his job." Damone finished with lacerating irony. "The sound system was perfect."

To a jury, Lord knew, this would spell cool-headed sanity. "Did the police ask that?"

"Yes." Damone watched him. "But not about Vietnam."

"He mentioned you were there," Lord offered. "I hoped maybe you could help me."

"What does *he* say?"

Lord tried to deflect the question. "It's more how he acts—remote, almost detached. I thought somehow the war might have caused that."

Damone was silent. "Nothing that happened there," he said finally, "justifies *this*."

"I guess I wondered about the nature of his service."

Damone still watched. Lord began to feel a wordless second conversation beneath the first, in which Damone was warning him off. "We were in a special unit," he answered tersely.

"What unit?"

"We didn't have a name. And I don't tell war stories."

Lord tried another angle. "I guess he was okay in Vietnam."

"Not exactly." Damone's tone grew flatter, quieter. "He'd been in the Long Binh Jail. For assaulting an officer."

At that moment, Lord saw himself as DiPalma, constructing a pattern of violence. "Was there a court-martial?"

Damone walked to the window. "No." The voice was soft now. "I got him out."

The answer had such resonance that Lord felt it in everything Damone had said or done before.

"What made you do that?"

"We were looking for volunteers." Damone's shoulders dipped. "Before, they'd processed us into 'Nam together."

"What was he like then?"

"Young." Facing Lord, there was movement in the black liquid eyes. "Only kids and suckers fought that war."

Lord paused. "But later, you hired him for Stacy Tarrant."

"He couldn't keep a job—I felt sorry for him." Damone looked at the floor. "Again."

Lord let that linger. "When you tackled Kilcannon, was there something about Carson that worried you?"

There was a long silence. "It was reflexes."

"War reflexes?"

"Yes."

"But Vietnam doesn't relate to what Carson did."

Damone's gaze rose to Lord's. "What makes you think," he said slowly, "that anything I'd say would *help* Harry Carson."

In his tone, Lord heard time running out. "What about the money?" he asked.

Damone gave a first, bitter smile. "Someone kicked in the door and ripped it off—happens all the time on the road. I forgot that when Harry shot Kilcannon." His speech suggested barely suppressed anger. "You could say I blew my job."

"That much cash would fill a suitcase. How could someone just walk off with it?"

Damone crossed his arms. "Did you at least see a *film* of the shooting?"

"Yes."

"The people there," he finished, "were watching Stacy and Kilcannon."

There was feeling in the words, a guilt and self-division far deeper than anger. "How is she?" Lord asked.

Damone's face and eyes went hard.

"Take off," he said.

"Remember where we were last night?" Marcia asked.

Lord ate chili from a can. It was ten o'clock; Christopher was in bed. He had not seen her since Kilcannon's death, had not slept in forty-eight hours. He did not answer.

The telephone rang.

Marcia answered. "He's eating," she snapped. "Don't call here." Slamming it down, she stared at Lord.

"I know how you must feel," he said.

"They've been calling all day—not just reporters. Some man said he'd find *me* if he couldn't get to you."

It startled him. "I'll call the police. . . ."

"How can you defend someone like that?"

Framed in the kitchen door, she was rigid. "I can't look at it as you do, Marsh. Sometimes I wish I could."

"But this is the big case," she said harshly. "Isn't it?"

He looked at the newspaper beside his plate. In black borders was a statement by the president, who had despised Kilcannon in life. "Today we mourn the tragic loss of a gallant young leader, so ripe with promises to keep. . . ."

"Yes," Lord said finally. "This is the big case."

"Even if it's a fucking *robbery*?"

"That's DiPalma's problem." Lord kept staring at the paper. "In one sense, I'm better off not knowing where the money went. It might be no help to Carson."

"I don't like you for that."

"You're not alone."

"Damn you. Don't you ever *feel* anything?"

He looked up again. "Maybe you should go to your folks. . . ."

"I'm not going to drop out of life because you've done this."

"Then we'll put in an alarm system."

"How can we afford that? Is Carson rich?"

Lord smiled faintly. "I'm afraid this one's at government rates. . . ."

"Tony, we can't take out a second mortgage. I won't sign."

Lord watched her. "I'll call Tom Mulvaney at the police department," he said finally. "How's Christopher?"

"Confused. The whole thing's over his head—he can't even understand why you couldn't go to the ballgame."

Moments ago, Lord had gone to Christopher's room, remembering that he had done this the night before.

"Drop it for *his* sake," Marcia said. Pausing, she finished in a lower voice. "After all, you're the one who wanted him."

In that moment, Lord forgot himself. "Hasn't it been kind of handy to have someone *else* to blame things on? You might have won the Nobel Prize by now. Hell, you might even have gotten a job. I don't recall telling you not to."

Marcia paled. In a trembling voice, she said, "That's unforgivable."

"So much is."

She turned away. Standing, Lord could not find words to cause the words before to vanish. "I'm sorry. . . ."

The phone rang again. Marcia started, but did not move. "We'll get an answering machine," Lord tried.

She was silent; the phone kept ringing. Lord spoke to her back. "I have to go out."

The phone still rang. "At ten-thirty," she said dully.

"Yes."

She folded her arms, hugging herself.

"Keep the dead bolt locked," he told her, and left.

Crossing the tracks on the edge of Potrero Hill, Lord passed through blocks of corrugated warehouses. It was like the underside of any city, except that the lights of downtown San Francisco were bright and close.

Lord parked near a brick warehouse on DeHaro Street and walked to the fire escape. Climbing to the second floor, he saw that the door was left ajar.

The warehouse was dark and silent; entering, Lord had an unwelcome thought of Kilcannon. Then he saw light coming from behind a wood partition.

On the other side were a cot, an old refrigerator, a sink, and a stove. A man sat at an easel, several beer cans next to his paint-speckled bench. His face glistened with sweat.

"So," he said, "the guy who shot Kilcannon is a vet."

Lord stepped closer. "That's right."

The man put down his paintbrush. He was thin and mustached, and though Lord knew him from television as David Haldane, leader of a Vietnam veterans' group, a certain withheld intensity reminded him of Damone. But what unsettled Lord was that he lived here. "And now," Haldane countered, "you want to scam some Vietnam defense."

"I'm here to learn."

"All right. You know how vets kill people when it happens?" Haldane snapped his fingers. "Like that—'cause something brought it back. Christ, Carson brought a fucking Mauser to work."

"I don't pretend to understand him yet."

"Understand *this*." Haldane stood to face him. "No vet I've talked to wants this guy to get off by faking post-Vietnam stress. There's too much at stake."

"Such as?"

"All the guys who *didn't* shoot Kilcannon." The blue eyes held Lord's. "Try out some numbers—a hundred and ten thousand suicides among Vietnam vets, fifty thousand more deaths in one-car crack-ups or from drugs or alcohol. What they need is jobs and help, not some lawyer trying to walk Carson on their backs 'cause that's all you've got going."

"Then you'd better educate me. If a defense won't fly, I don't want to screw it up."

"And what if it does fly? The whole country points at us."

"Maybe I can educate *them*. Look, can you really sacrifice Carson to help you politically?"

"It happened before," Haldane retorted. "Fifty-six thousand times."

As Lord glanced at the easel, he saw that Haldane's oil was of a Vietnamese child. "We're not getting anywhere," he said. "And I've got a vet in jail."

"What do you want to know?"

"How to tell Vietnam stress from something else."

Finally, Haldane shrugged. "For openers, take a real good look at Carson's life before, during, and after the war. Most combat vets with serious stress have two different lives—the war's like a fault line."

"Why?"

Haldane gave a sour smile. "It's real simple, man. Take your pet cat and start lobbing hand grenades all around him—by nightfall you've got a different cat."

Lord paused. "What was it like for you?"

"I was in the Iron Triangle, during Tet." Haldane's face closed off. "You were in college, right?"

"Then law school."

"And I'm a night watchman." Haldane lit a cigarette. "A lot of vets come back with an *attitude*, man. They remember when other people's self-promoting trips killed off their friends."

"Is that why Carson couldn't hold on to jobs?"

Haldane exhaled. "What else he tell you?"

"I've got a problem with the attorney-client privilege." Lord hesitated. "Let's say there was something about Kilcannon screwing veterans."

"Then he got that much right." Haldane leaned over, pulling up one pants leg until Lord saw discolored scabs. "That's Agent Orange, not poison oak. I showed that to Kilcannon."

"You met him?"

"Me and some other vets. We wanted this Senate committee he was on to vote money to study the effects of Agent Orange—lesions, screwed up brain chemistry, birth defects, the whole schmear. He did a little tap dance about how sympathetic he was and then told us to organize. He was off running for president the day they voted it down."

"How would Carson know about that?"

"One of the guys wrote an article called 'A Great Listener' about what a phony Kilcannon was. But nobody wanted the man dead." Haldane gave a shrug of laconic hopelessness. "I mean, what's the point?"

"Have any of you met Carson?"

Haldane shook his head. "I called some people in L.A. Never heard of him."

"What about Damone?"

"Just a name. Too busy with Tarrant to help out."

"He did give Carson a job."

Haldane stamped out the cigarette. "Fucked up there, didn't he."

Lord shrugged. "I'm going to need a shrink to examine him. An honest one who does therapy—not a professional witness."

Haldane thought. "Call Marty Shriver, in Berkeley. He's a good guy—works with vets who can't pay much. But do your homework."

"I will. . . ."

" 'Cause he won't like this either. And if Carson shot Kilcannon so some pals could boost the cashbox, no one's going to touch it." A mocking edge came into Haldane's voice. "You'd better figure this guy out."

"I understand."

"Yeah. I think you *do* understand that."

Haldane sat, staring at the half-finished child. When Lord left, he was painting.

Outside it was dark and cool. Lord took the fire escape, letting his eyes adjust to the night.

At the bottom, he heard something hit metal. He flinched, wheeling.

It was a cat robbing a garbage can. Its eyes glowed like yellow stones.

2

Lord and Cass sat watching Kilcannon's funeral.

The body had been flown to Princeton for a service in a Catholic church, broadcast by SNI. Cameras roamed the crowd outside—an old woman crying, two black children, a priest. Then their faces dissolved to the casket.

A silver-haired senator spoke with Irish eloquence:

"A novelist once wrote of his hero, 'He was born with the gift of laughter, and a sense that the world was mad.' Jamie Kilcannon knew too well that the world he wished to make gentle is too often mad. But even in madness, we remember the gift of his laughter. . . ."

The camera panned from the president and the first lady to a weeping man in a bow tie, then Stacy Tarrant, and stayed.

Lord leaned closer, taking in the haunted look, the way she held her head quite still. She had walked up the steps of the church with the same strong-willed dignity, so slowly that Lord thought she wished to pierce those watching with the wrong that Carson had done. Now he wondered whether law had stripped him of a normal response to tragedy. Yet the thought persisted: this purpose might sustain her.

As Lord watched, she listened to the senator's eulogy.

"And even in death, the terrible beauty of his last spoken words reflects his larger hope for mankind: 'Is everyone all right . . . ?' "

Stacy's gaze wavered, then fell.

"Jesus," Lord murmured.

The service ended.

Lord and Cass watched as she left with Damone, controlled again. Damone's face showed nothing; dimly, Lord tried to imagine the complexity of his feelings.

"We'd better go now, Cassie. We're due in court."

She nodded, facing the screen. As they left, Stacy stepped into a black limousine, and disappeared.

After this, the courtroom felt like a cathedral, the arraignment even more like the ritual Lord knew it to be. As Judge Rainey told him that he was charged with murdering Kilcannon, Carson stared as if listening to Latin. Reporters and artists filled the benches, scratching notes or first hurried sketches. When it was over, Lord touched Carson's shoulder, and then two deputies led him away.

Cass stared after him. "He looks stoned," she told Lord.

"He's high on life."

To his relief, Lord saw a small smile.

Outside, reporters spilled down the steps.

"What's his defense?" someone called out. Lord and Cass kept going, until he bumped into a trench coat with breasts.

Trapped, he saw unruly black hair, a mobile-looking mouth, then bright hazel eyes with an off-center glint. "Give me a break, Mr. Lord. I'm not pretty enough to make anchorwoman."

The misplaced flirtiness was so human that Lord almost laughed. "Who are you?"

"Rachel Messer—Channel 6."

"Okay, Rachel. Maybe when I know what to say."

"I can help you," she said cheerfully, and stepped aside.

Cass's Volkswagen was double-parked in front. Lord slid into the passenger seat, staring at the crowd.

"I wonder," he told her, "if Carson could get a fair trial on the moon."

She pulled away. "DiPalma hasn't found the money yet. Or co-conspirators."

"And Carson won't talk about Vietnam."

She glanced at him. "Looks like we'll get his records up to the stint in Long Binh Jail. With any luck, we can find someone who served with him to talk with us."

"But not Damone. And the impression he gave was that he can hurt Carson, not help him."

"Maybe you can find some way to appeal to him. Later."

"There *is* no way." Saying this, Lord realized he was certain of it. "Whatever Damone does is for his own reasons."

Carson puffed a Lucky Strike. " 'Nam?" he said. "Again?"

"Things you remember."

Carson laughed smoke. "Water."

"Wet?"

"Yes." The smile faded. "I can feel it on my skin."

Lord doodled on his notepad. "What else?"

Carson stretched out his free hand, watching it waggle. "Choppers, swaying before they'd drop you."

"When was that?"

"I don't remember." Carson's arm went slack. "Ask Damone."

"He won't talk to me. Where were you, anyhow?"

"The jungle." Carson's eyes closed. "It's all a blur—dark. I took a lot of dex."

For a moment, the skin around his eyes seemed to tighten. And then he was gone, Lord thought, absolutely gone. Staring at his useless notes, he wondered if Carson remembered DiPalma was waiting to try him for murder.

"Was that after you were in prison?" he asked.

Carson's eyes opened.

"The Long Binh Jail," Lord prodded.

Carson seemed to focus, intoning, "The LBJ."

"What happened when you got out?"

Slowly, Carson shook his head. "I don't remember, man."

"How'd you get there?"

"I butt-stroked a lieutenant."

"Why?"

"Fucker wanted us to count bodies."

"What did *Kilcannon* do?"

Carson stubbed his cigarette. "I don't see what the big deal is."

"The big deal is that he's dead."

"It's a rotten world, man." Suddenly, Carson's eyes seemed moist. "I remember when my kid was born, so pretty. I almost wanted to choke her so she'd never know."

"Where is she?"

"Somewhere. South Carolina—I can't find her."

"What happened?"

"I fucked up. Couldn't support 'em. . . ."

"What happened to the concert money?"

Carson watched the dying cigarette. "I don't know," he finally said. "I just don't know."

Lord wondered whether to believe him; only his child broke the litany of nonresponses. Half-curious, half-despairing, he decided to try another tack.

"What's it like, Harry? In the cell."

Carson thought. "It's like being numb. No people—sometimes I feel like my mind's just floating there."

"What do you think about?"

Carson stared at his hands. "I try to remember things. You know, *real* things."

Lord repressed the impulse to ask about Vietnam. "Real things?"

Carson paused. "Sometimes I think about being a kid."

Lord handed him another cigarette. "What's the first smell that comes to you?"

"Smell?"

"Uh-huh." Lord hesitated. "I can remember hugging my grandfather. He wore starched collars—he smelled like soap and starch to me."

Carson smiled faintly. Then he lit the cigarette, took a drag, and closed his eyes again. He was silent for some moments.

"Strawberries," he said.

Five hours later, Lord began dictating his notes, reorganizing the sequence, trying to capture the tone and feeling of what Carson had told him.

Strawberries.

He was maybe three, and the basement was full of them. Light came through a small square window. The strawberries were stored in corners: in the moist, musty basement, they smelled fresh and sweet and ripe. He would help his mother crate them. Much later, after his father had given them up, Harry still imagined that his mother smelled like strawberries.

The farm. Sometimes he thought about that.

He can feel its rhythms. Rousting Joey at 5:00 A.M. to milk the cows. They stumble through the darkness, Joey rubbing his eyes, and turn the light on in the barn. The cows wait in their stalls. Joey feeds them grain; Harry strains the warm clover-smelling milk, puts it through the cleaning equipment on the back porch, bottles it. At 4:00 P.M. he does this over as Joey cleans the barn. Cows don't know what weekends are.

Their wood-frame house sat on a crest surrounded by pines and oaks, overlooking the rolling fields and knolls which were all central New Jersey had. Before Mass Harry senior would stand out front to see what it needed. When the steps began sagging from thousands of footsteps, his father built new ones. You couldn't slip a fingernail between the boards.

His father had doled out projects between Mass, their 2:00 P.M. dinner, and "The Ed Sullivan Show" since Harry had been a kid—planting or repairing the tractor or cow shed or spreading cowshit through the crops or digging a new garbage pit or sealing the well. Harry and Joey never questioned him, except about the pine trees.

One Sunday, when Harry was ten, his father was trying to sell a few sheep off for cash and discussed this with a neighbor. Driving home he was quiet and the corners of his eyes were tight. Once they had parked he led the boys out back to an overgrown thicket. "We'll plant them here," he said. "Pine trees. To pay for college."

"How will they do that?" Harry asked.

"Once they're big enough, folks will come chop them down for Christmas trees. We'll use the money to start you off."

Harry didn't get it. "Everyone we know cuts their own."

"There'll be people. John Raskin told me someone from New York City was asking after his farm. They're looking to build an electronics plant."

"Will they buy any sheep?"

"No." His father turned to the thicket. "We'll dig this out with a tractor and plant them in rows. Maybe five hundred."

The trees became another job. Harry and Joey cleared the poison ivy and sumac and tore everything up by the roots. After they'd put in stakes with lines and planted the trees, his father designed a siphon method to irrigate that made Harry and Joey haul water in barrels. It worked well enough to make weeding a bitch. Pulling them that humid summer until his back ached, Harry felt the first stirrings of rebellion. Only the sight of his father inspecting the pine trees kept him silent.

But Harry didn't brood on it. Lying in his room, he preferred listening to the night sounds coming through the window screen. There was the throb of crickets and frogs thrumming in different pitches. There was every bird sound in the world—bobwhites and whippoorwills with their two- and three-beat songs ending on a rise—barking dogs and sheep bells tinkling, geese honking, and the distant ruckus of thousands of cooped-up chickens. Harry's senses got so keen that he could place the distance of summer lightning, counting a mile for each second before the thunder followed, and still catch the other sounds. The only noise which swallowed every other was the jets roaring from McGuire Air Force Base. In his early teens, these seemed to come more often.

Harry noticed that his father started watching Huntley and Brinkley after inspecting the pines. Usually, Harry senior had gotten what news he wanted from the *Readers' Digest*; now he watched the war. One evening Harry wandered into the living room, where Chet Huntley was reading the day's body count. "Looks like our boys mostly die on weekends," Harry senior remarked.

"Why's that?"

"Nobody watches then." His father turned. "Those pines are needing water."

A year or so later, after they got rid of their sheep, Harry senior spoke of college.

They were hauling water to the pines. "We can't afford sheep," his father said. "Better to try growing more tomatoes."

"I'll miss them, though."

Harry senior nodded. He put down the water and stood amidst the trees. The tallest came to his chin. "Didn't grow fast as I thought," he remarked. "Two more years, maybe."

Harry noticed iron in the black shock of hair. "Guess they need weeding."

His father turned to him. "I can't send you next year. Not right when you graduate."

Harry shrugged. "I never wanted to leave that much."

"Raskin's selling his chicken farm to some company—people always need a back-up." His father stooped to pick a weed. "Maybe the year after."

His senior year the recruiters started calling. Harry's father watched the news but did not talk about the war. The only time his anger showed was when some law student named Kilcannon put together an antiwar rally at Princeton. "They're not against *you* going," he snapped. "They're just scared we'll still be there when they lose their college deferments."

Harry remembered that when the draft board called him into Princeton for a physical. They stripped him down to his underwear and shoes and walked him and the other guys through a bunch of tests that showed they still had heartbeats and could piss in jars. Fifteen at a time, they ended up standing on crosses which were taped to the floor: for some reason, Harry and some black guy were in with thirteen Princeton kids who knew one another. Three doctors in white coats made them drop their pants and bend over, and then asked anyone with a doctor's letter saying he couldn't go in to take one step forward. Thirteen white guys from Princeton stepped off the cross holding letters and were sent off to see more doctors. The black kid, who didn't know what was happening, was bounced for having one leg shorter than the other. Harry just stood on the cross.

On the way home he was depressed. But when spring came without any letter he half-forgot. Beth Winship made that easier. They were in the same class at the regional high school: she liked him, she admitted, because he got good grades. Later she liked him for what they did in his car. She had kind of soft, pushed-in features which seemed made out of clay, but right in the middle were these green eyes that lit the whole thing. After a time the eyes were all Harry saw.

The night they graduated Beth let him. "I don't want you to go," she said afterward.

Her body felt warm. "Maybe they won't take me for a while."

The next month he got his notice. His father didn't say much, just stared at the pines.

One night, Harry joined him at the window. "Lots of kids are going to Canada," he said. "You can see it on the news."

Harry senior's mouth kind of moved. "That's them."

"Beth and I could go. We've talked about it."

"Maybe it hasn't supported us like it should, but I did this farm for a reason. Who'd take care of it, after?"

"Joey could."

"*No.*" When his father faced him, a vein stood out on his forehead, and his voice was thick. "Are you *scared*, Harry?"

Harry turned away.

But it was the old man who couldn't look at him when he left for the Army.

When the telephone rang, it was past ten-thirty, and Lord had finished.

"Is this Anthony Lord?"

A muffled voice—bland, without accent. "Yes."

"You have a son named Christopher."

Lord stood. "Who *is* this?"

The line went dead.

3

"Carson," Shriver said, putting down Lord's notes, "is a Boy Scout."

They sat in a house cut up into offices in a run-down part of Berkeley. Shriver's baldness, outsized earlobes, and hanging jowls made the otherwise youthful psychiatrist remind Lord of Grumpy in the Seven Dwarfs.

"Boy Scout?" he asked.

Shriver nodded. "You've got two types most prone to postwar stress. The first was scary to begin with. The second is a naive kid whose belief in authority was blown to shit in Vietnam. Like Carson, maybe."

"How did that happen?"

"Several reasons. As with Harry Carson, the draft sent the youngest soldiers in our history to fight a war that was meaningless *and* murderous —no one could explain why they were there, and they kept getting butchered taking and abandoning the same hills. And they knew most people *weren't* there. Like you, I assume."

"Uh-huh."

"You can bet Carson picked that up in a nanosecond. There's an axiom: veterans only trust other veterans. He doesn't say who his friends were?"

"Maybe Damone."

"What happened to them's critical. Which brings me to the rotation system."

"The thirteen-month tour?"

"Right. The average grunt measured his 'Nam time like a stretch on death row—each day he survived was another foot in the escape tunnel. Short-timers didn't trust rookies because they might get them killed; rookies didn't want to invest in guys who were leaving. So kids like Carson had a few close friends, and they kept getting shoveled into bags."

"Nice."

Shriver's smile was sardonic. "Nicer when their officers helped shovel them. By the time Carson got there we were bailing out, so only career officers punching their ticket had any stake in it. And the only success *those* guys could measure was counting dead VC." He gave a mock philosophical shrug. "To get some, you've gotta give some up."

Lord reflected. "My problem is tying Vietnam to shooting Kilcannon. For a Boy Scout, Carson's not very forthcoming."

"You make him sound like a recalcitrant witness. Truth is, what happened to him may have been so bad that he's repressed it." Shriver leaned forward, ticking off fingers on his hand. "First, the most intense combat experiences are often so fast or so horrifying that the memory doesn't really process them. Second, some grunts were so fucked up on smack or dex that they never *will* remember—again like Carson. Finally, what they *do* remember might be too painful to talk about—'cause it's traumatic, 'cause they don't trust you, 'cause they're so ashamed they can't. And," the smile flashed again, "because they're scared to face that it screwed them up."

Lord frowned. "To spend time with him, Carson's clearly 'screwed up.' But he could be howling at the moon and not come within forty miles of legal insanity. California law requires proof that *when* he shot Kilcannon he didn't know what he was doing or that it was wrong—even though he brought a loaded gun to work."

Shriver shrugged. "They got Hinckley off."

"That was in federal court, where the government had to prove him sane. In California, I have to prove Carson *in*sane, and after Dan White got off they changed the law to make that even tougher. Which is why the feds let DiPalma grab the case and borrow the FBI. Plus, in state court they can go for the death penalty." Lord paused, frustrated. "Without Carson's help on Vietnam, I've got a snowball's chance in hell. And no one's going to believe he thought that Mauser was a banana."

Shriver considered this. "In a way, I'd be more curious about shooting the camera. *I* find it hard to believe he thought he was destroying evidence." Leaning back, he tented his hands. "The dance between real and unreal in stress cases is funny. Last year, a vet was looking out at the Oakland Hills when suddenly he flashed on Vietnam. He grabbed a gun from the house, commandeered a station wagon for his escape, and told the woman driving to go fast enough to evade the VC without getting a ticket. Finally, they ran out of gas."

Despite himself, Lord smiled. "What happened?"

"They acquitted him of kidnapping—what he did was so pointless that it made no sense except as stress." Shriver examined his nails. "Unfortunately, he hung himself."

Lord hesitated before broaching the critical question. "If I plead him insane," he began, "I'm going to need an expert."

Shriver looked up. "I've never testified."

"You're clean. I don't want to use some witness for hire."

Pensive, Shriver shook his head. "It's not just that money was taken, it's that the murder itself seems planned. And that it was Kilcannon. No matter what you think of it, Carson gave you a clear reason—politics. That's the reason that *convicted* Sirhan." His eyes met Lord's. "I'm trying to help veterans with real problems—who do what they do because they served in Vietnam. As of now, they haven't gotten much understanding from the government, the VA, even their own families. I'm not sure I want to associate them with the most notorious assassination since Robert Kennedy."

Lord realized he was tired. "Sometimes," he said, "I don't think Carson's very convenient."

Shriver gave a shrug of sympathy. "He isn't."

Lord leaned closer. "Look, in less than three months, I have to know what to plead him. And *if* he's a stress case, he's going to need more than me or a witness. He'll need treatment, or going to trial will be dangerous in more ways than one." Lord paused, trying to keep Shriver from getting away. "Just don't give me a firm no, okay? Examine him."

Shriver stood. "Maybe you can do some more work with him and come back. I am kind of curious about what happened in 'Nam once he got out of jail."

"Thanks—so am I." Lord shook his hand. "Is there a back way out? I'd like to stroll down Delaware Street."

"End of the hall." Shriver hesitated. "And good luck."

Leaving, Lord emerged two blocks from his Datsun.

A half-block behind it, on the other side, was the black sedan which had followed him. Lord kept walking toward his car until he could read its license plate, and then crossed the street.

The driver rolled down his window. Casually, Lord leaned through. "Hello, Johnny."

"How's tricks, Tony." Johnny Moore's red beard and ruddy face made him look less like an FBI agent than a professor who enjoyed the outdoors. "Wouldn't have seen me if I'd been trying."

Lord nodded. "What's DiPalma want?"

"We're investigating your connection to the Kilcannon killing."

"Tell him the money's in Switzerland."

Moore smiled. "Not finding it is making him crazed. Seeing how his career depends on winning."

Lord shrugged. "The charm of stealing cash from a rock concert is that no one can trace it."

"Still, he can't accept coincidence. But I expect this is meant to scare you."

"And identify my witnesses."

Moore glanced at his mirror. "Just keep an eye on him, Tony—and whoever else might follow you. This case isn't going to make you very popular."

Lord slapped the hood, walked to his car, and went to see Carson.

That night, as was becoming his need, Lord transcribed more notes of what Carson had said.

In the shimmering afternoon heat, the barracks of Fort Benning stretched like a hallucination.

It had started out unreal. The Army marched two thousand newbies, hair shaved off, to a sweltering grandstand where a Catholic chaplain warned against "atheistic communism, dangerous drugs, and premarital sex." The last got scattered applause.

Since then, Harry's platoon had got a day's sleep a week and everyone was tired and pissed. Only the letters from Beth, and being in better shape than most others, kept him going. He couldn't believe he was here.

The black first sergeant, Pullman, was a soft-spoken guy who admired how Harry shot. But his platoon sergeant was brutal and dumb, and all he said about Vietnam was to hate the gooks on both sides. Harry mentally named him "Dickhead"; there was no way he was going to 'Nam.

How not to go struck him at Mass.

The priest-colonel who didn't like Commies or sex was losing his chaplain's assistant. The job promised safety, and Sergeant Pullman said he would help.

Harry waited to hear.

With one week left in the cycle, his platoon baked in the sun listening to Dickhead describe VC tactics and watching him stroke a pet rabbit he'd gotten. They were tired; when he kept saying not to trust dinks, they focused on the rabbit. It was so furry and soft-looking you wanted to pet it; when Dickhead slit its throat with a knife, its eyes were still big.

They sat there, sick, as he skinned it and threw the guts at them. A piece landed on Harry.

"The idea," Dickhead finished, "is don't warm to anything."

When he marched them off, Harry watched the back of his neck. "He got that from the Marines," someone whispered.

Sunday, Dickhead came around pushing savings bonds.

Harry couldn't forget the rabbit. "I don't think I want to right now."

"Listen up, Carson. I expect one hundred percent participation."

Staring at the ground, Harry slowly shook his head.

Dickhead grabbed the front of his T-shirt. "If you don't, douche bag, it's between us."

Harry looked up. This time, he nodded.

Glancing around, Dickhead squared off. "What's the matter," he taunted.

Harry thought of Beth. He was looking for a way out when Dickhead's fist struck his ribs. Staggering against the barracks wall, he saw the sergeant close in.

Harry split his nose with a lucky punch, and then Pullman ran up.

As Dickhead covered his face, Pullman pinned Harry, eyes filling with amazement and a kind of sorrow. "Man," he murmured, "you *had* that job."

Two months later, Harry landed in Vietnam.

The next morning, Lord stared at the cover of *People* magazine. The picture of Stacy bending over Kilcannon was captioned "Is Everyone All Right?"

"One more photo of St. James and the Widow Tarrant," Lord murmured, "and I'm going to throw up."

Cass watched him. "You've got a call," she finally said.

He jabbed the button.

"Tony? This is Rachel Messer."

He searched his memory. "Oh, sure—TV-6."

She laughed. "I know the whole world is waiting. But all I want is lunch."

He hesitated. "What's in it for Carson?"

"His defense needs to be humanized. Maybe I can help."

Silent, Lord examined the photograph of Stacy.

"Tony?"

"Maybe you can." He checked his calendar. "How's two weeks from tomorrow."

"Fine," she answered crisply. "Fournou's Ovens, twelve o'clock."

When she hung up, Lord slid *People* into the wastebasket, and stood.

Cass looked up. "Where you going?"

"To remind Harry there's a trial. Christ, DiPalma's got the FBI crawling all over."

He didn't return until night. Alone, he dictated the fragment he'd gotten of Vietnam, before Carson's eyes went dead.

The first bag hit the landing strip, rolled, and was still.

The sound as it hit was lost in the beating of chopper blades. The Hueys which followed grew larger in the hot, changeless sky. One after the other, they dropped their bags without touching down, as if suspended on vapor from the asphalt. Then they began beating their way back across the delta toward where the bags were from. The bags lay behind them in odd patterns and shapes.

Harry wondered who or what was inside. In front of him the guy from Knoxville started mumbling to Jesus: it seemed so feeble that Harry wished he'd stop.

There were more choppers coming.

It's your own fault, he thought—a thirteen-month walking tour of the fucking third world. All you need now is the shot you're waiting for and an M-16. It was his third day in-country; Beth's letter was still in his pocket.

They'd flown him and some other replacements into the Bin Hoa Air Base. It was about one in the morning, but the heat getting out of the plane was like a slap in the face, followed by the smell of shit burning in a used-up latrine. Then an E-6 who chewed gum said, "Welcome to Vietnam," and marched them off to some barracks like he was still at Fort Benning. On the way they passed some short-timers huddled together laughing as John Wayne charged a platoon of green-bereted actors across an outdoor screen at some Hollywood VC. "Those Cong haven't worked since *Flower Drum Song*," somebody mumbled. No one laughed. Harry didn't know the guys he marched with and didn't glance around: he was afraid they'd look scared.

The second wave of choppers neared, the guy from Knoxville prayed louder. Someone said, "It's only a shot, for Chrissakes"—there were comedians everywhere. Harry looked at the sky. The Hundred and First Airborne, he thought, but couldn't feel part of them.

The first morning in-country he'd seen one up close.

The E-6 had marched them past some palm trees to an enormous unwalled hangar full of people being processed in or out or hiding from the war awhile. There were hustlers selling dope and radios and watches, short-timers drinking and playing craps or poker, news- and cameramen looking for some action, a concession stand with soda and sandwiches, the roar of transports, a couple of sergeants on platforms, looking bored and cool like they'd set it all in motion. But what really got to Harry was when he walked off for a Coke like he was going to the corner store.

The Vietnamese vendor shoved a Coke at a GI in worn fatigues and turned to Harry. "Coke, GI?"

Harry nodded. The man gave him a lukewarm bottle. "It's not cold," Harry said.

"One dollar."

Harry couldn't tell from his face how much English he knew. He felt the other GI watch him.

"Thanks," he said, and left a dollar.

Turning, he saw that the soldier wore the insignia of the One Hundred and First. From a lineless face, his eyes looked through Harry as if staring a thousand miles on the other side of his head. Harry felt the need to say something.

"Where were you?" he asked.

The man nodded at nothing. "Custer Flats."

His voice and manner were so gentle that Harry began shifting from foot to foot. "What was it like?"

The man shook his head in a long, slow arc. Then he placed one hand on Harry's shoulder, regarding him with the detachment of a priest who has learned that the blessing he would give is pointless. Harry returned to line.

The next day they moved him to the Hundred and First.

They were herded to a bus with chicken wire strung around the windows. "What's this for?" someone asked the E-6.

"The dinks'll throw rocks and Coke bottles, sometimes grenades. Even the kids." Someone switched on a transistor and got the Airplane's "White Rabbit." As they left, Harry noticed that the base was surrounded by barbed wire.

They drove for half a day. Harry had never seen country that lush or people that poor. The road was nothing but potholes and dust, and the people in mud houses looked up at them with an air of weary fatalism. Passing, the bus kicked dust so that Harry could not see them. He imagined what they saw before the dust rose, a row of white faces criss-crossed by chicken wire. All he could do was listen to the radio and smell the other soldiers; it was hotter than hell.

Finally, he glanced at the guy next to him. He was sitting there with a look of self-containment, half-nodding with the radio like they were tooling down Route 66. Harry nearly turned away, and then the need to talk got to him. "It's unreal," he murmured.

The guy dipped his head to see him with an easy sideways motion. "Think so?"

Harry couldn't tell if he were mocking him or considered it an open question—it seemed safest to shut up. His companion slid back against the seat and closed his eyes until they reached Long Binh. Harry noticed that his dark, harsh-cut features did not soften as he slept.

Now, watching choppers, the guy's expression never changed.

The next chopper dropped two bags. One fell on the other; the guy from Knoxville murmured, "Yea, though I walk in the valley of the shadow of death, I will fear no evil . . ."

"For I am the meanest mother-fucker in the valley," the comedian interrupted. "Shut up, asshole."

The line inched forward toward a card table where two medics sat; one by one, the newbies got their shots and scurried away from the choppers and bags. Twenty minutes yet, Harry figured, and he'd begun to feel sick. Think of Beth.

They dropped another bag.

It broke open. What came out wasn't human.

Harry felt people sucking air. For one stupid moment he thought of the rabbit, then another piece spilled out. He turned holding his stomach.

Two hands grasped him. "Not on me, man."

It was the dark-haired guy. He looked past Harry at the bag, like some-one had told a bad joke. "It's okay," he said. "We'll figure it out."

"What's your name?" Harry managed.

"John Damone."

The next day, Damone was gone.

"What happened then?" Lord had asked.

It was like a screen had fallen. "They filled more bags," Carson answered, and asked to go to his cell.

When the telephone rang, Lord put down his notes to answer.

"You've been working hard, Mr. Lord." There was a pause; Lord recognized the voice, bland to the point of menace. "*Some* night, unless you stop, it's going to happen."

Lord sensed, rather than heard, a hand slowly putting down the telephone.

4

"What did you see?" Cass asked Lord.

For three nights running, on a rented videotape machine, Lord had studied the assassination. Now they sat with an instructor from the school for the deaf.

"I'm not sure," he answered. "I want Nancy to tell me."

Cass flicked on the machine.

Soundlessly, Kilcannon fell; Stacy dived to cover him. In close-up, his lips moved, then hers, then his. Watching, the instructor winced.

"Run that part again," Lord said.

Three more times, Kilcannon fell, spoke twice, lost consciousness. On the third, the woman webbed her fingers.

"Can you tell what they're saying?" Lord asked her.

Her throat sounded dry. "He asks if everyone's all right."

"And her?"

"She thinks so."

"What does he say back?"

The woman hesitated. "I'm not sure I got it."

"Shall I rerun the tape?"

"No—that's all right." She gave Lord a quirky, embarrassed look. "It's something like, 'Such a joke . . . but what does it mean?' "

"That's what he said?"

The woman nodded. Lord and Cass looked at each other.

"Thanks, Nancy," he said. Cass walked her to the door.

Lord ran the tape from the second station.

Carson shot the camera, shattering its lens. Suddenly his face filled the screen. Mauser dropped in front of him, he gaped at Kilcannon as they pinned him in a hammerlock.

Lord was studying Carson's face when Cass returned.

"What's happening with his records?" he asked.

Cass glanced at the screen. "I'm going through the list of names from the Hundred and First. Trying to track down someone who served with him."

"*If* they're still alive." He turned. "What about after they threw him in jail?"

"They say there's nothing—like he dropped off the earth." She frowned. "Maybe Damone will answer one of your letters."

"He hasn't yet. And I'll have to take DiPalma to court just to get his phone number."

"You could always subpoena him."

Lord shot her an annoyed look. "I can't have him testify without knowing what he'll say. He could devastate Carson."

"Won't DiPalma use him anyhow?"

"Damone's not on his preliminary witness list—it's like they're scared of him, too."

Cass looked toward the videotape. "I suppose," she said, "that Damone's perspective on all this is kind of complicated."

Lord followed her gaze. After a time, he said, "I keep thinking Carson looks surprised. Like he doesn't know what he's done."

He felt her hand on his shoulder. "I hope you're not trying to sell yourself an insanity defense."

Lord watched a moment longer. Then he stood, flipping off the machine. "I'm flying out to see Carson's mother."

The farm was so clear in Lord's mind that it was like returning to a place he'd remembered as better than it was. The surrounding countryside was broken into office parks for computer firms and homes for their executives; the Carsons' fields were fallow and unfenced, their house in need of paint. The porch sagged as Lord walked on it.

"I'm selling," Mary Carson told him. "Joey went to Canada, and what with Harry, that's the end of it."

Her face was grooved, and she walked with a heavy tiredness; it was hard to imagine the woman who had smelled like strawberries. Leaning on the railing, Lord watched clouds block the sun. He saw no pine trees.

"When did he come home?" he asked.

Her eyes narrowed. "June, I think. 1970."

"Were you expecting him back that soon?"

"We didn't think his time was up. Then all of a sudden there he was, not saying how or why."

"What was he like?"

She gazed out at the fields. "It was three in the morning when he got here, and he looked vacant, almost slow-witted. We sat in the kitchen, trying to talk. It was all about people dying—nothing made sense. I couldn't believe the language he used. Finally, I had to go upstairs."

"What about his father?"

"He didn't say much. But I could see him watching Harry like he didn't know him."

"How was he changed?"

"Every way. He drank and smoked—his room had a smell that made me think it wasn't always cigarettes. Maybe he took other things. Anyhow, nothing close at hand interested him anymore."

Near the porch, oaks began rustling in the wind. "Did he talk about the war?" Lord asked.

"Not even to his father. I think he felt like Harry blamed him." She flicked some paint off the railing. "What hurt was that he loved that boy so much."

"Did Harry ever write about it?"

"A few letters at first."

"Do you still have them?"

"I kept some for a while." She flicked more paint. "After what happened, his father burnt the rest. But there was really nothing from after he volunteered."

"Volunteered?"

"To extend his tour."

Lord turned to her. "You said there was something with his father."

She nodded vaguely. "One morning I went to his room and he'd crumpled newspapers all around his bed. They crackled when I stepped on them—he woke up with a start and was screaming at me to get out." She recited this like a tired family story which had been told too many times. "That's when his father came up the stairs."

The afternoon sky was lowering with the hard gray look of rain. "What did he do?" Lord asked.

"It was like he exploded with all he'd been holding in. He was red-faced —there was this vein that stood out on his forehead when he lost his temper, and then he had Harry by the collar shouting, 'Don't you *ever* treat your mother like that.'

"Harry was shaking. 'Damn you,' his father yelled. 'I went to war for three long years and still came back a man.'

"Harry just stared at him, and then he said the *F* word."

Her voice was thick. When Lord looked over she had raised two fingers of each hand to make a quote sign, and she was crying.

"Did they fight?" he asked.

She nodded blindly. "His father swung and missed. Then Harry hit him and was running down the stairs.

"His father's mouth was bleeding and I dabbed him with Harry's bed sheets. All the anger was gone—it was like he was helpless. We heard the chain saw then.

"I went to the window, his father behind me. It overlooked a grove of pine trees. Harry had the chain saw and was cutting them down, one after the other.

"Harry—my husband—didn't say or do anything. Just leaned against the windowpane with his mouth still bleeding, watching our son cut trees. Those pines were special to him."

"I know. . . ."

"And then Harry left. Beth Winship took him on."

Lord did not look at her. Finally, he asked, "Do you know where I can find her?"

"I promised I wouldn't tell where she was." Her voice grew harsh. "I want to keep seeing my grandchild."

"It would help me." More softly, Lord added, "Harry's not going to visit her now."

She straightened, hands on the railing. "Why did he do it, Mr. Lord?"

"I don't know yet."

She paused a moment. Turning, she said, "My address book's in the house." He heard the porch creak with her footsteps, and then the screen door opening.

He stayed there. The air had the fresh smell of ozone, before it rains.

The bleached blonde at the airport coffee shop looked older than Carson had described—that her face seemed to have no bone structure puffed and aged it. But he'd been right about her eyes; they were the clearest green Lord could remember.

"I'm sorry," she said. "I don't want him to know where I live. And I didn't want Cathy to hear us talking."

"How is she taking it?"

"Shaky. No one here knows who her father is, at least. But seeing him on television upset her."

Lord decided to be blunt. "Why exactly did you marry him?"

She smiled with one side of her mouth. "I thought I was Florence Nightingale. You know, if you love someone enough you can change what happened to them, even if they never tell you."

"What was he like?"

The smile faded. "Sometimes he could be so sweet, just holding my face in his hands, telling me about my eyes. But I guess what I remember most was waking up at night and realizing that he was crying, just sobbing." She looked past him. "I shouldn't tell you this, but at first I tried making love to get him out of it, telling him I loved him. He couldn't do it—when I asked what was wrong, he said, 'When you tell me that, I want to kill you.' "

Lord drank some coffee. "Did he let on why?"

" 'Because it hurts,' he said, and I finally caught on that he needed more than me.

"I think the crying was why he'd put paper around his bed—so his parents wouldn't sneak up and hear him. He kept saying he was fine, but he couldn't hold jobs—the person he worked for was always an asshole."

She shook her head. "He hated psychiatrists, like his father. What made me finally call one was the picture."

"I don't know about that."

"It was of some friend in Vietnam—he had curly, reddish hair, I think. About three days straight Harry stared at it like he was somewhere else. I called the VA."

"What did they do?"

Her eyes flashed. "Maybe he had a tumor, they said. We'll give him a brain scan."

Lord sipped more coffee. "Do you remember when that was?"

"June. I only know that because I started noticing that something always happened the beginning of June."

"Such as . . ."

She hesitated. "The fight with his father was then."

"What else?"

"One year I woke up at night and he'd covered my mouth. 'Shut up,' he said, 'they'll find us.'" Her voice fell. "He was sleeping with a knife."

Lord watched her. "Were there other things?"

Another slight pause. "He'd write poetry then like it would save his life."

"He wrote?"

She reached into her purse and pulled out a folded piece of notebook paper. "I kept one."

"Can I see it?"

She held the poem beneath her fingers a moment, then pushed it across the table.

Carson's writing was a slantwise scrawl that took Lord a moment to decipher:

> So that I can live with you
> I pretend that you're the woman I saw die
> In one bright flash of steel
> Brought back to life, because I cry

"Poor Harry," she said in a flat voice.

"Can I keep this?"

She looked away before nodding. "The funny thing is, Harry loved Cathy too—more than me, I think. But he couldn't support either of us."

"Did that bother him?"

"He was ashamed of it." She turned to him. "Did his mother say how Harry senior died?"

"No."

"He flipped a tractor, dragging fence posts by himself. Harry was a wreck—I think he felt guilty about not being there. But all he said was, 'Still trying to make it go.'"

"I don't understand."

"The farm. Because Harry couldn't go to college, he went to Vietnam. That's what made it worse when *he* couldn't take care of Cathy."

"Did he say so?"

She stared into his empty cup. "I'd get these calls after we broke up. His friend Damone was helping him, Harry was going to take care of us. But by then I was too scared."

"Of what?"

She lit a thin-smelling ladies' cigarette; the gesture, absentminded yet tense, reminded Lord of Carson. "The day he left, Harry was sulking around the house. I told him to stop it, please just stop. He didn't hear— just went vague.

" 'Stop it,' I screamed.

"He turned and slapped me across the mouth." She touched her lower lip; Lord saw where the stitches had been. "Right here.

"Cathy was crying in the door of her bedroom. I was so scared—I just wanted him gone. 'Get out,' I told him. 'You're no husband, no father, you've given us nothing but hell.'

"He blinked, like his eyes were clearing. He walked past me, kissed Cathy on the forehead when she was still crying, and left without a word."

Lord watched her cigarette burn in the ashtray. "When was that?" he asked.

"Last year." She stubbed the cigarette. "June."

5

"Tell me about Marcia," Rachel said.

Light and airy, the restaurant created privacy through smaller, separate levels. Sipping his martini, Lord answered cautiously, "We've been married seven years now."

"How did you meet?"

"One of my first prosecutions was a child abuse case. Marcia wrote a paper on it—she was a sociology major then."

"And Christopher's . . ."

"Six." Lord saw the unspoken question surface in the disturbing hazel eyes. "Frankly, Marcia and I don't see our marriage as newsworthy."

"People are interested, Tony. After all, you're young, attractive—and Harry Carson murdered another young, attractive man who might have become president."

It bothered Lord to have a symbiotic relationship to Kilcannon's perceived martyrdom. "Some days," he answered, "I can't believe my luck."

Rachel touched one finger to her lips; Lord caught a flash of red nail, the scent of perfume. "It's not luck—it's necessity. Ralph DiPalma's using the media for all it's worth, right down to Kilcannon's last words to Stacy. You've got to keep them from burying Carson before he's dead." Flashing a cocky, funny smile, she added, "And I can help."

Lord put down his martini. "What do you have in mind?"

She swirled her wine. "For Carson?"

"Uh-huh."

"Dodging all those interviews has been a mistake. I'd like to give your perspective to the public."

"And *you* get . . ."

"Everybody to watch me. 'Cause I've got you."

Her smile had an amusing child's jauntiness that made Lord wary. "Without throwing in my family?"

"Oh," she said innocently, "I just wanted to know you better." When Lord laughed, her eyes danced. "What else would you like to talk about?"

Lord feigned reluctance. "A little background that might help Harry. . . ."

"Yes?"

"Actually, there's something with DiPalma."

Lord sat holding Carson's diary.

"What his wife and mother were telling you," Shriver said, "is quite common among veterans. It's called the anniversary reaction."

"It's hard to believe he celebrates some unknown trauma every June."

Shriver frowned. "It's not voluntary. Look, do you ever associate songs on the radio to making love?"

"Sure."

"Okay—try to think of some other associations."

Lord riffled the diary. "It didn't happen to me, really, but I thought of it when you mentioned Bobby Kennedy. My girlfriend and I campaigned for him—we were watching the night he was shot after winning the primary out here. It was the last time I believed in politics or politicians." He paused. "I realize now that each June I still get angry."

Shriver gave him a look of irony. "How old were you?"

Lord smiled a little. "Eighteen."

"All right," Shriver went on, "let me try one on you where there's a known personal trauma. The children of suicides often kill themselves on the anniversary of their parent's death. In Carson's case, it raises the possibility of flashbacks—reliving some traumatic Vietnam experience as if he's still there."

"It's odd that Carson would have an intense reaction to leaving Vietnam."

"If leaving is what it was. You say he seems to have left ahead of schedule?"

"Yes. But Carson says he doesn't remember leaving at all—or what happened right before that. And we still can't find records for those last few months."

"Swell." Shriver glanced at the diary. "What's this you wanted me to read?"

"It's a poem in Carson's diary. I had to pry it loose from DiPalma—he thinks that poems still rhyme."

"That's another thing I should have mentioned—a lot of vets write poetry to try and deal with what happened." Putting on glasses, Shriver spoke the title aloud, "Golden Anniversary."

He read silently, quickly. "Kilcannon wasn't blond," he said when he had finished.

"He won't explain his reference to a camera, either. Won't say anything, really—it's just a poem. But I think DiPalma may use this to help beat insanity."

"How?"

"Because it reads like Carson *planned* to shoot someone—maybe over politics." Lord watched him. "He finished it the day he shot Kilcannon."

Shriver folded his glasses and returned them to their case. "I guess it's time I saw him," he said.

"Harry Carson," Rachel began, "poses an enigma."

Filmed at the Hall of Justice, she looked grave and intent. Her lips glistened with a faint gloss.

"Defense sources portray a rural youngster so shockingly different from the man who murdered James Kilcannon that there seems to be no connection between them. The break point—how those missing months in Vietnam affected Carson—is the central question defense attorney Anthony Lord faces in deciding whether to enter a plea of guilty, or not guilty by reason of insanity. . . ."

"At least," Cass told Lord, "someone's being decent for a change. . . ."

"A second puzzle," Rachel went on, "is whether the FBI is conducting surveillance of Lord himself. Though TV-6 has obtained the license numbers of agents allegedly involved, Prosecutor Ralph DiPalma declines comment. In an exclusive interview, Lord had this response. . . ."

Lord's tie was loosened and his desk covered with paper; he looked much younger than thirty-four. "In law school," he said earnestly, "they taught me that cases are to be tried in the courtroom. That's why, unlike the Soviets, we have a free and open jury system. That's the system Mr. Carson went to Vietnam for. I wish the prosecution showed a similar commitment . . ."

"*Oh, Tony.*" Cass shook her head, half-laughing. "I don't believe it. . . ."

Lord turned, stung. "DiPalma was screwing us. . . ."

"This is Rachel Messer, TV-6," she finished, and then Lord switched off the television.

Cass was no longer laughing. "He'll screw you back," she said.

"It can't get much worse, Cassie."

When Lord's telephone rang, he answered.

"Tony?" a male voice boomed.

"Uh-huh."

"This is Hart Taylor." Chairman of SNI, he didn't need to add. "I've just been watching you. I think it's time we met."

Taylor's private dining room topped the SNI building, overlooking the bay. It was lined with photographs of Taylor on a polo pony, at the crest of Mount Whitney, with two ex-presidents, a film actress, and his football team. In every shot he grinned like Errol Flynn's kid brother.

He grinned the exact same grin at Lord. "Sure tucked it to DiPalma, Tony. That was shrewd PR."

Lord finished his Bloody Mary. "I'm just trying to catch up."

"Still a ways to go, what with Kilcannon dead and Tarrant in seclusion." His grin narrowed in rueful sympathy. "It's the first time since Jehovah that someone's made such an impression by not being seen."

Lord swirled his drink straw. "I doubt she's given that much thought."

"Don't be sure. Can you imagine Stacy's impact when DiPalma calls her as his final witness?"

Where, Lord wondered, was this going? "It's crossed my mind," he answered dryly. "Once or twice."

"And that's exactly why I asked you here." Leaning forward, Taylor said in a caressing drawl, "We can put that moment in perspective, Tony."

"How?"

The grin returned full force. "By televising the entire trial, nationwide."

Lord felt like a fool. "You'd need the judge's approval."

"I think we'll get it, Tony—*if* both sides agree. And you lost your virginity last night." He grinned again. "This morning, Ralph DiPalma signed on."

Lord fought to control his anger. "That's because it helps him. Imagine you're a juror, Hart, with cameras watching. How easy would it be to return an unpopular verdict in front of the entire country?"

"It's your chance to tell them Carson's story."

"All I want is twelve people I might get to understand. Whatever else Harry is, he's not very promising for television."

Taylor shrugged. "Gary Gilmore was no charm boy either, and look what they did with him."

"Those were actors," Lord retorted. "Gilmore's dead."

Taylor stopped grinning. "What other problems do you see?"

"Witnesses. Cameras will encourage theirs and intimidate mine. DiPalma knows all this."

"He knows a whole lot else, too." Taylor stood, extending one arm to the window. "I don't want to sound cynical, Tony, but do you know what moves America in the nineteen-eighties? *Fame.*" His voice took on a rolling cadence. "Once you're famous, you can go from being a football player to actor to broadcaster and even to the White House. If you're a mass murderer, they time the paperback of your life story to come out with the miniseries; if you're a famous young lawyer, you might become a senator, even more. *DiPalma,*" he repeated, "knows all that."

"He also knows the judge is up for reelection." Lord's voice softened. "He may even know that you lost money last year. Because of low ratings."

Taylor scowled. "The way I look at it, the bigger audience the better—for us, Carson, *and* the judge. The Dan White verdict was unpopular because people didn't understand it."

"If you televise, there won't *be* an unpopular verdict." Lord paused a moment. "What I'm telling you, Hart, is that you'll be throwing the switch."

Taylor sat down again. "DiPalma says otherwise. Who am I supposed to listen to?"

"Your conscience."

Three days later, SNI petitioned the court.

6

DiPalma's hands were flat on the conference table, his voice precise. "It's my final offer. Guilty to premeditated murder—life sentence in a maximum security prison. He can die there."

"That's not much."

"All *you've* got is a hitch in Vietnam, with no detail."

"And you've got no motive." Lord leaned forward. "Where's the conspiracy, Ralph? Or the money? Even Carson would know he couldn't use it in jail. . . ."

"Doesn't it ever bother you that it just happened to get ripped off in the confusion, and that Carson had you all picked out? Not to mention the gun." DiPalma's eyes seemed flecked with light. "Pleading him insane risks the death penalty without knowing how the judge will rule on SNI's petition. You may end up on television with your cock hanging out."

"And an appeal I can take to the Supreme Court. They'll admire your use of SNI for leverage."

DiPalma turned up both hands. "Your client lives," he said, "and you get out of Vietnam. Let me know."

Lord nodded. "Before the hearing. One way or the other."

DiPalma left before Lord could close his briefcase.

"Twelve hours," Shriver said, "and Carson can't or won't talk about the war, leaving 'Nam, or that poem he finished. But he did open up on the subject of shrinks."

They walked in a park near the Berkeley campus. "In what way?" Lord asked.

"Doesn't like 'em. 'Cause he's perfectly sane."

"Does he mention politics?"

"Uh-huh, but I agree with you—he borrowed that somewhere. To give reasons."

"If he gives those reasons in court, he's gone."

Shriver ran a hand across the smooth top of his skull. "Unless you find *someone* to testify about what Carson did in Vietnam, you'll have a real problem connecting it to Kilcannon, or even knowing what this anniversary thing's about. . . ."

"But?"

"On his life story he's a classic stress case—only we've got no idea what was happening in his head that night. And that's where DiPalma nails me and Carson to the wall." He stopped, looking out at the park. "I can't say I envy your decision."

Lord gave him a crooked smile. "I wasn't looking for envy."

"What about guys who served with him *before* he got thrown in jail?"

"Haven't found any yet. Those names and addresses are fourteen years old."

"And Damone still won't talk to you?"

"Nope—after I saw him that morning, he just skated away."

"And nobody knows what *he* did in Vietnam, either."

"DiPalma may—for whatever reason he didn't put him in front of the grand jury, where I could get a transcript of his testimony. And *I* can't put him on without knowing what he'll say. As of now, he's out of the trial."

Shriver walked a few steps. "There may be things Damone and Carson *want* to forget—some pretty bad stuff went down over there." He folded his arms. "Strange there aren't any records."

"We had a hearing on that last week. The Army swears they don't exist, and Rainey accepts that. The only way it helps is there's also no record that Carson was jailed for assaulting an officer."

"You won't try to have him testify, I guess."

"Can't—don't know what *he'd* say, either. Besides, the postwar Harry lacks charm."

Shriver nodded. "The postwar Harry," he said, "is a mess. And we both know where he got that way."

They stopped at a park bench. On the grass a father played catch with his son; it reminded Lord that he and Christopher had not done so in weeks. He glanced sideways at Shriver. "Were you ever there?"

"Vietnam?" Shriver stared ahead. "Are you kidding? I was in med school. Incidentally, I see they want to televise the trial."

" 'They' is right. I'm opposing it. But there's no guarantee I'll win."

Shriver puffed his cheeks. "None of this sounds very promising."

"It isn't." Lord turned to him. "But if I go ahead anyhow, will you change your mind and testify?"

"Sure." For the first time, Shriver smiled. "There was never any question, was there?"

"Death?" Carson said. "No future in that, man. Life? Another fifty years of this."

He looked enervated; Lord wondered how many hours of thought had brought him to this mordant formula. "I don't lightly risk the death penalty," he answered.

Carson shrugged. "You won't be in a cell."

"Then let's talk about your defense, Harry. If I tell a jury you shot Kilcannon for his politics, there *is* none."

"That's why—"

"Is that why you slapped Beth," Lord cut in. "Because she offended you politically?"

Carson's mouth opened in a kind of croak. "Oh, man, why'd you *do* that?"

"It's a valid question—"

"*See* her."

"Because I'm trying to locate a defense. For whatever reason, you picked me as your lawyer."

Carson turned sideways. Then, quite tonelessly, he asked, "Is Cathy all right?"

"Beth says she's getting along."

"Beth—how did she look?"

"I knew her right away. It was the eyes."

Slowly, yet so completely that it moved Lord, Carson slumped, his hands covering his face. "I'm not crazy—I already told the shrink."

Lord watched him. "We're talking strategy," he said. "If I turn down DiPalma, an insanity plea's your only choice."

Carson's throat worked. "What happens if . . ."

"You get treatment. Years from now, if they decide it's worked, maybe you'll get out." Lord paused. "Maybe you'll see Cathy."

Carson's body was still. But when he looked up, grasping for a cigarette, his hand trembled. "What the hell," he said. "Anything beats this."

Christopher put his head on Lord's shoulder. "What are we reading?" he asked.

Lord could smell fresh skin, clean pajamas. "My favorite poem," he answered. "Grandpa used to read it to me."

"Did you have this book when you were a kid?"

"Uh-huh."

"It looks old."

"Thanks."

Christopher's eyes were crescents. "You don't look as old as the book. Just almost."

Lord turned in mock disgust. "Are you ready now?"

"Sure."

"That's a relief." With mounting drama, Lord began to read:

> "Isabel met an enormous bear
> Isabel, Isabel didn't care
> The bear was hungry, the bear was *ravenous*
> The bear's big mouth was cruel and *cavernous*
> The bear said, Isabel, glad to meet you
> How do, Isabel, now I'll *eat you. . . .*"

Pausing, Lord stretched out the surprise:

> "Isabel, Isabel, didn't worry
> Isabel didn't scream or scurry
> She washed her hands and straightened her hair up
> Then Isabel quietly ate the *bear* up."

Christopher's throaty chuckle reminded Lord of how his own father had delighted him with this inversion of the odds. "Does that mean you're going to eat *me*?" he asked Christopher.

"With peanut butter." His son's laughing voice turned skeptical. "Do you think a *girl* could do that?"

"At least as well as I could."

"Dad?" Christopher turned to him, suddenly tentative. "Mikie said you're a murderer. I said you're not."

Lord felt a deep, quiet anger. "You were right. 'Cause I've never murdered anyone."

"But the other man did, and you're helping him."

"Yes, because I'm not sure he knows why. Our country sent him to a war, Christopher. I think it messed him up."

"Were you in the war?"

Lord pulled him closer. "No."

For a moment, Christopher was silent. "When I'm in school again, will the policeman still drive me?"

"Maybe. Just until the case is over."

Looking up, Lord saw Marcia in the doorway, with a glass of wine.

"In a minute," he told her.

He turned back to his son. "There might be more about this on TV—other people may say stuff. If it happens, tell me, so we can talk."

"Sometimes you're not home."

Lord kissed his forehead. "I will be, okay?"

"Okay."

He stayed until Christopher slept.

Marcia was in the living room. She held the wineglass tightly in both hands.

"What is it?" she asked.

Lord sat next to her. "I may decide to plead him innocent, Marsh. It would mean a trial."

Her eyes widened, telegraphing astonishment. "Why?"

Lord hesitated. "I honestly think he's not responsible. . . ."

"My God, are you that eager for the big case?"

As if hearing herself, she turned, taking a hasty sip of wine. Lord decided to make light of it. "If I start sounding eager for this one, give me a saliva test."

She put down the glass. "What is it you want?"

"Understanding, to start."

"I can't be *you*." In the way she flung her arms, Lord saw that she had drunk more wine than usual. "I accept what you do. But you expect me to pretend I don't have feelings."

"I don't. But I have them, too."

She shook her head. "Here we go again, Tony—marshaling the evidence, marking our wounds as exhibits. Just like you and DiPalma."

Strangely, it made him smile. "Maybe you should go to law school."

"With what money?" She made her voice tired. "I remember asking what you wanted."

He faced her. "If I plead insanity, we'll need a second mortgage."

"For *Harry Carson*?"

"To pay the bills. I'd have another three to four months of not doing much on other cases. There're house payments, the new alarm system . . ."

"For Harry Carson," she repeated. "I told you this would happen the day you took the case."

He gave a broad, helpless shrug. "We're broke."

She watched, silent, until Lord's arms fell to his side.

"You're right," he said finally. "Domestic arguments begin sounding like trials, where nothing that's said is quite true or quite fair. Maybe it's that we lead such different lives. . . ."

"Oh, Tony, please—it's so hollow when you turn philosophical. It's not *you*. The man I live with burns to achieve, no matter what it costs."

He made himself wait to answer. "If I end up disappointed with my life," he told her, "it'll be because of what I've done, not failed to do."

"Then *do* it." She stood. "Go ahead, Tony. I'll sign the mortgage and watch you."

She walked briskly to the shower, as Lord had known she would.

Lord sat on the floor in a work shirt, blue jeans, moccasins. It was ten-thirty; his office was dark.

Silent and silver, Harry Carson shot Kilcannon like a robot. He fell, and then Stacy Tarrant was touching his forehead. Lord could feel the look she gave him.

"Doesn't it ever bother you," DiPalma had asked, "that Carson had you all picked out?"

Lord put on the second film.

Escaping, Carson saw the camera and knelt to fire. When he rose, it was not to run, but to stare at his hands. As he turned toward the fallen man, mouth opening, Lord froze the videotape.

If DiPalma knew the reason Carson gave was politics, he would win. Divorced from tactics and obligation, Lord knew, the morality of what he might do required a client who had acted alone, too deranged to understand his motives.

Staring at Carson, Lord pondered his own motives.

He sat there for moments. When he went to the telephone and dialed, Carson's dazed expression still filled the screen.

There were five rings and then a deep voice answered, "Yes?"

"This is Tony Lord."

There was a pause. "How did you get this number?"

"I went to court. I have to plead him tomorrow."

"I know." The voice was so flat it was hostile. "I watch TV. I even read your letters."

"Look, I need you to tell me what happened to him there."

"Ask the Army."

"There aren't any records—not for the last few months."

Damone paused again. "Then," he answered quietly, "you should ask yourself why."

"It doesn't matter—I have to know." Lord used his final, empty threat. "I can always subpoena you."

There was another, longer silence. Then, very softly, a click.

Lord watched Carson, until he heard the dial tone.

Four assistants flanked DiPalma. The five watched Judge Rainey as if Lord no longer existed.

"Case number 84-762," the clerk pronounced, "People versus Harry F. Carson."

There was the peculiar silence of massed bodies, poised for when the silence was broken. Rainey, a white-haired politician so concerned with appearances that Cass had dubbed him "The Great Oz," straightened as if posing for a portrait.

"Mr. Carson," he intoned, "the state charges that on June second of this year, intentionally and with premeditation, you shot and murdered United States Senator James J. Kilcannon. What is your plea?"

Carson gave Lord a tentative glance. "Not guilty," Lord responded. "By reason of insanity."

There was an intake of breath. Rainey slammed his gavel. "Very well. Trial will commence November first.

"The plea," he continued in a rich bass voice, "requires the court to rule on the petition of Satellite News International to televise these proceedings. We share Mr. Lord's concern that such broadcasts not prejudice the defendant's right to a fair trial, and take note of SNI's willingness to restrict itself to a single camera, without close-ups of any witness.

"We are also concerned that this case already has received massive, unavoidable publicity, to which *both* prosecution and defense have added. Nor are we unaware that in the past, political assassinations have resulted in continuing unhealthy speculation and widespread misunderstanding of verdicts reached in courts of law.

"Such a result in this case would compound the tragedy which led to it. Therefore, the petition of Satellite News International is granted."

The gavel cracked. Rainey stood, and then reporters filled the double doors as if sucked out by a vacuum.

Carson watched the bench where Rainey no longer sat. Touching his shoulder, Lord said, "I'll see you this afternoon," before the marshals led him away.

From the rear, Hart Taylor grinned at Lord.

An anger Lord could not control swept him past Taylor, through the corridors, out of the building. And then he found himself trapped with DiPalma on the highest step, facing more reporters, questions, lenses glinting in the sun.

A flash of superstition ran through him, growing to a kind of awe. Now, no one's life would be untouched—not his or Marcia's or Christopher's, not Carson's or Beth Winship's, or even Stacy Tarrant's. To *know* this, he thought, and yet be so unsure.

DiPalma had raised one hand.

"The people," he began, in a hard, rising chant, "know the rational, premeditated act of an assassin from the stupor of a so-called flashback. Mr. Carson did not murder at random or by accident. As thousands watched, he stalked a United States senator with a German-made Mauser and put a single bullet through his brain." He turned to Lord so that the cameras would record this, then faced them to conclude, "To seek another penalty than death would compound the contempt for reason which has brought us here today."

"Mr. Lord!"

Lord felt doubt and anger and necessity fuse into resolve. If this were to be tried on television, he would give them an opening statement to remember. As he framed his answer, he saw Rachel Messer pushing to be near him.

"The prosecutor," he began, "paints Harry Carson as a cold-blooded killer so that no one asks the question, Why? We intend to ask it for him.

"In 1968, when Mr. DiPalma and I were safe in law school, the government sent an eighteen-year-old boy to fight the most traumatic war in American history. That war returned to us a different Harry Carson. And it is that same war, not a 'contempt for reason,' which has brought us here today.

"If someone were to tie up their pet dog at nine in the morning and start lobbing hand grenades around him, by six that night they'd have a different dog. If, after that, the rest of us spat on the dog for having changed, then that dog would understand more about Harry Carson than either I *or* Mr. DiPalma." Facing DiPalma, Lord's voice was level but quite clear. "And if, after that, we shoot the dog, as the prosecution wishes, then none of us need understand at all."

There was a low whistle: as Rachel reached him, thrusting her microphone to his mouth, Lord saw how the news would open.

"But," he finished softly, "I believe a jury will."

Rachel grinned. Nodding to DiPalma, Lord began moving through the crowd.

THE TRIAL: STACY TARRANT

NOVEMBER 1–NOVEMBER 9

1

For the first two punishing weeks of trial, watching DiPalma prove Harry Carson an assassin, Lord waited for Stacy Tarrant.

His days ran together. He worked past midnight, awoke to scribble notes, cross-examined on a few hours' sleep. Through television, he relived DiPalma's attack in numbing third person.

Each morning he passed SNI's forty-foot broadcast truck, its satellite dish aimed at the sky like a silver web, its black cable climbing the steps to the lobby, past the usual shuffling defendants who stole for drugs, battered wives, charge-card deadbeats, jobless men and bag ladies, the half-insane who talked to themselves on the street and erupted into violence. More cameras looked past them, at him.

The cable ended at the high-security courtroom, bypassing the metal detector and theater-type seats where the press listened to piped-in sound and watched through a ceiling-high sheet of bulletproof glass. Inside, Rainey presided from a raised bulletproof bench. To his right front were DiPalma and four associates; Lord, Cass, and Carson sat nearer the jury to his left. Rainey had placed the camera behind a makeshift wood partition, so that the cameraman shifting angles would not distract the jury. But the effect was of an unblinking eye which hypnotized Carson.

Lord bought him a gray suit and had his hair cut short, trying to suggest the younger Carson he wished the jury to imagine. Instead, Lord sensed his stare at the camera remind the jurors of the violence which had brought them here.

* * *

For Carson to have a chance, Lord needed jurors with open minds. He tried to pick those who would listen to Shriver: opponents of the Vietnam War; older women with sons; young women who might prefer him to the prosecutor. But DiPalma saw this. Using peremptory challenges, he got rid of three young secretaries, a scientist from NASA, a nurse whose teenager had gone through counseling.

DiPalma's priorities were equally as clear to Lord: admirers of Kilcannon; order-givers who disliked weakness; ex-military officers or business executives; fundamentalists; feminists who would identify with Stacy Tarrant. They seemed to come at him without a break. With one juror left to pick, Lord used his last peremptory challenge to strike a female executive who kept smiling in his direction; hard experience had taught him that smilers voted against the lawyer they smiled at.

Cass was already watching the next prospect, a severe-looking woman with a Bible. "Get rid of her," she whispered. "Somehow."

Briskly, DiPalma found out that the woman was childless, a bookkeeper, had never traveled or known a psychiatrist. He blessed this life with an approving smile and sat.

Rising, Lord asked, "You *do* know that Mr. Carson has been indicted for the murder of Senator Kilcannon?"

The woman's thick glasses gave her a wary look. With a curt nod toward Carson, she answered, "Yes."

"But you're willing to presume his innocence."

She frowned. "I know that's the law."

"I gather you're afraid that the indictment means that he's *not* innocent."

She clutched her Bible. "Yes."

"Your Honor, I think we can excuse Miss Walker."

The judge leaned forward. "Miss Walker, if I tell you to ignore Mr. Carson's indictment, will you?"

After a moment, she answered, "Yes."

"Challenge denied," the judge said. "You may continue, Mr. Lord."

Lord turned to Rainey long enough to register amazement, then faced the woman. "I notice you've brought your Bible, Miss Walker. Do you sometimes pray?"

Her eyes brightened. "Yes," she answered firmly.

"Does God answer your prayers?"

"He *hears* them. He hears the prayers of all those who believe."

Lord looked puzzled. "But does He speak to you?"

She gave a resolute nod. "In my thoughts."

"Does that happen when you ask Him to?"

"No." She scowled at Lord's incomprehension. "When He wishes, He will speak to me."

"Even about decisions in your everyday life?"

"Yes."

Lord tilted his head. "Suppose He decides to speak to you about Harry Carson? Who will you obey, God or Judge Rainey?"

The woman was silent. "Take your time," Lord said mildly. "I know what a difficult choice that would be."

Behind him, Cass coughed.

"God," the woman answered.

Lord turned to Rainey with a half-smile.

"You're excused," the judge said tersely.

The next prospect, an older man with a crew cut, cool gray eyes, and a clipped manner, gave his name as George Kleist.

"What is your occupation?" DiPalma asked.

"I'm a retired naval captain."

"Whose navy?" Cass scrawled on her notepad.

Staring at it, Lord listened to more answers: that Kleist was an engineer by training; that he had served honorably in World War II; that both sons were business executives; that he had been married for forty-three years; that his family had never felt need of a psychiatrist.

"Whichever navy," Lord whispered to Cass, "they'll elect him foreman if he stays."

He had slept perhaps an hour, and now had brief seconds to decide how to approach a nightmare twelfth juror with his peremptory challenges gone and the first eleven watching. Standing, he faced a man whose strong jaw and steady gaze suggested neither hostility nor doubt.

"Mr. Kleist," he began. "I've just listened to the outline of an exemplary life. So all I ask is this: can you look at Harry Carson, and promise him *and* me that you will judge his actions with an open mind?"

Slowly, Kleist turned to Carson. As if startled, Carson's gaze snapped from the camera. For the first time, he looked confused, vulnerable. Across the gulf of age and experience, the two men stared at each other.

"Yes," Kleist answered finally. "I can."

Lord nodded. "Then we've got a deal, Mr. Kleist."

It was done, he thought. And then he saw Hart Taylor, grinning through the bulletproof glass.

The trial opened badly, with the coroner.

Lord addressed Judge Rainey. "I've already assured Mr. DiPalma that we'll stipulate the cause of death. The evidence he wishes to offer through Dr. Boyd has the potential to inflame the jury without adding one scrap of necessary proof."

Rainey scowled. "The prosecutor has a right to present his own case." Sitting, Lord could only hope that he had dampened the impact of what was coming.

It happened ten minutes into Boyd's succinct testimony.

"And did you," DiPalma asked, "photograph the deceased?"

"Yes."

As DiPalma held up three color photographs, the court reporter looked up from his machine. "Are these the photographs?"

"They are."

"Your Honor, I ask that they be marked as People's Exhibits One through Three."

"Mr. Lord?"

DiPalma placed each picture in front of Carson. He turned away. Staring down, Lord was glad that someone had closed Kilcannon's eyes.

"No objection."

DiPalma gave them to the jurors.

One by one, Lord watched them react—a young black cabbie, a Japanese professional woman, a retired Chinese businessman, a Korean draftsman of about Lord's age, several middle-class Caucasians, the two mothers he had managed to hang on to, Kleist. A jury more DiPalma's than his.

After a ballistics expert, the two guards who captured Carson, and a tearful young woman who had watched Kilcannon falling from front row center, DiPalma called Curtis Blake.

Lord saw a man with lank brown hair and sharp features, well-coached by DiPalma. But Carson eyed him as if he were a piece of furniture.

"So you helped Mr. Carson set up the sound system?" DiPalma was asking.

"Yes, sir."

"How did he behave?"

Kleist leaned forward in the jury box. "Just like always," Blake answered. "Maybe a little like there was something on his mind."

"But not crazy?" DiPalma asked.

"Objection," Lord snapped. "If Mr. DiPalma wishes to qualify the witness as a psychiatric expert, let him do so."

"Sustained."

DiPalma gave a faint smile. "How did the sound system work?"

"Real good. Stacy—she tested it out."

The witness's voice was artificially quick, Lord thought; his eyes moved more than his head. There was a faint glaze on his forehead.

"What did you do after that?"

Blake looked uncomfortable. "We just screwed around backstage. You know, waiting for Stacy and the senator."

"What was Carson doing?"

"Same thing. I remember about six, he called someone."

"Do you know who?"

"No." Blake darted a glance at Carson. "He asked me and Jesus to split."

Lord forced himself not to look at Carson. "What did he do then?" DiPalma asked.

"I saw him talking into the phone. When I came back he'd gotten real quiet."

"Did he go anywhere?"

Blake shook his head. "All I remember is him sitting against the wall, like he was waiting for someone."

Lord wondered how many hours it had taken DiPalma to make these answers so artfully artless. Kleist had begun taking notes.

"Were you there," DiPalma asked, "when Senator Kilcannon was shot?"

The witness looked at the floor. "I sure was."

"Did you see who shot him?"

As if on cue, Blake turned to Carson. "Harry did. I watched him do it."

Carson stared at the camera. "Could you tell the jury what happened?" DiPalma asked.

"Stacy was singing great, best in years—the crowd was calling her name. She introduced the senator. . . ."

"And then?"

"He comes forward. People are smiling and cheering. Then it just stops." Blake spoke much slower now, as if still shocked. "I turn and see Harry. He just walks out with a gun, real calm, like he's pacing out the distance on a floor."

"What does he do then?"

"For just a second he stops with the gun held out in front of him, like he's getting a better aim—"

"Your Honor," Lord cut in sharply. "I move that the answer be struck. Despite Mr. Blake's persistence in characterizing the defendant's actions, he is no more an expert in marksmanship than he is in psychiatry."

"It seems to me, Mr. Lord, that he's simply *describing* the defendant's actions. His answer will stand."

DiPalma still looked at Blake. "And after that?"

"Harry took one more step, and shot him."

"What did the senator do?"

"He fell." Blake faced the jury. "Stacy dived across him. Then I saw the blood coming from the top of his head."

As the jury filed out for recess, Lord saw reporters watching Carson through the screen, cynical smiles, mouths that made no sound. He had lost more weight, Lord thought—there was a closeness of bone to skin. His eyes had a lost quality.

"You've got to stop watching the camera," he said softly.

Carson stared. "It bugs me."

"It also looked like you don't care."

Carson began rubbing his eyes. "That's their problem."

"I know it's hard listening to people interpret you, Harry—even me. But I need your help about that phone call."

"It was to Beth." When Carson's hand dropped, his eyes were closed. "But I couldn't find her. Just the operator."

"So there's no record of it."

Slowly shaking his head, Carson looked up, gazing at Lord's red silk tie. "That's a nice tie, man."

"Thanks anyhow," Lord said.

As Blake wiped his forehead, Lord caught the sick-sweet smell of a speed freak, sweating.

"How well do you know Harry Carson?" he asked.

"I know him okay."

"Ever talk to him about his life?"

Blake twisted the handkerchief. "He didn't talk much."

"Do you know where he's from?"

"No, sir."

"Or that he had a wife?"

"Yes, sir," Blake said finally. "I knew that."

"What's her name?"

Blake hesitated. "I forget."

"Did he ever talk to you about Vietnam?"

"I don't think so."

"Do you know what Harry did after Vietnam?"

"Not until he worked for Stacy."

"You really don't know him at all, do you?"

Blake dabbed his forehead. "I know what he's like."

"About how many hours have you spent with him alone?"

"I don't know."

"Under ten?"

"Like I said, I haven't counted. . . ."

"As many hours as you spent with Mr. DiPalma, preparing your testimony?"

"Objection," DiPalma put in. "Irrelevant."

"Sustained."

"In whatever time you managed to spend with the defendant, did he mention James Kilcannon?"

"No, sir."

"And yet you saw him *shoot* Senator Kilcannon, you said. Does it strike you as normal to go about your work and then kill a United States senator in front of twenty thousand people?"

"Objection!"

Lord wheeled on DiPalma. "You can't have it both ways, Ralph."

"Overruled," Rainey said. "Calm down, Mr. Lord."

"Mr. Blake?"

"Maybe it's normal for Harry," Blake said to the wall.

"Did he tell you what was on his mind?"

"No, sir." As Blake turned to him, Lord saw too late the trap that DiPalma had set for him. "He was writing something down, though. In a book."

Lord's brain felt slow. Find a next question, he thought, don't look rattled. "What kind of book?"

"All I know is it was black."

End on an upbeat, don't show that you've been hurt. Shoving both hands in his pockets, Lord surveyed the witness with a quizzical, faintly contemptuous expression. "How many amphetamines did you take that day?"

"Objection!" DiPalma rose. "Harassing the witness, lack of foundation, unwarranted character assassination."

Rainey nodded. "Really, Mr. Lord."

"I believe Mr. Blake understands me, Your Honor. By this evening, I suspect some enterprising TV reporter will have made his recreational pleasures into dinner-table chitchat."

Rainey flushed. "I'll permit the question," he said after a moment.

"Mr. Blake?"

Lord saw the calculation moving through Blake's eyes—how much does this man know, how can he trap me? "One or two," he finally mumbled. "Just with my girlfriend."

"What other drugs?"

"A little coke, is all."

"And yet you're willing to offer us your perceptions of Mr. Carson."

Blake looked away. "I know what I saw," he told the jury. "So does everyone."

They were sitting in Lafayette Park, a reckless ten-minute drive from the Hall of Justice in Rachel's MG. The grassy knoll was sheltered by palms and lightly peopled with gay men or small kids and their mothers. It was one of the few places, Lord reflected, where he could eat lunch without being bothered.

As Lord took a bite of his apple, Rachel watched him. "I've been wondering where Marcia was, Tony. It might look more sympathetic if your wife were in court."

There was something kinetic about her, Lord thought, like a too-bright child who said things to see what would happen. "She finds this kind of thing depressing," he said at length.

"Anyhow, I think the jury likes you." Rachel took a sip of wine. "Did you see that the opening statements got the highest rating in SNI's history?"

"People will turn out to watch pit dogs, too, or executions."

"It's also *you*, Tony—like it or not, you're made for TV." She watched him. "I only wonder whether your case is made for *this* jury."

Lord gave a short laugh. "You have a way of beginning conversations, Rachel, that ends conversation."

Her look was funny, close to hurt. "I just was concerned. For me, not the station."

Lord began to watch a young mother, walking her baby a few short steps. "We've come up with one strong witness," he finally said. "A vet who can testify to Harry's service in the Hundred and First."

"But no one else?"

"No." Lord realized he felt uncomfortable. He covered this with a shrug. "DiPalma knows all that."

Rachel was quiet. "I'd like to do this again," she said after a while.

Lord watched the mother and baby disappear into a grove of trees. "You deserve better company, Rachel." He checked his watch. "I'd better get back. DiPalma's waiting for me."

2

When Lord returned, there was a bound black book in front of DiPalma. Now, as Johnny Moore testified on behalf of the FBI, he picked it up. Lord felt the jury waiting.

"What did you discover," DiPalma was asking, "when you checked the registration of the Mauser?"

"That Mr. Carson purchased it a month before the concert."

"Did you find other articles which belonged to Mr. Carson?"

"His motorcycle, for one. It was parked at the loading dock, the clearest route for an escape. After that we found his duffel bag."

"What did it contain?"

"Personal items—cigarettes, a newspaper." Moore paused. "There was also a journal, filled with Mr. Carson's writing."

Lord tried looking bored. DiPalma gave the book to Moore. "Is this the journal in question?"

"Yes."

"And what is its final entry?"

"A poem."

"Would you please read it to the jury?"

As Carson stared at the table, Moore took out glasses. Peering at the open journal as if at Sanskrit, he began reading in a flat, embarrassed voice:

> "Feeding the camera
> Hair golden, spirit dead
> Time circles back to you
> A bullet through the head."

"Does that suggest to you that Mr. Carson intended to kill someone?"

"Objection," Lord said casually. "The verse should speak for itself. Whatever it means."

Rainey turned to DiPalma. "We wish to prove premeditation," the prosecutor said.

"Objection denied, Mr. Lord."

"Yes," Moore answered. "Combined with the other evidence of preparation, the poem suggests planning by Mr. Carson."

"And after writing these words, and speaking with an unknown third party by telephone, what did Mr. Carson do?"

"He shot Senator Kilcannon."

"That night, did any other violation of law occur?"

"Objection," Lord put in quickly. "Whatever other alleged crimes took place are irrelevant to that charged to Mr. Carson."

"Your Honor," DiPalma replied, "I don't think it's reasonable to quarantine the circumstances surrounding Mr. Carson's crime in advance of hearing them."

"Overruled."

"The proceeds of the concert were stolen," Moore said. "Approximately four hundred thousand dollars."

Lord saw Kleist take out his pen. "Was the money ever found?" DiPalma asked.

"No." Moore paused. "It seemed to disappear."

"In the confusion?"

"Perhaps."

DiPalma paused. "Does a film of the concert exist, obtained from station KSRT?"

"It does."

DiPalma held up a can of film. "Is this the film?"

"Yes, sir."

"Your Honor, I move that this be admitted as People's Exhibit Thirty-three."

Cass whispered, "That's not the one that shows what Harry does afterward."

"Mr. Lord?" Rainey was asking.

"No objection."

The film began with Kilcannon and Stacy. As their hands touched, she smiled at him. Beneath the cheers, Lord could hear the jury's silence.

Harry Carson was suddenly behind them.

Each step he took was the same length and speed—the moves of a professional killer, in a straight line toward Kilcannon.

Then, as Blake had described, he stopped.

Kilcannon turned. Carson stood with the revolver aimed at his head. In that agonizing moment, Stacy's mouth opened.

Carson took one cool final step and fired.

The camera followed Kilcannon. Stacy fell on him; the film ended as she touched his face.

When the lights came on, Carson was staring at his hands.

Moore sat blinking on the witness stand. "You mentioned a newspaper," DiPalma asked quietly, "found in the defendant's duffel bag?"

"That's correct."

"Was it open to any particular page?"

"An inside page. The lead article involved a gay rights suit against Colby Parnell. The first name in the headline was Mr. Lord's."

"There *is* another film," Lord opened, "isn't there?"

"Yes," Moore answered. "From Station KQZT."

Lord held up a silver can. "This one?"

"Yes. I believe that's right."

DiPalma rose hastily. "We'll stipulate that the film exists, and that Mr. Lord has a copy."

"Thank you." Lord turned back to Moore. "What made you select the *first* film?"

Moore looked at him blandly. "I didn't."

"Then who did?"

"Mr. DiPalma."

"He also had you read a poem which referred to someone with 'hair golden.' For the record, was Senator Kilcannon blond?"

"He was auburn-haired."

"Did the poem have a title?"

" 'Golden Anniversary.' "

"Does that mean anything to you?"

"Nothing."

"In fact, you don't know what the *poem* means, either."

"I can only make an inference."

"You also inferred that Mr. Carson parked his motorcycle at the loading dock because it offered a clear escape route. It also offers the clearest route to McDonald's, doesn't it?"

Moore gave a small smile. "I don't know."

"Does it seem very reasonable that, short of levitation, Mr. Carson expected to escape from twenty thousand people?"

"It doesn't seem very reasonable to *me*."

Lord hoped the polite rhythm of his questioning might begin to get the jury past the film. At the corner of his eye, he saw Kleist taking notes again.

"There was testimony that Mr. Carson placed a telephone call. Is there any evidence that this call has the slightest relevance to what we're here for?"

"No."

Pausing, Lord could see the expectation in Moore's eyes, becoming bleak amusement. "And you also have no evidence to offer that the theft of Miss Tarrant's money was other than coincidental to the senator's death."

"We have no evidence either way."

"So the answer is yes, there is no evidence to offer."

"Yes," Moore repeated dryly. "There is no evidence to offer."

"The theft of money from rock concerts is common, is it not?"

"It happens. Loose cash can't be traced."

"During your investigation, did the bureau advise Mr. DiPalma that there was no evidence he could offer linking this theft to Senator Kilcannon's death?"

"Objection!"

"On what grounds?" Lord snapped. "There's no privilege."

Rainey pondered this. "Overruled."

"We told him," Moore replied. "Yes."

"How many times did he ask about this?"

One side of Moore's mouth twitched again. "Several."

"He also prepared you for your testimony, did he not?"

"Yes."

"Did he state his intention to ask about the money?"

"Yes."

Walking toward the witness box, Lord asked, "And did you tell him yet again that there was no evidence linking that theft to Mr. Carson?"

As DiPalma half-rose, Moore looked at him and then Lord. "What I told him," he said carefully, "was that there was no connection to which I could testify."

Lord turned to Rainey. "Your Honor, I move for a mistrial."

With the courtroom empty, Lord was reminded of a space capsule. Even the cameraman was gone.

"Mr. Lord?" the judge said sternly.

Lord stepped forward. "Nothing is more devastating to an insanity defense than proof of a conspiracy. But Mr. DiPalma *has* no proof. So instead he insinuated the robbery, knowing he could not connect it to Mr. Carson. That his only purpose was to prejudice the jury demands a new trial."

"The motion is spurious," DiPalma retorted. "Having seen how badly the trial is going, Mr. Lord wants out before Miss Tarrant's testimony. So he asks this court to make itself a public spectacle by reversing its rulings where no prejudice resulted."

Nodding agreement, Rainey turned to Lord.

"The trial is tainted, Your Honor. The lingering implication is that Carson phoned a co-conspirator and that the murder *and* a robbery resulted—after which he called his lawyer."

DiPalma smiled. "Why don't you have him testify, Tony, and straighten us out?"

"I agree that a mistrial is uncalled for," Rainey broke in, "and would damage the credibility of the justice system. Motion denied."

It had gone as Lord expected. Still facing DiPalma, he waited a moment to follow through. "Don't you think," he said evenly, "that there's something strange about cheating Carson into the gas chamber?"

"Mr. Lord!" Rainey said with frank distaste. "If you precipitate another personal exchange, I'll find you in contempt."

For a moment, Lord was shaken at what he must do. "That," he responded finally, "would be impossible."

Reddening with comprehension, Rainey spun his chair. "Where's the deputy—"

"Hear me out," Lord snapped. "I gave you a chance to avoid this motion. But you let Ralph proceed, knowing what he meant to do. You've screwed me on TV coverage, on jury selection, and on evidence—because you're afraid that if Harry wins, *you* lose—"

"That's it, dammit—"

"But if *I* lose, I'll spend the next three years trying to reverse you. One more lousy ruling and you'll be the judge who blew the Kilcannon case on television." Lord lowered his voice. "I've got to cross-examine Stacy Tarrant, then put on a Vietnam defense. I want all the latitude you've given Ralph."

DiPalma turned to Rainey, as if demanding him to call the deputy. But the judge still stared at Lord. "Of course I regret it," Lord added softly, "if passion has caused me not to choose my words with care."

Rainey drew himself up. "I'll let it pass," he answered in a monotone. "This once."

"Unbelievable," Cass said.

It was ten forty-five. "No choice," Lord told her. "The trial's going to hell, and tomorrow DiPalma puts on Stacy Tarrant. I need Rainey to give me more leeway, or Ralph to go too far."

"I think the jury's still listening."

"Then pretty soon they'll figure out I can't give them one good reason to believe Harry didn't know what he was doing. In a way, combat experience argues that he *did*." Lord's headache was a dull throb which started in his eyes. "I've got no Damone or second year—no way to explain the anniversary thing or relate it to Kilcannon. And DiPalma's holding back a heavyweight psychiatrist to say that just as soon as I finish."

Cass began to straighten Lord's desk. "At least none of the jurors have smiled at you."

"Wait till Tarrant gets through." He turned to her. "You interested in the truth, Cassie?"

"Sure."

"If it had been my decision, and not Harry's, I'd have taken DiPalma's deal."

"I know." She finished the desk. "I'd better take off. Jeannie says I'm never home."

Lord smiled faintly. "See you in the morning."

When she had left, Lord began flipping dials.

On every station, a confident DiPalma wore the caption "Courtesy of SNI."

But SNI was looking ahead. As a voice-over summarized her life, Stacy Tarrant sang in Amsterdam, collected her second Grammy, waved from a motorcade with James Kilcannon, bent over his body.

"In seclusion since the funeral, Miss Tarrant will appear tomorrow at the trial of Harry Carson. . . ."

Lord turned it off and walked to his desk.

It was neater now—Cass had stacked the requests for interviews to one side. Next to these, on five sheets of a yellow legal pad, was his outline of potential question areas for Stacy Tarrant, and a single can of film.

There was nothing more to do now, but go home.

Leaving, Hayes Street was quiet—the opera was over, the restaurants closed. Two blocks away, the dome of City Hall glowed.

Lord took the middle of the street, avoiding doorways or parked cars. Beneath the streetlights, his shadow moved forward, retreated, moved forward again. The fog was penetrant and damp on his face.

Near the corner, Lord stopped short of his Datsun, staring at the windshield.

In the scrawl of a child or a maniac, red paint spelled out the words "You die."

Glancing over his shoulder, Lord saw no one. He unlocked the door, checked the rear seat, and quickly got in. Gazing at the inverted scrawl, he wondered if Marcia would see it.

He would park on the street, he decided. As he pulled onto Van Ness, the red letters glowed in the lights of oncoming cars.

3

The jury began turning, straining to see her, until Lord turned with them.

Damone stood behind the bulletproof partition. Next to him was Stacy. Even through the glass, the look she gave Lord had the clarity and astonishing directness he knew from the Parnells'.

As DiPalma faced the jury, her face merged with his reflection in a double image.

"The People call Stacy Tarrant."

She glanced at Damone. Then he moved to a front-row seat, a deputy opened the glass door, and Stacy entered the courtroom.

Her movements had the tensile awareness of someone used to people watching her. She wore a simple blue dress, light eye makeup, no jewelry or nail polish; that she was quite slender added to the sense of a vulnerable woman trapped in the consequence of her gifts. But there was something electric about her, Lord thought, which would draw people to the smallest gesture.

Taking the stand, she did not look at Carson, or at Lord.

DiPalma stood to one side, so that she faced slightly toward the jury. Their profiles turned as one. Rainey sat straighter; Carson stared at the foot of his bench, as though caught between the camera and Stacy. The taut silence around her had a delicate, explosive quality.

DiPalma began softly. "Would you state your full name, please."

"Stacy Lynn Tarrant."

Soft yet smoky, the voice startled with its familiarity. "And what is your occupation?"

"I'm a singer."

"And you've enjoyed some success?"

A slight hesitation. "Yes."

It was like a play, Lord thought; even her stillness was involving, the soft questions and answers. "Is that why you became a performer?"

"I really didn't expect what happened." Stacy flicked back her bangs; Lord realized that this characteristic gesture was resonant with public moments. "I wanted people to hear what I wrote."

"Will that be your work in the future?"

Stacy paused. "I don't know."

"When did you last work as a singer?"

Another pause. "The night of June second."

"What happened that night?"

She folded her hands. It drew her shoulders in, making her seem more fragile. "Senator Kilcannon was shot."

Lord could sense her drawing the jury into a kind of intimacy. "What was your relationship to the senator?" DiPalma asked.

"We were very close." She paused, as if brushing away some memory. "I also believed in him."

"How did he come to be at the concert?"

She raised her head. "I wanted to help him become president."

DiPalma waited a moment. "Who was it," he asked quietly, "that shot him?"

For the first time, she faced Carson. The cool, clear gaze had an impact all its own, Lord thought, so that the quiet answer which followed became an indictment. "Harry Carson."

Carson watched the floor. "How did it happen?" DiPalma asked.

She turned to him, distracted. "I introduced Jamie to the crowd," she finally said. "Something made me look up at the screen."

"What did you see?"

"Harry Carson was behind us." She spoke as though the memory came to her a moment at a time. "He had a gun."

"Did you turn to him?"

She shook her head. "At first, it was like a film. The way he moved was so perfect." The smoky voice became softer, lower. "Somehow I thought if I didn't turn, it wouldn't be real."

The jurors seemed not to move; Lord kept himself from glancing at Kleist. "What happened then?" DiPalma asked.

"Jamie's hair seemed to lift." Another pause. "When I turned, he was falling."

"What did you do?"

"I fell across him."

"Weren't you afraid Carson would shoot you?"

A slight nod at her lap. "Yes."

"But you covered Senator Kilcannon."

She looked up again, to DiPalma. "I didn't want him to die," she said simply.

Lord saw one of the jurors, the Japanese woman, turn away. "Was he still alive?" DiPalma asked.

"My eyes were closed. But I could feel him breathing. After a while—it seemed longer than it was—I looked at him."

"And then?"

"I brushed the hair back from his face."

"For what reason?"

She paused. "It was the only thing I could do for him."

The stillness was eerie, Lord thought—no coughs, papers shuffling, nothing.

"Did he speak to you?"

Stacy breathed in. "He asked if everyone was all right."

"What happened then?" he asked.

"John Damone—my manager—cleared the way for a stretcher. I went in the ambulance."

"Did you see him after that?"

"Yes." She stared at some middle distance, voice echoing her disbelief. "He was dead."

DiPalma stood quite still. Stacy turned, as if hoping he would do something.

"Before the concert," he asked, "did you see Harry Carson?"

"Yes." Her voice was drained of feeling. "He set up the sound."

"That's a complex job, isn't it."

"Yes."

"Did you discuss it with him?"

"Yes," she repeated tonelessly. "I told him the sound was great."

"Was it?"

"It was perfect."

Carson bent forward. "Did you say anything else?" DiPalma asked.

Stacy looked away, like someone caught in bitter recall. "I thanked him."

"What did he say?"

" 'No problem,' he told me." Her voice had the first tremor of anger. "He seemed almost detached."

DiPalma moved closer. "At any time, were Mr. Carson's actions in any way less than competent?"

In Stacy's pause, Lord replayed the careful phrasing of the question. "No," she answered. "He was always competent."

"Judging from this, did he seem rational?"

A second odd question, Lord thought; he was certain that DiPalma was avoiding something, perhaps something that Stacy might say. "Yes," she told him. "Very rational."

DiPalma stood next to her now. "Even at the moment he shot James Kilcannon?"

"Yes." Turning to Carson, she spoke in a clear, quiet voice. "Especially then."

The courtroom was silent.

"No further questions," DiPalma said.

The red car hit a crack on the hardwood floor, spun, and flipped on its back near the sofa.

"That's not very good, Daddy," Christopher said, and zoomed the car up *The New Yorker* and the shoe box he had made into a ramp. It flew into the air, landing against the coffee table.

"Not bad," Lord told him. "But the driver's three feet shorter."

Christopher laughed. "How tall are you, anyhow?"

"Around six feet."

His son considered this. "I saw you on TV again, before Mommy changed the channel. You were just sitting there."

Lord smiled. "Some days I like to watch."

Christopher's look suggested that he knew this was funny, but didn't know why. "You're cuckoo, Daddy."

"And you're the proof." Lord picked up the car and rolled it to his son. "I hear you've been making some noise in class."

Christopher's expression changed with his father's. "I feel funny sometimes."

"Do you know why?"

Christopher shrugged at the car. "Do you love Mommy?" he asked.

"Sure. What makes you wonder?"

Christopher rolled the car a few inches. "She says you don't do things with her anymore."

Don't let her start this, Lord thought. "I miss that, too. But it's only till the trial's over."

"I hope it's soon."

"So do I." Suddenly Lord grabbed Christopher and flipped him backward, holding his wriggling, laughing son aloft. "Because you're getting too big to deal with."

Trying to scowl, Christopher slid down on top of him, nose to nose. "Can we play now?" he demanded in his oldest voice.

"Just let me change into jeans. And no more acting up in school, okay?"

"Okay."

He found Marcia in bed. "What's wrong?"

"I'm tired," she answered in a flat voice. "There's a frozen pizza in the icebox."

Shrugging, he hung up his suit coat. "I'll need the car tomorrow, by the way."

"What's wrong with yours?"

"Carburetor." He turned, ready to ask what she had said to Christopher, then heard his son's car in the hallway. She watched him, expectant. "I've been thinking," he finally told her. "Tomorrow night, let's go out to North Beach."

She hesitated, testing. "I wouldn't mind tonight, actually."

He shook his head. "I got the early recess so I can cross Tarrant tomorrow, when the jury's had some time to get over her. I've got to figure out how to keep her from finishing Harry off."

Marcia's glance turned more oblique. "Because she's so sympathetic?"

"Because she's so smart." He paused. "Are we on for tomorrow?"

For an instant, they looked at each other. Then her eyes lowered. "That would be nice, Tony."

"*Daddy!*"

Lord stepped into the hallway. "Here comes," Christopher called, and the red car raced toward Lord. He bent to catch it.

4

Walking toward Stacy, Lord could feel the crowd gathered outside, reporters standing to see, the camera following him to her. She waited with a wariness so deep and quiet that he could almost touch what had happened to her. For a fleeting moment he imagined two people, caught in a glass cage.

"I'm sorry we have to do this," he said.

She looked surprised. "So am I."

The jury's silence was like breathing suspended. "You're a graduate of Berkeley, aren't you?"

"That's right."

"With honors in music and a drama minor?"

"Yes."

"What did your drama studies emphasize?"

She paused briefly, as if to tell him that she had been warned. "Acting."

"Did you take any psychology?"

"Not formally."

The perfect prosecution witness, Lord thought, coached to give minimum answers. He kept his tone soft. "You mentioned that you and Senator Kilcannon were 'close.' In what sense?"

She gave him a long, level gaze. "We were lovers."

"For over two years, I think."

"Almost that."

"I imagine you were in love with him."

Her brief hesitance had a self-questioning quality. Lord watched the decision form in her eyes. "Yes," she said. "I was in love with him."

"His death must have been devastating, then."

The offended look she gave him vanished in her answer, close to inaudible. "It still is."

"You mentioned that you haven't performed since then."

"No."

"Nor for a year before?"

Her eyes never left his. "It may have been that long."

"Because of stage fright, I understand."

As she flicked back her hair, Lord saw that the gesture had an absent quality; she was thinking as she did it. "It's harder now," she said simply.

DiPalma had not stood to help her, Lord realized, because she did not need it. Quietly, he asked, "How does that make you feel about Harry Carson?"

There was the slight hesitation again. But her look and answer were direct. "I hate him, for what he did to Jamie."

"Do you have a preference as to the jury's verdict?"

"Yes."

"Doesn't that affect your testimony?"

"It can't." Her toneless voice underscored the words. "Nothing can affect what happened, now."

Lord nodded in sympathy. "For the record, we've met before, haven't we."

It seemed to startle her. "I saw you," she amended.

"At a party for supporters of Senator Kilcannon?"

Lord watched the comprehension surface in her eyes. For the jurors, he was suddenly a fellow mourner, defending Harry Carson because he believed in him, forced to question her despite their empathy. The choice he had left her was to disclose the reason he had been there, seeming hostile to the jury, or put the party behind her.

"Yes," she answered coolly.

"When had that party been arranged?"

"Once I decided to do the concert."

"At what point did you decide that?"

"Jamie asked a week or so before."

"And when did you first tell anyone else?"

"The next day I called my manager." She hesitated. "To book the Arena."

For a reason Lord could not discern, her eyes seemed to widen at the answer. "So if Mr. Carson purchased a Mauser three weeks before that, he couldn't possibly have known that he'd be anywhere near Senator Kilcannon. Because no one knew—not you, the senator, or Mr. Damone."

She looked away. "I suppose not," she said at length.

"Yet you're certain that Carson's behavior on the day of Senator Kilcannon's death was rational."

Her voice grew stronger. "Yes. I am."

"What do you know about Vietnam stress syndrome?"

She resumed watching him. "Very little."

"Are you close to anyone who served there?"

A slight hesitance. "Only John Damone."

"Has he described any of his experiences?"

She shook her head. "I think he wants to forget it."

"But he did remember Harry Carson."

She paused. "That's why he hired him, yes."

"Did you ever discuss how the Vietnam War affected Mr. Carson?"

Stacy brushed back her hair. A long moment later, she answered, "Once."

In his surprise, Lord was suddenly certain why DiPalma had not called Damone, and why his final questions to Stacy were so carefully phrased. He paused a moment, planning his next questions.

Quite softly, he asked, "When was that discussion?"

The look she gave him was wounded, close to angry. "The day of the concert."

In the silence, Kleist reached for his notebook; tension made the rest of the jury look oddly alike. "Because he seemed so 'detached'?" Lord asked.

Her nod was slight, reluctant. "Yes."

"How did the subject arise?"

She seemed to steel herself. "I mentioned it to John."

"What did he say?"

"That maybe it was Vietnam."

Lord tilted his head. "Before today, have you mentioned this to anyone?"

She hesitated. "Mr. DiPalma."

"Anyone else?"

She was silent for a moment. "Jamie."

Startled, Lord's question was almost involuntary. "When?"

"On the way to the concert." She paused, finishing softly, "Before I saw what Harry Carson had been thinking."

The answer, and the way she said it, were devastating.

Lord forced himself to sound incredulous. "So the shooting resolved your question about his state of mind?"

"The shooting," she answered quietly, "and the way he did it."

"But that happened quite quickly."

Her voice was softer yet. "It didn't seem to."

Lord gave her a pensive, puzzled look. "By any chance, has Mr. DiPalma shown you a film of what happened?"

She hesitated, surprised. "Yes."

"And did the film refresh your recollection of how Harry Carson behaved?"

"It's not something I can forget." She paused briefly. "The film preserved it, that's all."

DiPalma had risen; Lord saw that he understood what was coming. "For the record, Ralph, was that the film to which you stipulated, or the one you chose as evidence?"

DiPalma flushed. "It was Exhibit Thirty-three."

Lord turned to Rainey. "Your Honor, Mr. DiPalma has asked Miss Tarrant to characterize Mr. Carson's behavior after watching his chosen view of what happened. He forces me to ask that she and the jury view a second version."

"Objection," DiPalma snapped. "Mr. Lord may reinvent reality when he presents his own case."

"But by then," Lord retorted, "Miss Tarrant won't be here to ask about it."

Rainey gave Lord a long, unhappy look. "Objection overruled."

Lord turned to Stacy. Her mouth parted.

DiPalma's fault, Lord told her silently. He took you a step too far.

She said nothing.

On the screen, she spoke Kilcannon's name.

The crowd responded. "Kil-cannon."

From the witness stand, Stacy watched herself with a look of appalled fascination. Her recorded voice grew more insistent. "Kilcannon."

In the dark arena, fists appeared, pumping like pistons on some strange machine. Above them, Stacy smiled as the chant rose higher, "Kill-*cannon*."

He stood next to her now. As their hands touched, the cry became hypnotic, each repetition echoing in the smoke and haze and light.

"Kill-*cannon*. . . ."

As if drawn forward, Carson moved toward them, gun extended.

Suddenly, he stopped; his last step before firing was like a trance being broken.

Kilcannon fell. In the courtroom, Stacy flinched.

The camera followed Carson.

He moved as if from muscle memory. A film camera rose from the side; seeing it seemed to change him. He came to a jerky stop, knelt, and fired three times. With the last shot, he dropped the gun, looking toward Kilcannon in dumb amazement, and then at his hands.

"Now," Lord said.

The technician froze the image for Stacy and the jury. Behind them, Damone had stood, staring through the glass.

The lights came on.

In the courtroom, Carson was staring at himself. Stacy did not move; her stunned, sick look was an odd reflection of Carson's.

"Miss Tarrant?"

Slowly, she turned to Lord.

He was standing a respectful distance back. "I'm sorry," he said. "You hadn't seen the rest of what he did, had you?"

Her voice sounded parched. "No."

"Does his behavior still seem rational?"

Facing Carson, she seemed to reach for some reserve. "Yes."

"But how can you ever know that?" Lord asked softly. "Or is it that you want to?"

"Objection!"

Lord turned to DiPalma, as though to remind the jurors that he had opened this.

"Overruled," Rainey said, and then looked back to Stacy.

Her shoulders raised, and then her face, waiting.

Lord shook his head. "No further questions."

He sat down. Stacy walked from the courtroom without looking at him, and was gone.

Entering the New Pisa, Lord had felt glad to be in the kind of public place with bright pictures on the wall and couples smiling at each other, heedless of him or Harry Carson. Then he realized that he had chosen a booth with a clear view of the door.

"See someone we know?" Marcia asked.

He smiled automatically. "Just ravenous strangers, waiting for our booth."

"You look tired."

"Long day." He examined her. "You watched my cross-examination, didn't you? On television."

She hesitated. "Yes."

The woman who had come through the door looked wrong for the restaurant, Lord thought—alone, haggard, close to anorexic. Her straight black bangs seemed cut with a hatchet, and she carried an oversized purse. Watching her, Lord mentally replayed his wife's tone of voice. "I'm not the judge, jury, or prosecutor, Marsh—I'm there to protect Harry. I had to use that film."

She sipped her Chianti. "I guess I was surprised you mentioned the Parnells'."

The woman took her place in the line. "Tarrant could have said what happened there." He turned to Marcia. "She surfaced to help DiPalma, right down to pronouncing Harry rational. All I did besides create even more sympathy for her was to keep doubt alive—barely. It'll be a cold day in hell before I apologize for that."

"I wasn't looking for an apology, Tony. Just trying to understand you."

The woman was watching them. Perhaps he had drawn her attention, Lord thought, and faced his wife again. "Not your fault," he told her. "Some days I enjoy more than others. Let's forget it."

"I'd like that."

Awkwardly, he covered her hand. "I think Christopher was glad to see us going out."

She glanced downward. "I guess he worries sometimes."

"So do I." The last impulse to confront her flickered and died. "Let's not let him, all right?"

"*I* never have."

Looking sharply up at her, Lord saw the woman, watching his hand on Marcia's with the bright-eyed look of a bird.

"Tony?"

There was something wrong, he thought sluggishly, even as the woman started forward.

As Marcia turned, he stood without thought. Staring fixedly, the woman moved toward them, purse raised in front of her.

Three feet away, she said dully, "You're *him*."

Grab the purse, he told himself. But he couldn't make his hands move. Marcia's mouth and eyes stretched open.

Lord stepped between them.

The woman spat in his face.

As Lord's hand went to his eyes, the woman stooped and spat in Marcia's wine.

Lord wrenched her away from Marcia. With mad intensity, the woman shrieked, "*Fucker!*"

Marcia ran from the restaurant. Throwing the woman to one side, Lord went after his wife, shoving through the line of startled patrons.

He found her bent over the steering wheel, crying.

Lord put his arm around her. He could feel her shoulders trembling. "It's okay," he tried. "We'll go somewhere else. Please, we can't let this ruin things. . . ."

"Your *job's* done that," she said with sudden vehemence. "Nothing will be okay until you quit."

He kept his arm where it was. She turned, not crying now, demanding an answer. Strange, he thought, that you can look at someone and yet see anyone else—Christopher, his father, even Stacy Tarrant.

"I can't," he finally told her.

She turned from him, staring at the parking lot. "Take me home, Tony."

THE TRIAL: JOHN DAMONE
NOVEMBER 12–16

1

Monday morning, when Lord opened with Shriver, Damone was there.

He watched Shriver intently, as if comparing what he heard to what he knew. Edgy, Lord wondered if he were there for Stacy Tarrant, or himself; the unanswered question of what Damone and Carson had faced in Vietnam ran through Shriver's testimony.

"So your opinion," Lord summarized, "is that service in Vietnam changed Harry Carson."

Shriver nodded. "It's like a fault line—before and after are two different people. There's no clue in his childhood or adolescence to what he's become."

"Does that apply to shooting Senator Kilcannon?"

"Yes." Lord could hear conviction in the calm, slow rhythm of his answer. "To me, it's inconceivable that Harry Carson would be here if not for Vietnam."

"Can there also be a pattern to the way that some *particular* trauma affects postwar behavior?"

"It's called the anniversary reaction." Facing the jurors, Shriver explained, "It's like recalling when a parent died or got divorced, but much worse. To survive for one year was the draftees' obsession—they counted each day they had left. So their postwar subconscious may revive a traumatic event on the date it originally occurred, sometimes to the day."

"How does this reaction surface?"

"Through depression, moodiness, volatility. A severe traumatic memory will cause some vets to respond as if they're still in Vietnam."

Lord paused. "Does the poem Harry completed on June second, the date of Senator Kilcannon's death, seem to fit this pattern?"

As Shriver glanced at him, Carson looked unsettled, oddly young. "The title, 'Golden Anniversary,' suggests that," Shriver answered, "and its images—blond hair, sunglasses, a camera—have no apparent relationship to Senator Kilcannon."

"And does June second also relate to Mr. Carson's Vietnam experience?"

Shriver gave Carson a puzzled, contemplative look. "It's the date he returned from Vietnam," he answered. "An entirely different man."

"Let's talk about murder," was DiPalma's sardonic lead-in. "Isn't violence caused by so-called Vietnam stress typically spontaneous?"

Shriver hesitated. "It can be."

"Caused by a real or perceived threat which triggers war reflexes?"

"That's often the case."

"So that the victim is dictated by circumstance rather than careful planning?"

Shriver paused. "As in combat, who gets hurt is usually a random matter of threat or opportunity."

"So this isn't the typical case?"

Lord recalled his own first questions, David Haldane's skeptical response. "Not typical," Shriver answered. "No."

"Did Senator Kilcannon threaten Mr. Carson?"

Shriver raised one eyebrow. "Not as you and I would define it."

"Then can you point to some specific in Carson's war experience which would make *him* view Kilcannon differently?"

Shriver frowned. "As is often the case, Mr. Carson's memory of Vietnam is suppressed except for fragments—plus no records exist for the latter part of his service. Which," he added pointedly, "is *not* usual, and no fault of his."

"But you can't tell us, for example, why the memory of leaving Vietnam would impel him to murder a senator."

"What I don't have," Shriver retorted, "are facts to tell me how the anniversary reaction might fit with what he did."

"In their absence, Dr. Shriver, isn't there equal reason to believe that Mr. Carson used a convenient date and a helpfully titled poem to cloak a simple assassination?"

Shriver's frown became pensive. "That would require sufficient understanding to manipulate what I am convinced is a genuine psychological condition. There is nothing here to suggest that level of sophistication."

"Then," DiPalma pursued, "what your opinion comes to is that but for events fourteen years past, he would not have shot Senator Kilcannon."

"Without the irony, yes."

Folding his arms, DiPalma summoned a tone of amazement. "But can you state, Doctor, that Mr. Carson did not appreciate the *consequence* of shooting the senator, or that murdering him was wrong?"

It was the only test that Rainey would allow the jury to apply; their faces, cautious and alert, registered Shriver's pause. "I believe that," he finally answered. "But I don't yet have the facts to tell you why."

DiPalma stared, as if stupefied by inexplicable foolishness. "No further questions," he murmured and walked to his table, leaving Shriver's frustrated look for the jurors.

Mary Carson's courtroom voice was flat, and she would not face her son.

Lord spoke softly. "Before Vietnam, then, Harry was a normal farm boy."

Her mouth compressed in a bitter line which made other lines appear. "He was his father's son."

"Was he violent?"

"No."

"And afterwards?"

"He was lost to us." As if caught in a crosscurrent of feeling, she added, "It killed my husband. . . ."

She stopped herself, mouth ajar. As Carson looked up in sudden, palpable hurt, Lord realized he had her eyes.

"That was after the fight you described," he ventured.

She faced him, seemingly surprised by this intervention. "Yes," she said at length. "Harry left that day."

"When was that?"

She gave her son one long look, and turned from him. "Early June," she said in a tone of final reckoning, "almost a year to the day after they sent him back to us."

"During the fight," DiPalma asked her, "did your son do anything that told you he didn't know where he was?"

She gave him a bewildered look. "No."

"Or who he was hitting?"

"No." The look became chiding. "My husband had rebuked him for cursing me."

DiPalma nodded. "What was the significance of the pine trees?"

"His father had planted them."

"So cutting them down was a specific act of hatred against his father."

"Objection," Lord snapped. "The question assumes Mrs. Carson's clairvoyance."

"Overruled. You may answer, Mrs. Carson."

She held herself straight, as though strengthened by bitter memory. "Yes," she said finally. "It was."

Glancing toward Carson, Lord noticed that Kleist's blue notebook had been replaced by a red one, in which he wrote now. But Carson's eyes were shut.

"No further questions," DiPalma said.

Faced with his past, Carson looked smaller. It was a trick of his mind, Lord knew, and Carson's posture; as Beth took the stand, he seemed to curl in a shell.

She sat with a tentative delicacy, as if poised to run. Through the glass, Damone watched her.

"Before Vietnam," she was saying, "Harry was different."

"Different than afterwards?"

"That, and from the other boys I knew." Her voice became softer, reminiscent. "He knew how to see things and not to be embarrassed by it. Like he had a second way of looking."

"How do you mean?"

"He saw the farm like that. He said the reason he wanted to keep it was because he could smell and touch and feel things, see the work he'd done." Lord sensed her groping to make the jury understand. "He could name all the sounds and smells—I remember he took me for a walk once, down to this bog they had. Afterwards, he asked what smell I remembered. . . ."

"Objection," DiPalma cut in. "Unresponsive."

"Sustained."

Beth turned to Rainey. "It smelled like wild mint," she finished.

Lord saw Carson's quick, sideways glance at Beth, as if afraid looking would hurt him yet afraid she'd disappear. "After the war," Lord asked, "did he still notice things like that?"

"No. But in a way I could still see it in him—like that second part of him was hurt now." Her neck gave an embarrassed twitch toward Carson. "He used to cry in his sleep. . . ."

"Objection—unresponsive."

Lord turned. "What are you afraid of, Ralph?"

"Sustained, Mr. Lord—and that's sufficient." To Beth, Rainey added less severely, "You'll have to confine yourself to answering the question."

She nodded, then answered softly, "I thought I was."

The judge gave her a look of perplexity. "You may proceed, Mr. Lord."

"When he would cry, did you try to wake him?"

"At first." Her gaze flickered toward Carson again; she picked at a fold of her dress, like a smoker without a cigarette. "One night when I did, he rolled on top of me and clamped his hand over my mouth. 'Shut up,' he whispered. 'They'll find us. . . .' "

"When was that?" Lord broke in.

"June." She looked down. "I just lay there, trying to breathe through my nose and feeling his heart beat against me. Then he drew back his head— it was like he knew who I was then. But he could never talk about it."

She shot another half-glance at Carson. "I think that's where the poetry came from. . . ."

"Objection." DiPalma made this dutiful, bored. "Unresponsive."

"Sustained."

"Did your husband write poems?"

"Yes."

"What were they about?"

"He'd never say. But I knew they were about the war—death, dying. . . ."

"Did you show them to anyone?"

"I tried to show Harry's mother. They were too ugly, she said."

"That was after the fight."

"Yes." Her glance at Carson was longer. "I wanted them to understand."

"Did they?"

Her eyes stopped between Carson and Lord. "They couldn't."

Lord paused. "But there came a time," he said, "when Harry was violent with you."

"Only that once." She turned a fraction more toward Carson. "He looked so surprised. . . ."

"What did he do?"

"When I told him to leave, he did—like he was ashamed to argue. But I was just so scared it happened."

She was no longer speaking to him, Lord thought, or to the jury. "When was that?"

"Last year." Slowly, she faced Carson, as if seeing what they could never have. "I never saw him again."

"Do you remember the date?" Lord asked.

"June." She said this quietly, to Carson. "June second."

"So when your husband hit you," DiPalma asked, "you think he was confused?"

"Yes."

He eyed her with melancholy skepticism. "But he also told you he hit a sergeant, didn't he? In boot camp."

"Objection," Lord said, startled. "Hearsay—the witness wasn't in boot camp."

"Your Honor, the question falls within two exceptions to the hearsay rule. First, a pattern of violence would indicate Mr. Carson's persistent intent to commit violent acts. Second, it would negate the Vietnam stress defense advanced by Mr. Lord."

Rainey nodded. "Objection overruled. You may answer, Miss Winship."

"He wrote me about it." She hesitated. "But the sergeant tried to make him buy savings bonds."

"So he *hit* him?" DiPalma asked. "Tell me, was this before or after he went to Vietnam?"

Beth stared at her lap. "Before."

DiPalma drew himself up. In a tone of pity which underscored her crestfallen answer, he said, "No further questions."

"Mr. Lord?"

As Lord hesitated, Carson took his pen and wrote "Cathy," and then his lips formed "Please."

Lord stood. "Did Harry also write you that he'd seen this sergeant skin a rabbit alive and throw its entrails into an audience of recruits?"

"Yes." Her voice firmed. "Harry hated animals being mistreated."

Recalling Kilcannon's autopsy photos, Lord mentally winced. "Would you call him a good father?" he asked.

"A gentle father." She glanced toward Carson. "Even with his problems, he tried to listen to Cathy."

Lord paused. "How is she taking this, now?"

"Objection. Irrelevant."

Lord gave DiPalma a weary look. "You mean harmless."

Rainey frowned a moment. "I'll allow it."

"Miss Winship?"

"For Cathy's sake, I wish this weren't on television." She faced Carson again, finishing softly. "But I think she'll be all right."

"Thank you, Miss Winship."

Lord lay on the bed, motionless. Marcia did not look at him.

"It's coming down to Damone," he finally said. "He's the only one who knows what happened to Harry up to June. And DiPalma may have put him there in front of me, knowing he can devastate our defense, until I'm desperate enough to risk that."

He heard Marcia flip a page. "What does it matter," she answered evenly, "as long as it's the truth about him."

"I wonder if we'll hear the truth." He stared at the ceiling. "Today reminds me of what an old defense lawyer said before my first case: 'A trial isn't about truth—it's where twelve people vote for who constructs the best story.' "

"I thought this was what you wanted, Tony. The big case, where people can see how good you are."

Lord turned to her. "I'm getting killed," he said softly.

"And *I've* given up security, a career. . . ." She closed the book. "Everything."

He watched her, silent. Since the incident of the woman, she had withheld herself in small, clear ways—silence, a certain space between them, a book on her knees, as now. There would always be a reason, he was suddenly sure, for what she did or had not done. But it would never be her.

"I'd better say good night to Christopher," he said.

His son's room had the warm musky smell of a child and the stuffed animals he slept with. Each night last year, he recalled, when Christopher still believed they had feelings, he would place a different animal near his pillow.

"Daddy?"

His son's voice, sleepy in the dark. Lord kissed the top of his head.

"Good night," he murmured, "don't let the bedbugs bite." Said this to reassure himself, because his father had said this to him. Said it in his father's tone of voice.

It scared him not to care if they made love.

He stopped in the hallway.

What he had told her about law, he had lived by for years. But it was painful now to watch as each piece of Carson's life was sifted by rules and divorced from context, to become another building block of someone's self-serving hindsight. A lie, like the lies he and Marcia spoke to each other, telling two stories of a single life.

He entered their room, and took his keys from the dresser.

"Preparing another witness?" she asked coldly.

"A good one, I hope. Named Bramley."

2

The witness was stocky and round-shouldered, with curly brown hair and a wide-eyed way of looking, as if fearful he would sound like a fool. Glancing at Damone, Lord put both hands in his pockets and turned away.

"Would you state your full name?" he asked.

"Robert Lee Bramley."

"And what is your occupation?"

"I'm an accountant." Though his voice was light and quite young, he had forced it into a monotone. "In Chicago."

"Are you also a veteran of Vietnam?"

"Yes."

"How did that come about?"

"I was drafted."

"At what age?"

"Eighteen."

"How long were you in combat?"

Bramley eyed the ceiling. "Two hundred and thirty-four days."

"Did your tour end early?"

A small shrug. "When I was wounded, they sent me back to the States."

"Can you describe your return?"

"We landed in Oakland." He paused. "Some demonstrators were chanting 'Babykillers.' "

He could have been reading a repair manual, Lord thought. "After Vietnam, did you receive any counseling from the Army to help you readjust?"

A second, fractional shrug. "They discharged me."

"Could you have used some help?"

"I still have nightmares." An embarrassed pause. "I get angry for no reason."

"Are you in counseling now?"

"Yes."

"For what problem?"

"My wife left me." There was a faint echo of surprise. "I could never talk to her—explain what happened to me."

"But you'll try to tell the jury."

"Yes."

"Why is that?"

Turned to Carson, the wide-eyed look registered disbelief that they were there. "Harry saved my life."

As Kleist leaned forward, Carson glanced away. "He served with you then," Lord asked.

"In the Hundred and First." Bramley began to watch the ceiling again. "We were near Khanh Duong, walking up and down these hills with three-foot grass. It was rainy and cold—there were leeches and red ants, jungle rot, hepatitis, parasites—" He shrugged, cutting himself off. "Harry came in to replace a guy who'd been booby-trapped."

"Did you strike up a friendship?"

"Replacements got you killed—my only friends, Stillman and Cook, had been there long as me. And Harry came in with a picture of his girlfriend, all spooked about some body bag breaking open." When he shrugged again, Lord recognized it as a kind of tic. "It might have been the guy he replaced."

"At first, how did he do?"

"For five days, I think it was, he stumbled around while we tried to find some VC." He seemed to count mentally. "Sixth day, they found us."

"Objection. Unresponsive."

"Sustained."

When Bramley looked confused, Lord knew that DiPalma would start trying to rattle him, making his account lifeless and fragmented. Stepping between them, he asked, "What happened when they found you?"

"We were in triple canopy jungle." Pausing, Bramley retrieved his monotone. "A thirty-caliber machine gun opened up from somewhere—you could never see where it came from 'cause it sent up this echo all around. So you watched for bullets splitting the foliage." His speech became so careful that Lord imagined him repressing a shrug. "I saw the jungle splitting in a straight line toward me."

"What happened?"

"I froze. Someone hit me. Falling back, I saw the grass fly up from where I'd been." An odd, inappropriate smile. "Harry was on top of me."

"After that, how did you feel toward him?"

"I wanted to keep him alive—Cook and Stillman did, too." He gave a furtive glance at Carson. "We began calling ourselves 'brothers.' "

"Cook and Stillman—what were they like?"

"Objection. Irrelevant."

It was time, Lord thought, turning to Rainey. "Mr. DiPalma and I can either go through this piece by piece, Your Honor, or let the witness put Harry Carson's introduction to the Vietnam War in context."

Rainey pursed his lips. "I'll allow it—provisionally."

"Cook . . ." Bramley seemed to blank out, start again. "He was from Kentucky, with glasses, big ears. Stillman was funny, from New York."

"Who was your battalion commander?"

"Colonel Bast." The witness nodded to himself. "First day he chewed Harry's ass 'cause his hair was too long. He was wanting to find us a fire-fight."

"Did he?"

"Uh-huh. One night he put us on top of some hill about five hundred feet high—with helicopters, so Charlie would know we were there."

His voice still showed no emotion. "What happened?" Lord asked.

"It was dark—first we heard them shouting, 'Kill GI, kill GI.' We dug trenches. It was drizzling—the choppers dropped our reserve ammo in the wrong place. Charlie got it. . . ."

"Objection. Unresponsive."

"Sustained."

Bramley's mouth remained open; it gave him the look of a runner, tired and a little detached, deep in the thoughts he ran with. "I . . . it started with mortars, was all. The four of us were together—like brothers, Stillman said. Dumb—there were bodies flying up around us, then pieces of bodies. People screaming. . . ."

"After the mortars, did they attack?"

"Used a human wave, around oh-one-hundred." The shrug was like a spasm. "All around us—you could see them in the tracer bullets."

"Did you take casualties?"

"Most of us died. Stillman got it through the eye." Bramley paused, scratching one side of his face. "I couldn't stop looking at that. Then they got Cook in the calf—"

"And Harry?"

"He pulled Stillman on top of Cook." He paused, as if recalling something. "When the VC overran you, they bayoneted the bodies to make sure you were dead."

"Were you overrun?"

"No." Another shrug. "Bast called artillery in on our position."

"What happened to Cook?"

"They medevaced him out."

"At the time, where was Colonel Bast?"

"Battalion HQ. He came later, with five choppers for security and a combat photographer."

"What did he do?"

"Had his picture taken with one foot on top of a dead VC." To Lord the words seemed to come, one at a time, without emphasis or inflection. "By the time he got there, there were flies crawling in the eyes and ears of the VC. Like on Stillman."

"Where was Harry?"

"Next to Stillman, staring at the colonel." He paused, looking down. "When Bast saw him, his face kind of changed. He told someone to put Stillman in a bag, and went back to his chopper."

"What did you do?"

"We evacuated the hill—went back to the base camp."

"And Cook?"

"He got back three weeks later."

"Did you have further contact with Colonel Bast?"

A nod. "There was another operation—a hill, like before."

"What happened?"

"Nothing—they never came." He looked past Lord with the inexplicable smile. "One dumb VC stuck his head up and Harry shot it from about two hundred feet. Fell right back in the grass and disappeared, like at a shooting gallery."

"Dead?"

"Uh-huh."

"How do you know?"

"Bast showed up later, wanting a recon patrol to confirm the dead VC for his body count." A glance at Carson. "So he picked Harry."

"What did you do?"

"Cook and me—we knew they'd be waiting. . . ."

"You went with Harry."

"Yeah."

"Did you count the body?"

"Uh-huh. There were four live ones next to it."

"What happened?"

"They gut-shot Cook—he was holding in his stomach with both hands." The monotone was softer. "Harry shot two VC and then I got one. The fourth got me in the knee."

"Who shot him?"

"Harry. When he fell, the VC's bayonet was sticking in Cook's brain. It was weird—I don't think I'd seen him without his glasses before."

Lord paused a moment. "How did you get back?"

"Harry got me in a fireman's carry and then a sniper hit my arm."

Bramley examined his left wrist. "He was running zigzag—I could feel the pulse in his neck and hear the bullets ping. It seemed like forever till we got to the perimeter."

He hadn't shrugged, Lord noticed. "What happened then?"

"He went back for Cook.

"It was crazy, what with him so hung up on Beth. I screamed after him, 'He's dead, man.' Then some other guys laid down covering fire—there were VC bullets all around him, like a movie. Bast just watching.

"Harry made it back with Cook.

"With his eyes closed, Cook looked like a baby except for the blood. That was how Harry held him, standing in front of Bast.

"Nobody said anything, just waited for Harry to catch his breath. When he did, his face was still wild but his voice was real soft. 'Here's your body, sir,' he said, and laid Cook at the colonel's feet. So gentle, the way he did that.

"Bast was still staring down at Cook when Harry butt-stroked him in the mouth. . . ."

Bramley's voice didn't change, just stopped. As Lord waited, tears began running down his face, and then he shrugged.

"See," he explained, "I would have killed him."

Carson put a thumb and finger to his eyes.

"Thank you, Mr. Bramley." Turning, Lord checked the jury.

Kleist's pen had frozen above his notepad. "We'll take a ten-minute recess," Rainey said.

"In the last ten years," DiPalma asked Bramley, "have you held the same job?"

Composed again, Bramley nodded. "Yes."

"Ever shoot at anyone?"

Bramley seemed to force himself to look down. "No."

"Or strike your wife?"

"No."

"Or anyone else?"

"No."

"What did Colonel Bast look like?"

"Red-faced, sort of squat. Crew-cut brown hair."

"Ever see him in sunglasses?"

"It was always raining."

DiPalma folded his arms. "Do you know of any connection whatever between the events you've described and the murder of Senator James Kilcannon?"

Bramley's eyes slowly raised. "All I know," he said in a new, taut voice, "is what happened to Harry."

DiPalma paused, seeming to frame another question, then think better of it. "I have nothing more."

"A brief redirect, Your Honor." Standing, Lord glanced toward Damone, and then faced Bramley. "After he hit Colonel Bast, what did they do with Harry?"

"Sent him to the Long Binh Jail."

"Did you write him?"

"My letters came back." Bramley paused. "It was like he disappeared."

Turning, Lord saw Cass on the other side of the partition, and nodded. She touched Damone's shoulder, handing him the envelope.

"Mr. Lord?"

Damone looked up from the subpoena, at Lord.

"No further questions."

3

Images moved across Lord's television: Bramley crying, Carson looking away, Damone's intent angular profile, turning from one to the other.

Seeing him again, Lord had thought the tempered harshness of his face remarkable—the penetrant black eyes, corners etched with premature grooves. As they faced each other, Lord began, "We have to talk first—"

"You've made your choice," Damone interrupted curtly. "Tomorrow we'll see how you enjoy it." So Lord sat roughing out questions for his own key witness, to which he did not know the answers. The cardinal sin.

His telephone rang.

A reporter, he thought reflexively—the desk was littered with phone slips. He picked it up.

"Mr. Lord?"

Bland yet intimate, a voice imprinted on Lord's inner ear.

"Yes?"

"You've read our message." The voice paused, waiting for Lord to absorb this. "If you continue . . ."

A soft, incisive click.

It changed, somehow, the look of Lord's office. A dim-lit yellow, starker than it had been, with the window behind him a black rectangle. Replacing the telephone, he drew his blinds.

It was the intelligence that troubled him, he saw. Careful touches, carefully spaced—Christopher's name, Lord's car, the teasing interval without a call. Knowing the worst moment.

He was not sure how long he had been standing when he heard the echo. Perhaps ten minutes.

He walked to the reception area, listening. Through the door, an old-fashioned grid of glass pentagons, the hallway was dark. The echo was footsteps, closer now.

A janitor, Cass returning—they wouldn't call first. Then the footsteps stopped, too long.

He flicked on the light.

A shapeless figure, broken into pentagons. No key, dark hair, holding something. He groped for a heavy object.

A rap on the glass.

"Tony?"

A muffled, woman's voice. When he opened the door it was Rachel, with a bottle of champagne.

She was wearing a raincoat, hair curly from fog. "Can I come in?"

Lord bent his head, put one hand to the bridge of his nose, and started laughing.

"What's so funny?"

"I just had a threatening phone call." He shook his head, smiling at himself. "I was preparing to die like a fool."

She stepped inside, closing the door. "What kind of a call?"

"Oblique—I've had them before." He looked up at her. "How'd you get past the guard?"

"Told him I was your wife." With her tilted smile, she shrugged open the raincoat. "He searched me for weapons."

Lord watched her. "You didn't pick the best night."

"I know—I checked your witness list at the clerk's office. As of yesterday, Damone wasn't on it." She paused. "You're trying to fill in the blanks, aren't you? You don't know what he'll say."

Lord smiled faintly. "You'll go far, Rachel."

"What about you?"

He exhaled, feeling the adrenaline fade. "On a scale of one to ten, it's the worst night of my career."

Walking past him, Rachel set the bottle on the reception desk. "I know," she said. "That's why I'm here."

When she turned, her eyes were serious. As Lord looked at her, silent, she gave an embarrassed smile, a small movement of her shoulders.

The telephone rang behind her.

Lord glanced at it, then Rachel, waiting. The phone kept ringing.

"Not here," he said.

Her apartment had the luxuries of someone living alone—signed prints, a thousand-dollar stereo, a brass bed—luxuries that Lord could no longer afford and had forgotten to care about. Passing the stereo, her fingers grazed it. Everything was neat; the absence of a child seemed strange to Lord. She lit two candles at the side of her bed.

"The champagne's getting warm." She smiled.

He opened it, releasing the cork gradually so that none was lost. When they were first dating, he remembered, the trick had impressed Marcia.

"Not a drop," Rachel said.

"It's all in the wrist." Part of him felt like someone in a movie he'd seen before.

Sipping champagne, she watched him over the rim. He could see resolution form in her eyes.

He had forgotten what it was like to be in a woman's apartment. Forgotten what this was like.

He kissed her. Her mouth was full, insistent, a memory.

Rachel stood back from him. Slowly, she began to undress.

Her body was full-breasted, compact yet smaller than her energy made it seem. An ankle chain caught her stocking; she began to fumble with it. Suddenly Lord felt selfish.

"Here." He knelt, finding the clasp, and unfastened it.

She kissed his hair, touching the top button of his shirt.

The sheets were cool and clean-smelling. Only her body was warm.

"Oh God, Tony."

He felt lost again. All he understood was where to touch her. She moaned softly, encouragingly, at what he did. A kind of guide.

When he was inside her, she pulled him close.

He moved with her, controlled, as if some part of him could not join the rest. He kissed her neck in apology, closed his eyes. He felt her climax, then again moments later, with him.

Afterward, they drank champagne.

"Unbelievable, Tony—you make love like you look."

"Scared," he joked. "Or tired."

She smiled. "Beautiful. And aware."

He had forgotten this, too—the knowledge he once had, unflaunted and half-thought-of, that he could move a woman. But he felt jangled, out of place.

"Why so quiet?" she asked. "Postcoital tristesse?"

And insensitive. "Hardly that," he said lightly. "Best first time in history."

There was a long silence.

"Where is it with Marcia, Tony?"

It snapped him back. Why push it, he thought, and then guilt mingled with the sad, second thought that she had asked the wrong question. He turned his face on the pillow. "That's not for tonight, Rachel. Really."

"Please, I'm just trying to understand what makes you tick."

Had Marcia wanted to be pregnant, Lord suddenly wondered, to blame him for her dependence? And then he wondered what he was doing here— with Harry Carson's fate in his hands, a witness to face, a wife and home. Christopher. "It hardly matters," he answered.

She watched him. "Do you want to leave?"

"I think I'd better."

She snuffed out the candles. They left, two half-filled champagne glasses on the bed stand.

"Where do you want to go?" she asked.

"Just to the car."

Driving from Pacific Heights, they talked quietly, about nothing much. Lord could feel her calibrating what she said, to suggest she wanted him without looking for commitment. Experience, he thought—she was not naturally a careful woman.

When they turned onto Hayes Street, Lord saw the station wagon. A green one, parked by his.

Lord couldn't react—read the license plate, he thought dully. Couldn't speak, as Rachel stopped next to it.

Through the windows of two cars, Lord and Marcia faced each other.

As Rachel turned to him, Marcia's face looked white and pinched. Her mouth was open; Lord thought, perhaps, that she was saying something.

"Who is that, Tony?"

"Marcia."

Marcia's head spun. Her car pulled jerkily forward and then sped away, taillights careening around the corner.

"I'm sorry." As Lord kept staring, Rachel touched his shoulder. "She had to know sometime."

Lord turned to her in disbelief. He saw it mirrored in her eyes, even before he opened the door.

The hallway was dark; a crack of light came from their bedroom. Passing Christopher's room, Lord could hear their son breathing deeply, asleep.

Their door flew open. Wet from the shower, Marcia looked slight and wounded and vengeful. Her hair hung in strands.

"Don't come near me, you bastard."

He glanced at Christopher's room. "Not here," he said in a low voice, and then realized he had said this to Rachel.

"Fucker." Her tight voice became a shiver. "I knew there was someone."

Part of her wants Christopher to hear, he thought to hurt me by showing her hurt. Softly, he closed his son's door.

"There really wasn't," he tried. "Not before tonight. I know you feel betrayed. . . ."

"You're an emotionless, cold-blooded liar—you *couldn't* know."

Say something else, he thought, anything different. "Why did you go there?"

"Someone called, a man." She raised her head. "When *I* called, you were gone. He told me who you'd left with and where I could see her."

He felt sick. "It's so hard to explain, Marsh. I'm not sure it's good to try yet. . . ."

"Then go fuck her. But I don't ever want you to touch me."

She was still, arms folded. "I already knew that," he answered.

"If *that's* your excuse. . . ."

"It isn't. Please, not here. . . ."

"Then get out."

"Not with Christopher sleeping."

"Then tell him—right now. Or I will."

The hard, rasping demand had a rehearsed sound, as if she were possessed by the drama of her anger.

"I can't do that. . . ."

She took one step toward him. "That's all you care about. Him. . . ."

"Don't use him, Marsh. Don't try. . . ."

She fled into their room. In two convulsive jerks she spun again and threw the alarm clock at his head. It shattered on Christopher's door.

"That's it," Lord snapped. "Get the hell back from here."

The door opened behind him. Frightened, Christopher was trying to smile, to make it a joke, looking from one to the other. Lord scooped him up. "It's back to bed, mugwump."

"What's wrong?"

Over his son's shoulder, Lord looked at Marcia. She had not moved; he knew she would not move now. "My fault," he murmured to him. "I hurt Mommy's feelings, and made her mad. But not at you."

She seemed to hesitate. As he quickly turned and carried Christopher inside, her door clicked behind them. Christopher sat on the bed, rubbing his eyes.

"I've got a problem," Lord said gently. "Where do I sleep?"

His son patted the bed. "Here," he managed, and rolled to one side, so that his father could hold him.

Lord could feel his son's heartbeat, the rise and fall of his breathing. How much more frightening for a child, he thought, when the people you depend on are so angry and so lost.

"I love you," he promised. "I'll make things okay."

At last, Christopher fell asleep. Lord never did.

While it was dark, and Christopher slept, Lord showered in the second bathroom. Shaved for court.

The house was eerily quiet. Except for glass in the hallway, Lord felt what had happened as the vestige of a bad dream.

In the kitchen, Marcia was drinking coffee in jeans and a crew-neck sweater. The sun through their window had a pitiless quality.

"I want you gone," she said. "Today."

It still sounded like a script, unreal except for his son. "Not without Christopher."

Her eyes blazed. "What do you know about taking care of him?"

"I love him. The rest I can learn. . . ."

"That *is* all you care about."

"No." He hesitated, fumbling. "It was just, standing in the hallway, I could remember so many things. But I couldn't imagine the future—couldn't find a vision of the life that I'd be pleading for, anywhere."

"Except for Christopher."

"I can't leave him here. Not after last night."

She set down the coffee. "I'm sorry, Tony. You're not getting him."

He couldn't think, only react. "That's not for you to say."

"Isn't it?" She stood with sudden, angry confidence. "*I* raised him, while you tried cases and fucked other women. If you even try for custody, he'll be dragged into court with both of you. And you know better than anyone what that's like, don't you?"

Lord faced her with a cold, returning anger. "Last night," he said quietly. "I couldn't believe what I'd done. Now I can."

She turned from him.

Kissing his son, Lord told him to have a good day, and went to court before Christopher could see his face.

4

Don't think of that now, Lord told himself. Tonight, something will come to you.

Next to him, Carson met Damone's stare with a furtive, anxious look. Touching his client's shoulder, Lord stood.

"Would you state your full name, please."

"John Anthony Damone."

A deep voice, soft with latent power, a street kid's inflection. "Are you a veteran of Vietnam?"

"Yes."

"What is your current occupation?"

"I manage Stacy Tarrant."

His tone made this personal, between the two of them. "After Senator Kilcannon was shot," Lord asked, "did you help rush him to the ambulance?"

"Yes."

"And before that, in Chinatown, you tackled him when he was speaking from a cartop."

"Yes."

"For what reason?"

"I thought firecrackers were gunshots."

Lord gave him a quizzical look. "Were you an admirer of the senator's?"

"No."

The answer was so flat that Lord heard a faint contempt. "Then what made you do that?"

Narrowing, Damone's eyes reminded Lord of their first confrontation. "Reflexes," he answered tersely.

As if sensing antagonism, Kleist leaned forward. "From Vietnam?" Lord pursued.

"Yes."

They watched each other, Lord knowing that the trial might turn on his next question, knowing that only Damone knew the answer. Then he asked, "What was the nature of your service?"

Placing both palms together, Damone touched them to the edge of his beard. With equal quiet, he answered, "I was an assassin."

The word had a shocking, literal sound. Covering his surprise, Lord amended in feigned puzzlement, "You mean you were in combat."

Damone gave a slow shake of the head. "I mean I murdered people. On assignment."

Stunned, Lord thought too late that Damone's desire not to testify involved more than Stacy Tarrant, or himself. "At whose direction?" he managed.

"A CIA officer. Named Glennon."

Rainey leaned toward Damone, as if to interpose a question. Reluctantly, Lord asked, "How did he recruit you?"

"I'd been wounded, following orders." Lord caught a faint, sardonic undertone. "Glennon promised me more independence."

"Did you work alone?"

Damone hesitated. "In teams of three."

Lord felt the jury's instinctive stiffening. "Where did Glennon find the others?"

"In military prisons. He went to people charged with murder or assault, and gave them a choice."

Several jurors glanced toward Carson. Calmly, Lord asked, "Is that the choice he gave to Harry?"

"No." Damone's tone grew quiet. "*I* gave it to him."

"For what reason?"

"I knew him, from processing into 'Nam."

"Do you know why he accepted?"

"He wanted to get married." Turning toward Carson, Damone finished with terrible irony. "Harry would have been in prison for a very long time."

Silent, DiPalma must believe the last three questions to be fatal. But Lord had no choice but to finish.

Quietly, he asked, "How did your team work?"

Damone's eyes betrayed surprise, and then went hard. "They dropped us at night, near a village, with scarves, knives, and grenades." Pausing, he added coolly, "Plus a map of the hooch Glennon wanted."

The last phrase, Lord thought, conveyed a warning, or a dare. He forced both hands in his pockets. "And once you found it?"

"We knotted our scarves and slipped in to where they were sleeping."

Damone's stillness, like his answer, had the tension of withheld violence. "And then?" Lord finally asked.

"We pinched their nostrils, so they'd open their mouths to gulp air." Pausing, Damone's voice took on a laconic fatalism. "Then we stuffed our scarves in all the way to the larynx, to muffle screams, and cut their throats."

There was suffocating silence.

Lord stared at him. "Whose throats?"

"VC officials and whoever else was there." Even the pause seemed sardonic. "Glennon gave us names off a CIA computer run."

Appalled, Lord remembered something Shriver had told him. "Did he also give you drugs?"

Damone kept watching him. "Dexedrine," he said at length. "And some stuff left over from the French."

"What was their effect?"

"They killed memory and inhibitions." A brief, bitter smile. "Glennon didn't want his people feeling or remembering too much."

Lord hesitated. "Why do *you* remember?"

The smile faded. More quietly, Damone answered, "I didn't need the drugs."

Lord heard his own silence. "But Harry did," he ventured softly.

Slowly, Damone nodded. "The work didn't agree with him."

An ironic inflection, Lord thought, yet close to tender.

"When did you discover that?"

The faint smile. "On his first mission."

"What was involved?"

"Glennon sent us to kill a VC tax collector."

Lord tilted his head. "Did Harry have some particular assignment?"

"To kill the wife." Damone paused. "Glennon wanted him to 'get wet.' "

" 'Get wet'?" Lord repeated automatically.

"Cut her throat so blood spurted on him." Each word was tight. "Glennon liked to see the proof."

Carson covered his mouth. Everyone else—Rainey, Kleist, the court reporter—was still. Damone had stripped the last veneer of normal cross-examination; his dialogue with Lord had turned visceral and explosive.

"The woman," Lord said. "Was that usual?"

Damone nodded curtly. "Glennon's rule was to kill them."

"To what purpose?"

The jurors looked back to Damone. "If she cried," he finally answered, "someone might hear her."

Lord's fists bunched in his pockets. "Did something go wrong?"

"The wife was young." Damone glanced at Carson. "Harry couldn't kill her."

"Did you?"

"Capwell, our scout." Damone folded his hands. "Then he laid the flat of the blade against Harry's face, to leave blood, and whispered, 'Now Glennon won't send you back.' "

Lord saw the Japanese juror touch her throat. "What did Harry do?"

"We got him out of there."

At the edge of Lord's vision, Kleist was writing with slow deliberation, the others looking everywhere but Carson. "How did Glennon react?"

Damone raised his head. "Capwell lied to him."

"In fact, would he have sent Harry back to prison?"

"He'd done it before." Damone paused. "With others. Capwell knew that."

Lord removed both hands from his pockets. "And after that," he finally inquired, "Harry took the drugs from Glennon?"

Once more, Damone's response was soft with irony. "He knew we depended on him."

Kleist stopped writing.

Lord stepped forward, drawing the jurors to him. "How did he come to leave?"

For the first time, Damone looked away. "It was after a special mission," he said. "In daytime."

"Why daytime?"

"Glennon wanted it filmed."

Astonished, Lord felt the phrase "feeding the camera" on his flesh. "For what reason?"

"A newsman found out that the CIA was running death squads—they called it the 'Phoenix program.' Glennon decided to use our team to solve their PR problem."

"How?"

"By having a combat cameraman film us bringing in a live VC. Problem was, the guy cc'uldn't film at night."

"So Glennon sent you out in daytime?"

Now the pause suggested pain. "He sent Capwell and Harry."

"But not you?"

"It was suicide." Damone seemed resolved not to turn from him again. "I told Glennon to try and kill me himself."

"What did he do?"

"He preferred to send me on an errand." The touch of dryness vanished. "I told Harry to come with me."

"Why didn't he?"

"Capwell. Harry said he owed him."

"What happened then?"

Damone kept staring. "I left."

"And when you came back?"

A brief flicker. "Capwell was in a body bag."

"How did he die?"

"He'd bled to death." The steady eye contact had begun to seem like self-punishment. "From a bullet wound."

"Who told you that?"

Damone paused. "I opened the bag."

It broke the rhythm of Lord's questions. He felt the jury and Carson, waiting.

"Did you ask Glennon about it?"

Damone's eyes seemed to darken. "He wouldn't talk."

"Did he get his film?"

"I don't know."

"Where was the cameraman?"

"I never saw him again."

"And Harry?"

"Gone." Damone snapped his fingers; the startling gesture galvanized the courtroom, and then he added, "Glennon sent him home, just like that."

Lord waited. "Since then, did he ever tell you what happened?"

"He doesn't remember."

When Lord turned, Carson was staring at his hands.

"The final mission," he asked quietly, "when was that?"

For a long moment, Damone watched Carson. "The first of June," he said.

"Mr. Lord forgot to ask," DiPalma began. "Did Harry Carson become an assassin?"

Damone leaned forward, elbows on knees. "Yes."

"How many people did he kill?"

"Five."

DiPalma looked contemptuous. "Any women?"

Damone seemed to consider him. "Harry took the men."

DiPalma's mouth opened, closed, and then he asked, "What was his weapon?"

"After the first mission, Glennon let him use a Mauser."

DiPalma let the answer resonate. "Did he kill in any particular way?"

Damone's eyes lowered. "He was a headshooter."

Lord saw DiPalma's surprise becoming confidence. "How did he identify the man he shot?"

"Glennon gave us photographs."

DiPalma crossed his arms. "So Carson memorized the faces of his victims."

"Yes."

"Despite the drugs."

"Yes. . . ."

"And then murdered the specific person he *intended* to."

It was the key point, Lord knew. Damone looked off, as if reflecting, then answered softly, "Unless there was some mistake."

The lethal joke was so oblique that DiPalma seemed to comprehend it in slow motion, so that the jury registered his confusion, then his anger. "But you still hired him," he shot back.

Suddenly, Damone's stillness suggested control. "I knew what he'd been through," he answered. "Not what he'd do."

"Or what happened on this 'special mission'?"

"No."

"Or even *if* it happened?"

"I saw Capwell." Damone's voice was still soft. "Something 'happened' to him."

DiPalma flushed. "Whatever that was, do you know of any bearing it has on Mr. Carson's prior experience in shooting preselected targets?"

"No."

"Or his murder of Senator Kilcannon?"

Damone turned to Carson. "Only Harry knows that," he finally answered.

When Carson looked away, DiPalma raised an eyebrow for the jury. "Then I have nothing more for Mr. Damone," he said to Lord, and sat down.

Walking toward Damone, Lord hesitated. "Glennon," he began. "How old was he?"

"Late twenties."

"How would you describe him?"

"The all-American boy—used to play Beach Boys albums in his hooch." Damone paused. "He was saving his Vietnam pay to buy a Porsche when he got home."

The description was such a fun-house mirror of what Lord expected that he searched Damone for some heartless joke. But Damone's eyes were not laughing, or even smiling.

"What did he look like?" Lord asked.

"Southern California." Damone's voice was lower now. "He'd bleached his hair blond."

"What color were his eyes?"

"Blue." Damone hesitated, then added quietly, "But he usually wore sunglasses."

The courtroom was hushed.

"Where," Lord asked, "do you suppose I might find him?"

Damone gazed at the floor. "He's dead."

He sounded so certain that it jarred Lord. "Are you sure?"

"I saw him." Rising to Lord's, his eyes were preternaturally bright. "He'd bled to death, like Capwell."

Lord felt a kind of chill. "How?" he asked reflexively.

Damone's eyes didn't change. "Someone," he said quietly, "cut his throat."

Lord could not look away from him. "Did Harry know?"

"No." Damone's voice was almost a whisper now. "I didn't want to stir bad memories."

Carson's mouth was ajar, face filling with shock and confusion. Seeing Rachel through the glass, Lord thought suddenly that he should not leave the city now, for Christopher's sake.

"Your Honor." His voice seemed someone else's. "In light of this last testimony, I move for time to locate any film of the defendant's last mission."

Rainey was staring at Damone. From the witness stand, he still watched Lord.

Almost absently, Rainey murmured, "Recess granted."

THE TRIAL: TONY LORD

NOVEMBER 19–DECEMBER 1

1

At fifty thousand feet, Lord felt his life in suspension, the trial behind and ahead of him.

Boarding the 747 to Washington, he had noticed passengers turning to watch him. He sat alone in the darkened cabin, staring at the tops of heads and scattered reading lights.

There was no Glennon, the chief counsel of the CIA had told him, at least no record of such a person. But Lord had seen a blond-haired murderer, dying in Carson's eyes.

There was no Glennon, he knew, because John Damone had killed him.

"Cocktail, sir?"

A pert flight attendant was smiling at him. He ordered a martini; swirling the plastic cup, he wondered if the warmth of her smile was imagined.

Why had Rachel happened, he asked himself.

Was it fatigue or loneliness or fear? Or memory, turned to anger that he might never feel that for a woman again, or a woman for him. That he would serve out his marriage to Marcia, pay the bills and be blamed for it, send Christopher to college.

As his father had done for him.

Fool, he thought. To hurt for Christopher now, filled with martini regret. Now, when Marcia knew that the one way she could hurt him was through their child. Why hadn't he lied?

For what reason, he suddenly wondered, had Damone not wished to testify?

An ice cube splashed in his cup.

Startled, he looked up at the flight attendant. "Another cocktail?" she asked.

"Thank you."

She poured it expertly. "You're the lawyer, aren't you? Anthony Lord."

A gaunt man in the middle row turned to listen. Lord nodded, then remembered to smile.

"Good luck." She glanced at his wedding ring, and went on. The man watched Lord drink.

It's all changing, he thought. You don't know what will happen, and you're scared.

When he deplaned, TV cameras were waiting.

"Mr. Lord," someone called, "do you expect to locate the film?"

Sluggish from gin, he stood blinking in the TV lights, obscuring the faces behind them. "I hope so," he finally answered. "Harry Carson deserves at least that much luck."

Angling through them, he took a taxi to his hotel, and dialed Christopher.

"Hello," Lord's own voice answered. "This is Tony Lord. Neither Marcia nor I can come to the phone. . . ."

"Christopher?" Lord said above the tape.

"But if you'll just leave a message. . . ."

Damned machine. Lord's voice rose. "Christopher, it's Daddy. . . ." Please, be there.

"Daddy?"

Breaking in, his son's voice was cautious. "How's things?" Lord asked in relief.

"Fine."

"Good." Lord smiled into the telephone, trying to coax animation from the space between them. "I'll bring something back," he promised. "A surprise."

"Okay."

At seven, had he been so reticent on the phone? Or was Christopher starting to protect himself? "What are you doing, son?"

A pause. "Mommy's letting me watch 'Dawn Rider.' 'Cause she knows I like it."

Why didn't *he* know that, Lord wondered. "Then I don't want you to miss it, mugwump. I just called to say I love you."

"Okay." I love you, too, Lord silently added for him, and then Christopher finished, " 'Bye."

Hanging up, Lord stared at the telephone.

By calling Marcia, a stranger had done to him what threats could not. Who could hate him so intelligently?

Lord double-locked the door.

There was a wad of pink slips in his coat pocket—reporters' calls, the last from Rachel. He threw them away, and asked the desk to hold his messages.

Lying on the bed, he inspected the signs of his disorientation. A still life, the whirring air conditioner, a Gideon Bible, the TV bolted to the·wall. Strange channels.

SNI was running highlights of the trial.

Lord watched himself, as he would watch a stranger. Saw someone fluent, graceful, never confused—an illusion, losing to DiPalma. Turning it off, he could not sleep.

The next morning, he presented himself at the Army film archives, followed by reporters.

A huge metal warehouse—green metal shelves, lamps hanging from high ceilings. At one end were rows of file cabinets with Asian names, battalion numbers, vague dates. In some strange way, the sheer volume convinced Lord that the film did not exist.

The Army's politeness reinforced this. A smooth-faced employee explained the filing system in a drill sergeant's cadences, until Lord was sure that he was being taken on a Kafkaesque tour of the irrelevant. Trapped, he felt the trial, waiting to be finished and lost.

They'd set up a projector in a cramped room to the side. Alone with each day's cans of film, Lord watched half-forgotten reconnaissance missions in black and white, silent movies of people dying and killing. But not Carson.

Returning to the hotel, he would pass reporters asking what he had found. He developed stock answers to their questions, suppressing his tense anger over the flickering, endless films which would not save Carson. After the first night, he ordered from room service.

On the morning of the fourth day, Lord found the film.

A nineteen-year-old boy, his movements jerky from drugs and fear, his eyes unmistakably Carson's.

Alone in the witness room, the same eyes watched Lord, much older. "You look tired," Carson said.

Lord tried to conceal his tension. "It's a long flight home."

Tapping a cigarette, Carson still watched him.

"There's a film, Harry."

A change in the eyes, like dilation—fear, perhaps hope. "Does it show what happened?"

"Some." Lord lit Carson's cigarette. "Can you remember anything?"

"Capwell. . . ." Carson's fingers twitched. He inhaled deeply, then exhaled, watching the smoke as it vanished. "He's bleeding. . . ."

"And then?"

His eyes flickered. "I'm landing in Oakland."

The cigarette burned in Carson's hand. "I want you to see this," Lord said finally.

A quick, shallow puff. "When?"

"Tomorrow." Lord hesitated. "On the witness stand."

Carson's eyes flew open. "In front of them?"

"Yes."

A tremor of one hand, covered with the other. "Why then?"

"To help you testify."

The cigarette kept burning. "I don't want that," Carson murmured.

"Want what?"

A flush appeared on his neck. "To know what went down."

"Why?"

"The stuff I remember—what John said. It's bad, still."

Lord watched him—cornered, fearful-looking. "Is there something else you didn't tell me?" An ash fell on the table. "Maybe something you told Damone."

Staring at the ashes, Carson shook his head. "Why, man?" he murmured finally. "Why do you want me to talk?"

"Because I can't prove you didn't plan to shoot Kilcannon." Lord leaned forward. "You're our only chance, Harry. . . ."

"Then show me the film. Before."

"DiPalma's waiting for you." Lord paused. "If you watch now, then he'll say we put together a story to go with it. I'd rather you try to remember in court—whatever comes out."

Carson opened his mouth, but could say nothing.

Lord clasped his arm. "You said you wanted to see Cathy someday, away from this. However it goes tomorrow, I'll do my best to make that happen."

There was a long silence. Finally, Carson nodded.

Lord waited for his own tension to ease; it wouldn't.

"Let's get ready, then." He took the cigarette from Carson's fingers, before it burned them. "I'll be DiPalma."

There was something wrong.

Finishing the milk shake, Lord stared at the ceiling of his motel room. In the role of DiPalma, he had done too well. Except that DiPalma might falter on motive.

If Carson had no rational motive, what had made him mention politics the night he shot Kilcannon? To cover his own confusion?

Who had called Marcia?

He looked at the stuffed bear, hastily purchased at National Airport, still in its bag. His wristwatch read 12:01—too late to call Christopher.

In nine hours, the trial would resume, and he would gamble everything. Now he waited, in a motel room near the courthouse. Registered under his father's surname, the Polish one, before his father had changed it.

Another cubicle, he thought. Another television. He crumpled the empty milk shake carton.

He had to win. There was no margin in his life for losing.

2

Except for Lord, the courtroom was still.

The bailiff's finger rested on the light switch. The gallery had stood, including Shriver, pressed to the glass. Inside, the jury faced a blank screen. Kleist had put away his notepad; DiPalma and his assistants formed a silent row. Behind the partition, Lord saw Rachel with Hart Taylor, watching Carson.

He had borrowed Lord's red silk tie; jittery on the witness stand, he kept checking the knot.

"Harry," Lord said, "I'd like you to watch the screen."

In a seeming reflex, Rainey nodded for him, and then Carson's eyes moved, head following.

Lord saw the TV camera turning with him. A hall of mirrors, he thought, then realized he had forgotten to signal. He glanced at the film technician, then the bailiff.

The room went dark. On the screen, numbers flashed downward.

A picture—the burnt stalks of trees, silvery black and white. As the camera swept them, a figure appeared.

Carson was dressed as a Vietnamese.

He walked bent, disguising his height, sandy hair concealed by a conical hat. It might have been more comic than frightening, except for the trees and the look of his eyes, like burn holes.

The focus widened.

Dressed like Carson, two other men moved with him in what had once been forest—on a hillside, sloping downward, its trees seared with an eerie uniformity. That there was no sound made it surreal; the midday sun looked like the moon.

They stopped together—Carson, a radioman, a third man with a beaked nose and white, sudden grin, pointing forward. Capwell, Lord was certain.

The camera followed where he pointed.

At the bottom slope, the burnt forest became lush green jungle, so thick its treetops merged in a canopy. Perhaps a mile farther was a clearing, with thatched huts that looked like toys. Four inches of film from Capwell's finger.

Facing him, Carson nodded.

The film was crisp, astonishingly professional. As the camera recorded them, the three men started down the hillside with knives, machetes, M-16s. The village disappeared from view, and then they reached the jungle.

In front of them, odd-shaped leaves and shrubbery came from every angle. Swinging his machete at the wall of foliage, Carson hacked his way inside, toward the village.

Suddenly, it was dark.

A flash of white sun on a machete blade—an adjustment in the lens, admitting light. The three men reappeared as shadows, swinging machetes between shafts of sunlight, filtered by trees. The effect was claustrophobic; dense, shapeless leaves, a few feet of vision, the drugged, frenzied rhythm of blades hacking darkness. A figure knelt—Carson, then the others, to rest.

As Capwell wiped his forehead, the camera zoomed in on Carson's foot. It was bare; the leech became a stain when Carson slapped it. His eyes fixed on the camera, hostile.

Capwell pulled him up.

Their blades beat forward again, feet at a time. The light gave off a kind of steam.

Lord tensed, waiting.

Suddenly the radioman dived; what looked like a grenade rolled between his legs. Carson jerked up his rifle. It recoiled; something fell from above; someone in the courtroom gasped.

The camera veered.

On the ground, near the radioman, was the headless body of the monkey Carson had shot. Capwell reached, grasped the grenade, and held it to the camera. His smile was fixed, unnatural. The grenade was a coconut.

He turned to Carson; as if synchronized, their heads tilted. Lord imagined them listening to the echo of the bullet, wondering how far the sound had carried.

The radioman rose, fumbling with his equipment. His fingers did not seem to work. When Capwell lobbed the coconut, it bounced off his chest.

The three men stood in a semicircle, staring at each other, surrounded by dark. Deciding.

Capwell's neck twitched toward the village.

Carson turned, facing the same direction. Slowly, he nodded.

Across the courtroom, Lord looked toward Carson. The beam of the projector was between them; in its light Carson's face was yellow, older, as he watched the boy he had been start cutting toward the village again.

They seemed even tenser now; every few feet, they stopped to listen.

All at once, the men sheathed their machetes. As they crept forward, there was a change in the quality of light—the leaves were sharper, the darkness at their feet became damp ground and brush.

Over Carson's shoulder, framed by leaves, was the clearing.

For minutes, the camera was still. Pieces of life moved past—a chicken, a covey of children, a woman bearing water. Normal, even banal, except that there were no men.

Carson and Capwell turned to each other. Capwell's lips opened; somehow Lord knew this had been silent, a warning. Carson's eyes were hollow.

Together, they looked at his watch. From the angle of light before them, Lord guessed it was late afternoon.

Jerkily moving on the balls of their feet, the three men broke from the jungle.

The village was nine or ten hooches, surrounding a center courtyard. The women and children there were already still, backs to the camera. Loping toward them were three other men in pajamas, too tall for Vietnamese, their rifles unslung.

They began raiding hooches.

Turning from them, the camera followed Carson.

Necks turning from side to side, he and his team entered a hooch with their M-16s pointed.

The hooch was dim, cramped, with three cushioned chairs and a thatched table. On the wall was a wooden carving of Ho Chi Minh; beneath that was a washbasin, half-filled with filmy water, scissors, and a straight razor balanced on its edge. A primitive barber shop, Lord guessed.

Carson was staring at the table.

There was a bamboo cup, next to a bottle that looked like rice wine. The bottle seemed empty. Carson grasped the cup; wine sloshed when he slapped it down.

The camera kept moving, to an indentation in the cushion of one chair.

Carson reached out, touching it, turned to the others. Lord mouthed it with him: "Warm."

Capwell spun as if startled. Suddenly they were running past the camera, Carson holding a grenade.

Swinging wildly, the camera stopped in the doorway.

Outside, the women and children were gone. Five men were running with rifles; behind them the taller men sprawled dead at various angles. As Carson and his team appeared, they opened fire.

The radioman's head snapped backward; Capwell crumpled; Carson threw his grenade.

The camera caught its parabola—a perfect arc, spreading the Viet Cong as it fell among them.

The ground rose first. Then a second grenade hit, wafting dead or dying VC to various heights. The camera followed one. He seemed to rise in slow motion, arms flailing like a rag doll, then snapped in midair, falling in a precipitous heap.

Except for bodies, there was no one in the courtyard.

Slowly, the camera panned the village.

The radioman had fallen on his back. There was a hole in his eye socket; only his lower body moved at all. The camera kept circling.

Carson held Capwell, hands clamped across a stain in his chest. As he tried to lift him, Capwell's hat tumbled off, exposing curly, reddish hair.

Staring up at the camera, Carson's eyes seemed disbelieving. His mouth opened—it might have been a curse or plea for help—and then he reached out for the dead man's radio. Grasped it, finally, to sling on one shoulder.

Capwell's eyes moved, trying to follow.

Cradling his head, Carson rose with him. Capwell's legs stretched limp but straight in front of him, resting on their heels. From the two men's shadows, Lord could see it was dusk.

Carson began dragging Capwell toward the jungle.

The two men moved backward, Capwell's head on Carson's shoulder, gazing up at him, tears running down Carson's face as he staggered, blood on his fingers now, trickling from one corner of Capwell's mouth. They reached the edge of the jungle; first Carson vanished, then Capwell, the bare heels of his feet leaving trails as they disappeared, and then the film went black.

When the lights came on, Carson was blinking at the screen. The rest of him didn't move.

"After that," Lord asked softly, "what do you remember?"

He didn't react; the jurors' looks held nervous empathy.

"Harry?"

Mechanically, Carson's head turned to Lord.

"The first thing that comes to you."

Carson's face twisted. "Uh . . ."

There was dull pain in the sound. "VC?" Lord prodded.

Carson looked up at the ceiling. "There were more."

"Where?"

"In the jungle." His mouth stayed open. "At night."

Lord put both hands in his pockets. "What happened?"

"I shot them." Carson touched his forehead. "We made it to the paddies. You could hear rice, moving in the wind. . . ." The odd, poetic detail seemed to widen his eyes.

"Was it still night?" Lord asked.

"Uh—yeah."

"How long did that take you?"

A strange, surprising smile. "A long time."

Lord watched him. "Where was the cameraman?"

The smile vanished. "With us."

"Do you remember his name?"

Silence. "No."

Lord watched him. "Was Capwell alive?"

"I bandaged him." Carson's tone was wondering. "The water was at our necks. I couldn't tell if he was bleeding. . . ."

"Could he walk?"

"I carried him." Carson's gaze fell. "There was blood on his face."

Lord moved closer. "The VC," he began. "Did they . . ."

"He was moaning." Carson angled his head. "They heard him."

Gripping his notepad, Kleist did not write. "Who?" Lord asked.

"A VC. In the rice. . . ." The voice trailed off.

Lord leaned forward. "What happened?"

"I dragged Capwell out. . . ."

Please, Lord thought, remember. "Where?"

"Up on the mud." Carson hesitated. "He kept moaning. . . ."

Lord nodded encouragement. "What did you do?"

"I . . ." A hesitance, then sudden clarity. "I covered his mouth and shot him full of morphine."

"They gave you morphine?"

"If you got captured, see, you couldn't tell them shit for a while . . . couldn't remember. . . ."

Lord's stomach felt empty. "Did he stop moaning?"

"Yeah." The strange smile again. "He started asking for beer. . . ."

"Beer?"

"Schlitz." The rueful tone became frightened. "In the middle of the fucking delta, with Charlie hunting us. . . ."

"Did you try something else?"

Carson's eyes shut. "I left him there with the camera guy, calling for Schlitz."

Rainey's mouth was a tight, thin line. "Did they capture him?" Lord asked.

A long pause. "No. . . ."

Pain again, reluctance. Lord moved next to him. "What happened?"

Carson shut his eyes. "I hid till Charlie found them. He aimed his rifle . . ."

The sentence died. Gently, Lord said, "The VC killed them?"

Carson's mouth opened; there was no sound, and then he answered, "I cut the VC's throat."

There was utter silence.

Breaking it, Carson's voice held quiet amazement. "First time. . . ."

His eyes opened. Lord moved in front of him, to help. "Were there others . . . ?"

"I dragged the dead VC to the water and ripped his head back, so the water would go through the slit." Carson's eyes didn't move. "See, when their lungs fill up with water, they sink. . . ."

"You didn't want him found. . . ."

"His lungs were filling up, and Capwell's still calling for beer."

Lord's throat was dry. Jurors stared down, one with hands to her face, and the gallery was a stunned, silent frieze. Lord realized that he was searching them, for Damone.

Turning to Carson, he saw a new focus in his eyes. "Capwell," Lord said. "What did you do about him?"

Carson seemed to recall something. "He'd have choked if we'd covered his mouth anymore." A short pause. "I told the camera asshole to not touch him or he'd die."

The last had an unnerving lucidity. "Could you move him?"

Carson stared at the floor. "I radioed Glennon."

"What did you tell him?"

"That we had his film and the prisoner he'd wanted us to get—to send out a patrol boat." A sly, sheepish smile. "I said to bring beer."

"Was Capwell still asking for it?"

"For a while." Carson's voice was gentle. "I held him, then he was quiet."

Lord studied him. "Did Glennon come?" he finally asked.

"With three others." Carson's speech was becoming trancelike. "In a patrol boat, before dawn."

It sounded final, somehow. "What happened?"

"I took a beer from Glennon and poured some in Capwell's mouth." Carson paused in disbelief. "It just came back out."

Someone coughed, once.

Softly, Lord asked, "What did Glennon do?"

Carson's mouth worked. " 'You lying asshole,' he tells me. 'He's stiff. You dragged me out here for a fucking corpse.' "

Distractedly, Lord touched the bridge of his nose. "Did you answer?"

A small headshake. Raising one arm in front of him, Carson answered, "I took out the Mauser to kill him."

"Did you fire?"

Carson stared at his arm. "They grabbed me."

"And then?"

"Glennon shot me full of morphine."

There was a tightness in Lord's chest. "After that," he ventured, "what do you remember?"

Carson lowered his arm. It hung loosely, like his head. "I'm home. My mother's pissed at me for swearing. . . ."

His voice stopped. He didn't speak or move, nor did anyone.

"And what do you remember," Lord asked finally, "about the night you killed the senator?"

Carson's eyelids fluttered. "Oh, man. . . ."

"Anything at all."

Carson hunched, as if from a blow. "There was shouting, over and over, in my head. . . ."

"What was it like."

" 'Kill Glennon, kill Glennon. . . .' " The voice rose, then broke, whispering, "Kill Glennon."

Lord felt the whisper shudder through him. "What happened then?"

"There was a flashbulb." His voice tremored. "I saw him. . . ."

"Who?"

"I shot at his head." Carson swallowed. "The camera was there. . . ."

"On the mission?"

"When I turned, he was lying on the stage, with Stacy over him. . . ."

"Kilcannon?"

"Yes—him." Carson touched his eyes. "God, I can't believe he's dead. . . ."

Lord tilted his head. "Who?"

"Him." Carson's face bent to his knees. "Glennon. . . ."

His shoulders began shaking, and then the sounds came, keening and arrhythmic.

Over Carson's head, Lord and Rainey looked at each other. "No further questions," Lord told him.

Filing in, the jurors stared somberly at Carson. He sat with his hands folded, withdrawn. DiPalma watched him keenly, his body a line of tension. When Rainey banged his gavel, Lord started.

"Mr. DiPalma?"

In an instant, DiPalma was moving toward Carson. "This morning," he began, "Mr. Lord showed us a film. When did *you* first see it?"

Good, Lord thought. Nervously, Carson smoothed his mustache. "This morning."

DiPalma's surprise showed in the briefest hesitation. "Then when did you first *hear* what was in it?"

Carson wouldn't look at him. "I didn't."

Kleist made a note. DiPalma paused, frustrated, then summoned a skeptical expression.

"You purchased the Mauser four weeks before the concert, did you not?"

Carson bent forward. "Yes."

Lord folded his hands. Almost casually, DiPalma inquired, "Were you thinking about Glennon then?"

Carson seemed to flinch. "I don't know."

"That was the first revolver you'd bought since Vietnam, right?"

"I guess so."

As he mumbled, Lord put both hands under the table, where the jury couldn't see them. "And when did you first learn," DiPalma went on, "that there would be a June second concert including Senator Kilcannon?"

"Uhh—" The sound died in Carson's throat. "I don't remember."

DiPalma scowled. "Whenever it was, did you think of Glennon then?"

Carson shook his head, as if to clear it. "I don't know."

"How did you hear about the concert?"

Carson hesitated; the jurors' sober, inward looks were evolving into sharp attention. "John, I guess," Carson murmured. "Damone."

DiPalma put both hands on his hips. "And when did you first plan to shoot Senator Kilcannon?"

"Objection!" Lord stood at once. "It's not established that the defendant *planned* to shoot the senator at all."

Brow furrowed, Rainey watched Carson. "Sustained."

DiPalma directed his faint smile at Carson. "That morning, you brought the Mauser to work. Had you ever done that before?"

Carson hesitated. "No."

"You didn't show it to anyone, did you?"

Carson shook his head. "I guess not."

"Or tell anyone you had it?"

His head continued shaking, as if to ward off questions. "No. . . ."

"Were you planning to shoot the senator *then?*"

Lord realized he was gripping his knees. Look at him, dammit, he thought. Carson's voice rose. "I don't know—"

"You don't *know.*" DiPalma straightened in astonishment. "You're telling the jury you killed a presidential contender onstage, in front of twenty thousand people, yet you don't know how you happened to be out there with a gun?"

"Objection." Now Lord tried sounding weary. "Only a short time ago, on direct examination, the witness described his state of mind at the moment of the shooting."

The camera turned to Rainey. "Sustained," he ruled, and then Lord saw that DiPalma's eyes were bright.

"Very well," he said to Carson. "That morning, where did you wake up?"

"Uh. . . ." Carson's voice was light, surprised. "The Holiday Inn."

"Did you think you were in Vietnam?"

Through the glass, Shriver looked angry; Carson stared at the floor. "Uh—no."

"Did you shower and shave?"

"Yes."

"Did you think about Vietnam then?"

"Uh—" Fleetingly, Carson glanced up, then rubbed his eyes. "Sometimes, in water, I feel scared. I don't know. . . ."

His voice stopped; the gallery began standing. DiPalma seemed to discard his next question for another. "How did you get to the concert?"

"My motorcycle."

"How did you know the route?"

"Uh—I think I asked someone."

DiPalma narrowed his eyes. "When you got to the Arena, what did you do?"

"Help set up the sound system."

The answer was a monotone. DiPalma smiled again, as if about to ask Carson where he thought he was, then snapped abruptly, "Did you also read about Mr. Lord in the newspaper?"

Carson's eyes shut. "Yes—"

"Because you thought you'd be needing a lawyer?"

Carson shook his head.

"Speak up," DiPalma prodded.

"I don't know."

"Why?" DiPalma asked softly. "Because you thought you were in Vietnam?"

Carson turned away. "I don't know."

DiPalma stared at him. "Did you also park your motorcycle by the loading dock?"

"Yes."

"And later, did you use the pay phone?"

"Yes."

"To call whom?"

"Beth. . . ." Carson's eyes were still closed. "But her number was unlisted."

"Did Information tell you that?"

"Yes."

"Which Information?"

"South Carolina—Columbia."

DiPalma shook his head, as if overwhelmed by Carson's rationality. "Tell me, Mr. Carson, who stole the concert money?"

It seemed to startle Carson, then deflate him. As if no one could believe him, he murmured, "I don't know."

DiPalma's eyes were cold. "Perhaps you know if Senator Kilcannon was blond."

Carson wiped his forehead with two fingers. "He wasn't."

"Then did he remind you of Glennon in some other way?"

Slowly, Carson looked up. "I thought about him all the time."

"Who?"

Carson's tone held sudden returning anger. "Glennon. . . ."

"You saw Senator Kilcannon backstage, didn't you?"

"Yes."

"Did you recognize him as James Kilcannon?"

"Yes."

"Did you know you were at a rock concert?"

Carson's voice began to waver. "Yes. . . ."

DiPalma moved closer. "Did you mean to kill him *then*?"

A shiver ran through Carson's body. "I don't know."

"You don't?" DiPalma asked in an incredulous tone. "Then what made you bring the Mauser?"

Kleist leaned forward, waiting. Lord saw Shriver in the gallery, mouth open, as if speaking for Carson. But the witness was mute.

"Mr. Carson?" Rainey asked.

Slowly, miserably, Carson shook his head. "I don't *know*."

"You—don't—know." Moving forward with each word, DiPalma stood over Carson. "But after you murdered James Kilcannon, you asked for Mr. Lord."

Carson's tone was chastened. "Yes."

DiPalma paused, stretching out the moment. Quite softly, he asked, "Did you think you were in Vietnam?"

Carson's eyes opened. "No," he said in a clear, quiet voice. "I was in jail."

DiPalma nodded his satisfaction. "Yes," he finally murmured. "You did know that."

Lord rose. "Was that a question?" he asked.

Staring down at Carson, DiPalma gave a small, scornful smile. "I *have* no more questions," he said, and sat down.

"You also finished a poem that day," Lord began. "Called 'Golden Anniversary.' Did it include the line 'feeding the camera'?"

Carson stared to one side. "I think so . . . yeah."

Lord moved closer. "After you shot the senator, what was the next thing you did?"

"I turned. . . ." The vague voice grew stronger. "That was when I saw the camera."

"And what did you do?"

Carson gave a bewildered shrug. "Fired at it."

"Instead of trying to escape?"

Carson grimaced. "Yeah."

Lord's expression was quizzical. "For what reason?"

Carson shook his head, as if at his own foolishness. In a parched, embarrassed tone he answered, "I don't know."

Lord let the three words linger for the jury, half-turning to DiPalma. "Why?" he asked gently. "Did you think you were in Vietnam?"

DiPalma's eyes widened; Carson's closed. "I don't know." The words held a kind of agony. "I just don't know."

Lord nodded. "I know," he answered.

3

The trial concluded with the psychiatrists. Though their testimony was critical, Carson stared past them, as if he had been leeched of interest in his fate.

"Glennon," Shriver told Lord, "is the missing piece."

He had a new assurance, Lord saw. "In your opinion, Doctor, how did Glennon affect Harry's life since Vietnam?"

"He haunted him for fourteen years." Turning to the jury, Shriver ticked off fingers. "First, Glennon symbolized the horror of what Carson was forced to do—as exemplified by the poem he wrote for Beth. Second, his half-repressed memory of Capwell's death became fused with anger over the death of other friends, *and* guilt that he'd survived without avenging them. Third—and this is important—working for Damone would suboonsciously remind him of Glennon." He paused, touching the fourth finger. "Remember that in Harry Carson's mind, Glennon never died until this trial. That's what 'Golden Anniversary' is about."

Kleist listened, Lord noticed, with the air of someone straining to decide. "And what," Lord asked, "was the influence of Glennon on the shooting of James Kilcannon?"

"Decisive."

"Even in connection with carrying a weapon?"

Shriver nodded. "That seems a classic instance of the anniversary reaction—compounded by all the drugs he took there, which would operate to repress memory *and* help telescope time. Under those circumstances, Carson wouldn't know why he did certain things in the real world—fight his father, slap his wife, even bring a gun to work."

Lord felt the gallery, the camera, the jury watching. "And what about the actual moment of the shooting?"

"Harry reacted in terms of his training—to shoot specific people in the head. In his mind, the chant Miss Tarrant started—'Kill-cannon'—became a summons to kill Glennon." Pausing, Shriver gave Carson a pensive look. "It's tragic, really. Harry Carson shot the wrong person, on the anniversary of trying to kill the right one."

Carson touched his mustache. He did not look up.

"When we first met," Lord said to Shriver, "I asked how vets can live part in the everyday world, and part in their memories of war. Do you recall the example you gave me?"

"Yes." Shriver took out his glasses case. "It was the vet who commandeered a woman with a station wagon, then told her to go fast enough to escape the Viet Cong but not so fast the cops would stop them.

"He was charged with kidnapping. His psychiatrist's opinion was that the crime had no rational explanation—that the veteran had coalesced real and unreal. The jury agreed, and acquitted him."

Lord paused. "After that," he asked at length, "what did the veteran do?"

Shriver glanced at Carson. "He hung himself."

"I'm curious," DiPalma began, "how you explain the rational things *Harry Carson* did up to the moment he shot the senator?"

Shriver frowned. "I can't, really, beyond what I've already said—that stress victims can function with apparent normality."

"I note the word *apparent*." DiPalma placed both hands on hips. "Isn't it also possible that Carson came to work planning to shoot the senator, and succeeded?"

"That," Shriver said in a dubious tone, "is always a possibility."

DiPalma's voice rose. "And isn't it further possible that in the execution of a preconceived plan, Carson had some temporary confusion with certain details of a Vietnam experience?"

Shriver hesitated. "It's conceivable, yes."

"Even that he made the whole thing up?"

Shriver's tone sharpened. "Conceivable, but unlikely."

"But possible?"

Shriver gave a reluctant nod. "Yes."

Glancing sideways, DiPalma underscored Carson's averted gaze. "No further questions."

Dr. George Ford was a blocky man with black horn-rimmed glasses, a square face, and lips he pursed to show authority. He taught at Berkeley, wrote articles, and had a thriving practice; his brusque tone suggested that he was being inconvenienced.

"In *my* opinion," Ford said briskly, "there is no basis for isolating the murder from the rational conduct which preceded it."

DiPalma nodded. "Even in light of Vietnam?"

"Yes." Ford looked toward the camera. "Don't misunderstand me—part of Mr. Carson's service there was unfortunate, even unfair. But lots of people lead unfair lives, and remain capable of making rational decisions." Turning to the jury, Ford concluded, "Put bluntly, I do not believe that a fourteen-year-old trauma made him kill a well-known stranger at a concert he helped set up."

DiPalma raised an eyebrow. "What about the 'anniversary reaction'?"

"Certainly, intense memories *do* follow traumatic incidents." Ford pursed his lips. "It's the notion that this one would seize him from morning to night, causing him to carry a gun, which strikes me as fantasy."

"Even at the moment of the shooting?"

Ford gave a heavy shrug. "Oh, he might have had associations then. But how did he *get* that far?" Another pursing of lips. "Here is a man with experience in killing those he'd planned to kill, hours or days before. I don't view this as some sustained mistake."

He was good, Lord thought—Kleist had begun taking notes. "Can you enlighten us, then," DiPalma was asking, "on the motives common to assassins?"

"Objection," Lord cut in. "The question asks Dr. Ford to speculate on the motives of others, using them to tar Harry Carson."

"I'm soliciting an observation," DiPalma retorted crisply, "not unlike Dr. Shriver's on the veteran who killed himself."

"Overruled," Rainey said.

"Motives other than money?" Ford answered DiPalma. "Fame is one, political differences another. However disagreeable killing may be to most of us, these are clearly understood motives, common to many assassins."

"Even if the assassin never states them?"

Ford examined Carson. "Absolutely."

"Thank you." With an air of satisfaction, DiPalma turned to Lord.

Standing, Lord watched Ford until he felt the jury's anticipation. "How would you describe your practice?"

"Wide." A tacit gibe at Shriver. "And varied."

"Varied enough to include veterans of Vietnam?"

"Of course." Ford looked nettled. "In my career, I've treated veterans of four different wars."

Including the Crimean? Lord considered asking. "For stress?"

"Their problems may *include* that—people can be quite complex."

Lord gave him a quizzical look. "In the midst of all this complexity, have you also found time to testify in criminal cases?"

Ford paused. "On occasion."

"How many occasions?"

"I'm not sure."

Lord tilted his head. "If I said fifty-six, would that seem wrong?"

Ford's lips pursed. "It may have been that many."

Lord smiled faintly. "Perhaps it would be simpler to count the times you've testified for defendants."

"It wouldn't, actually." Ford began sounding nettled. "As you suggest, I'm quite busy. . . ."

"Try seven."

Ford stared at him. "You've obviously counted—"

"What did they have to do to impress you?" Lord broke in softly. "Bark like dogs?"

"Objection!" DiPalma snapped. "Harassing the witness."

Lord turned on him. "Let him answer," he shot back. "Lots of people lead unfair lives—"

Rainey pounded his gavel. "Mr. Lord, I'll thank you to restrain yourself. Objection sustained."

But the jury was riveted. "Isn't it true," Lord demanded in a low, angry voice, "that four of those defendants were previously diagnosed as paranoid-schizophrenics?"

Ford sat straighter. "Paranoid-schizophrenics," he intoned, "are a particular interest of mine."

"But not Vietnam veterans."

"No." The quick, curt answer was that of a man eager to be rid of someone. "Not as such."

Lord's smile returned. "Thank you," he said politely. "No further questions."

They recessed before closing arguments.

Lord sat alone at the defense table. "Hi," Cass said behind him.

"Hi, yourself. And thanks for the stuff on Ford."

"I saw your cross," she said, sitting. "That was some fine indignation."

"Had to make him look bad." Lord felt himself coming down fast. "I knew I couldn't shake his opinion."

Cass contemplated him. "You know," she said, "the first time I saw a psych defense, I kept waiting for *the* answer. There never is one, is there."

"No." Lord gazed at the jury box. "Finally, they just vote."

The jury waited, opaque but for their nervous attention.

Rising to face them, DiPalma held an open magazine.

"Ladies and gentlemen, it is the aim of the defense you've witnessed to make Harry Carson seem the victim. But the victim is not here." Pausing, he flipped the magazine to its cover. "*This* was James Kilcannon."

Hair tousled, Kilcannon grinned from the cover of *Newsweek*, poignantly alive.

"For millions of his generation, and millions more from every race and circumstance in life, he was the last best hope in a dangerous world."

As the jury watched, DiPalma placed the magazine face down.

"In one brief moment," he said softly, "Harry Carson changed that.

"For fourteen hours, he had waited with a concealed weapon, hiding his intentions by going about his normal work. And when his moment came, he walked onstage, took one step forward, and murdered James Kilcannon with a single perfect shot."

DiPalma stood straighter, as if to reign in his emotions. "Mr. Lord," he said, "must ask you to believe—must *prove* to you—that this rational moment, the climax to all those other rational moments, is one of stark insanity.

"Well, Mr. Lord has surely proven that his client is far from perfect." DiPalma turned to Carson, voice etched with scorn. "And the surest proof we have is that Harry Carson failed to escape.

"But even then, did *reason* fail him?

"No—he called a lawyer whose name he'd memorized from the morning paper, fourteen hours before. And now this lawyer asks you to believe his client killed because of what he'd suffered in Vietnam, fourteen *years* before."

Once more, DiPalma faced the jury. "This incredible suggestion slanders every other man who suffered there. But even slander will not save him, for the question is not whether Mr. Carson's service there is worthy of our sympathy, or even whether it changed his mental makeup or the stability of his life. For as the judge will tell you, Mr. Lord must now have proven that, at the moment he shot James Kilcannon—not some other moment—Harry Carson did not understand what he was doing *and* that it was wrong.

"To manage this, he asks you to forget what Harry Carson *did*, and believe only what he *says*—and then only about Vietnam."

DiPalma placed one hand on hip, in his now-familiar pose of disbelief. "Specifically, he presents the murder of James Kilcannon as a curious mental misunderstanding, the annual resurrection of an attempted murder in a rice paddy." Pausing, he added softly, "The attempted murder of a shadowy figure which only Harry Carson, and only at this trial, claims to have happened at all."

Too sarcastic, Lord hoped, perhaps an opening. But the jury listened closely; the rhythm of DiPalma's speech and logic was tight, effective. "Even if we knew nothing of Mr. Carson's cool and rational conduct prior to the murder, this excuse stretches the bounds of psychiatric reason. But we *do* know what he did. And all that Mr. Lord can place in the balance is a poem, and the shooting of a camera.

"Do these truly mean—in spite of everything else—that Harry Carson murdered by mistake? More to the point, do they *prove* it?

"To even ask these questions is as absurd as wondering why he needed a revolver to set up sound for Stacy Tarrant."

Moving to his table, DiPalma seemed to gather himself. "As he lay dying, James Kilcannon asked Miss Tarrant, 'Is everyone all right?' Fortunately, neither she nor any others were wounded—not physically. But everyone is *not* all right, and never will be. For Harry Carson killed not just a man but the hope—the *right*—of a free people to chose those they wish to lead them."

Slowly, DiPalma turned up Kilcannon's photograph for the jury. "James Kilcannon is dead," he told them. "Harry Carson murdered him. Justice demands that Harry Carson answer for it."

Lord spoke his first quiet words to Kleist.

"I hope that all of you listened closely to Mr. DiPalma. For he is a very able and experienced prosecutor, and he has very ably told you what this case is *not* about."

They watched him now, interest caught.

"It is not," he went on, "about whether Harry Carson shot Senator Kilcannon. Everyone knows that.

"It is not about whether his death was sad beyond redemption. It was.

"No, what this case requires is that you ask and answer the simple question, Why?

"Why did a boy from a close rural family, with hopes for the future and not so much as a parking ticket, become the man who shot James Kilcannon?

"What," Lord asked with sudden anger, "does Mr. DiPalma think his motive was?

"To go through this trial?"

The jurors' heads snapped back, surprised, as he pointed to Carson.

"Where is the profit, or the passion, or the principle which would motivate the act?

"There is none." Turning, Lord's gaze swept each juror. "For this so-called cool and rational killing was a crime bereft of reason, and Harry Carson is its final victim.

"It is this," he added softly, "the *prosecutor* asks you to forget.

"In contrast, he has suggested that the trauma my client sustained in Vietnam is a distraction, that I wish you to ignore the things that Harry

Carson *did*. But all I ask is that you consider with me certain *other* things he did—and what they mean.

"I do not believe that the so-called attempted murder in a rice paddy is simply an excuse.

"Nor do I conceive the fight with his father—exactly one year later—as the beginning of an alibi.

"Or that he was merely aiding his defense a year ago *last* June, when he slapped his wife and left his daughter behind.

"If I am wrong, then the writing of a poem, and the shooting of a camera, are just the final touches." Lord turned slowly to DiPalma, with Carson slumped between them. "If I am wrong," he said with quiet irony, "how very clever Harry Carson has always been. And look at *all* he's gained."

Across the courtroom, Lord and DiPalma stared at each other, and then Lord turned to Kleist.

"What was done to James Kilcannon can never be undone. All Harry Carson brings to this courtroom is the hope that you will look at him, and ask the simple question, Why?" Pausing, Lord finished softly. "And, in the end, I believe that you will find the answer—not guilty, by reason of insanity."

Lord stood there, watching them, and then Kleist smiled.

At that moment, Lord was certain he had lost.

4

Christopher watched Lord toss clothes in his suitcase. "I want you to live *here*, Daddy."

Stopping, Lord stared at the suitcase. "I'll just be at Laura and Ray's— till your Mom and I can talk better."

"Promise?"

His son was about to cry, Lord knew. Before Christopher could see his face, he scooped him up. "It's not your fault, honey. It's mine."

Christopher clasped his neck. When Lord put him down, he turned, running to his room.

A moment later he returned with a school photo of himself. "You can have this. So you don't get lonely."

He was trying to smile. "Thanks, mugwump," Lord said. "I'll put it near my bed."

Christopher watched his face. "Do you have a picture of Mommy?"

"I'll be sure and ask for one." Taking his son's photograph, he knelt. "You know what the best day of my life was?"

Christopher leaned his forehead to Lord's. "What?"

"The day you were born."

Marcia was waiting at the front door. "Are you moving in with *her*?"

Lord shook his head. "Since that night, we haven't spoken."

Her eyes narrowed in mistrust. "I'm not sharing Christopher," she finally said, "if that's what you're angling for."

"Look—"

"I've already talked to a lawyer, Tony. No joint custody—you're not getting your way this time."

He glanced down the hallway. "Or what? You'll use our son again?"

The anger he saw was barely controlled. "If that's what it takes to defend my rights."

Lord stared at her. "Jesus Christ," he said, and left.

In his friends' guest room, alone, he unpacked the suitcase. For a moment Lord sat on the bed, gazing at the photograph of Christopher. Then he picked up the phone and dialed Cass.

"No word," she said. "I'd have called you."

"Yeah. Okay."

There was silence. "That bit about smilers," she said. "It's folklore, Tony."

For four days, Lord went to his office, awaiting the verdict.

There was a split in the jury, he knew; with each hour, a mistrial grew more likely. He slept fitfully.

On the afternoon of the fourth day, Cass called him, sounding tense. "Better get over here."

When Lord arrived, they'd brought Carson down from jail.

The bailiff announced Judge Rainey. Standing, Lord felt numb; DiPalma was pale; Carson shifted his weight from side to side. The jurors filed in, looking at no one.

Kleist stood front row center, the foreman.

Reporters watched through the glass, ready. The camera turned to Rainey. He seemed shaken, smaller than his robes.

"Do you have a verdict?" he asked.

"We do." Kleist looked grim; his voice had wavered slightly. His eyes never left the judge.

"Will you read it?" Rainey asked.

Kleist squared his shoulders. "Not guilty," he said. "By reason of insanity."

To Lord, the next minutes were a blur.

There was an explosion of sound, followed by reporters running for cameras or phones. Kleist nodded to him, followed by other jurors, but no one smiled. When Lord grasped Carson's shoulder, he looked away.

"It's a start," Lord told him.

Carson watched the floor. "Thanks," he mumbled, and then Rainey gaveled them to order.

Judicial calm recovered, he ordered Carson to a state mental facility. Two deputies took him away.

It was over.

Cass hugged him awkwardly. "You did it, Tony."

"Both of us."

She looked at him, shaking her head. "You'll need me to bring the car around," she said, and was gone.

Turning, Lord saw DiPalma.

They faced each other, winner and loser; Lord remembered in surprise that he was taller than the prosecutor. Silently, he extended his hand.

Eyes filled with anger and humiliation, DiPalma stared at it.

Lord's arm fell to his side. Shrugging, he headed toward the glass partition.

The lobby was filled with reporters and spectators.

"Hey, Tony—"

Lord kept going through flashbulbs, newspeople, TV cameras. "You fucked up my picture," someone whined, and then he reached the door.

More cameras formed a semicircle, blocking his way. From the top of the steps, a crowd flowed across the lawn and sidewalk and into the streets. For the rest of his life, Lord realized, people would remember this.

A piece of metal glinted, coming toward him. Like Kilcannon, he thought crazily, then saw it was a shotgun microphone.

"Tony," someone shouted. "Do you view this as a vindication of Vietnam vets?"

Lord composed himself. "They don't need vindication," he answered. "They didn't shoot James Kilcannon. What they *and* Harry Carson need is a more intelligent appreciation of what we asked them to do."

Another microphone. "But do you believe the verdict was warranted?"

Lord nodded. "The jury's verdict is both warranted and courageous. The ultimate credit goes to them. . . ."

"Some people think DiPalma blew it."

"He just couldn't find any motive." Lord gave a half-hearted smile. "You're not supposed to make one up."

"Tony!"

A familiar, woman's voice. Turning to find it, Lord saw Damone, leaning against the wall.

Faintly smiling, Damone nodded.

"Over here!"

Lord watched him an instant longer, then faced his questioner.

It was Rachel, gazing at him from behind the microphone. "How do you feel now?" she asked.

"Tired."

She pushed closer. "But don't you have any personal reaction?"

As their eyes met, he felt Damone still watching. "It's history," he said, and then brushed past her, starting through the crowd.

PART 3

TONY LORD
and
STACY TARRANT

THE SEVEN DAYS OF PHOENIX

APRIL 8–14, THE FOLLOWING YEAR

Day One: Monday

1

Within twenty-four hours of Stacy Tarrant's call, Lord was on a plane to Los Angeles.

The night before, he had worked late with Cass, preparing to leave. They worked quickly and quietly, both stunned by what Phoenix had done. Lord made a list of lawyers to call, putting off meetings or hearings; Cass culled the coming week's files and then the Saturday mail. Alexis Parnell's kidnapping replayed in the background, on SNI.

With the volume low, the distorted voice of Phoenix seemed to come from some great distance:

"John Damone will die unless Stacy Tarrant can persuade you to pledge five million dollars, through a unique and public act of selflessness which I will disclose on my first broadcast, tomorrow night. . . ."

As Lord turned to watch, Alexis stumbled once more, beneath the door of the terrorist's white van.

"As for Alexis Parnell, in the days that follow you will judge her husband's televised compliance with my demands. Then, on the seventh day of her captivity, you will cast an advisory vote through SNI as to whether she will live or die. . . ."

The camera zoomed in; the fallen woman gazed up at it, in shocked close-up.

"And on the final day you will witness her release or execution—live."

The picture changed. At night, a body lay in a darkened patch of grass.

Then a light flashed in its face; Colby Parnell, blindfolded, an audiotape stuffed in his mouth with a gag.

The voice which replaced that of Phoenix was Rachel's.

"Early this morning," she began, "SNI rescued Colby Parnell from a deserted hillside in Sonoma County, after a call from the terrorist. But like the authorities, Parnell has no clue as to who would take his wife, or where they are. Tonight, one day after the kidnapping, Phoenix seems to have vanished.

"As for Stacy Tarrant, she is unavailable for comment. . . ."

Glancing at Lord, Cass muted the volume further.

Lord finished his work. Opening the last piece of mail, a department-store box, Cass gazed at it silently. Then, without speaking, she handed it to Lord.

Lord stared at the lump of feces inside. "Pity," he said at length. "No return address."

"Another anonymous admirer." Closing the box, Cass took it to the farthest corner of his office. "At least it had time to dry."

"That's the post office for you."

For the first time that evening, Cass smiled a little.

"Being famous," Lord told her, "has changed my whole life."

Her gaze moved across the messages on his desk—requests for interviews or speeches—then back to the television, stopping until Lord followed this. SNI was running the film of Stacy Tarrant; in the silence of the too-quiet streets beneath his office window, Stacy Tarrant turned from the fallen James Kilcannon, to them. "I wonder why she called you," Cass murmured.

"I don't know." Walking to the television, he turned it off. "One call, Cassie, and I'll leave with you."

He picked up the telephone, dialing. When Marcia answered, he said, "It's me. Look, I've got a favor to ask."

"What is it?"

"I promised Christopher I'd take him to see *Star Games* this week, and I've been called out of town. I may be tied up for a while. . . ."

"Another big case?"

Lord waited a moment. "Anyhow, I think we'd better go tonight."

"You can't." The words came quickly, rehearsed. "Fred and I are taking him—I don't want him near what's been on television."

"He and I were planning on it, Marsh. . . ."

"Then tell *him* that," she said flatly.

Lord heard her put the phone down, then say, "Tony wants to talk to you."

"Daddy?" His son's voice fell off. "I told Mommy you were taking me. . . ."

Lord could envision his seven-year-old mumbling into the telephone, with Marcia close by. As too often lately, he found himself trying to guess in seconds the effect of some response on Christopher; he was at once afraid that Christopher would choose his mother, and that choosing him would make his son's life harder. "You really want to see it, right?"

"Well, Mikie says it's good—"

"Then you can tell me about it, okay? And don't forget to thank Fred."

"Okay."

Christopher's voice was muted. Lord wished that he could see his face. "I love you, Christopher."

"Me too."

"Then let me speak to your mom, all right?"

"Okay." Another pause, then, " 'Bye."

" 'Bye."

"What is it?" Marcia snapped.

Lord leaned forward. "Two things. First, tell that idiot if he drives my son when he's stoned again I'll see you both in court. Second, I'm tired of watching you use Christopher. Next time I come over, don't make him stand on the porch with his suitcase like a fucking orphan. . . ."

"I don't want you in this house. For *any* reason."

"Listen—"

Marcia hung up.

Lord sat back in his chair. "Jesus."

Cass had busied herself with the Rolodex. Almost shyly, she looked up through wire-rimmed glasses. "Marcia puts him in the middle, huh." She paused, then added, "And you're paying her too much for it."

"I wanted to keep him in that house." He shook his head. "Whatever else, Marcia's not a fool. The choices she gave me were intended to inflict pain."

"You got joint custody for Jack Cole. . . ."

"Public trials may be my perverse idea of fun, but not for Christopher." Lord put on his sportcoat. "Did I tell you that *People* wanted to do a piece on our divorce?"

Cass watched him. "I guess," she said finally, "there's no way of knowing who called her that night."

"No." Lord found himself staring at the blank face of the television. "I blew it, that's all."

They left in silence.

Standing by her car, Cass asked him, "How's Harry doing, anyhow?"

Lord shrugged. "Not great. Marty Shriver says he doesn't take much interest."

"Give him time." She dipped into the front seat, put her key in the ignition, then leaned back through the window.

"You're nervous, aren't you, Tony."

"Uh-huh. For Damone, Alexis, *and* Stacy Tarrant. Phoenix wants more from her and Parnell than money—this remote broadcast thing he's trying goes way beyond that."

"And you're not sure you can help her."

Lord shoved both hands in his pockets. "She'll be under incredible strain, and the only real conversation we've had was on the witness stand, when I made her watch that film. It's hard to call that quality time."

Cass winced. "I suppose not."

"It's funny—I've stopped counting how many times in the last ten months some fool or another has asked me, What's Stacy Tarrant really like? As if I'd know."

Cass was momentarily quiet. "She must *think* you can help her, Tony." She gave a sudden crooked smile, then blew him a kiss. "Good luck," she said, and drove away.

Now, flying Los Angeles to meet Stacy, Lord listened as the men sitting in front of him discussed the kidnapping.

"I don't think this Phoenix can do it," the first one was saying.

"This guy at work says he *can*," the authoritative one answered, "but they'd need to have a satellite dish. You've seen them—on those TV trucks."

The first man was more subdued. "I feel sorry for the Parnell woman. I mean, they already lost their kid." He paused. "Maybe they'll just do a Patty Hearst number, then let her go."

"No one's sure what this guy wants, though."

"He'll say tonight, he promised. About the other one too—Stacy's boyfriend or whatever."

"Yeah, look at *her*," the first man mused. "Like I tell my kids when they get hot about some punk rocker—get famous, and end up screwed."

The elderly woman next to Lord noticed his expression. "I feel so sorry for that girl," she ventured. "She seemed like such a nice person somehow, though no one has really seen her since the trial. Of course, that must have been hard for her."

Lord nodded. "I imagine it was," he responded, and lapsed into silence.

The woman kept watching him. "Excuse me," she asked. "Don't I recognize you?"

Smiling, Lord shook his head. "I'd remember you."

The woman looked pleased. Reaching into her purse, she pressed a Bible tract into his hands. "You seem like a nice person too," she said. "This tells how we can all be saved."

The moment stirred memories of his mother watching him at Mass, dubious but hopeful. Thanking her, Lord opened the pamphlet. For the rest of the flight he pretended to read it, still pondering how to give advice on something as wrenching as Damone's abduction to someone who no doubt despised him. Every so often, he flipped a page.

Deplaning, the woman grasped his sleeve. "God bless you."

Lord smiled again. When she was out of sight, he slid the pamphlet into a wastebasket.

Though people noticed him, no reporters knew he was here. But the newsstands were filled with customers reading headlines. The afternoon paper used pictures of Stacy and Alexis to dramatize "The Tragic Lives of Two Women"; its photo of the bound and gagged Parnell was credited to SNI. Lord did not linger. Stacy had refused to postpone the last day of shooting; her limousine took him to Paragon Pictures.

Passing through the marble arch which had symbolized movies since he was Christopher's age, Lord saw reporters and photographers and fans waiting for Stacy. A clearly surprised security guard checked his name against a list, placed two phone calls, then gave him a slip of paper marked "Soundstage Twelve—Anthony Lord for Stacy Tarrant."

Waiting for Lord, Stacy closed her eyes.

She sat alone in a canvas chair, preparing to reshoot her final scene. She could not get it right, could not believe in it. Voices and footsteps echoed through the giant soundstage: for an instant, what was happening to John Damone seemed more real than that she was here, an actress.

Her new career at least, she remembered with high-strung irony, she owed to Lord.

It had begun the night after he'd cross-examined her, as she sat like this with John in her suite at the Mark Hopkins, staring at nothing.

"It was like I was catatonic," she had murmured to Damone. "Lord kept asking questions, and I heard myself answering."

Damone lit a cigarette. "It was that film he showed you."

"How could he do that?"

"You're nothing to him." Damone sounded neither angry nor surprised. "Neither was Kilcannon. Lord likes to win."

"Will he?" she asked.

"No." Damone's eyes narrowed. "Not without help."

She turned to him. "I can't go on like this, John. It's so pointless. . . ."

"Perform." The word was so soft that it asked a question.

"I can't."

He shrugged. "The longer you go—"

"*No.*" She stood. "I watched that slime murder him—I can't walk on-stage again."

"Are you afraid some psychopath will shoot you?"

Stacy hesitated. "I'm afraid of the second before that," she answered. "When I know it's going to happen."

He watched her, silent.

Finally, she sat again, glancing away. "It would be like walking on his grave."

Damone bent to stub his cigarette. "And you still can't write."

"I can write—all about absurd death for no reason." She looked up at him. "I won't make money from it."

Damone drifted to the wet bar and poured himself a drink.

Somehow, his quiet brought her close to tears. "Damn Lord," she said.

Turning from her, Damone answered in a monotone. "The man I hired killed him, Stacy. Lord just brought it back."

She closed her eyes for a moment, heard him swirling ice in his glass. "That question he asked me—about Carson buying the gun *before* I said I'd do the concert?"

"Uh-huh."

"Did Carson ask if you'd reserved a date, in case?"

"No." Damone's voice was quiet again. "There was no need for Harry to know about it."

When she opened her eyes, he still drank, with his face to the wall, pensive. "Mark Steinberg called," he finally said. "He wants to see you."

She remembered brushing back Jamie's hair. It took a moment to ask, "The director?"

"He doesn't mind that you've never acted." Damone faced her. "Do you?"

She paused. "No—not tonight."

Damone gazed at her, then the suite, and began packing. That night she flew back to Los Angeles.

The next morning, before dawn, the dream came for the first time.

It began without sound. She was onstage; raised up by the crowd, Carson suddenly aimed his revolver at her face. As she waited to be shot, Carson glanced past her, then nodded. In slow motion his arm moved away from her. The revolver seemed to jump in his hand; on the screen above them, she saw Jamie fall. When she turned, the curtain had closed, and they were alone. "But what does it mean?" Jamie asked, and then she awakened. For an instant, her waking was so blurred in the dark that she reached out to touch him.

In the days that followed, the dream came repeatedly. But Damone was at the trial; she could not talk of her dream to anyone, or explain it to herself.

A week later, returning from the trial, Damone gave her Steinberg's script.

They did not discuss her dream then, or what he had said in court— neither wanted to, though both knew that she had watched him. For the rest of Carson's trial she reviewed the script as if her life depended on it, scribbling notes in the margin and learning the shorthand for each camera shot, trying to imagine the film frame by frame.

The story was spare. After divorcing her husband, a young mother finds that she is dying. The ex-husband she despises will raise her daughter. Awkwardly, she tries to teach him to be a parent, until they achieve an understanding of each other, and themselves. The film ends with the mother sending her daughter to live with him.

The day after the verdict, Damone and Stacy met with Steinberg.

That morning, Steinberg had offered to cancel the meeting, without giving reasons. When Stacy declined, he drove out to her new retreat in

Malibu. No one mentioned the trial or attempted small talk, nor did Steinberg look at Damone. "You've read the script," he began.

Stacy nodded. "But I haven't acted since college."

"You're not a twenty-year-old model, either." His voice was matter-of-fact. "There's a lot I won't have to tell you."

Stacy smiled at one corner of her mouth. "I'll sleep on it."

The next morning, she told Steinberg she'd agree if the set were closed to the press. When filming began, she attacked her role with total concentration.

Part was insecurity; her costar was a Yale-trained actor. But Stacy used herself more ruthlessly than she had when singing. Reaching for a mother's feelings, she became so lost that sometimes silence hung over the set. To help her relax, Steinberg installed a piano in her trailer. This was her only music. Her life assumed a rhythm—studying the script, doing takes until Steinberg was satisfied, imagining the next scene. On weekends she wrote down ideas. It was the purest work she had ever done; she did not watch dailies, or care what happened to the film when it was finished.

It had been only yesterday—a few moments before she learned Damone had vanished—that Stacy realized what the film had meant to her.

She'd awakened before dawn, alone, as she had since Jamie was shot. Sitting up, she stared at the darkness; her dream had been the same.

Stacy made coffee and went to the deck.

It was part of the ritual; she no longer cried. Staring at the ocean, she let the espresso drift to her nostrils, subconscious sifting the dream.

The air was heavy and smelled of salt. In the first morning light, a runner traced the line where waves struck the sand. A hundred yards out, kelp in long strands undulated with the ebb and flow. When she glanced back down the beach, the runner had vanished.

Once more, the dream meant nothing. Only Carson might know, she thought—or Carson's lawyer.

Retreating, she went through her exercises. As always, they took thirty-five minutes; showering and washing her hair added forty. It was seven-fifty by the time she had dressed.

Like a prisoner, Stacy reflected, measuring out the weekend in time-killing habits. Restless, she phoned her driver. "Can you pick me up early?" she asked. "My meeting's not till ten, but I'd like to look at the lot when nobody's there."

As he cruised it, revolver spoiling the line of his coat, Stacy leaned against the window.

The back lot of Paragon was quaint as the Cotswolds. It had sprung up in the twenties, when films were a cottage industry, and the buildings were modest white stucco. They passed a mock-Tudor house, built for Valentino beneath a gnarled and incongruous palm tree, a blithe juxtaposition which reminded her of the home she'd had to sell after Jamie's death, for security's sake. Then they reached a street of the 1920s.

Each detail was perfect. A billiard parlor; a gold-filigreed sign; ornate wooden balconies; a worn brick hotel with rococo lettering; chimneys and smokestacks at various heights; a wrought-iron stairway; stone pavements; a horse trough; gaslights. Block by block, a slum alley, Brooklyn neighborhood, frontier town, and fieldstone mansion seemed remnants of an eclectic civilization that had recently vanished. Then the limousine turned the last corner and Stacy saw the scaffolding behind them. She was not sure why this depressed her.

Steinberg was waiting in front of the executive offices. When the limousine stopped, he opened the door.

"Hi," he said. "Where's Damone?"

"I haven't called John in three or four days. Was I supposed to?"

"He wanted to see this."

Stacy grimaced. "If he's smart he changed his mind."

He glanced at his watch; Steinberg was the only man Stacy knew who could pace standing still. "We'll give him ten more minutes."

He led her past an oak reception desk, down a hall lined with modern art, to the private screening room.

No one went inside without permission; Stacy had never seen it. When Steinberg unlocked the door and flicked on some overhead lights, it seemed like a bunker, simply furnished and still dark. There were red plush carpeting, white walls, four rows of executive chairs; the room looked empty, as only a stage or a courtroom can look empty. Its floor slanted upward from the screen to a back wall whose upper third was the window to a raised projection room. A dim form stood at the projector, the sole technician given access.

"I feel like a political prisoner," Stacy said.

Steinberg began walking in circles. He wore blue jeans, Adidas, and a Disneyland T-shirt; beard, rimless glasses, and bright anarchist's eyes made him look like a grad student who never slept. As always, he chewed gum with such absentminded fury that Stacy, who had come to like him, wondered if he'd been chewing the same piece since UCLA film school.

She sat, watching him. "How's your metabolic rate this morning?"

Still pacing, he grinned. "Like a python—I could eat forty-two Snickers bars and never know it."

"What's this about, anyhow? You didn't want me to see dailies—I'd get self-conscious, remember?"

"I thought by now you deserved to." He shoved both hands in his pockets. "I've never seen a novice work this hard."

Stacy shrugged. "I did it to get sane, Mark."

His smile turned quizzical. "Like needlepoint."

"Something like that."

He gave a half-shake of the head and continued his circles. "You're making me nervous," she said.

"Where's Damone, anyhow?"

"You really think I'm hiding him?" When Steinberg did not answer, she angled her head at the projector. "Is it that bad?"

He stopped to look at her a moment. "Okay," he said, and turned toward the window. When the technician saw him, he nodded, then switched off the lights.

A stream of light hit the screen. Stacy remembered watching the film of Carson, and then her face appeared.

It was the final scene, filmed out of sequence. Stacy's character was preparing to send her daughter to live with her former husband. Their dialogue was deliberately underkeyed—matters of brushing teeth and packing a lunch—so that its effect depended on nuance. Stacy had cut her mannerisms to the bone: now she saw that this restraint allowed the moment to speak for itself. With concentrated ordinariness, she buttoned the top of the child's coat. Then she looked into her face; gently, Stacy brushed back the girl's bangs with two fingers of her hand.

Watching, the gesture hit her with a physical shock; she did not remember having done this. She felt an ache in her throat, and then some second part of her saw that she was made for the camera. When the screen went black, she realized Steinberg was next to her.

He didn't look at her or switch on the lights.

"You're going to be a film star," he said finally. "It's time you knew."

She turned from him.

"It's going to happen, Stacy. The studio people started watching dailies weeks ago. They saw what I did."

Standing, she walked to a corner. "It's too close to Jamie."

"You couldn't help that, in your state of mind."

"I should have tried."

"Even if you had, this thing would have followed you." He hesitated. "That film of you and Kilcannon—it's like being Jackie Kennedy. People will see whatever you do in terms of that."

She turned. "That's being an icon, not an actress."

"You make it worse by hiding out." His voice became more passionate than she had heard it. "Do another picture, then another and another, until you *are* an actress."

Stacy could not sort out the reasons she felt ashamed. "You know," she said finally, "I can't even *have* children."

Rising, Steinberg switched on the lights. "Look, Stacy, why don't you tell your chauffeur to circle the block. We can take in brunch somewhere, drink a little champagne, and maybe kick this around. It's past time."

It was a measure of what had happened, Stacy thought, that she wondered what he wanted before she felt his good intentions. "Thanks, Mark. But I'd be bad company for you—I've got too much to think about." When Steinberg looked obliquely hurt, she added gently, "Anyhow, I'd better wait for John."

He shrugged. "Another time."

As Stacy wondered what else to say, there was a knock on the door, and then a security guard leaned in. "Miss Tarrant?"

"Yes?"

"Two men from the FBI want to see you." The man sounded bemused. "It's something about Mr. Damone. They asked me if we have a television. . . ."

"Stacy?" A tentative hand on her shoulder.

Her eyes flew open; it was Jack Harris, the associate producer.

"The security guard just called," he told her. "Lord's here."

At the end of the maze of false building fronts, her driver let Lord out beside a sprawling concrete soundstage from the thirties. It was barnlike inside, with extension cords strewn on wooden floors, bare walls covered with insulation, props and catwalks dangling overhead. Behind a metal reception desk there were more guards, blocking a passway through some partitions erected to hide the sets. Giving his slip to the receptionist, Lord watched her place another call.

"You're Anthony Lord," someone said.

It was not a question. Lord turned to see an ascetic-looking man in a work shirt and chinos, standing between the guards. "That's right."

"I'm Jack Harris." He paused, frowning at Lord. "Stacy's four takes into the final scene. It may be a while—she's having trouble."

"I'm not surprised." When Harris scowled at the floor, half-turning, Lord asked, "Mind if I go in with you?"

Harris looked up, silent. "She asked you here," he said finally.

Lord followed him through the partition, past a series of partial interiors: the sterile lobby of an apartment building, one corner of a day-care center, a bar with stained glass chandeliers, a kitchen with a butcher-block table, an off-white living room with track lighting and abstract prints. Only voices from deeper within told Lord they were nearing the actors.

Rounding half an office cubicle, Lord saw Stacy Tarrant.

She sat with her eyes closed as a woman applied makeup to traces of sleeplessness. Uncertain, Lord stopped ten feet back. But as the woman finished, she opened her eyes, and saw him.

Her cool expression did not change; had her gaze not lasted so long, Lord would have thought himself invisible. Then she turned to the makeup woman and murmured thanks.

A buzzer sounded, twice. Without speaking to Lord, Stacy walked toward a restaurant with Russian decor and half a ceiling. The other half was canvas, casting indirect light.

"It's the Russian Tea Room," Harris explained, and entered the set.

Perhaps twenty people were there. A black woman paged someone on a walkie-talkie; a cameraman focused his lens; three others adjusted the shutters of lights at various angles; two more held microphones on long poles. At one table, a blond man and a slender woman close to Stacy's height sat for someone with a light meter. Next to them, Lord picked out Mark Steinberg, talking to Stacy and her costar. No one smiled.

Listening to Steinberg, Stacy nodded. Then someone put glasses of wine on the table, and the two leads replaced their stand-ins. Voices dropped; the camera lowered; lights focused on the couple; booms hovered over them. The atmosphere reminded Lord of an operating room. Stacy was quite still.

The buzzer sounded.

There was silence, and then she began speaking.

Lord could follow the scene. Stacy and her leading man disliked each other but were meeting out of some need she had. It was tense enough that Lord guessed why Steinberg had saved it for last; she spoke to the table, a woman under pressure who had rehearsed an emotionless speech, finger tracing the rim of her wineglass. Impatient, the costar asked questions. Her voice became taut, her responses more controlled and rehearsed. Lord was not sure she was acting.

Then her costar asked one question too many.

Her eyes rose from the glass, direct and quite luminous. "Damn it." Each word was low, succinct, angry. "I need you."

"Print it," Steinberg said crisply. "That's a wrap."

Stacy's costar clasped her hand. Someone began clapping; it spread until Stacy looked up in confusion. Then Steinberg called out, "Super," and grinned at her.

Managing a smile, she got up from the table and hugged him. "I'll call you," he said.

"Okay."

She turned to the others. One by one, she took their hands, kissing the makeup lady and two or three more. Most would never see her again; Lord sensed they had come to admire her, and felt for her now. As she walked toward him, head down but still smiling a little, he felt the vacuum she was entering.

She stopped smiling when she reached him. "I'm ready," she said.

"You were good," Lord said.

Nodding, Stacy watched darkness fall, charcoal through the tinted windows of her limousine. She did not know how long they had driven without speaking.

Moments passed like this.

"Why did you call me?" he asked.

She turned, examining him. His face was older; that the last year might have cost him something seemed right.

"Yesterday morning," she finally answered, "while I was still in shock, suddenly there were all these people telling me what I should do. The FBI, poor Mr. Parnell—even Ralph DiPalma called." She turned from him again, speaking in a lower voice. "I want John back. I'll need someone independent to advise me how to do that, period. I don't have to like them."

"It might help."

Stacy clasped the armrest on the door. "You *know* John," she responded coolly. "*And* the Parnells, the SNI people, and the authorities in San Francisco who are handling it all. For *this*, you make sense. Let's leave it at that."

Narrow-eyed, Lord glanced at the soundproof glass between them and the driver. At length, he asked, "Why does Phoenix think you'll agree to a 'unique act of selflessness' to save Damone?"

"We've been together since I started." She flicked back her bangs, uncomfortable. "John's a loner—I'm probably his closest friend."

"Any family?"

"Once, in New York City. John was a career foster child—that's how he ended up in the Army." Fear welled inside her. "To go through that . . ."

"He's no use to Phoenix dead," Lord said, "Not yet."

She turned, angry at his prescience. "You *owe* him, dammit. . . ."

"Look, how did the FBI say he'd been taken?"

She had to stop this, Stacy realized; hatred was a luxury until Damone was safe. "Someone broke in," she finally answered. "The house was torn up, and his car was still there."

"Anything else?"

"I was too rattled to remember it all." She stared past him at the lights of Malibu. "*You* saw Alexis. . . ."

"I'm just trying to imagine who could take him, and how."

But Stacy felt the film of Alexis washing over her again. "What does it matter now?" she murmured.

Lord was silent. "That depends," he told her finally. "On exactly what it is he really wants you to do."

Stacy realized how tightly she gripped the armrest.

Her watch showed 7:20.

2

It was 7:37.

Back against the shed, Phoenix watched the clouds change colors. Vanishing in the Pacific, the sun tinged them a deepening pink. Then pink shaded into gray, and he knew that search planes could no longer see him. Turning, he opened both doors.

Behind them, two satellite dishes were aimed at the sky. Four feet high, four feet across, the fiberglass webs were smaller but more powerful than those used at the Carson trial. Cables ran from their antennae to his replica of a satellite control room: monitor screen, tape cassette, color controls, sound equipment. Checking his watch again, the low thrum of the generator made him restless.

It was 7:40.

Twenty minutes, a nation waiting, and still he did not know if this would work.

To calm himself, Phoenix thought of his good fortune since the morning he had captured Alexis Parnell.

It had begun shortly before dawn, at the bottom of a deserted limestone quarry, an hour north of where he would take her.

The three men had been waiting there since dusk, with the white van. They had bought it for cash in Rhode Island, filed off the serial numbers, stolen its New York plates from a junkyard. Each man was as anonymous. Two years before, in Boston, they had asked Phoenix to finance a drug deal; in return, he had dangled the future prospect of a multi-million-dollar kidnapping. Now his plan had sucked them in. The men had driven west from Massachusetts without knowing his targets, encountered no trouble on the way, had no connection to California. Like Phoenix, they wore gloves.

As one held a flashlight, they began switching tires from his black van to their white one. Then, silently, they got inside the back. Their keys were waiting for him on the seat.

In night's last darkness, he left the black van, climbing the steep road from the quarry.

The white van stopped again at an abandoned campsite, forty miles from the Parnells'. They waited there for five more hours, hot, reviewing his plan. No one saw them.

At 2:00 P.M., Phoenix drove them toward the Parnells'.

His mouth was dry. Seeing their red brick guardhouse, he realized that he had driven the last stretch of country road with both hands tight on the wheel.

Yards from the iron gate, he slipped on his hood and took the Mauser from beneath the seat. When he braked suddenly, tires squealing, a head popped into the guardhouse window. In one continuous motion, Phoenix slid from the van, raising his revolver with both hands. Through the glass, the man gaped in his revolver sight; Phoenix saw his own reflection aiming.

Neither moved. Phoenix fought back panic—he could not shoot him with the gate still locked.

With a deliberate air, he beckoned.

Tentative, the man stepped from the guardhouse, arms raised. When he came through the gate, Phoenix clubbed him on the skull.

In a fireman's carry, Phoenix hauled the guard to some scrub brush, unlooped the rope from his belt, then bound and gagged him; what seemed agonizing slow motion had taken four minutes. He rushed to his van and began driving in the same direction, steadily as before.

A mile past the gatehouse, a firebreak branched left from the road. Phoenix took it. When he stopped again, the van had climbed another half-mile. To the left, through a line of oaks, he gazed down at the tennis court.

It was two hundred feet from the house, a sloping mile from the van. Between them, on the path snaking toward the court, he saw two figures in white. As he raised his field glasses, the woman bent to touch the hem of her tennis dress, sunlight glinting on blonde hair.

His throat constricted.

He lowered the glasses, motionless. Then he slowly got out, walked to the rear of the van, and unlocked it.

The three men blinked at the sunlight, jerkily stretching their joints. Two unloaded rifles, one a camera; sliding from the van, they lifted out the motorcycle, and then Phoenix waved them through the tree line. Sheltered from view, he studied the terrain. Weeks before, he had walked it at night, with the Parnells sleeping inside. As then, underbrush and gullies concealed the route he had taken to the court.

Satisfied, he stationed the cameraman, then synchronized his watch with the two others. The Parnells began playing as they pulled on burlap hoods; at a movement of his hand, the gunmen started down the hill.

He found it hard to turn away.

Driving back down the break, it took him twenty-seven minutes to reach the road again, and turn toward the Parnells'.

At 3:57, he reached the undefended gate.

Opening it, he imagined the two gunmen, huddled in the last gully beneath the court—frightened, doubting him. They could not see the players, only hear their voices and the catgut ping of tennis.

Phoenix slipped on the hood.

As if in a dream, he passed the manmade lake, bordered with cattails, then drove through the symmetric double row of dogwoods Parnell had planted to please his wife. In the afternoon breeze, a pink blossom fell on the windshield; then the dogwoods ended in a circular drive, a tailored green lawn.

As Phoenix veered across it, two masked gunmen burst onto the court.

The players froze; Phoenix felt a savage explosion of joy. And then Parnell turned to the sound of his van, as if hoping to be rescued.

Phoenix leaped from the van, camera resting on his shoulder.

Parnell gaped in disbelief; the shock on Alexis's face seemed to focus on his camera. Then the two gunmen moved to each side of her, one binding her hands, the other with a revolver to her temple.

Phoenix began filming her.

Turning from his wife to the whine of the camera, Parnell blurted, "Take *me*. . . ."

Tears sprang to her eyes. As Phoenix filmed them pushing her toward the back of the van, staring helplessly at Parnell, she stumbled.

Time stopped.

Even as she gazed up at him, fallen near his van, Phoenix felt the moment as if it were his last: the woman with her hands bound, the slanting clarity of four o'clock light, the green, retreating sweep of hills, the geometry of the white-lined court. Then Parnell moved, a raising of his hand.

Unshouldering the camera, Phoenix drew his Mauser.

"No—" she cried out.

Without turning, Phoenix placed the revolver to her husband's forehead. Parnell's mouth fell open; the hooded men beside him seemed to flinch.

Phoenix swung his arm wide, cracking the revolver against his temple.

There was a dull thud as the shock ran through Phoenix's arm. Parnell slumped heavily, glasses falling beside him in the dirt.

Slowly, deliberately, Phoenix stepped on them, and looked up at Alexis. Her gaze rose in horror from her husband's shattered glasses to the hooded man who had struck him.

Turning from her, he signaled his confederates.

In rapid sequence, the two armed men trussed and blindfolded Parnell, threw him in the van, tied cloth across Alexis's eyes. They stacked the weapons and camera before pulling her inside with them. Running to the driver's side, Phoenix stuck his Mauser beneath the seat and stepped on the accelerator. Dust rose in his rearview as he left the court behind.

Ahead was one straight mile of gravel; then a twelve-hour escape had to be flawlessly timed. He checked his watch, read 4:11, and pushed the pedal to the floor.

The Parnells' iron gate and guardhouse grew larger in his windshield. Suddenly, a motorcyclist appeared outside the gate and opened it. Jamming on his brakes, Phoenix stopped.

The cyclist held up the film he had taken. A second camera was strapped to his motorcycle.

Phoenix left the van.

In silent haste, they opened its rear door; as the two gunmen lifted his motorcycle, the cyclist ran with Phoenix to some scrub brush fifty feet from the drive. The guard lay where Phoenix had left him, bound and unconscious. Lifting him by his hands and feet, they trotted to the van and threw him beside Parnell. Then the motorcyclist sat next to the others against one side of the van, facing their two prone victims. Huddled in a corner, Alexis turned her blindfolded face, as if to hear. Phoenix threw his hood at her feet, and slammed the door.

As he drove away, the gate looked as before.

His heart still raced.

He breathed in, foot easing on the accelerator. For the next eight hours, he must drive steadily, drawing no attention.

The country road they took wound through pastures and hillsides of grapes and crops. Now and then oaks overhung the asphalt, some with Spanish moss; creeks ran beneath them, one so swollen it murmured through his window. Two or three trucks passed in the other direction. Hat shoved over his eyes, Phoenix drove by like a local with his mind on sheep or cattle or planting grapes. He could feel the heat in the back of the van, the fear of those trapped there, and his own.

For another half-hour, he followed his circuitous route, northwest through Sonoma County.

Ahead, sun fell between the first scorched trees. Years ago, a fire had seared miles of hills; above the greenness of recent growth—oaks and brush and younger firs—the blackened pines gave him a kind of chill.

Leaning forward, Phoenix spotted the gnarled oak which marked his path, and turned abruptly from the road.

In the time it took to climb the path, twisting upward between scrub oaks and scabrous pines, it became dusk. Phoenix could scarcely see the ruined farmhouse. It was enough that the surrounding acres had been sold to the next farm, that no one lived here now.

He stopped at the crest of the hill, taking out the Mauser. When he opened the van, the sound carried.

The three men gaped at him. Alexis was hunched in the fetal position, near her husband. As she whimpered, Phoenix threw Parnell's near-dead weight across one shoulder, snatching a duffel bag.

For minutes, he carried Parnell across the ridge line toward a stand of oaks, dark shapes in moonlight. There was no sound but the rise and fall of crickets, a few leaves in the wind, Parnell moaning softly, blind-folded.

At the base of an oak, Phoenix put him down, loosened the gag. Parnell's voice was a croak.

"Why . . . ?"

Phoenix pushed the Mauser down his throat. As the bound man moved his head from side to side, gurgling, he pulled the trigger.

The click of an empty revolver echoed in the trees.

Parnell sobbed when he removed it. Reaching into the bag, Phoenix knelt beside him, looping two videotapes around his neck with twine. Then he forced the audio cassette between the older man's teeth and jammed it tighter with the gag. Parnell choked, gulping, then was silent.

Returning to the van, Phoenix walked softly, to slow the beating of his heart.

* * *

It was an hour before Phoenix descended the quarry again. When he stopped, the black van was a swatch of intensified darkness three feet away.

Opening the white van, he heard Alexis's muffled crying.

She was lighter than he had imagined; beneath the tennis dress, her legs felt cold. As he carried her to the black van, her sobs turned to ragged breathing, like a hunted animal afraid of its own sounds.

The three men shuffled in beside her, carrying their equipment, so that only the unconscious guard remained locked inside the white van.

Eyes narrow, Phoenix searched the starlit sky for helicopters or surveillance planes, listened for their sound.

Tomorrow, someone would find an untraceable van, with no fingerprints but the victims', and match its tire prints to the sites of two kidnappings. A perfect circle, leading nowhere, if Phoenix could evade them for eight more hours.

In minutes, the other van had taken the path from the quarry to a county road, veering west toward Highway 101. Phoenix began checking the gas gauge.

It was three-quarters full when he hit the highway, heading north for Humboldt County.

Five hours distant, yet like another country—rugged, isolated, hostile to strangers. Fifteen years ago, it had been a wilderness, with a few logging towns and Eureka on its northern coast. And then the trickle of burnt-out cases had begun moving from cities where the drugs had gone bad, the rip-offs grown too frequent, the crash pads turned weird or gone condominium. In the mountains, living in tents or lean-tos without electricity, they'd begun to plant their own marijuana, and then to sell it.

Dying towns thrived; realtors sold land no road could reach. Strangers began raiding crops, careless hikers disappeared, Mexicans brought in to harvest vanished before they were paid. Poachers were shot near their trucks. Now people moved there to grow dope, or not at all.

Phoenix checked his gas gauge.

He could not buy gas until he was deep in Humboldt; Alexis might scream, someone could remember the van.

The gauge edged toward half a tank.

For four hours he drove toward Humboldt with agonizing slowness, as the two lanes on each side became one and the look of the country changed as it rose, wide vistas closing in, oaks becoming pine, scattered towns growing smaller, and the road higher and more winding, until he ran along the cliff of the Eel River, a hundred-foot drop to the right. The radio thinned to a crackle; redwoods towered at the edge of the road, blocking the moon. The darkness ahead of him looked like Alaska.

The gauge moved toward empty.

The only safety was hours ahead, the carefully chosen shelter he had bought for cash from a realtor in Garberville, posing as a novice grower with thick glasses, earrings, a southwestern drawl. A hunter's cabin so remote that it had not been used for years.

Twenty miles from Garberville, the gas gauge began merging with the line marked "E."

Turning the knob, he found the Garberville station.

The twang of country-western music made his nerves raw; the break for news was almost a relief. The newsman's voice became a drone he only noticed when it quickened.

"In a late bulletin, the Napa County Sheriff's Office reports the disappearance of San Francisco publisher Colby Parnell and his wife, Alexis. The Parnells were reported missing by their attorney, John Danziger, whom they had earlier invited to dinner. Authorities theorize that they may have been abducted while playing tennis. . . ."

Instinctively, Phoenix grasped his Mauser.

He cranked down the window, to clear his head. His T-shirt was soaked; night air chilled his face and chest. Redwoods bounded his right, the steep cliff of the Eel his left. He had nowhere to hide short of where he was going.

At the bottom of the grade, the Eel veered abruptly beneath a bridge marked "Humboldt County." Looking from the sign to the gas gauge, Phoenix saw that it was empty.

Moments later, he passed the Garberville exit without stopping for gas. To his right now, moonlight on the water shone like obsidian.

Turning from the river, Phoenix took an unmarked path between two redwoods.

As the van disappeared in the grove, his headlights caught the massive dirt-red trunks. Those and the road were all he saw; he drove ten miles an hour. The radio stopped making sound.

Slowly, he climbed through eight more miles of redwoods as the gauge slipped beneath empty. At the crest was a bowl of darkness, a valley without lights. The road turned gently south.

Turning with it, Phoenix took his foot off the accelerator.

For several miles, he idled downward, braking to save gas. Then, abruptly, the road hit bottom, crossing a wooden bridge. Beneath it, the Mattole River ran gently. The sign just beyond it read "Honeydew, population fifty." One quaintly marked general store, with a gas pump.

Phoenix stopped by the pump, wiping his forehead, then honked.

A light went on; a face peered through the window of the store. Finally a figure emerged, shirtless in overalls, walking to the van. Phoenix imagined the gunmen holding Alexis, hand over her mouth.

"Sorry," he drawled. "Gas gauge is fucked up."

The man nodded. "Recognized your truck. Hardly recognize you. You look different."

Phoenix handed him ten dollars. "I feel different."

With each click of the gas pump, he waited for a noise from Alexis.

"Eight gallons," the man said.

"Thanks." Starting the engine, Phoenix watched him disappear inside. Sweat beaded his forehead again.

Two hundred feet farther, he stopped and got out.

The Mattole River was to his back. Facing him, more rugged than the country before, loomed the King Range.

He was standing at a phone booth.

Putting in four quarters, he dialed a toll call, so there would be no record. There was the hum of long distance, three rings, and then a woman answered, "Satellite News International."

Phoenix placed a handkerchief over the mouthpiece.

Quickly but calmly, he told them where to find Colby Parnell.

A few hundred feet past the phone booth, Phoenix took the final path. Within two miles, he reached the first locked gate.

It was galvanized metal five feet high, lashed shut with heavy linked chain and a combination lock. Using a flashlight, Phoenix opened it, unwrapped the chain, drove through, and lashed the gate behind him.

Ahead the jeep trail began its precipitous climb to the summit of the King Range. A mistake could drop them down miles of ravine; the hours he'd spent memorizing its dangers must serve as his eyes.

Through three more gates, the trail narrowing as it grew steeper, he reviewed his trips in minute detail.

Each piece of equipment had become a new scrap of memory, a building block of cover.

One by one he had bought components in different names through different outlets, ordering in other states or overseas and always paying cash, so that tracing them in seven days' time would be impossible. He had driven each piece up the mountain like a grower hauling fertilizer and irrigation line, mind photographing every spot where leaving the path would be fatal. At the end, he unloaded what he'd carried.

Two cameras. Videotape. A sound system. The components of a simple control room: transmitter; videoswitcher; a generator to power them. Cable for two satellite dishes. One to receive; the other toward a specific azimuth —the satellite for SNI.

He had planned well. By the final trip he had assembled a broadcast station of the kind which had transmitted the wedding of Prince Charles and the trial of Harry Carson; people at the store in Honeydew had begun to recognize his truck, then to know the name he gave them, then to pigeonhole him as a rustic grower with earrings and thick glasses; he had memorized the route from Honeydew to his broadcast station as clearly as he could.

It veered upward at a sharper angle, piny cliffs on one side, a two-mile drop on the other. Ahead, a jet of white water cut across the path, a permanent stream. His headlights caught the quick splash of its waterfall and then the van hit it, tires spinning, catching, pushing forward as spray covered the windshield. Beyond, the road grew narrower and steeper; as Phoenix saw that darkness and the water had made him drive too slowly to make the grade, he pushed the pedal to the floorboard. The motor whined in protest.

Six feet from the top was the final gate.

Straining, the van climbed for it at a forty-five-degree angle, losing speed too quickly. The iron gate in his headlights seemed to move closer by only feet, then inches. Three feet from the gate his wheels began spinning again.

The van inched backward toward the ravine, then lurched.

For agonizing moments, he was caught in equipoise between gate and ravine, tires spitting dirt; in the seconds remaining before he skidded back into the ravine, the van must start.

It shuddered, tires catching.

Spinning, they inched forward—one foot, then two, and then the van crept to the gate, stopping at the crest. When he threw the brake on, it held.

Phoenix got out; his limbs had a malarial feeling. He opened the gate and sat with it in the middle of the road, looking back into the ravine.

In minutes he was driving through meadow on the Cooskie Ridge.

A doe flashed across the trail. For an instant she turned as if shot, black eyes reflecting the lights of his van. Then she skittered away, part and then all of her vanishing in the black, trackless meadow. Phoenix wiped both palms on his pants.

The van reached more woods, so thick with timber that no light came through. The trail was steep and too narrow to turn; in his headlights, pine boughs seemed to leap into the road, snapping on the windshield. Phoenix smelled sap as they broke.

He drove from memory, knuckles tight on the wheel. As the van strained upward, he felt the country swallow him in its tunneling effect, and then the trail opened.

The van broke into moonlight.

A meadow, beneath the crest of a ridge. To each side now there were only sky and stars. The air was crisp; the van climbed gently toward the pines at the top of the ridge. He stopped thirty yards from them. When he got down, Mauser in his belt, the meadow felt damp. Its shadow around him merged with the sky.

He walked to the back of the van and opened it. A man crept forward, then two others, staring out at him. The vastness made them silent.

From the meadow, Phoenix motioned them forward.

Stiff, they got down, half-dragging Alexis. Phoenix pointed toward the ridge line. They bore the half-conscious woman ahead, arms and feet still bound. Following, Phoenix thought they looked like a thin line of wounded.

As he aimed the revolver, Alexis stumbled and fell.

Phoenix fired.

His silencer popped; the man to the left flung one arm in the air. Feeling this tremor, the next man looked across as his friend fell to earth, then fell on top of him. Only the third knew what was wrong.

As he turned, Phoenix shot him in the heart.

He walked toward their shadows. The third man lay on Alexis. As Phoenix rolled him off, she whimpered. He noticed with disgust that she smelled like urine.

One by one, he dragged the three men toward the pines, to the grave he had dug. The third man was cold. It took a half-hour to cover them with the dirt he had piled; as he stepped back into the meadow, the night was thinning like smoke.

Dawn broke behind him.

Northwest across the ocean, white-blue with first sun, the distant outline became a jutting promontory of rock—Cape Mendocino, the western-most point in California. The meadow glistened with dew.

He turned straight to the west.

The ridge of pines blocked the ocean, shadows still covering the cabin. But planes might fly over soon, looking for something or nothing.

In slanting light, he drove Alexis to the cabin.

Phoenix carried her inside.

In the dim light, he saw his cabin in pieces: a photographer's lamp, a wood-burning stove, walls sealed with pine tar, his mattress on the floor, the sink, a mousetrap, a window covered with air-raid paper, an ancient refrigerator with an irregular hum, his picture of Stacy Tarrant. The television.

He unlocked the second room.

Inside was a narrow cot, a small refrigerator, the jerry-rigged shower he'd connected to his well system. In the makeshift closet were the clothes that he had brought for her.

Placing her on the cot, Phoenix put on his hood.

Slowly, he unbound her hands and then removed the blindfold.

The look in her eyes was different from a stare. It was shock, so profound that she seemed not to see him. Only her shallow breathing said she was alive.

He felt himself trembling.

Turning from her, he locked the door between them.

For twenty-four hours, he did not let himself go near her. Solitary, he slept, awakening to watch Alexis on SNI, listen to the sound of his distorted voice, feel their power growing. Waiting for fear and isolation to change her, until she would do as he pleased.

This morning, he had put on his hood again, and unlocked her door.

She lay on the cot, covers pulled to her shoulders. Her hair hung in oily strands.

"Please . . ."

He put one finger to the mouth of his hood, and again walked toward her. Waiting, she did not move.

Slowly, he pointed to his room.

It took a moment to change her expectations.

Rising at last, she seemed drained, yet circled away from him. Half-withdrawn, half-indifferent to self, afraid only that he would kill her.

The moment she saw his camera flickered in her eyes.

It faced a canvas chair, with black cloth pinned to the wall as a backdrop. She sat there without orders. The chair was too large for her; the effect of that and her expression was of utter helplessness.

Phoenix framed this shot, ready to complete his tape.

The light was wrong. Considering, he focused the photographer's lamp on Alexis. The revision pleased him; surrounded by darkness, she looked even smaller, more fragile.

Stepping forward, he placed the microphone around her neck.

She sat with dumb, frightened patience. Then, as he backed away, she touched the cord at her throat.

"What do you want?" she mouthed.

Standing behind the camera, he pointed to the microphone. It did not matter what she said, only that her voice would wrench Parnell. As he focused the lens, her eyes were blank. Then she patted her hair by instinct.

Phoenix began filming.

Now he held the tape in his hand, waiting outside the cabin for the last pink tinge of dusk to vanish. Behind him, the generator kept on droning.

Across the country, he felt them waiting for his broadcast. Most of all, Colby Parnell and Stacy Tarrant.

It was 7:48.

It would be all right, he told himself.

His theory was taught in the military, at community colleges, in books at any library. Properly angled, the up-link dish sent a microwave to the SNI satellite in one quarter of a second, transmitting pictures and sound. Broadcasts of Muhammad Ali's prizefights, the funeral of Princess Grace, even Stacy's foreign concerts had originated from control rooms like this. But there had been no way to test *this* control room without his hostage.

It was 7:52.

If it worked, the awe he'd create through Alexis would be magnified tenfold; should it not, shuttling tapes to SNI would be dangerous and feeble-looking. Only remote broadcasts could reinforce the illusion of armed guards, explosives wired to his heartbeat, two hostages. As Stacy and Parnell restrained the FBI, two hundred million others would watch each surprise he had planned for them.

It was 7:55.

Behind the blackout paper, Alexis watched SNI. Night had fallen, silent and cool.

Phoenix went to the control room.

It was 7:57.

The tape he held was waiting to be broadcast.

For a moment, he hesitated. Then he pushed it into the cassette player and glanced up at the monitor. Bars of color appeared. He turned a knob on the monitor, breathed in once, and pushed a button.

It was eight o'clock.

3

Stacy's glass and redwood beachhouse was decorated with bold modern prints, Bokhara rugs, Ming vases, and some pleasing curiosities seemingly bought on impulse—a hand-carved rabbit, an old magazine rack stuffed with *New Yorker*s and a *Rolling Stone*, an antique pedal organ. They were arranged with care but fit in another home; Lord guessed she'd bought nothing for this one. Drapes blocked its view of the ocean.

On the bookshelf, a small TV from the primitive days of color faced her white wool couch. She sat on its edge, Lord by one arm, waiting. Neither spoke.

"To protect his hostages," Rachel read in pious tones, "SNI stands prepared to broadcast transmissions by Phoenix. But, to quote the president, 'This act of electronic terrorism has drawn the horror and condemnation of civilized people around the globe. No idea can be advanced, no purpose served, by the public torment of innocent men and women. . . .' "

Lord wondered how many millions watched her.

Stacy's wall clock read 8:03.

Nervous, Lord glanced at the bookshelf. Some Ann Beattie short stories, a few books on psychology, several piles of sheet music. No plaques or gold records. No pictures of Kilcannon, or anyone else.

When he turned, SNI was showing clips. In sequence a younger Parnell reported on his missing son; Stacy bent over Kilcannon, Carson stared down at them.

It was the film that Lord had shown her.

She did not move or look away. Watching her was painful; it would not take much, Lord suddenly knew, to break her self-control.

"It's filler, Stacy."

She turned on him. "Filler—"

"I meant that maybe he can't broadcast."

Rachel was sounding startled. "We have a picture. . . ."

They both turned. At first it was grainy, a shadow; for an odd split second, Lord thought of Neil Armstrong on the moon. Then the shadow became a hooded man announcing, "I am Phoenix—"

"No," Stacy said softly. "This can't be happening. . . ."

A mouthpiece distorted the terrorist's speech. "I hold John Damone and Alexis Parnell. My death will trigger theirs within fifteen seconds. . . ."

Lord stood; leaning forward, Stacy balled her fists.

"There is no hope," Phoenix told her, "but cooperation.

"Each hostage is to be freed or executed on separate conditions. These conditions are political: that Stacy Tarrant and Colby Parnell assist those stepped on by a murderous economic and social system—the poor, the unemployed, soldiers who protect the special interests which profit from their death. Only Tarrant can save Damone; only Parnell can spare his wife a public execution. And only you can help them, through the medium of SNI.

"There will be no negotiations.

"There will simply be compliance by Parnell and Tarrant, broadcast over SNI, or their loved ones will die at any time.

"You will judge their actions.

"John Damone will live only if Stacy Tarrant can persuade you to donate five million dollars to provide food and shelter for those in need."

For a moment, he paused.

"She will do this," he said slowly and succinctly, "by performing the night of April eleventh at the Arena in San Francisco—the site of her last concert."

Lord heard her intake of breath. He forced himself not to watch her.

"This concert will be broadcast live on SNI. During the performance only, the audience may pledge donations through its local affiliates.

"If you contribute five million dollars, then I will give her John Damone.

"If not, I will execute him on the night which follows, as the world watches with her.

"Do not feel too sorry for them. Both have prospered from her career without sharing its benefits with others. If they had, my intervention would not be necessary.

"Now it is required.

"At eight o'clock tomorrow evening, Stacy Tarrant will appear on SNI, to tell you whether John Damone will live to see eight-thirty. . . ."

Lord felt sick. As he turned to her, Stacy's eyes seemed to glisten in the faint electronic glow.

Parnell touched where Phoenix had struck him.

His skull throbbed, and he had not slept or eaten. His weakness was like a fever which floated him in and out of clarity. Both Danziger and the red-bearded FBI agent seemed like strangers, inhabiting his library in some vague, depressing dream. As they watched his television, reporters waited outside.

The screen went blank.

In that instant, eerily, he felt himself lying in the field again, dew on his face, the tape in his mouth, visions of what this madman was doing to Alexis becoming a hallucination. Writhing on his side, trying to drain saliva from the back of his throat, his brain losing oxygen. Trying to stay alive, to save her.

Then gagging, a rattle in his throat. Choking to death.

Footsteps.

Hallucinating. Passing away.

Leaves cracked.

"He's choking."

The blindfold grew yellow.

A blinding light, the tape ripped from his mouth, gasping for breath. A camera filming him.

"It's all right," the dark-haired woman had said. "We're from SNI. . . ."

On SNI, the hooded image reappeared.

Returning to the present, Parnell felt this as a double shock.

"Alexis Parnell," Phoenix was telling him, "will live or die as her husband deserves.

"Colby Parnell is a wealthy man. The price for the woman he supposedly loves must be more than the pittance he pledges to charity.

"In order that we can fix this price, Colby Parnell will reveal to you, directly following Stacy Tarrant, his tax returns and charitable contributions for the past twenty years.

"Together, you and I will gauge the depth of his generosity. We will assess the true motives, in dollars and cents, behind his newspaper's opposition to programs for the poor.

"And then we will decide what is appropriate.

"On the third and fifth days of his trial, at eight o'clock, I will order him to carry out separate acts of contrition. He will complete each act on the day following my broadcast, or Alexis Parnell will be executed.

"You will be his jurors. On the fourth and sixth days of the trial, again at eight o'clock, he will report to you the state of his compliance. As with Stacy Tarrant, if he displeases me in any way, the following night I will execute his dependent as he watches.

"But if he keeps her alive, then at the end of his report on the sixth day, *you* will cast an advisory vote through SNI on what her fate should be.

"And on the seventh day, you will witness her release or execution— live."

The picture changed.

"My God," Parnell whispered.

Alexis looked frail, vacant. Remembering the moments before SNI had found him, Parnell thought that she had broken. Then her lips moved. "Please. . . ."

Parnell stood.

"Please, Colby—get me away from here."

The screen went black. As Danziger turned to him, shaken yet half-querying, Parnell knew he was thinking of Robert.

Parnell's voice was thick, and he could look at neither man.

"Don't try to rescue her," he managed. "I'll do anything he asks."

It had been some moments, and Stacy had not spoken.

"A terrorist miniseries," Lord murmured reflexively.

Standing, Stacy whirled and slapped him across the mouth.

Her eyes shone. Tasting blood on his lip, Lord saw that the slap had been instinctive, as though Phoenix had reminded her just how much she hated him.

"That one's free," he told her. "But it's the last."

She backed away, breathing hard. Then she turned and walked to the deck.

Switching off the television, Lord gave her a moment before he followed.

Head bent, she leaned on the railing with both hands. Lord thought, but was not sure, that she was crying.

He stopped a few feet from her. "I came to help you," he said. "I still want to."

Her face raised to the ocean. "I have to do the concert—no matter what."

"You wanted my advice on getting him back. The first step is demanding to see him, like Parnell just saw Alexis. . . ."

"I don't *want* to make demands. I don't want him dead."

"Phoenix hasn't proven he isn't. Until he does, you lose your leverage by promising him anything."

She turned to him, in shadows, speaking in a lower voice. "You think Phoenix has already killed him, don't you?"

Lord wished that he could see her face. "What I think," he said finally, "is that unless you ask, we're not doing all we can to prevent that."

"I don't know. . . ." Her shoulders turned in. "I need some time, to think."

He waited a moment. "Whatever you decide, we'll have to fly to San Francisco. To go to the FBI, *and* to SNI."

She touched two fingers to her eyes. After a time, she said "Tomorrow morning, then."

Feeling her aloneness, Lord wondered if to be with him only made it worse. "Can your driver take me to a hotel?"

"Yes. I'll have the guard let you out."

He had started through the sliding door when instinct made him turn, to find her watching. "I'm not Harry Carson," he told her. "I don't have any answers about him. You should know that."

She did not answer. Leaving, he heard waves lap on the beach, deep yet steady.

Day Two: Tuesday

Reporters began scrambling down the steps of the Federal Building in San Francisco. As Stacy watched from inside the limousine, their faces merged with those at Carson's trial in a surreal collage. From one side, a photographer sprinted across the plaza with the building's glass and concrete as his backdrop. Stacy saw him grow larger, camera case flying as he came toward her at an angle. At the moment he aimed his camera, using a flashbulb to penetrate the window, she flinched at her dream of Carson.

"Are you all right?" Lord asked.

She nodded without looking at him and opened the door.

For a superstitious moment, the press of people and lenses meant that Damone was dead. She stopped, disoriented. "Hey, Stacy," someone called, "you going to sing for him?"

Don't let Phoenix do this to you, she thought—not in public. "Let's get through them," she murmured to Lord, starting to move, and then police were hurrying them up the steps. As they moved, there were exclamations of surprise when the crowd saw who she was with. Realizing she and Lord would be photographed together, Stacy kept her head down.

Near the entrance, the hazel-eyed SNI reporter watched Lord from between two police. "Well," she said to him, "it's the odd couple." Stacy saw Lord's sharp returning glance, and then they were inside.

The tile lobby was sterile and rectilinear. As an elevator opened, she recognized Parnell.

There was an ugly bruise near his temple, and his look at her was pleading; the crisp suit and breast-pocket handkerchief somehow made this sadder. She went to him instinctively.

Face to face, Stacy could not remember his first name. She touched his arm, half-whispering, "I hope Alexis will be all right."

His eyes were puffy. "And Mr. Damone."

When she nodded, Parnell leaned closer. "Please," he said under his breath, "don't take any chances with them."

She felt Lord watching. "I won't," she answered.

He pressed her hand. Then they went on with their lawyers, Stacy toward the elevator, Parnell to face the crowd.

They sat in a windowless conference room, sealed from the jangling of phones and extra FBI agents crowding the halls and offices. Across from Lord and Stacy were Ralph DiPalma, a red-bearded FBI agent named Moore, and United States Attorney David Johnson, a thin man with a wary, anxious look.

"As this is a federal investigation," Lord was saying, "I'm curious why Mr. DiPalma is here."

Johnson hesitated. "The U.S. attorney," DiPalma answered in a monotone, "is allowing me to probe any connection between John Damone's kidnapping and the murder of Senator Kilcannon."

As Stacy turned to him, Lord's expression did not change; the sense of lightning thought behind this self-control fascinated and angered her. "Do you have evidence of that, Ralph? Because any conflict of interest on my part would be unfair to Miss Tarrant."

As DiPalma gave him a quick, nettled look, Stacy noticed the FBI man's curious watchfulness. "In both cases," DiPalma retorted, "Miss Tarrant can be viewed as a victim. And the theft of money from her concert is still unsolved."

Lord examined him. "If you *do* find anything," he told Johnson politely, "please let me know."

Johnson shifted his chair. "As far as we can, Mr. Lord."

Moore turned to Stacy. "The investigation is being run out of Washington," he explained. "But I'm case agent for San Francisco. My job right now is to get more background on Damone, and it seems like you're the only person who was close to him."

Unsettled by DiPalma, Stacy hesitated. "John had a kind of defensiveness," she finally said. "Like being close would hurt him."

Moore raised an eyebrow. "In what way?"

"The way most people get hurt." That she hadn't slept, Stacy realized, made her more irritable. "I don't think he had much love when he was young, that's all. Maybe Vietnam—it could have made him feel apart."

"Did any of that affect his work?"

Stacy shook her head. "He had this absolute conviction that was almost magnetic—when he said something, people believed it. It was just that he didn't care about building a reputation. Except for me."

"Did you ever ask him about that?"

"As you said, we were close. Part of being close with John was knowing not to push. . . ." She stopped, turning away.

"Would you like coffee or something?"

"No—it's okay. It's just that you don't know him, and I'm talking like he's dead." She looked at Moore. "Do *you* think he is?"

Moore appraised her with clear blue eyes. "I'm sorry. But we just don't know. . . ."

"What I've suggested," Lord put in, "is that Miss Tarrant at least demand that Phoenix put Damone on camera."

Moore kept looking at Stacy. "What if I make him angry?" she murmured. "Then John dies."

Moore glanced at Lord, then Stacy. "We agree with Mr. Lord's advice—it's a way of protecting him. If Phoenix thinks he has to keep Damone alive to get you out onstage, maybe he will."

For a moment, Stacy closed her eyes. "Then I'll try."

Nodding, Moore seemed to search for a more neutral topic, in present tense. "Does Damone have interests outside music?"

"Getting away from it all." Stacy flicked back her bangs. "He's got a pilot's license and travels all over the world. And when being cooped up makes him crazy he goes backpacking in the Sierras, maybe once a month for four or five days. . . ."

"He goes alone?"

"I think so." Stacy smiled fleetingly. "He told me as long as I sold records, he didn't need friends."

That Moore did not smile made her feel isolated. "Did he have *any* other friends?" he asked. "Maybe from Vietnam?"

Stacy's smile faded. "Except for Harry Carson?" she asked coolly.

Moore glanced at Lord again. "Yes."

"I don't think so—he never liked being reminded of it." Stacy paused. "Why?"

"I'm looking for someone who might kidnap him, or know how that might hurt you. It might be the only lead we get."

She shook her head, embarrassed by the whipsaw of her emotions. "I'm sorry—really, that's all I thought about last night."

As Moore nodded, Stacy felt the others watching her. Lord broke their silence. "Miss Tarrant has two days left. What are your chances of tracing his signal by then?"

Johnson frowned. "It's theoretically possible. But until next year, the Soviets have the only satellite that can do it."

"Have they been approached?"

"By the State Department. The Russians refused on grounds of national security. Given the political content of Phoenix's first broadcast, Washington thinks they're loving this."

Stacy thought of a surrealist play, hours of absurd dialogue which would end in shocking violence. "You must have some idea where he is," Lord pursued.

Johnson turned to Moore. "Based on where he kidnapped Mrs. Parnell," the agent said, "the probability that he's not in a city, and the time of his broadcast, we think Phoenix is somewhere in Northern California. But unless we can find out who he is or locate him through some tip, that's an enormous area, and a random search by choppers might only spook him. With this little time . . ."

"If there is some tip, would you try a rescue?"

"There're problems. To start, Colby Parnell doesn't want us to—it's more than possible that his wife or someone else would end up dead. I know what you're looking for, Tony, but there's no realistic chance of a successful rescue operation before this theoretical concert."

"Then how does learning his identity help the victims?"

"If we can use that to find *where* he is, then we might consider surrounding it and trying to negotiate." Moore paused. "If time's too short, then we may have to tell him *who* he is on SNI."

Lord watched him. "There are risks to that," he finally said. "Whether you're right or wrong."

"It's a last resort. The idea is to shrink him to human size, including in his own mind, and get the hostages out alive." Moore's speech became emphatic. "We think he might be less likely to kill, and more afraid we'll hunt him down, if we've already identified him."

"How do you plan on doing that?"

"We've got over four hundred agents running down every potential lead or tip, trying to trace unusual purchases of broadcasting equipment, combing the records of prospective terrorists, and going through the lives of everyone involved for at least the past ten years. That's why all the questions about Damone." Moore leaned back so that his gaze took in both Lord and Stacy. "At the most, we've got two days until her concert date, and five before the deadline on Alexis. And the more excited Phoenix gets, our psychiatrists think, the more likely he is to kill at any time. So if either of you think of anything that might lead us to him, call me right away." He turned to Stacy, quieter. "If we can't stop this, I'm afraid that what to do about Damone comes back to you."

Stacy found that she couldn't say anything; really, there was nothing left to say. Without glancing at Lord, she nodded.

Smoking dope, Phoenix watched himself on SNI.

The images he saw were a collage of all his hopes: his own hooded visage, people watching in bars and airports, the president denouncing him. Millions waiting to see what he would do next.

To the moment he disappeared, each step of this drama was meticulously planned, except that he did not know how it would end.

The missing piece excited him. It was part of the challenge he had set himself, to pit his mind and instincts against theirs, proving his transcendence until he saw the climax he should give them. The ultimate act of improvisational genius.

He grinned at the thought, their struggle as the raw material of art. So much like a trial.

Instinctively, he turned to the locked door.

She lay behind it, the center of his drama, her fear of him a magnet. The feeling this gave him—that anything could happen to her—had become his threat on television.

Phoenix stopped smiling.

His plan was to preserve her for the end. But if then he let her live, how could he give them the last thrill they'd be waiting for?

So much depended on what he saw through SNI.

Taking another drag, Phoenix faced the television.

They were showing Stacy now, wondering if he had the power to make her step onstage again, for John Damone's sake. Though Phoenix feared her answer more with each hour that passed, for this moment they were paired before the world.

Her face leaped out at him.

She and a blond man were pushing through a crowd. Still the television, he realized, though the voice of the hazel-eyed newswoman seemed a thousand miles off.

"Emerging from seclusion, Miss Tarrant appeared at the Federal Building in startling company. . . ."

As he turned, Phoenix could see that the man was Tony Lord.

Phoenix stared at him in disbelief.

"Both refused comment. But despite Lord's successful defense of the man who murdered Senator James Kilcannon, Miss Tarrant's former companion, a government source confirms that she has retained him to help secure the safe release of John Damone. . . ."

Phoenix ground the joint beneath his boot. Her picture was still beside his mattress. He gripped it in both hands, fighting the impulse to tear it apart.

Angrily, he pinned her face above his bed.

There were more reporters in front of the Mark Hopkins—SNI had found out where she was. Why couldn't they wait, Stacy wondered; in three hours she would come to them.

Lord turned from the window. "We need to talk," he said. "Do you like sandwiches?"

"Anything."

"Let's take off," he told the driver. "Head down California."

As they drove away, Stacy saw a woman running toward them in the rearview. "Where are we going?"

Lord shrugged. "I'm making this up as we go along."

They dropped from Nob Hill, crossing Van Ness, and headed up Washington Street, past a wooded park, elegant apartment houses from the twenties, private homes and consulates. Away from downtown, Stacy thought, San Francisco was still human-scale, and then she recognized the neighborhood where Alexis had given the party. She turned from the window.

"What about beer?" Lord was asking.

They were stopping near a delicatessen. "Just not light beer," she said finally.

He looked into his wallet, grimacing. Stacy gave him ten dollars.

Through the window, she saw him call someone from a pay phone. Then he came back with a bag and directed the driver two blocks north.

They stopped at the garage of a white nineteen-thirtyish apartment building. "Let's take my car," Lord said.

Parked near the exit was a beat-up Datsun. Getting out, Stacy saw that it was equipped with a break-in alarm and lock for the hood.

Lord watched her hesitation. "It's okay," he told her. "The radio still works."

"I wouldn't mind just quiet."

Leaving the garage, Lord wound through the Presidio, passing views of water framed by pine boughs, then downhill to a beach at the mouth of the bay. He parked facing the ocean; near them, Stacy saw a police car.

"Better view than at a restaurant," Lord remarked, and gave her a beer and sandwich.

Stacy took a bite, looking out. A trace of fog made the setting sun an orange, hazy disk. A terrier ran at the water's edge; his owner chased him; a man and woman built a bonfire. To their right, the ocean narrowed to the Golden Gate; on the left was a cypress-covered cliff, dotted with stucco houses whose colors caught the light.

Lord followed her gaze. "It's how I imagine an Italian hill town," he said. "Portofino, maybe."

"You've never been there?"

"I come here instead." He smiled briefly. "Every time I see my son."

Glancing across, Stacy realized he no longer wore a ring. "When I was his age," Lord was saying, "my mother bought a Woolworth's painting of the Golden Gate. I think that's when I decided to come here—I didn't know it was so cold I'd have to look at this through windows. But Christopher loves it."

That for once he seemed unguarded made her hesitate. "What did DiPalma mean?" she finally asked. "About connecting Carson to this."

Lord's eyes narrowed. "I don't know—considering that Harry's a high-security patient in a state mental facility."

"It doesn't sound that simple." Her voice rose. "My God, remember what Moore said? We're talking about two people's lives."

Lord glanced at her half-eaten sandwich. "You've got the broadcast yet, and we've got to decide what you'll say—"

"I never asked you to decide what we should talk about."

Lord watched as she put down the sandwich. "In that case," he said evenly, "you should have noticed at the trial that DiPalma goes too far. Always."

Stacy felt herself redden. "And you just wait until he does—always. But that doesn't make him wrong."

"Why don't we just get this out." Lord's voice was tighter. "Conspiracy theories are the last resort of people who can't let go. DiPalma can't let go because he lost the case. You can't let go because you lost Kilcannon. About which, believe it or not, I'm very, very sorry."

"*Sorry. . . .*"

"Sorry," Lord shot back. "In spite of all you think it's done for me. And I was also as sorry about pulling that film on you as anyone with a client to defend could afford to be. But I'd do it again, because that's my job. Now, which is your reason for hating me—the film, the verdict, or that I once admitted not admiring Kilcannon?"

Stacy fought for control. "All of them," she retorted softly. "But what scares me is how smart you are."

For an instant Lord looked so stunned that it mingled with her own surprise at quoting his words to Jamie. She felt their taut, trapped emotion, and then Lord smiled without humor. "In other words, you're afraid I won a case when I knew better."

"Yes."

"That can happen. But if I tell you I honestly don't know what DiPalma's talking about, will you accept that? Because *you're* my client now, and I'm as concerned with that as Moore is. Not to mention Alexis and Damone."

She turned away—drained, obscurely embarrassed. "Go ahead."

"Your immediate problem is whether to do that concert. I'm not sure you should."

Distracted from anger, Stacy imagined standing behind a curtain, but the impulse to perform seemed something from another life. "If John's alive," she answered, "that's nonnegotiable."

"My thought is that Phoenix may release him if there's nothing to gain. And you won't become a target again—for him or whoever else."

"That's what Colby Parnell tried, with his son." She turned. "Did you see him this afternoon?"

Watching her, Lord's expression became one of resignation. "You're fairly attached to him, aren't you—Damone."

Stacy faced the windshield. A half-sun tinged the fog and dusk pink-gray, making the couple's bonfire a yellow, flickering shape. It made her feel cold.

"Yes," she said. "I am."

"How did you meet?"

"John was at Berkeley on the GI Bill. After a while, he got involved booking concerts with student money. I'd started doing clubs, and he was wondering what to do when he got out. One night he came to see me."

The last sun slipped beneath the water. Tentative, Lord asked, "Were you lovers?"

Stacy turned to him. "You asked me that before," she said with equal restraint. "About Jamie."

Lord expelled an audible breath. "Someone's blackmailing you, Stacy— in a particularly perverse and intimate way. I want to know what strings he's found to pull."

His face was covered by darkness; like Jamie's, she thought suddenly, as they'd ridden to the concert. "It doesn't matter," she told him. "Not this time. Let's go now, okay?"

Lord regarded her a moment, then started the car. Two sets of head-lights lit the beach, his and the police car's. Stacy watched them, silently reliving what she had not said.

Gazing from her apartment, she'd felt John's lips on the nape of her neck.

For that instant, her senses took in everything: nighttime, Berkeley, the smell of fall, the way his beard felt. Then she turned in half-surprise; he had never touched her as a lover.

As his mouth pressed into hers, she felt his chest and arms, then his hardness. She closed her eyes.

His hand covered her breast.

Stacy broke away before she knew it. "No—"

It seemed to change the meaning of their empty wineglasses, the soft Carly Simon record, her unmade bed. John was breathing hard.

She tried sounding more controlled. "It's not right. Not with what we want."

His own voice was thick. "We can have both. . . ."

"I don't want a lover-manager." The hurt dulling his eyes reassured, then disturbed her. "It's not you," she tried, "it's me. I want to know you ten years from now, okay?"

He gave a bitter, one-sided smile. "Can I quote you when some other guy moves in?"

Slowly, her tension became disappointment. "Whoever else," she answered, "is temporary. Please, let's not change things."

He watched her, three feet away. Something in his look seemed so thwarted and then so sad that it was as if he had wanted her for years. It made her feel selfish, and much younger than twenty-one.

"Stop it, John."

The sour smile returned. "I have a problem, as they say, with rejection. You're paying for it."

His hurt and latent anger unsettled her. "I'd feel better if you talked to me instead."

After a moment he lay back on the bed, shoulders against the wall, staring up. His Bronx-edged voice was flat and distant, as though he were talking of someone else.

"When I think about being a kid," he began, "I remember the light catching my mother's hair. The same picture every time—black hair, olive skin.

"She's listening to a Frank Sinatra record in this walk-up we had, waiting for my father.

"He'd split because he didn't like having me. I used to hear him—I was a pain in the ass, a millstone, she could have gotten an abortion. I hid in my room, pretending he wasn't my father, or that I could beat him until he begged me to stop."

Stacy turned to him, wondering if he was inventing this to get her into bed. But his eyes had closed as if he were transported.

"After he left, she used to meet him and stay overnight. When she came back she'd always hug me, like an apology. But each time I got more sure she'd leave.

"When I was thirteen, he came back. I saw them whispering in the doorway—I can remember the look she gave him, so quiet and cool." Damone shrugged. "They left me there. I never saw either one of them again."

His eyes remained shut. Realizing his story had ended, Stacy was still unsure of what to believe. She sat quite still, confused.

"I'm sorry," she finally told him, and felt foolish for it.

Opening, his eyes glinted. "It's not all bad," he said. "Part of me still hates him, and wants her attention. That was what kept me going in Vietnam, getting my high-school equivalency, then through college. It's like I had a family to make it for."

As Stacy looked at him, quiet, his own eyes changed.

Hesitant, she touched his face. Then, slowly, his forehead came to rest on hers.

Moments later, without her asking, Damone left.

He never spoke of this again, or touched her, except as the friend he became. Now, staring at the lights of the SNI building, Stacy wondered what would have happened, or not happened, if she'd made love with him.

"We're here," Lord told her.

Alexis took one sip of wine.

He had spread cheese and fruit in front of the television. But she would not eat until he had backed away. She still wore the soiled dress.

"The Phoenix Countdown," Rachel said. "Day Two."

When Stacy Tarrant appeared, Phoenix leaned forward, tense with hours of waiting for her answer. At the corner of his vision, Alexis glanced toward Stacy's photograph.

She faced the camera with the directness which was peculiarly hers. Yet this made her seem more vulnerable, he thought, a woman forced to become tougher than she wished. It moved him.

"What I have to say is simple," she began. "I'll do the concert."

Her voice was level but huskier than usual, a little hard to hear. As relief coursed through him, Alexis turned from the photograph with a puzzled, frightened look.

"You know what John means to me. You know I'll sing if he's alive." Pausing, Stacy's timbre changed. "All I ask is for you to show me that he is."

More than her words, the pause made him regret the cruel thing he had planned for her. For a moment, he wondered if he could truly use the Damone tapes he had made, and then remembered she had gone to Tony Lord.

"All I want now," Stacy finished, "is to see him. I'll be watching at eight o'clock tomorrow."

When the picture changed, he saw Alexis wince.

Parnell sat at a table, a stack of documents in front of him, waiting for a signal. Then he blinked, once.

Voice raw, he began reading from his tax returns.

"In nineteen sixty-five," he said, "we had approximate income of three hundred and fifty-seven thousand dollars. Our contributions to charity, inclusive of money and other gifts, were nine thousand, two hundred. . . ."

He looked down, fumbling with the microphone clipped to his tie. Alexis placed one hand to her chest.

"Nineteen sixty-six," Parnell resumed. "Income of three hundred seventy-nine thousand, gifts of eleven thousand."

Between each year, he caught his breath. "Nineteen sixty-seven," he fought on. "Income, three hundred sixty-one thousand . . . gifts were ten thousand."

Alexis stared now. There was sweat on Parnell's upper lip.

"In nineteen sixty-eight . . ." His voice cracked.

Alexis seemed to stop breathing—as if, Phoenix saw, she and Parnell were alone. He gripped the return in both hands. "Nineteen sixty-eight," he rasped, "income of four hundred eleven thousand . . ."

As Parnell swallowed, Alexis's lips parted.

"Gifts . . ." He coughed, finishing miserably, "Two thousand . . ."

The returns slid from his hand.

He stared at them dumbly, then his head jerked up. "That was the year Robert, our son . . ."

Watching, Phoenix saw the pain on Alexis's face. Parnell's voice broke. "If you only knew our sorrow. . . ."

As he turned from the camera, Alexis's eyes seemed to harden. Parnell looked back again, mouth open but silent, as if beseeching her.

He was certain now. He could break Parnell on television, as part of his entertainment. In front of his own wife.

Phoenix wondered how this ordeal would change her.

As she watched, mortified yet unable to look away, Parnell slowly picked up another piece of paper. "Nineteen sixty-nine," he managed. "Income, five hundred thousand . . ."

Day Three: Wednesday

Stacy sat upright, and then the scream died in her throat.

Her heart was pounding. Brushing back her hair, it felt damp. The sheets were kicked off the bed.

"Damn you," she murmured.

She switched on the lamp, fumbling for her glasses. Dawn was a crack of light at the edge of her drapes. She had slept for perhaps two hours.

Jerking the drapes open, she thought of the last morning she'd awakened with Jamie.

"You can't let go," Lord had said, "because you lost Kilcannon."

Morning came blue-gray across the rooftops, bringing the promise of sunlight. She wondered if Damone could see it, and if it looked the same.

"Imagination," Jamie had once told her, "is a curse."

In thirteen hours, she would know if John still lived.

She went to the stereo, turned on a New Wave station, and sat at the edge of the bed. Her breathing had eased; when she repeated "Damn you," almost as if practicing, her voice was close to normal.

Her dream had started out the same.

She was singing at the Arena; as before, the crowd held Carson aloft with his revolver aimed at her face, setting off a sequence she could never stop. Glancing backstage, Carson fired past her; she turned to find Jamie dying; he asked her what it meant. But this time the dream did not end there. At the moment Carson shot her, she awakened, calling out for Damone.

He was the only one she'd ever told about the dream.

"What it means," he had answered after a time, "is that you'll have it till you sing again."

She wished that she could tell him how scared she was.

Lord ran faster.

In front of him, Pacific Avenue rose between gabled Victorians and stone mansions, shade trees, manicured gardens. The street was quiet—a few cars, birds calling, some kids walking to private schools. Ahead the same old woman with flinty eyes peered over one shoulder as her poodle decorated a bush. Lord's Nikes kept pounding the sidewalk. Turning left up the steep grade that was Pierce Street, he glanced behind him at a mile of houses, slanting toward the blue circle of the bay. Then he started up the hill.

Above, Pierce stopped at a knoll of grass and trees overlooking the view to Lord's back. Reaching the top, Lord saw a bearded man on a park bench, drinking coffee and reading the morning paper. Steam rose from his thermos cup.

As Lord ran into the park, the man put down his paper. Stopping next to him, Lord pressed the timer button on his wristwatch and said, "Twenty-nine minutes."

"What distance?" Moore asked.

"Five miles—I'm getting faster."

"You'll need it to outrun the cameras." Moore glanced toward the front page; beneath "Tarrant and Parnell Say Yes," the photograph of Lord and Stacy entering the Federal Building was captioned, "A Stunning Pair."

Lord sat down. "They just don't have her sense of humor."

Moore looked at him keenly. "Why'd she want you, Tony? Bullshit aside."

"You mean aside from what she tells me?" Lord paused. "My theory is that she thinks I know something about Carson no one else does."

Squinting, Moore blew on his cup. "Do you?"

"Nothing I can relate to this." There was dew on the grass, Lord noticed, glistening in the sunlight. "Not, seeing how I am his lawyer, that I could tell you if I did."

"In which case, you'd have what they used to call a moral dilemma. Seeing how you might be able help us stop this guy from killing two more people."

Silent, Lord stared across the rooftops at a destroyer heading into port. "How do you suppose," he finally said, "that he got that broadcasting equipment without stealing it."

"With cash." Moore gave him a sideways glance. "We don't know from where."

Lord turned. "What's DiPalma have, Johnny?"

"Outrage." Moore's smile didn't change his eyes. "He thinks you fucked him—and consider how you'd like to be the jerk that lost the Carson case.

Phoenix is his last chance to bring you down in public and keep from losing reelection."

"If that's all it is, the bureau wouldn't play along."

Moore shrugged. "What if he's right, Johnson keeps asking, how will we look—the pressure from Washington's unbelievable. Me, I'm never happy with questions I can't answer."

Lord kept watching his eyes. Quietly, he asked, "Is Damone part of his own kidnapping?"

Unscrewing the thermos, Moore poured some coffee. "Is that what she thinks?"

"I doubt it's occurred to her." Lord's tone sharpened. "Come off it, Johnny."

The faint smile returned. "There's no preparation for flight, odd financial transactions, or association with known crazies. In fact, nothing strange since that charming little stint in the Army." Moore's eyes remained a blank. "But maybe you know why Damone would abandon a good career and considerable personal assets to become a fugitive, or what his motive might be. Considering that he's close friends with one extortion victim and never met the other."

Lord had no answer. "If it's real," he finally asked, "how did Phoenix take him?"

"With difficulty. The door was kicked in, and Damone's blood was on the dining room table." Moore sipped coffee. "This morning we matched a tire track near his drive to the van that took Alexis."

"You found it?"

"Last night, pretty close to there. Plus the guard, alive but no help at all. The hooded wonder scared the piss out of him."

"Any fingerprints?"

"Uh-huh. The guard, both Parnells, *and* Damone. His are less clear— maybe older." Moore paused. "Maybe he's dead."

Lord was quiet again. After a time, he said, "I can see Damone trying to escape and getting killed, or just being too dangerous to chance taking with them—it would be much easier for Phoenix to work on Alexis by herself. Frankly, if I were him, I wouldn't keep Damone alive any longer than I needed him."

"I guess we'll see tonight."

Lord shoved both hands in the pockets of his running suit. "What about the Parnells?" he asked slowly. "One family, two victims. Any chance it's the same kidnapper?"

Moore considered him a moment. "That file is seventeen years old, Tony. And it's absolutely cold—they never even found the body."

"Who was the agent?"

"Frank McCarry. But he died last year. There were no prints left at the scene, and the MO's different—not jazzy, no politics. Just money for the kid."

"Did McCarry know why Parnell didn't ransom him?"

"From his notes there were family problems—the boy moved out abruptly, six months before it happened. But Parnell insists he didn't pay for the same reason you don't want Stacy to ransom Damone. Though that didn't work out very well." Moore turned toward the bay. "As Parnell demonstrated last night, for the edification of millions."

"How's he holding up in private, Johnny?"

"He's not."

Lord considered this. "You know," he finally murmured, "I almost hope he *is* dead."

"Damone?"

"Yes."

"You're worried for her, aren't you?" Moore faced him. "Specifically, you're thinking there's no way to stop Phoenix from slipping into the Arena and blowing her away."

They stared at each other. "You don't know who Phoenix is or what he looks like," Lord said. "Imagine what he could get out of Parnell by harming Stacy."

Moore's look turned curious. "Has *that* occurred to her?"

"She doesn't say. But I'm sure it has—what with Kilcannon."

"And if he shows Damone?"

"Then I hope you can protect her."

"From twenty thousand people? We'll put cops around the stage, snipers on the catwalks, metal detectors to snag guns coming in. But there's no guarantee, especially where Phoenix could plant bombs or plastic explosives and maybe get away unharmed." Moore finished his coffee. "A hundred million more are going to watch on SNI. Pretty tempting to a psychopath—which I absolutely think this asshole is."

"Not political?"

"Sometimes they go together. But if I were as sure of what he wanted, and why, we'd be closer to who he is." Moore paused. "What he's done is much too risky for simple extortion, so one thing he clearly needs is the worldwide attention he's commanded. Which makes him more unpredictable each day that goes on."

"By inspiring him to new heights?"

Moore nodded. "Each night he has to top himself. And no one knows what could anger or excite him to the point that he explodes."

Lord turned back toward the water. "SNI's become his partner," he said after a while. "When I woke up, their tapes were all over every channel, and a horde of cameras and reporters were waiting for me on the sidewalk. One of them said that at eight o'clock last night downtown was near-deserted."

"It'll only get worse. And given what I've told you, I don't think we're close." Moore gazed at him. "I didn't want to say this in front of your new client, but DiPalma's raised a question about Carson that maybe you alone can answer, at least in time. I can't tell you what to do, except that we'll try to use whatever people can give us to stop this. So I'd feel better if you'll keep thinking about it."

Lord rubbed the bridge of his nose. "Okay," he said at length. "Thanks for the clandestine meeting."

"Anytime." Moore began screwing on the cup. "By the way, what does his name mean to you?"

"It's a mythic bird." Lord stood, looking out. "As I recall, it burned itself on a pyre, then rose from its own ashes."

"Anything else?"

Lord turned to him. "The Carson trial. Of course."

Alexis finished speaking.

From behind the camera, Phoenix watched her, afraid to move.

He must think, to stop himself from feeling. That she was now becoming his weapon meant that he must protect her from himself.

As he watched Alexis, his picture of Stacy gazed over her rigid shoulders in a confusing double image. Full mouth, fresh skin, clear eyes. Every man's fantasy lover, or daughter, or mother; the woman he needed to step onstage for him.

Now she was with Tony Lord.

Lord was almost as intuitive as Phoenix himself; this much was clear from watching the trial. That his own need had driven her to Lord had kept him sleepless and tormented.

He beckoned Alexis forward.

As at his apartment, the sidewalk near Lord's office was crowded with reporters, cameras, sound trucks. He pushed through them, ignoring questions.

Cass had set up the videotape machine. "The clerk released a copy of that film," she said.

"Good enough. Did you phone Stacy?"

"Uh-huh. She's safely at the Mark, arranging the concert with Bill Graham. Asked you to call if there's anything about Damone."

He glanced at the yellow slips on his desk. "All Phoenix?"

Cass nodded. "Mostly people wanting interviews." She paused. "*Us* would like a cover on you and Stacy."

He stared at her. "That's grotesque."

"Look at the bright side—*People* wanted Marcia."

They both smiled a little. "Same thing for everyone," he said at length. "No comment until both hostages are returned. Moore thinks the worst thing we can do is give Phoenix more inspiration, or make him angry."

"Sure." She left the room.

Lord dialed Marty Shriver.

He sounded surprised. "I've been watching you on television," Shriver said finally.

"That's what I'm calling about, in a sense. DiPalma's intimating that Phoenix is tied to Harry."

There was a startled silence. "Do you have any reason to believe that?"

"None. But under the circumstances, Harry has to be approached."

"How, exactly? 'By the way, are you tied in with the biggest maniac of the eighties?' I'm still trying to get him out of Vietnam."

"That's no better, then?"

"No. He won't communicate."

Lord hesitated. "Look, I need you to be the one who broaches this. I can't go anywhere without media trying to figure out why—it would be like damning Harry."

"And this just undercuts what we're trying to do for him. . . ."

"I'm in an impossible position, Marty, and the question has to be asked." Lord paused. "*Before* Stacy Tarrant's concert."

He could almost hear Shriver thinking. "And then?"

"Call me."

There was silence on the other end. "I'll cancel some appointments," Shriver said, "and go down tomorrow morning."

"Thanks."

Shriver hung up.

Pensive, Lord switched on the machine.

On its screen, Carson and two other men began a fifteen-year-old kidnapping mission, carrying semiautomatic weapons down a barren hill.

Moments later, still watching, Lord picked up the telephone again.

The number he dialed rang for several minutes. As Carson burst into the village, a harried-sounding receptionist answered, "Hart Taylor's office."

Phoenix pushed the door open, motioning her outside.

She took off the microphone with hesitant fingers, and edged slowly past him.

Sunlight dazed her. Placing one palm between her shoulder blades, Phoenix gently pushed her through the door.

Alexis stumbled into the grass. When she turned, he pointed to the ridge of pines where he had buried the three men.

Quiet, cool, they smelled of spring dampness, rustling boughs which filtered shafts of light. Phoenix felt more peaceful; the woods distracted him from Lord and Stacy.

Alexis scrambled ahead, neck turning to see him.

Lighting a joint, he inhaled through the mouth of his hood. From the back she seemed much younger; the slacks and black turtleneck fit her as he'd known they would. The first perfume-tasting hit seemed to rush to his head.

Her eyes locked on the joint.

Phoenix took a second drag, waving her forward. She crab-walked sideways, afraid not to see him, and stumbled across the new-dug dirt.

She stopped, gazing down as Phoenix waited for her to understand. Then her eyes changed, and she knew what it was.

She turned to him, arms stiff at her sides. The pines were close to still, the faintest stirring at the corner of his mind. Her face turned white as he put the joint to his mouth again, watching her imagine her own death.

For a moment, he imagined it himself, and then Alexis stepped slowly off the dirt.

When he crossed it, she still moved backward, the ten feet between them like an invisible rope. She did not know that she had reached the edge of the pines.

As he motioned her to turn from him, he watched her shudder, then comply.

Suddenly she was staring in surprise as the ocean appeared in front of her, sparkling with afternoon sun. She took one instinctive step forward and then stopped, looking back. He pointed; moving from the trees, sunlight glinted on the crown of her head.

She stopped again, fearing to go near the cliff. Wind rippled her hair. She seemed to respond, standing straighter and brushing back a strand. There was color in her cheeks now. He wished he could take off the hood, feel sun and wind on his face.

Reluctantly, he waved her back.

When she passed, leaning away, he saw that she was still not certain that he had taken her out for a walk, not to murder her. Though fear was transforming her as he wished, he was suddenly, deeply angry.

At the cabin, he shoved her inside her room, locking the door. Closing it on himself.

Finishing the joint, he made himself envision how he could use her against Parnell.

The plan was working. All he needed, now that fear had begun opening up the past for her, was the help of SNI.

As Stacy entered the SNI dining room with Lord, Hart Taylor rose to greet her.

"This would be such a pleasure," he said, "if what made it happen weren't so terrible." Turning to the hazel-eyed woman next to him, his grin flashed. "Tony, you know Rachel Messer. We've stolen her from TV-6."

Their eyes met. "Congratulations," Lord said after a moment. When Rachel gave Stacy an appraising look that lasted beyond her cool "hello," Stacy was certain that what she sensed between her and Lord was as simple, or as complex, as sex.

Still smiling, Taylor told Lord, "Rachel will be covering this Phoenix Countdown."

"Is that what you're calling it?" Lord inquired. "Catchy."

Taylor's smile contracted. "Just journalistic shorthand," he said. "In any event, I'm glad you requested we get together."

A waiter seated them at a table with a sweeping view of the Bay Bridge. Car lights moved like soldier ants above the water, a black void with a foreground of too many high rises, dim rectangles with patchwork squares of yellow. Where the window ended, Stacy saw an alcove arranged like the private screening room, with one wall a TV screen.

"Cocktails, anyone?" Taylor asked.

Lord glanced at Stacy. "Not tonight. Thanks."

"Okay." Taylor spread his hands. "You wanted to exchange ideas."

Lord nodded. "For openers, Miss Tarrant's trying to save Damone from a terrorist no one knows. Because his plan depends on television, you might have some notion of his sophistication, what he's hoping to achieve, even what kind of person he might be."

"I've thought about that since you called." Tenting his fingers, Taylor leaned toward Stacy. "Despicable as it may be, his opening is brilliant. He takes Alexis on a weekend, when news is slow, leaving a spectacular tape to assure it's the lead story worldwide. It sets out the ultimate drama—life or death. And by making its climax depend on two celebrities, he recruits a hundred million 'jurors' to vote on their response."

Stacy's arms and wrists felt cold. She placed them in front of her, one covering the other, and caught Lord's glance.

"Phoenix," Taylor went on, "then starts nightly broadcasts to give the jury full knowledge of compliance. But they're also more hypnotic than saturation advertising, because each packs its own surprises, up to and including the potential murder of a hostage. You don't dare miss one, right to the bitter end."

It struck Stacy that his tone was close to admiration. "I guess," she said softly, "he may have a future as a program director."

Taylor turned to her, unsmiling. "Actually, I think he understands the average program director perfectly. Because you're who you are, Stacy, Joe Shmoe at Station X can reach into the morgue for one of a million file clips —including with Senator Kilcannon. Same for the first Parnell kidnapping. So Phoenix creates a wave of subsidiary programming. . . ."

"I'll give you an example." Speaking for the first time, Rachel had a certain brightness in her eyes. "An hour ago I saw on the wire that a UHF station in East Lansing is running Alexis's old movies as an 'Alexis Parnell Film Festival.' "

Stacy stared at her. "What Rachel's saying," Taylor cut in quickly, "is that it's like 'War of the Worlds,' and Phoenix is Orson Welles." He finished with a kind of intimacy. "I think he knows the media cold and has the instincts of a great entertainer. In fact, he may be a genius."

"Considering all that," Lord interjected, "how were last night's ratings on Stacy and Parnell?"

Turning, Taylor's face set. "We've just got overnights. But in layman's terms, about eighty percent of the audience."

"What's your usual share at eight o'clock?"

Taylor hesitated. "Six percent."

"And then other stations share your clips, captioned 'Courtesy of SNI.' "

"Free of charge, naturally."

Lord tilted his head. "Has Phoenix affected your ad revenues?"

"I really have no idea. Obviously, we've had calls from advertisers. . . ."

"I was only wondering," Lord observed, "if Phoenix knows *that*, too?"

Stacy caught Rachel's faint smile before Taylor faced her. "We're hostages as well, Stacy. If I'd refused to broadcast, then Damone and Alexis would be dead."

She paused. "Will *you* do other things on Phoenix?"

"The standard news coverage. Perhaps a segment on the Parnells. . . ."

"Is that all?"

Taylor put one finger to his teeth. "We did think we might do something on *you*, to create some sympathy before the concert. After all, it *is* news, and you'll be asking for votes, as it were. Contributions, really—"

"Perhaps," Rachel broke in, "we might do an interview."

Stacy turned to her. "No. Thank you."

As Rachel glanced at Lord, Stacy checked her wristwatch. In twenty minutes, she thought in disbelief, she would see what this terrorist had done with John.

"Actually," Lord told Rachel, "I have a request on that subject. Given that I agree with Hart that Phoenix's plan is geared to the media." He turned to Taylor. "What I want is simple. No interviews, speculation, or programming beyond the Phoenix broadcasts. No leaks from DiPalma or anyone else. No clips of the Kilcannon shooting. Absolutely nothing on Stacy. In fact, nothing to excite Phoenix, make him angry, or give him new ideas until *both* hostages come back alive."

Taylor shook his head. "What you're asking, Tony, is a quarantine no newsperson can accept. For my part, I can't agree that *covering* news makes us responsible for it."

"Really? Before the Carson verdict, didn't SNI poll viewers on how they'd vote?"

Taylor shot Stacy a furtive look. "Just once."

"Do you happen to recall which witness drew the highest ratings?"

"Probably Stacy's testimony, Damone's—Carson's, of course. . . ."

"Because one thing that came to me this morning is that the tape of Alexis's kidnapping is almost identical to the film of Carson's last mission."

Both Stacy and Taylor stared at him. "Using that film was your tactic," Taylor answered pointedly. "Like the film you turned on Stacy. . . ."

"And in the process I showed millions how deeply Kilcannon's murder still affected her. Then I dragged in John Damone." Lord finished in an incisive voice. "While I was defending Carson, I think we also prepared an audience for Phoenix. Perhaps gave him his basic script—'Courtesy of SNI.' "

"Alexis wasn't there—"

"The Parnells *did* come up, though. In a question I asked Stacy." Lord watched him. "We're back at the same old stand, Hart—right where we were with Carson. I hope this time you'll agree with me."

Lord kept surprising her, Stacy thought. "Despite how you felt about the Carson trial," Taylor was retorting, "SNI can't be held responsible for every psychopath who might get notions from the news we cover."

"Except that *this* one called you, and now you're giving him massive coverage." Lord leaned forward. "It's dangerous. And if this continues, you're morally implicated in whatever he does."

As Rachel watched him with a curious, almost neutral look, Taylor folded his arms. "*If* Damone is still alive," he answered finally, "we'll consider your request."

Stacy waited a moment. "It's also *my* request."

Taylor turned to her. "It's nearly eight," Rachel interrupted.

Nodding to Stacy, Taylor rose and led them to his alcove.

Following, Stacy found herself with Lord. "You didn't want it televised?" she murmured.

"God, no." He gave her a sharp, sudden look. "That was your friend DiPalma."

Parnell and Danziger waited in Moore's office. When Moore switched off the lights, the glow of his television turned the tile a sickly green. Distractedly, Parnell noticed smudges, a scuff.

"We've received a picture," the anchorman said. Looking up, Parnell saw a blurry hood between Danziger and Moore.

"Mr. Parnell," the slurred voice said. "Your charitable donations are an affront to those in need. They expose your politics as self-aggrandizement.

"The jury and I will help you find a conscience."

Parnell moved toward the screen. Please, he thought, just let me see her.

"Before noon tomorrow, Pacific time, all those requiring your financial help are to call the offices of SNI. From among them, the network will transport the five it thinks most desperate to San Francisco.

"Directly after Miss Tarrant's concert, on SNI, they will appear with you to personify the suffering of those crushed by a society which permits you to ignore them. As your jury watches, you will select one among them to receive the donation you *now* deem appropriate. For your wife's sake, I hope the jury agrees."

The picture changed, and at last he saw Alexis, dressed in black.

His fear became a sick, humiliated relief. Then her lips opened, closed, opened again. "Colby." The word was almost spat. "This is how it was for Robert."

Danziger turned to look at him. Suddenly Parnell felt helpless, unable to speak or move. He just watched, fighting tears.

Then Alexis vanished, and he turned from the screen and Danziger.

Stacy felt Lord move behind her. Almost to himself, he murmured, "It'll be okay. . . ."

The second face grew clearer, a man's.

"My God," Lord said.

It was Damone.

As Taylor clutched at a telephone, Stacy's nails dug into her palms. There was the shadow of a bruise above Damone's beard, what looked like a scab at his temple. The barrel of a shotgun rested there.

"Stacy," he said. "Don't do it." Following something off screen, his voice became less steady. "Don't . . ."

Stacy was still, as though moving would endanger him, and then he disappeared.

Phoenix replaced him. Through his hood and mouthpiece, he said simply, "He has one more day, Miss Tarrant. The choice is yours."

The screen went blank. "What a fucking foul-up," Taylor snapped into the phone. "How are we going to screen all those calls?"

Instinctively, Stacy turned to Lord. As Rachel watched them, he slowly shook his head.

"I have to," Stacy told him.

Intently, Alexis studied the face in front of her, John Damone's.

When the screen went blank, she turned to Phoenix with a haunted look. He saw the question half-forming on her lips.

Silently, they formed the words, "Where is he?"

Phoenix placed his index finger to his temple. As if pulling a trigger, he slowly curled it shut.

Alexis blanched. She could not see him grinning through the hood.

Day Four: Thursday

1

Phoenix could hear her breathing in the darkness.

He shut the door behind him. It clicked, softly; the pattern of her breathing changed. As he went to her cot, blankets stirred. He could sense her looking up at him.

Kneeling, he cracked open the refrigerator near the bed.

Its thin light startled her. She clutched the blanket to her throat, eyes frightened. He could almost feel her heartbeat.

Taking a pear from the refrigerator, he held it out.

She seemed uncomprehending. Finally, watching him, she reached for it.

As she took one hesitant bite, Phoenix uncovered her legs. She stiffened, staring over the pear. When he touched her ankles, her flesh raised beneath his fingertips.

His hand was still. Wondering how this felt to her, he imagined Parnell watching them, then forced himself to stop.

Carefully, Phoenix bound her ankles with a rope.

Finished, he looked up at her. She took a second bite, as if to keep him there.

He waited until she was done. Then he stood, placed one palm against her breastbone, and gently pushed her back onto the cot.

She lay there, waiting. Standing over her, he unlooped the second rope from his belt and held it tight in both hands, inches above her throat.

Shaking her head, she pressed both wrists together and held them out for him.

He tied them, staring down at her.

When he was done, Phoenix shut the refrigerator, and the room was dark again.

For another moment he stood over the bed, wondering if any part of her wanted him to stay, and why. Wondering if she were grateful to him yet, for living.

He turned and walked from the room, locking her inside.

Removing his hood, he shaved in front of his picture of Stacy Tarrant. Then he put on his glasses and broad-brimmed hat.

Outside, it was not yet light. Starting the van, he drove from memory across the meadow, headlights off. By the time he reached the edge of the ravine, dawn would have come. The morning of her concert.

Rain began spattering the windshield.

Lord and Cass sat drinking coffee. It was 7:15, but barely light, and wind from the northwest blew gusts of rain on the window.

"All right," Lord said, "you've read my notes on Johnny Moore."

She nodded. "It's like he's making you responsible for one corner of the case. Given what they hope to do, that's a lot of pressure."

"Granted. But on what theory?"

"That you know or suspect something that may connect Harry to Phoenix, but can't directly say because of the attorney-client privilege." She paused. "It has to be the stolen concert money."

"Which would make my defense total bullshit."

Sipping coffee, Cass watched him over the rim. "Or so they think."

"I ruled that out again, about one-thirty last night. The evidence of his anniversary reaction came from too many people to be faked. Plus, it's too extreme to kill a presidential candidate just to set up a robbery. And Harry swears he didn't know about that—"

"He did fabricate a little," Cass interposed mildly, "about his supposed political motive."

"But take the robbery one step further. Harry couldn't steal the money, and neither could anyone who stayed at the Arena once Kilcannon was shot." Lord finished his coffee. "Among others, that lets out Damone, his one known friend. So Harry becomes part of a larger conspiracy of which there's no evidence."

"Then what do *you* think?"

"That *Moore* knows or suspects something—maybe concerning the robbery—that he won't say to me directly because I'm Harry's lawyer. But I don't know what it is."

"Maybe," Cass said finally, "he thinks there's someone out there with a personal vendetta."

"The problem is that no one I can think of even *knows* her, Damone, and both Parnells, let alone hates them all." Lord gazed at the cover of *Time* on his desk, Phoenix dangling television inserts of Stacy and Parnell from puppet strings. "No, I think his connection is with the Carson *trial.* It's just that he's such a sadist."

Cass raised an eyebrow. "How did she react last night?"

"She got very quiet." After seeing Damone, he had driven her to the Mark in silence, with nothing left to do but keep his fears to himself. "I think it sank in that she was really going back to the Arena."

"I wonder if she still can sing." Cass eyed her cup. "Need some coffee?"

"Sure. Thanks."

As she went into the outer office, a light flashed on Lord's telephone. A moment later Cass leaned back in, hurriedly saying, "I think you'd better take this."

"Who is it?"

"He won't tell me, Tony." She looked and sounded unnerved. "Except that you'll want to hear from him."

Lord picked up the telephone.

"Mr. Lord?"

After a moment, he knew the voice. It was the caller from Carson's trial.

"Yes?" he finally answered.

"She never should have chosen you." Lord heard a hum, perhaps long distance. "Now if she begins her concert, she will not end it."

There was the same soft click.

Slowly, Lord dialed her number.

He counted seven rings before a man's stoned-sounding voice answered, "Yeah?"

"May I speak to Marcia."

"Who's this?"

"Tony Lord."

"Yeah?" Lord imagined him sitting up in bed. "Well, this is Fred, and I don't think she wants to talk to you, man. Frankly, seeing you on this TV horror show is like a bad dream. . . ."

"It wasn't my idea. Please, this is important."

There was an audible breath, to show his listener's tolerance. "All right, Tony—it's like this. I've been hearing bad reports about you, you know? Like picking Christopher up at day care when you've got no right."

Lord's grip tightened. "I'll take that up with her."

"You're just not *getting* it, man. Marcia's *vulnerable* right now—she feels *threatened* when you do that—"

"It's because I'm a real bastard," Lord cut in softly, "who's about to put a stop on her support check. So why don't you just remove her from the cross, nail by nail, and gently place the telephone to her ear."

There was silence. Lord heard a muffled conversation, then Marcia said, "Hello, Tony."

"Hi. Sorry to bother you, but I need your help with something."

"What is it?"

"A bad subject, I'm afraid." Lord hesitated. "That phone call—the night we broke up. Do you remember it?"

Her tone chilled. "I can't forget it."

"What was the voice like?"

"This is very painful." Marcia paused. "Why do you want to know?"

"I think maybe I just heard from him."

There was quiet. "It was very flat," she said coolly. "Very precise. But soft, almost muffled."

"No accent?"

"No."

Lord was quiet for a moment. "Was it the man who threatened you the night I took the case?"

There was the silence of thought. "That was so long ago, and I hadn't put them together. I can't be sure."

Lord exhaled. "Okay. Thank you."

"You can thank me by being civil to Fred."

Pausing, Lord answered quietly, "When Christopher was born, Fred wasn't what I had in mind for him. I was."

"Then you should have been faithful." Marcia's voice took on an edge. "Though you always thought Stacy Tarrant was beautiful."

"She's just a client, Marsh."

"So you won't have any divided loyalties, for once." Her tone softened. "Good-bye, Tony."

When Marcia hung up, Lord pressed the telephone button and placed a second call.

Rain depressed her.

It always had, even when she was a child and feared nothing but what children fear. She would sit at the window of her parents' home and imagine it would never stop.

When she was five, she still remembered, she had formed a plan. Her mattress could float; she and their Doberman would sail away with a box full of marshmallows and dog food. Much later she realized that her fantasies were solitary—those of an only child, she supposed, who sensed the tensions in her parents' marriage—and that she always overcame some fear or danger.

Turning from the window, she looked at the messed-up bed.

She did not know what in the dream most scared her—that she could not stop it, or now was killed at the end. She couldn't ask John what he thought or felt. She had to sing in eleven hours and didn't know if she could.

The telephone rang.

Her callers were being screened except for Lord and Bill Graham. She answered it.

"Hi, Stacy. . . ."

"Is there something about John?"

"Nothing, I'm afraid. But I need to see you."

"I'm working out a program. Really, I don't know what I'm doing yet. . . ."

"This won't keep."

She hesitated, glancing at the bed. "I'd like to get away from here."

He seemed to think. "Then my place is best. It's ten minutes from both of us, and reporters don't hang out there once I've left."

Lord's apartment seemed furnished with whatever he'd hung on to and a few things he had liked. Entering, Stacy saw a framed Kandinsky poster above a shelf of books which marked when he'd had time to read—*Sexual Politics*, a biography of Robert Kennedy, *The Gulag Archipelago*, some Vonnegut. A few stories for children told her that he still read to his son; the school picture beside these was of a blond-haired boy so much like Lord that Stacy surprised herself by smiling.

"That's unbelievable," she said. "All your wife did was to store him."

"I'd forgotten you saw her."

"Her back, mostly—she was leaving." Stacy sat next to him. "What's so urgent?"

Lord's gaze was uncertain. "Someone called this morning. To threaten you."

Stacy flicked back her bangs; the reflex felt like self-impersonation. "What exactly did he say?"

"That you wouldn't finish the concert. Because you'd hired me."

She gave an automatic shrug. "It's no surprise, really. I mean, you get this kind of thing. . . ."

"I've heard from him before, Stacy. During the trial."

"To threaten *you*?"

Lord nodded. "He seemed to wait for the worst times. Like before Damone appeared."

Stacy looked up. "Then he's doing it to me now, that's all."

"He also followed me, Stacy." Lord paused. "The night before you testified, he left a message on my windshield, just to let me know that. On the way home I realized that he could have wired the ignition and they'd be burying me in a bell jar."

With exaggerated care, Stacy straightened the folds of her dress. "He didn't, though."

"True. He found another way to hurt me."

"How?"

"It's personal, and not important. But when he called this morning, I had no choice but to tell you. He knew that."

She looked out the window. The rain had become a steady, windless downpour that showed no sign of changing. "Do you think he's involved with Phoenix?"

"The clever meanness is the same. But I'm not sure why Phoenix would want to screw up my defense of Carson then or drive you away from me now. Not by threatening you about the concert."

Hands folded, she touched them to her chin, turning to him. "But you didn't want me singing *before* this, did you!"

Lord looked away, then back at her. "By demanding that the money you raise go to charity," he finally answered, "Phoenix doesn't *directly* benefit from the concert. But he also gets you from behind your security. That creates some possibilities I can't ignore."

Stacy shook her head. "I've already promised him. If I let some crackpot back me off, he says John dies."

"I'm not so sure he's just a crackpot."

"I'm *scared*, all right?" She stood, walking to the bookshelf. "God, I wish I hadn't said that."

Stacy heard him move behind her. "Did you think I'd missed it?"

"Talking makes it real. And that only makes it harder." She turned to him. "What do I tell myself if I don't go on tonight, and never see John again. Or maybe Alexis."

Lord tilted his head. "I don't know."

"Then if you want to help me, Tony, help me do this." She gave him a tired, ironic smile. "Really, there'll be no living with me if I don't."

It was four o'clock.

Lord stood atop the second tier of the Arena, three hundred feet from the stage. Both tiers formed a horseshoe overhanging the floor where five thousand fans would stand. As janitors swept it, amplifiers blasted "Lucy in the Sky with Diamonds." Their heads looked like dots; the Beatles echoed off concrete; the place felt vast and cold and empty.

At the end of the horseshoe, where Kilcannon had stood, a crew carried equipment boxes from the loading dock to the stage. Between cuts on the tape, Lord heard their footsteps and metal boxes unlatching.

After some time, he moved to the exit ramp. The route he chose took him down two flights to the corridor surrounding the floor; Lord followed the right arm of the horseshoe until he'd passed the last entrance. Three police who blocked the remaining corridor nodded him through. Behind them were a series of doors: the ones on Lord's left concealed stairwells to the stage; the right-hand door were offices.

He stopped in front of the last office. The door seemed to have a new lock; the dent beside it was the size of a boot heel.

Turning, he opened the door across from it and climbed the stairwell to the stage.

He stopped next to the telephone Carson had used, checking his watch. It was less than four hours to the concert now, and there was no one close enough to hear.

Quickly, he called Shriver. "I just got back from seeing Harry," the psychiatrist said. "I've been trying to reach you. . . ."

"What did he say?"

"Nothing. He went into a shell—absolutely refused to talk about it."

Pausing, Lord watched the stage. "Do you know why?"

"Maybe I insulted him." Shriver sounded weary. "Maybe anything."

"Okay. Thanks."

"Anyhow, good luck."

Lord replaced the telephone.

In front of him, Curtis Blake directed the crew. Their work was silent, abstracted. Where Kilcannon had fallen, the stain had been scraped off with sandpaper; the wood was now a slightly different color. Curtis stepped around it.

"Hello, Curtis."

His look was guarded. " 'Lo, Mr. Lord."

"Your crew works fast. How do they know to put which box where?"

Curtis shrugged. "You can tell by the shape, usually."

"And weight?"

"Yeah. Sometimes."

Lord nodded. "I guess you're setting up later than last time."

Curtis's eyes flickered toward the discolored wood. "Stacy didn't want to do a sound check."

"Doesn't she need one?"

He shrugged again. "I think maybe the band'll run through it."

"Then I won't interrupt you." Lord followed Curtis's gaze. "By the way, a little wax might help cover that up."

Curtis stared at him. Then he nodded, turning to the crew, and Lord took the catwalk to the loading dock. Through its entrance, he saw SNI's satellite truck, then more cameras panning a long line of fans who stood with stolid patience in the drizzle. Behind a line of police, the crew off-loaded boxes from the truck to the freight elevator, passing through a metal arch wired to a detection device. A cop sat watching it.

Lord climbed the catwalk three flights up.

Standing above him, Johnny Moore checked vantage points with two police snipers. Lord turned to watch the crew.

After a while, he heard Moore's hard-soled shoes clanging down the steps. When they stopped behind him, Lord said, "Glad the bomb squad's here."

"Ain't gonna happen that way, Tony—not on my watch." Moore spoke in an undertone that didn't carry to the stage. "Still drawing a blank on that call?"

"Uh-huh."

Moore paused. "How about on DiPalma's question?"

"I don't see any connection but the trial." Lord turned. "I was hoping your gang of four hundred might be doing something more relevant."

"Oh, Phoenix was spotted near Gillette, Wyoming, today. Turned out to be a hunter in a ski mask." He scowled. "We're wallowing in tips, all of them bad, and no closer to helping the hostages than we were two days ago."

"Swell." Lord leaned on the railing. "Only three and a half hours now."

"It's a real event." Moore slouched next to him. "I saw some asshole in the parking lot selling Phoenix T-shirts."

"Jesus."

"We ran him off. Incidentally, did you hear the tickets are free? Courtesy of Stacy and the Arena."

"At least she can't get ripped off." Lord kept watching the crew. "While we're here, tell me how that happened last time. Because I've got no idea at all, let alone any notion of what Harry would stand to gain. . . ."

"You've gotten a lot of mileage out of that one, Tony."

"At the moment," Lord answered quietly, "that's not a very useful observation."

"My theory's still evolving, actually. I can tell you what the police reports say—I was up all last night reading them." Moore began to watch with Lord. "Once he was shot, all the security fell back around Kilcannon —no one watched the office when Damone ran in with the paramedics. So the cops think someone kicked the door open, grabbed the bag of money, closed the door again to look normal, and split in the general chaos."

Beneath them, Jesus Suarez took another box off the elevator. As he crossed the stage, Lord responded, "There's no witness to anyone leaving with a satchel."

"According to conventional wisdom, Tony, her fans were too shocked to notice."

Jesus opened the box. Lord felt Moore's gaze, moving from the roadie to him. As if he could see his thoughts.

"Of course," Lord said finally, "someone could have waltzed it out of here in a box."

Moore's eyes glinted. "Which means the crew."

"After the shooting, did anyone check that out?"

"More or less—given Kilcannon, the cops' initial work on the robbery was pretty screwed up. But they questioned the crew and impounded the truck and any equipment boxes lying around. Nothing there."

"Sorry. Because that's my best shot."

"Still, it's a thought." Moore kept watching Jesus. "It really is a thought."

2

Stacy got out of the limousine.

She moved toward the loading dock, wearing blue jeans and a khaki work shirt, carrying a travel bag. It was like a dream repeating, except that the crowd was so silent, and she was alone.

Police trotted her up the ramp, and then the iron grid of the freight elevator was closing behind her.

It was 7:30, and she'd heard nothing from Lord.

She rose past concrete and catwalk. On the darkened stage, Curtis waited with a flashlight.

They looked at each other. Then Stacy nodded, and followed him toward the dressing rooms. Instinctively, she glanced at the wall beneath the telephone. No one was there.

The band was in the tuning room. She hugged them, Leon Brennis last. "Thanks for coming," she said.

"No problem, Stace." Leon gestured at the others. "We went over what you told me. Think of anything else?"

"Not yet. Let's run through the list before I go on."

When he nodded, she kissed his cheek, and went to the dressing room.

Opening the door, she half-expected Damone to turn from the mirror. Then she walked to the empty stool, trying to imagine that this was the last time she would sing.

There was no sound at all.

She began to do her makeup in a kind of trance. Vaseline, then kohl for her eyes, half-hoping that Lord would call with something to keep her offstage. Her watch read 7:50.

Her hand slipped.

"Damn," she murmured. Reapplying kohl, she found that her fingers were trembling.

Someone tapped on the door.

She started. "Yes?"

Lord leaned through the door frame.

It gave her a momentary frisson. A split second's hope followed, and then she saw that he was holding a dozen roses.

"If you don't like them," he said lightly, "I've got peonies outside."

"No—they're lovely. Come in."

"Just for a moment." When he put them on the table, she noticed the small envelope.

Leaning forward, she began to open it. "I don't seem to talk to you too well," he was telling her, "unless it's about some disaster. So I thought I'd say this with flowers."

The card was in his handwriting:

"Will you have dinner with me tonight?" it asked. Beneath this was a P.S.:

"Truth is, I really like you. It's just sometimes you make me a little nervous."

Smiling, she picked up the flowers and smelled them. "You buy dinner," she said, looking up, "and I'll forget the ten dollars you owe me."

The way Lord's grin changed his face surprised her—it was careless and youthful and made her want to it see it again.

The thought startled and embarrassed her. "I'm really hungry," he was saying, "so I'd better let you go. Good luck, huh?"

"Okay. Thanks."

He stopped in the doorway. "Moore and the cops have covered this place like a blanket. So your biggest problem is knowing when to quit."

"I hadn't quite gotten that far."

"SNI will give the audience telephone numbers for call-ins, and after that they'll start a computerized count of contributors. I'll be on the catwalk to your right, watching on a battery TV. Look up every once in a while— when SNI's count hits five million, I'll raise one hand."

"All right." She hesitated. "The roses really *are* nice, Tony."

" 'Tweren't nothing," he said, and closed the door.

She stared at it for a while. Then she took an envelope out of her bag and scratched more notes on it.

Outside, she found Leon and Greg going over the list. "Let's do 'Equal Nights' second," she told them, "so this doesn't get too downbeat, okay?"

Leon nodded. "Anything else?"

She gave him the envelope. "I've scratched some of my nightclub stuff in the margins. If I decide to change something, I'll just tell you."

"Fine with me, Stace. Sure you'll be okay without a set program?"

"Tonight doesn't have to be perfect—just different. We'll see how it works out."

She followed them down the hallway.

As she waited, Curtis led the others to the platform, then aimed the flashlight so that Leon could tape her envelope on his keyboard.

Alone in the wings, Stacy looked around her.

There was a cameraman near the telephone, poised to film over her shoulder as she went through the curtain. Lord's dim figure stood above her on the catwalk. One flight up was a police sniper stationed to protect her; Stacy could see his cap and the outline of a rifle.

She folded her arms, staring down as the sick feeling came to her again. Then she saw the beam of light at her feet, Curtis waiting for her.

He glanced at his watch. She nodded, and then he was leading her forward. There was silence on the other side of the curtain.

Stacy stopped behind it. Curtis retreated; she felt the camera waiting, the invisible audience twenty feet from her. She couldn't move.

Taking two steps back, she looked up to where the sniper was, then Lord. What the hell.

She turned to Curtis. "Just open it," she said.

* * *

Lord could see how scared she was.

Then she stepped into the spotlight, face appearing on the overhead screen, and began to sing "Reruns at Midnight."

For the first few notes, her voice was shaky. She sang without moving, a straight, slim figure beneath him, shirt-sleeves rolled above her wrists. On the screen, her gaze was blue and wide; the simple beginning had a quality of nakedness foreign to past concerts. In front of her there was darkness— smoke, massed bodies, silence. Three more cameras.

Lord glanced down at the mini-TV. There were no numbers beneath her face. Her voice would break, he thought, or she would; something else would happen. He bent back to check the police sharpshooter standing above him.

Below, she kept on singing. It came to him that her voice sounded rawer, older, a little smokier.

When she finished there were still no figures on the television, and no applause.

She gazed up at her face on the overhead screen. "This really isn't it," she said softly.

The quiet in front of her was like a caught breath. She turned from them, backstage. "Could someone turn off that screen," she asked, "and switch on the hall lights?"

When the lights came on, her audience was standing, even in the tiers.

She was staring at where Kilcannon had fallen; Lord realized that she saw the discoloration.

Her eyes rose to the screen. "I look at that thing," she explained, "and it's like singing to a mirror. What I really wanted is to see you."

The screen went dark. She seemed to think, then went on in a clear, quiet voice.

"I guess you know how strange this is for me. But I'm really glad you're here. And I think I'd feel better about *my* being here if we had a moment's silence."

On the television beside him Lord saw her head bend forward, her eyes close. The audience did the same.

There were still no figures.

Stacy looked up. "A few minutes ago," she began, "someone told me I made him nervous. I think it was his way of apologizing for not being able to say things quite right and also, in a funny way, to put me more at ease." She smiled a little. "So one thing I wanted to tell you is that you make me kind of nervous."

There was a soft, appreciative murmur.

She flicked back her bangs. "Anyhow, backstage, I was trying to figure out how I got here.

"One part was that when I was eleven or so, I had a crush on Paul McCartney. It got pretty convoluted—I even reset my bedroom clock to know what time it was in London." A second fleeting smile. "And then I decided that Paul would never notice me unless *I* got famous, too. So I started writing songs."

In front of her, the audience seemed to relax.

"But the part I didn't know," she told them in a softer voice, "was that I had thoughts and feelings I could only express that way. By hoping someday you'd be here for me." Walking to the edge of the stage, she added quietly, "And here you are for me, still.

"Only somewhere I stopped seeing your faces. And when that happened, I got afraid you wouldn't come.

"Being afraid like that gets lots of things screwed up. One thing that did was my idea of you.

"So this is kind of my apology."

She was so exposed, Lord thought, that anything could happen.

On his screen, SNI flashed $400,000, in print beneath her face.

"But a second thing that happened," Stacy continued, "was that the rest of life passed like shadows at the corner of my eyes—I was hardly looking. I guess that was what brought me here last June, to be part of something bigger. And you were here for me again."

She paused, looking down at the stage. "You know what happened," she told them softly, "and while I was trying to come to terms with it, this stuff got started in the media about *my* tragedy. And now someone's found a new way to exploit that."

Her head snapped up. "Even before this, it really hacked me off. 'Cause it's so obvious that the worst thing about what happened isn't what happened to me.

"So that's another thing I need your help with. If they put me on some magazine cover, and I'm looking sad, don't buy it, okay?" She stopped, grinning suddenly. "Boycott tragedy."

There was startled laughter, then applause.

Stacy cocked her head. "You know, when I *did* meet Paul McCartney, he was married."

As the laughter rose, Lord realized he was smiling.

"I don't know what that means exactly, but I think there's a metaphor there somewhere."

She seemed looser now. "So this concert really is it for me," she said. "Not to escape what happened here, because you've been great, and I've been luckier than I knew sometimes. But just because I'm old enough to find some other ways of saying what I feel. Maybe something private to be proud of."

She held the microphone close to her mouth. "But first," she asked gently, "I'd be proud if you'd help me do one last thing I can't do without you. And that's help save John Damone from whatever *this* thing is.

"He's been my friend for ten years and in our way, we love each other. That's why I'm here."

On Lord's television, the figure had risen to $675,000.

"Of course it all may sound like hell, but for once I've got some great excuses." Stacy paused, gaze sweeping the crowd. "Still," she finished quietly, "I really hope you like it."

Before they could applaud Stacy turned to the band and then they broke into "Equal Nights." With a loose swing of her body, she began to sing.

The band had slowed the tempo a bit, Lord noticed; her voice wasn't as strong. But it sounded better now.

On television, she was smiling.

The figure below her face was $1.1 million. Some of the audience began singing with her; when the song ended, $1.5 million flashed on the screen.

Lord wondered how long she could keep it up.

The crowd was cheering. Stacy shook her hair back. "Thanks," she said. "What's next . . ."

Lord heard three sharp pops.

There were shrieks; Stacy straightened, then reeled back.

Running down the catwalk, Lord saw her catch her balance. She stood there, staring out.

To the right of the stage, the crowd had caved in on something. There was fighting, pulling; then police pushed through and extracted a skinny young blond man. "Free El Salvador," he yelled.

One cop held up a silver object. There were scattered cries of "Cap gun . . ."

Like Chinatown, Lord thought.

She was utterly still, head turned toward the blond man. The audience seemed stunned, afraid of how she'd react.

Climbing the catwalk, Lord saw her face on SNI.

Her eyes flashed with anger as they dragged the man away. "El Salvador's one thing," she said to the retreating figure. "But *you're* something else."

There was a nervous ripple of laughter.

On the screen, the total jumped to $2.3 million.

Stacy turned to the crowd. "Let me find something to sing, okay? Kind of get me back in the mood."

She said a few words to Leon, and then the band began playing "Love Me Right."

The tempo was an easier, swaying rhythm, and she sang without frenzy or artifice. After a while, her body caught the music, swirling her hair. On the television, Lord saw her smile again.

Her voice slowed for the end:

> "You know the fire
> Lives through lovers
> This night the fire
> Burns in *us*."

The Arena echoed with applause and whistles, the reactions of a normal crowd.

Suddenly, the figure jumped to $4.1 million.

It startled Lord. One more song, and she could get off. He leaned over the railing.

"So what do *you* want?" Stacy asked the crowd.

A man called, " 'Desperado.' "

With a mock grimace, she turned to Leon. "Can *we* do that?"

"*I* can."

Quit screwing around, Lord thought. Leon played the first few notes, and then she began singing it as a soft, smoky love song:

> "Des-perado
> You know you ain't getting younger
> Your pain and your hunger
> Are driving you home. . . ."

She missed some notes, a little unsure. Her only backup was Leon on the keyboard.

Five million dollars flashed on the television.

As Lord waited for her to finish, her voice became stronger. On the final slow stanza, it was high and clear and beautiful. The last notes seemed to float there.

Applause came rolling over her. She bowed her head, then turned to look up at him.

Lord raised one hand.

Almost imperceptibly, she nodded. The crowd kept applauding.

Stacy waited them out. "Okay." She smiled. "So what's next?"

Lord stared in disbelief. " 'My Funny Valentine,' " a woman cried out.

"*That* was nine years ago." Shading her eyes, she found the caller. "Were you there?"

"*Yes.*"

"You know," Stacy said slowly, "I'm really flattered you remember."

She looked back to Leon, and began.

Her version gave the lyrics an upbeat, comic lilt. Tensely searching the audience, Lord realized that Johnny Moore was watching him.

As Stacy continued, he saw, a benign feeling seemed to spread over the Arena. It was only at the end that her voice lost a little.

She touched her throat. "I'd better make this one the last," she said with a quick smile. " 'cause I never promised I wouldn't cut a record."

The crowd laughed in response, and then her smile vanished.

"A while ago," she went on, "someone signaled that we've done what we set out to do. I can't thank you enough for that, for me and for John Damone." She looked at the camera. "Really, I'd like to thank everyone."

Pausing, her voice became cooler. "It's time now," she said, "for John and Alexis to come back."

There was total silence.

She looked back at the crowd. "Okay," she said, "I used to do slow, sad songs to close, 'cause they seemed to work better. But I don't want to finish tonight with one. So I've come up with a familiar song that isn't, and maybe you can sing it with me."

There was a drum riff, and then Stacy launched into a jaunty version of "That'll Be the Day":

> "That'll be the day
> When you make me cry
> You say you're gonna leave me
> You know it's a lie
> 'Cause that'll be the da-a-ay
> When I die. . . ."

Stacy grinned.

There was laughter and applause, and then the whole place was moving. The band tore loose, cymbals crashing and drum pounding as the crowd sang with her to the final line:

> "That'll be the da-a-ay
> When I die."

When the audience began calling her name, she didn't move.

It went on for minutes. When it ended, Stacy was still standing there. "I love you," she said, and it was over.

If only she had not left him so off-balance, Phoenix thought.

When the picture changed, he saw Alexis's face change with it.

On the screen, Parnell sat like a wax dummy between five tense supplicants, three men and two women. Alexis seemed transfixed.

Her husband's voice was halting. "The choice you've given me—it's too hard." His eyes fell to a notecard. "Too hard—"

Phoenix began to smile at his confusion.

"Ah, this is Valencia Cruz of Taos, New Mexico." Belatedly, Parnell's head twitched toward the wiry, olive-skinned woman closest to him. "She's the mother of six children," he read on, "whose husband has lost his job and health insurance. Now she needs a costly bone marrow transplant in order to live—"

As the woman stared at him, Alexis reddened.

"Beside her is the Reverend Howell—" Stopping, Parnell squinted at the card; a black man in a dashiki leaned closer to correct him. "*Harlell* Cleveland," Parnell amended, "of Washington, DC. Mr. . . . the Reverend

Cleveland runs a successful drug rehabilitation program for teenagers which has lost its federal funding."

For a moment, Parnell spoke faster. "To my left is Theresa Licavoli of Saint Louis, Missouri. Ah—Theresa has the problem of trying to house elderly people without families—" Interrupting, an intense, sharp-featured woman said something in his ear. Giving her a cornered look, Parnell murmured, "Uh—Ms. Licavoli tells me this problem affects thousands across the country. . . ."

So far, Phoenix thought, SNI had chosen beautifully.

"To my right," Parnell struggled on, "is David Feldstein of here—San Francisco. David is director of a food program for low-income families which was recently defunded." Parnell stopped at something in the card. "Mr. Feldstein would like to make a statement. . . ."

"It's shocking," the bearded man said over him, "when we can spend billions on some so-called Russian threat and starve our own people."

Parnell nodded dumbly, to indicate sympathy or perhaps to cut him off. When there was silence, he looked back at the card.

He stared at it for several seconds.

"Last," he read haltingly, "is Jon Gustafson of Bemidji, Minnesota. . . ."

His mouth kept moving, speechless, then murmuring, "Head of 'Parents without Children.' . . ."

Distractedly, he wiped his forehead. In her husband's silence, Phoenix realized that Alexis's face was pinched.

"Ah, this is composed of parents whose children were abducted. . . ."

Phoenix began laughing.

The sound made Alexis start. She turned to him, tears welling.

"Three years ago," Parnell said woodenly, "Mr. Gustafson's four-year-old son was . . . kidnapped by his former wife. So far he has spent $110,000 in an effort to find Matthew. . . ."

Suddenly and completely, his voice broke. Tears ran down Alexis's face. Someone at SNI, Phoenix knew, was a genius.

"So," Parnell went on abruptly, "he founded—ah, PWC to computerize all information which might assist recovery of kidnapped children. . . ."

The stolid, brown-haired man bent forward. "Marie," he said to the camera, "if you're watching, please, bring Matt home and I won't do anything. I just want to see him again. . . ."

Parnell gaped at him, then turned as if at a voice in the studio, gripping the card in front of him. "Ah—I've been deeply moved by meeting these four—five fine people." He glanced at Gustafson. "It's hard to choose—"

Turning, he pushed his glasses up the bridge of his nose. "I've decided . . . to give them each two hundred thousand dollars. . . ."

Alexis had stopped crying; suddenly, Phoenix felt the explosive mix of her captivity with what she saw and heard.

"I also would like to do something—ah, personal." Belatedly, Parnell remembered to face Gustafson. "Jon, I'd like to pledge an additional two hundred thousand in the name of my own lost son, Robert. . . ."

She was pale, Phoenix realized, trembling.

Abruptly, Alexis stood, mouth tight with anger and emotion. It twisted as she turned to him, struggling to form the word "Please. . . ."

Instinctively, he put the microphone around her neck, and stepped behind the camera, to let her speak.

Something about the first kidnapping, he sensed with rising excitement, had divided her from Parnell. Something he might open like a wound.

Lord knew to stay on the catwalk.

Below him, Stacy looked back at the empty hall, the stage where Kilcannon had fallen. Then she walked toward the dressing room without glancing up.

The band waited near the corridor. As she hugged them, it became a collective embrace. Then she put an arm around Leon and Greg Loughery, and they all went to the tuning room.

Only then did the crew start loading boxes. From the back wall, Moore watched them.

When the band reappeared, Lord climbed down the catwalk. They filed past him, talking among themselves. Catching Lord's eye, Leon Brennis smiled.

There was no one in the tuning room except a guard.

When Lord knocked, there was a muffled, "Come in."

Stacy sat facing the door.

He closed it behind him. "Two of you," he finally said, "would make a dozen."

There was the hint of a smile at the corner of her eyes, and then it passed. "I hope it was what John needs."

He nodded. "Still hungry?"

"I don't know. Really, I think I'm too wired to eat."

"Sure," he said automatically, then felt his disappointment.

She watched him, hesitant. "Can you drive me somewhere, Tony? I'm kind of up to here with limousines and hotels."

He tilted his head. "Where, exactly?"

"I own a place no one knows about." She paused. "At Sea Ranch, three hours up the coast."

He gazed at her. "That's a fairly long drive at night."

"There's plenty of room." She flicked back her bangs. "You can stay over."

He sat on the edge of the dressing table. "A late dinner's one thing," he ventured. "But there's some pretty fair evidence that I'm bad news for you."

"Nothing happened." She smiled faintly. "Nothing's going to happen."

They watched each other. "Then you'd better tell Johnny where it is," Lord said finally. "He likes to know when we're out past eleven."

Her smile lingered. "Okay," she said, and picked up her bag.

They walked together to the stage. Lord stopped there, looking out at the Arena, as Stacy talked to Moore. Then she headed toward the loading dock.

Moore's gaze as it moved from Stacy to Lord was curious, almost pitying. He stepped forward as Lord passed.

"On the other hand," he murmured, "he could have waltzed it out *before* Kilcannon was shot."

When she finished speaking to her husband, for Phoenix's camera, Alexis seemed defenseless to him.

He watched the anger she had spoken drain from her. In its place, arising from the shock of her own outburst, was an embarrassed sense of their new intimacy.

Was this his imagination, Phoenix wondered, some fantasy of his aloneness? Or suppressed emotion, running between them like a wire?

Her hand moved slightly. Just a fraction, as if she wished to reach out in her confusion, for comfort or for warmth. As if what was happening brought her closer to him than to Parnell.

He stayed behind the camera, fighting panic and desire. He did not know if this was self-projection; if he reached for her, he did not know how it would end.

For a moment, he fiercely wished that she could see his face, *see* him as he really was.

She must not.

His own hand moved.

With an effort of will, he raised it, pointing toward the door.

Her eyes shut. For that instant, she seemed not to breathe; Phoenix felt her solitude as his.

He could not permit himself to learn if what he saw was the numbness of a captive, or desire, or simple self-disgust.

She turned—almost brokenly, it seemed to him—and walked to where he pointed.

Locking the door, he leaned his back against it, feeling her behind him.

At first, watching SNI was only a distraction.

"Whatever the outcome," their woman reporter said outside the Arena, "this concert was in at least one sense a personal triumph for Stacy Tarrant. But it appears unlikely that her own feelings will soon be known. . . ."

On film, two police began running Stacy toward a white Datsun.

"After the concert, Miss Tarrant left with attorney Anthony Lord for an unknown destination." The newswoman skipped a beat before adding, "As a result, she is unavailable for comment. . . ."

Phoenix mashed the off button, a slow, deep anger building within him. And then from his hatred and self-division, an alternative climax to his drama started forming.

If he did not kill Alexis for them, perhaps there could be someone else.

Day Five: Friday

Dawn jarred Lord awake.

Throwing back the quilt, he heard beams creaking, remembered he was upstairs. The house surrounding him was redwood, with lofts and skylights over spaces which opened to the first floor, where Stacy slept. The breeze through his window screen smelled of salt.

It looked across a hundred yards of sea grass to the ocean. The first ribbon of sunlight, brightening the water, revealed jagged, blue-gray rocks. Waves pounding against low cliffs sent jets of spray rising to a graceful peak above his line of vision, then falling back again. The muffled roar came seconds later.

Leaning out, he looked along the coast. Here, ninety miles above San Francisco, the seascape turned rugged through Humboldt County and beyond. Even to the south, battered cypresses grew sideways in the wind, and the Coast Range overlooked the water. The waves of sea grass were like heather.

It was six-thirty, and he had managed three hours' sleep.

They had driven from his apartment in relative quiet, talking little. What Moore had said about the robbery kept turning in Lord's mind.

He walked to the telephone beside his bed and dialed.

"Tony?" Cass sounded drowsy. "Where are you, anyhow?"

"I drove Stacy up to Sea Ranch." He kept his voice low. "I want you to call Atascadero. Tell them I need to see Harry after the broadcast tonight, or as early tomorrow morning as possible."

"Is something wrong?"

"I'm not sure." Lord gave her the telephone number. "Just call me back with a time."

Waking came to her slowly, from a deep, dreamless sleep. It took a moment to recall where she was, and how she had gotten there; suddenly the thought of seeing Lord out of context made her edgy.

She found him in the L-shaped window seat at one corner of the living room, wearing jeans and a green-wool turtleneck and drinking coffee. The ocean seemed to absorb him.

"Hypnotized?" she asked.

It took Lord a second to turn, as if part of him were elsewhere. So much like Jamie that the thought startled her.

"It does that to me," he told her. "Actually, I was thinking that it would be impossible to look at the ocean for any length of time and still be impressed with yourself."

As he sipped some coffee, she leaned her shoulder against a beam. "God," she said finally, "I am so relieved I feel guilty."

He tilted his head. "You've done everything you can. Except drink this coffee I made."

She poured some and sat against the corner where the windows joined. "How long have you been watching?"

"A couple of hours." His look of curious interest told her he had followed the thread. "Does the ocean affect *you* like that?"

"Sometimes, but not in a bad way." She sipped coffee, looking out. "It's just that when I feel smaller, I start looking at what's closest to me, if that makes any sense."

"Sure." He glanced around him. "This is a terrific place. For contemplating, and otherwise."

"I've always loved it here. My father used to say he didn't want to know anyone who didn't."

"Is this your family's?"

"Not exactly—my parents used to rent it for vacations. I'd sleep in the loft upstairs, listening to the sounds, and pretend it was ours. I couldn't believe we weren't special to the house." Talking, she felt the relaxation of memory. "I used to personify things—trees, cars, houses—and this one has such nice associations. So five years ago I hired a real estate agent to tell me if it ever came up for sale. Two days after that happened, I bought it."

"Instant gratification."

"Longest two days of my life . . ." Stacy responded automatically, then cut herself off.

Lord watched her over the rim of his mug. "This waiting for eight o'clock gets so hard," she said at last. "I just want to see them both."

He nodded, turning back to the ocean. "Think you can take me for a walk?" he asked after a while. "You must know everything about this place."

Staring at the locked door, Phoenix took a deep drag off the joint.

He began to imagine her on the other side, waiting for him. He had not slept.

Was she thinking, he wondered, of what she had said last night?

He knew that prisoners, out of helplessness, need to identify with their captors and, in the end, to please them. But he had not known how much this knowledge would divide him: millions watched him, and yet Alexis was the only audience he saw. They shared this, alone.

Smoking, he tried to distract himself with Stacy's picture. But the image she brought to him was Lord's.

He turned toward Alexis's room again.

For moments he was still, postponing his decision. But his own need to know her feelings was too strong.

Slowly, he walked to the door and opened it.

Alexis was awake.

She watched him from the bed, not knowing that what she had said to the camera had changed things, or that what she did a few moments from now would help decide who would live and who would die. He felt their silence as a delicate thread, their stillness as two figures on a frieze, one not knowing the choice he would give her, the other waiting for her answer.

He turned away, leaving the door open behind him.

Stepping outside, Phoenix took off his hood, and dropped it on the porch.

He stopped there, considering. There was little chance she could escape him, although she might not know this. But what he did from here on out would depend on whether she tried, or stayed behind, to live.

Phoenix got in the van and drove off, to begin the act whose ending she would write for him.

They walked along the promontory, water glistening beneath them. Stacy stopped to look at some wildflowers.

"Dad and I started taking this walk when I was nine or so," she told him. "He loved nature, even the smallest things, and he had this absolute patience—it wasn't what he said so much as how he watched. I guess all the time I was learning from him."

She needed to talk, Lord knew, perhaps to anyone. "Parents and children are interesting," he remarked. "The pieces of myself I see in Christopher are often pieces of my father. Except that sometimes Christopher's a wiseass."

"Is that genetic, or environmental?"

"Environmental. Dad's a very nice man."

"Then he's not a lawyer."

"No, but he's been very sporting about that. Speaking of which, where are the seals you promised?"

She led him to a finger of rock where the surf pounded at both sides. When they reached the end, she said, "Down there."

Seals covered the rocks below, and more gray-brown heads surfaced from the water, looking for space. Stacy raised the binoculars. Surprisingly, she smiled, then handed them to Lord.

He focused on two seals sliding from the water. Wet and glimmery, they collapsed on the rock with forepaws and flippers sprawling, sunning themselves. Every so often they looked up, inquisitive yet lazy, the supreme pacifists. "I wonder what they think about," Lord remarked.

"Fish. Sleeping. Sex, in season."

"They don't seem afraid of us."

"They've been hunted enough. But it's okay—we're not too close."

"Hunted?"

"Clubbed in fishnets, or harpooned, or even shot." She sat next to him on the grass. "When we first came here, I found a seal on the beach someone had shot through the head. I couldn't go back until it washed out to sea again." She paused. "I dreamed about it for weeks. Because I couldn't imagine who would do that, or why."

Something in the way she said it made Lord face her.

She had picked a wildflower, turning it in her hand. "The problems between us," she murmured finally. "It's more than just the trial. Part is something I never told you."

Her eyes seemed darker, Lord thought. "What was it?" he asked.

Stacy hesitated a moment. "I've had this dream. Carson shooting Jamie, over and over."

"The way it really happened?"

"Not exactly." She kept turning the flower. "Before he fires, Carson looks backstage, then nods. I can never figure out why."

"Or what it means to you?"

"No. But at the ending, that's what Jamie asks me."

He watched her. "Do you recall when you first had it?"

"Yes." She looked up at him. "It was the morning after you cross-examined me."

He felt his eyes narrow. "Do you know why?"

"No."

Lord gazed out at the seals. At length, he told her, "I guess you've left me without much to say."

"I'm not asking you anything." When he turned, she was watching him. "Just stay for a while, okay? That's part of why I told you now."

Would she still be there, Phoenix wondered, when he returned?

Miles passed, trees and mountain trails he hardly noticed, waiting to find out. When at last he reached the meadow, the cabin was a dot only two hundred yards away.

At seventy yards, he braked, taking the binoculars from his dashboard. His palms were wet with anxiety.

She was sitting on the porch.

He stared through the binoculars, watching her face, she unable to see his. Her gaze at the van was expectant.

Still here. Waiting.

He remained there. For a moment, he could believe that she admired his genius, was more than just a prisoner. Had chosen him above Parnell.

Yet, if she saw his face, he must kill her.

They stayed like that, van in the meadow, Alexis waiting on the porch. He was uncertain how long he could sit and watch her, so tense with wanting to step on the accelerator that he could feel his own pulse.

Suddenly, Alexis understood.

She rose, looking out at him. Then she turned, entering the cabin, slowly and reluctantly. As the door closed, quite softly it seemed, a tremor ran through him.

He felt the tightness in his throat as he drove to the cabin. When he stepped down from the van, slamming its door shut, he half-thought the cabin door would open at the sound, with Alexis standing there to see him. Half-wanted this.

The only sounds were his footsteps on the porch, stopping abruptly.

The hood was left for him, next to where she had sat.

At that moment, he knew his drama would end, not with Alexis, but with Tony Lord.

It was late afternoon. They sat in Stacy's kitchen finally eating a desultory snack. In the last few hours, he had told her a little of his marriage, and his son; it was meant as a distraction, Stacy knew, to help time pass with something other than what had happened to her. But that he seemed more human brought her back to it.

The silence, Stacy realized, was hers. Tentative, she broke it.

"At the Parnells'," she asked quietly, "when you said that Jamie was so smart it scared you, what did you mean?"

Lord looked startled, and then considered her. "I really don't want to go where this would take us."

"It won't change what I saw in him." She hesitated. "I guess I'm asking what made you say it."

Picking up his wineglass, Lord turned it in his hand. "Just as well," he said at length. "Because it has more to do with me than him."

He hunched back against the chair, still contemplating his wineglass. "I grew up believing in politics and politicians," he began. "Before Robert Kennedy was shot, I wanted to be one. Then, like a lot of people, I saw that we'd begun electing presidents by whoever could finance the glitziest ads and cleverest thirty-second media events, none of which says anything real about them or what had made me care. I was young and had ideals, and like someone young, I took it personally.

"Kilcannon didn't invent that. But he was too smart not to excel, and too dimensional not to understand what was happening to him." Lord hesitated, still examining his glass. "I didn't know him, but that much was obvious. And the really smart ones are the most dangerous, at least to themselves, because the tension between ambition and contempt for where it takes them starts tearing them apart." He looked up. "Or does that seem too presumptuous?"

Stacy watched him. "No," she said finally.

"When you saw me that night, I was angry that a client of mine had been caught up in it. Since then, I've understood a little more about ambition, and about the pressures on Kilcannon." He paused, still watching her. "Enough to be sorry for what I said."

"Are you sorry you defended Harry Carson?"

"Not for itself, no. What I'm sorry for is that Christopher paid a price for that." He looked away. "And that anyone else did."

"Then you believed in your defense, all along."

Lord's eyes narrowed. "I never had a compelling reason not to," he answered, then glanced at her quizzically. "Did you ever have a subject in school where sometimes you got the right answer, and sometimes the wrong one, but never quite knew why?"

"Calculus."

"For me it was chemistry. Anyhow, an insanity defense is like that— win or lose, you're never sure."

Stacy reached for a tone of dispassion. "So you live with it."

"It all came down to the date, really." He rubbed the bridge of his nose. "How *did* you happen to pick June second, anyhow?"

"Chance. As I told you at the trial, Jamie didn't ask me until the week before. So I called John."

"Did Kilcannon name the date?"

She'd begun gauging his expression. "John had it reserved," she answered slowly, "so we'd have a place. He always said I'd end up raising money."

"He was right," Lord shrugged, and then Stacy realized that the court-room look was a kind of screen which fell across his eyes.

The telephone rang.

Pensive, she cocked her head toward the sound, asking if Lord would answer. He did.

"You've got a problem," Cass told him.

When Lord glanced back, Stacy started clearing dishes. "What is it?" he asked.

"Harry doesn't want to see anyone. He's gone into a shell—"

"This can't wait." Stacy turned to him; more calmly, Lord added, "Tell them I'll be there early morning."

As they watched each other, Cass asked, "Have you found out something, Tony?"

He hesitated. "I hope not."

Turning, Stacy put their leftovers away.

After a moment, Lord said, "Is there anything else?"

"Moore called," Cass responded. "This morning, their Tulsa office got a call from someone claiming to be Phoenix, directing that SNI tape the first five minutes of his transmission in strictest confidence. A 'private screening,' he called it."

"Did he give reasons?"

"No."

As she closed the refrigerator, Lord saw Stacy rest one hand against it, quite still.

"Then we'll have to wait," he said to Cass.

Parnell was alone, waiting. It was 7:30.

The drapes were drawn, and his television ran without sound. In his mind, Alexis lay beneath her captor, crying out.

He no longer trusted his reactions. The six days since she had vanished stretched like years; meeting Lexie Fitzgerald seemed closer in time. This morning, he had lacked the will to shave.

His moods swung wildly. In moments of elation, he imagined her coming home, thankful and deeply changed. And then he knew that she would die on television.

Suddenly, he recalled the revolver in his desk drawer.

He passed the flickering screen, taking the gun in his hand. His own face was on SNI, a rerun. The idiot host of a sadist's "Queen for a Day."

Parnell held the revolver out in front of him. In his mind, Phoenix knelt there, begging.

Parnell put a single bullet through the mouth of his hood.

The click of the empty revolver brought him back. He was being punished, he knew at once, for murdering Robert in his heart.

Climbing the stairs, he realized he was counting steps.

She had kept his room the same; the rock albums, the projector, the photo of John Garfield. Opening the window, he saw Alexis through the glass of her own dressing room.

Get a hold of yourself, Colby.

He left quickly. When he reentered the library, it was 7:45.

There were reporters waiting in front of his house. To steel himself, he imagined they could see him.

He put the gun away. Turning up the volume, he sat as if he were waiting for a film to start. Except that ten minutes seemed endless.

At 8:01, Phoenix had not appeared.

Parnell's hands clenched into fists. He was making him wait, to see if he had pleased this terrorist enough for his own wife to live.

At 8:06, SNI was showing a clip of Lord cross-examining Stacy. Each question seemed like torture.

When the picture changed, Parnell rose from his chair.

Tears were running down Alexis's face. "I've watched you with these people, Colby. . . ."

She seemed to choke as he moved toward her, and then her face raised to the camera.

"You gave them money in *Robert's name*." Her voice filled with scorn and anger. "Why didn't you do that while he was *alive* . . . ?"

Twisting away, he knew he had felt her thinking this so often and so long that now he had imagined her saying it. Then he heard the slow, deep words, "Charity does begin at home. . . ."

She had said it, in front of strangers. Millions of strangers.

"Tomorrow," the hooded figure went on, "the jury will advise me to spare or execute the remaining member of your family. But you must have completed two final acts of penance.

"First, you will prepare five million dollars in unmarked bills, to be used as I direct." The blurred hood moved toward the camera, finishing with distorted softness. "Then, on SNI, you will answer your wife's question.

"If you refuse to do so, she will die within seconds."

Parnell sat on the rug, where he had imagined killing Phoenix, and began to sob.

Stacy sat in the window seat, hands folded. Lord kept himself from touching her.

The end of the shotgun was inserted in Damone's mouth. Only his eyes moved.

The voice of Phoenix droned on.

"There are also two conditions on the life of John Damone. First, Stacy Tarrant must pledge her concert money to Greenpeace, the Committee for a Nuclear Freeze, Homes for the Homeless, and the Food for People Program. . . ."

"Yes," Stacy said. "All right. . . ."

"The second condition must be fulfilled by her attorney, Anthony Lord. . . ."

Stacy half-reached for him. It was sudden, instinctive.

"He alone can effect the release of John Damone *and* Alexis Parnell, should she survive. At 8:15 tomorrow, he will appear to give Miss Tarrant's answer, and to state his willingness to follow whatever instructions I shall give. . . ."

She flinched when the phone rang again. "Keep watching," he said quickly. "I'll get it."

"If Mr. Lord does not, *both* hostages will die at 9:00 P.M. tomorrow, on SNI. . . ."

"Yes," Lord snapped into the telephone.

"This is Johnny," Moore said. "He's already told us part of it on tape."

"What does he want?"

"The money." Moore paused. "He wants you to be the courier, Tony."

Lord sat down. Quietly, he asked, "Did he say why?"

"He doesn't want us to slip an agent in on him. But he'll recognize *you* from SNI."

It numbed him. "Does that sound right?"

"It's a reason. Dealing with an amateur is in his interest."

"Are you any closer to who he is?"

Another silence. "*We're* not, no."

Lord couldn't think of anything more to ask.

"After you watch the tape," Moore said finally, "we'll talk. There's a lot for you to think about."

Standing, Lord walked toward the living room. The extension cord stopped him short of seeing Stacy.

"Shit."

"Yeah, I'm sorry about this." Moore waited a moment. "What time will you be here tomorrow?"

"Not much before noon."

"Can we make it sooner?"

"No," Lord answered, and hung up.

Pacing his control room, Phoenix imagined what Lord must think. He would try to put together reasons, then weigh his chance of surviving against his son. Put him in the balance with two hostages, or one.

He turned to Alexis.

Watching her husband, she had wept—not with pity, he hoped, but catharsis. Yet she still sat at the console, eyes averted. Where he needed admiration, he saw doubt.

He watched until her gaze met his.

Her mouth opened, forming words. Her look made it a statement: "You won't kill Lord."

He shook his head, in sheer relief that she asked nothing for her husband. And then he stopped. As if, he realized, she might sense his lie.

When she began walking toward him, he could not move.

Each step was trancelike, eyes wide and unsmiling, as if desperate for warmth and reassurance. Two feet away from him, she hesitated.

Shaken loose from Parnell, Phoenix realized, she had no one.

In his imagination, she was straining to see him through the hood. Lifting it from his face.

With the last vestige of self-control, he moved his head from side to side, and pointed to the cabin.

For a moment, she was still, awaiting some new signal. Please, he thought, let me be. Live to hear Lord's answer.

She turned, briefly looked back, then walked to the cabin.

He dared not go there for five minutes. When he did, her door was still ajar.

He took one deep breath, then crossed the room, locking her inside again. His forehead rested against the door.

He sat on the floor, shaken.

Forty-eight hours more, he thought, to spare her life and wait for Tony Lord to come.

They sat on her porch. Fireflies flashed and vanished, and crickets thrummed above the deep, distant echo of the ocean. The air had a coolness which would turn to dew.

"Do I have a vote?" she asked him.

He turned to her. Quietly, she said, "I don't want you to go."

His head tilted. "Even for Damone?"

"Yes." There was a long silence. "What I do for him is different."

"What about Alexis? Yesterday, you asked me what you'd tell yourself if something happened to either of them."

Stacy hesitated. "What about today?" she asked. "When you told me about your son."

He could not answer. When the telephone rang, it sounded harsh through the window screen.

Stacy stood quickly, as if to keep him there. He heard her answering, then silence, and walked inside.

She held out the phone, mute. When he took it, she stepped back.

"Harry wants to see you," Cass said tersely.

Lord kept watching her. "Did he say why?"

"No. But right after Phoenix mentioned you, he told some shrink he'd changed his mind."

Lord saw Stacy become quite still, mirroring his reaction. "I'll be there as soon as I can," he said finally, and hung up.

She did not move. "What is it?"

"Carson wants to talk with me."

"Why?"

"I don't know." Lord hesitated. "He's a client, Stacy."

Her head bowed. A moment later she looked up again, flicking back her hair. "I'll call my driver," she said coolly.

Day Six: Saturday

The drive south to Atascadero State Mental Hospital took seven hours. It was still night when Lord got there, and he had not slept.

An iron gate surrounded the complex. Driving through, Lord parked near a dark, sprawling rectangle that only sunlight could make worse; it would not hide the bars in several windows, or the armed guard at the entrance.

The guard led him up some battered stairs to a labyrinth of cinder block and tile. The echo of their footsteps brought back the night he'd first met Harry Carson.

At the end of the high-security wing was a locked metal door. Through its observation window, Lord saw a chair and a Formica coffee table. Carson sat on a worn sofa whose color had probably been green, tapping a cigarette on the table. The rhythm had no purpose but passing time.

Someone in another room began shrieking. When the guard opened the door, admitting Lord, the screams didn't register on Carson's face. A fluorescent light flickered overhead.

Quietly, Lord said, "Never give us a good place to talk, do they, Harry?"

Carson did not answer. When the door shut, cutting off the shrieks, Lord took the chair across from him. In a flat voice that his first soft tone made harsh, he said, "Tell me about Damone."

Carson stopped tapping the cigarette.

A moment passed. As if to stretch it out, Carson put the cigarette in his mouth. He struck a match, took one deep drag, and softly answered, "John asked me to shoot Kilcannon."

Lord felt his eyes close. For some period of time—it may have been a minute or only seconds—he could think of nothing to say.

"*Why*," he asked.

"For Beth and Cathy." Carson exhaled. "John knew I couldn't take care of them."

Leaning back, Lord studied him. Something in his face made Carson look away.

"You told him that."

Carson nodded miserably. "I could talk to him, man—he said *he* flashed back, always at the same times, even when he couldn't remember why." He paused, groping. "See, he understood why I hit Beth. . . ."

Lord became quite still. In a low voice, he asked, "When did he first mention Kilcannon."

"Later—a couple of months before it happened." Carson watched the cigarette burn in his hand. "It was more like something to consider."

"What were his reasons?"

"Someone he'd met in Vietnam—he never told me who—wanted Kilcannon dead. Because of his politics, John said." Stubbing the half-smoked cigarette, Carson added quietly, "Like I told you that first night."

Lord took out a pen. He clicked it, once.

"And that was all right with you."

A slight, embarrassed shrug. "John knew that I could do it."

Lord realized he was staring. At length, he asked, "Did he tell you the date?"

"No—it depended on if Stacy did a concert. Even when I bought the Mauser, I kind of hoped she wouldn't. . . ."

"When did he tell you she would?"

"Maybe a week before." Carson's throat worked. "The time was wrong. I kept reminding John I had fucked-up thoughts then—like maybe I couldn't concentrate. . . ."

"What did he say?"

"It was bad luck, that's all." Carson turned from him again. "He offered me five hundred thousand dollars."

It was a moment before Lord became aware of his own silence.

"How," he asked softly, "were you supposed to collect it?"

"The guy had money. In three years, if I didn't give up John, they'd get the cash to Beth." Carson seemed to grasp at this. "Like on 'The Millionaire,'" he said. So she wouldn't know."

Lord rubbed the bridge of his nose. "And you trusted him."

"I *had* him—I was the only one who knew." Carson looked up for confirmation, and then his gaze broke.

"When did you decide?"

"Only that morning." Carson's voice fell. "He showed me that article about you. He'd heard you were good. . . ."

Lord said nothing.

"I'm sorry, man. . . ."

"Just tell me what happened."

Carson tried to gather himself. "It was like I said at the trial. I kept going back and forth—here, 'Nam, Beth. Glennon." He began to shake his head. "It was just the wrong time for me—even when I shot him, I couldn't get it straight. That fucking camera . . ."

Once more, Lord's pen clicked.

"Who did the robbery?"

"I didn't know about it." Leaning forward, Carson touched his eyes. "When you told me it had happened that night, I figured that was the money they meant for Beth."

Lord waited a moment. "They meant you to die, Harry. Trying to escape."

Carson's hand fell.

"You fucked up," Lord told him softly. "By stopping to shoot at the camera. So we had a trial instead."

Carson fumbled for another cigarette. Sticking it in his mouth, he mumbled, "I had to tell you. . . ."

"You're ten months late." Striking a match, Lord held it out. "If I were to tell them now, they'd try you for perjury, and then for Kilcannon's murder. In federal court."

Carson's cigarette stopped short of the flame.

"On your side," Lord told him quietly, "the attorney-client privilege still protects you. But that only complicates my problem, doesn't it."

Carson's face was pale. Looking into his eyes, Lord blew out the match.

"Tell me about Phoenix."

"I never heard of him." The eyes seemed naked. "Except when this guy took John, I thought maybe it had to do with the thing we did. That it was all going bad."

Lord nodded. "I don't think you'll see him again—any more than Beth will see that money."

Carson's head bent to his knees. "I don't want you to die, man. . . ."

Lord did not trust himself to answer. His silence seemed to rest on Carson's shoulders.

He looked up, almost shyly. "Do you want to tell them?"

Lord put the pen away. At length he answered, "I don't think I can do that."

"Why?"

For a last moment, Lord watched his face. Then, very softly, he told him, "Because I'm your lawyer, Harry, and I was right the first time. You're insane."

* * *

Lord hardly noticed the four-hour drive to San Francisco.

He had no time to stop and think. Only when he arrived at the Federal Building, surrounded by reporters, did he realize that part of what he'd lost was his idea of himself. He brushed past Rachel without looking at her.

Upstairs, the FBI had installed a second receptionist to transfer calls from citizens with tips. Silently retrieving him, Moore stopped at a large room housing several agents, a bank of telephones, a television, two computer terminals, and a map of the United States and Canada. The map was dotted with pins where Phoenix had been sighted.

"We've talked to over five hundred callers," Moore explained in an undertone. "Waiting for just one person to tell us something useful."

On their television, Lord saw himself enter five minutes earlier, to the accompaniment of Rachel's voice. "Inside," she began, "Anthony Lord faces a decision on which lives may depend. . . ."

"Let me see the tape," Lord said.

Without answering, Moore led him to the conference room.

Johnson and DiPalma were waiting with a videotape machine. Neither stood.

"We hear you saw Carson," DiPalma told him.

Lord turned to the screen. Glancing at the others, Moore switched it on.

"This is a private screening," Phoenix began, "for Anthony Lord."

Bordered by black, his hood faced the camera. The slow, distorted voice seemed relentless.

"If Parnell makes final penance, and the jury approves, I will return his wife and John Damone for five million dollars in cash.

"Their return must be to you alone."

Part of him still did not believe it, Lord thought. He strained to see the eyes.

"By enabling me to know you from an FBI agent, SNI has supplied the perfect courier. I will accept no one else. . . ."

No color showed through the dark holes of the hood; Lord had only imagined his eyes were black.

"Directly after Parnell," his voice commanded, "you will state Miss Tarrant's compliance, and your own desire to 'reclaim' the hostages.

"If you do not, they will die directly following your refusal.

"But if you do, they will live for one more day, while I privately tell you the route by which we two shall meet."

Pausing for emphasis, Phoenix filled the screen. "And if at its end, you do not appear alone, they will die *tomorrow* night, as you watch on SNI."

He vanished.

Lord sat down.

The others watched him. Finally, he asked Moore, "Do you really think he'd kill someone on television?"

Moore simply nodded.

"What did Carson tell you," DiPalma demanded.

For a moment, Lord could not look at him. Finally, he answered, "Whatever Carson says to me is privileged, Ralph. You know that."

DiPalma's voice rose. "If *you* know something about Phoenix. . . ."

"Dammit, *Carson* doesn't know who he is. . . ."

"What about the robbery," Moore put in softly.

Lord turned, pausing. "Carson wasn't in on that."

Moore was silent. Lord watched him consider the possibilities his denial did not cover.

"You have an obligation," DiPalma said, "to help us try and find him, *before* tomorrow."

Lord kept watching Moore. "Does Parnell have the money?"

Moore nodded. "He wants to see you."

"I'm not ready for that." Lord's own voice seemed to come from someone else. "Tell me how an agent would handle this exchange."

"He'd give Phoenix the money, get his hostages, and split. No tricks, no gun."

"Could someone follow?"

"Depends on where the route leads." Moore leaned forward. "Let's cut the hypotheticals, Tony. *You* won't know the route until after you've agreed—"

"And if you back out then," DiPalma snapped, "you've killed them one day later. Which comes back to my question."

Lord still faced Moore. Quietly, he asked, "Suppose we're down to that, Johnny. Would you rather take a stab at Phoenix, with one day left, or send me with the money?"

Moore's gaze moved to DiPalma, and then back to Lord. A private look of comprehension passed between them.

"If that were my only choice," Moore answered finally, "I'd send you."

Lord felt himself nod. "Then I'll think about that," he said, and left without acknowledging DiPalma.

Hurrying through reporters to his car, Lord was unsure of where to drive. Stacy seemed a thousand miles away.

Such a joke, he thought. But what does it mean.

When he turned toward Noe Valley, he had six hours to decide.

Fred sat on their porch, reading a paperback called *Positive Self-Fulfillment*.

"Where's Christopher?" Lord asked.

"Inside." Fred's chin raised. "I want to be real definite, Tony. We don't like you coming around when it's not your weekend, no matter what's going on with you."

Stepping onto the porch, Lord stood over him. "Just keep reading," he said, "and you'll hardly know I'm here."

He turned and walked through the door.

Christopher was alone in the living room, racing toy cars. Seeing Lord, his eyes lit up, and then he sneaked a quick look down the hallway.

Smiling, Lord nodded in that direction. "Is your mommy here? 'Cause it's a perfect day to take you to the park."

Christopher jumped up. "You wait here," he said. "I'll ask her. . . ."

"Hello, Tony."

Marcia was wearing a bathrobe. Lord saw that she had changed her hairstyle, as she did when depressed.

"I like your hair," he ventured.

Defensive, her look said that she knew what he was thinking. "Why are you here?"

"To play with Christopher."

"It's not in our plans." Her eyes changed slightly. "I'm surprised you're not too busy."

"I may be. Later."

Christopher stood to the side, watching them. In an undertone, Marcia asked, "What does he want you to do?"

"Nothing much." Lord looked quickly toward his son, catching her eye. Marcia shook her head.

"It's just that I may be gone tomorrow," he told her.

Marcia stared at the hands in his pockets. "Fred and I can do some things around here," she said finally. "Can you have him back by four?"

"Yes."

"I'll count on that."

All at once, Christopher was at his side. Marcia looked at their son, then Lord, and walked back to her bedroom.

When they drove around the corner, Christopher asked, "Are you going on a trip, Daddy?"

"Maybe. Just for a while."

His son hesitated. "But you'll always be my dad, right?"

"Of course." Lord smiled across at him. "You're stuck with me."

They drove to Golden Gate Park, past museums and bicyclists and cherry blossoms, stopping at the Polo Field, an immense bowl of grass several football fields long and wide, with goalposts at each end. As Christopher waited, Lord reached into his trunk for their foam-rubber football.

"Dad," his son was saying, "how come Mommy won't let me watch TV today?"

Lord hesitated. "I don't know," he answered, then turned with the football. "But when boys under eight watch too many cartoons, they can't catch passes."

"*I* can . . ." his son challenged, and then Lord threw the football.

Christopher clutched it in both hands. "Amazing," Lord called.

Laughing, Christopher ran out onto the grass. Lord's stomach felt hollow. Five more hours. An hour with his son.

Just enjoy him, Lord ordered himself. Let him enjoy you.

Near some goalposts, they started playing catch. As their game settled into a rhythm, it struck Lord that the short runs and drops and catches were a kind of conversation. Both began throwing spirals, orange ball floating across the green. His son had never thrown so well.

He caught the ball and held it, head tilted in a mirror of his father's. "Why are you looking at me like that, Daddy?"

"I was thinking how good you are."

"You looked sad, though."

Lord shook his head. "Part of having a boy is watching him grow up. It's fun to watch you get bigger and better."

His son stood taller. "If I have a little kid, I'm going to bring him here, like you."

"I bet he'd like that."

"Will you still come?"

He senses it, Lord thought. The divorce has made him keener.

"Of course."

"Good." Christopher became quite still. "Then you can *watch* us."

"Watch?"

"Yeah." When his son's eyes began dancing, Lord realized that he had been slow to understand the game. " 'Cause you'll be too old to play. . . ."

Christopher dropped the ball and began running.

Lord ran after him. "Christopher Lord," he yelled, "I'm taking you prisoner."

"*No.*"

"Then tickling until you beg for mercy. . . ."

Christopher's shoulders began shaking with laughter, and then he ran out of breath and out of control, chuckling deep in his throat as his father swooped and pinned him to the ground. They laughed into each other's eyes, and then Lord began tickling his stomach.

"Repeat after me," he demanded. " 'I will always treat my daddy—' "

Wriggling and squirming, Christopher gasped. "I will always treat my daddy—"

"With total reverence."

"With total—whatever—"

Lord held him for an extra moment. "Thank you," he said solemnly. "You are free to go."

Christopher jumped up with crossed fingers. "I can't trust anyone." Lord smiled, and retrieved the football.

They played catch, man and boy, until shadows began to stretch across the field.

Four hours left.

"It's time to go," Lord told him.

His son's shoulders slumped. "Don't you want to stay?"

Lord didn't trust his voice. " 'Course," he said at last. "But I promised your mom."

Christopher watched his face. "One more catch, okay?"

When Lord waved him toward the crossbars, Christopher began running. As the ball sailed in a high, soaring arc, Lord thought he had thrown it too far. Christopher's run became steps too big for his body, then a headlong stumble barely converging with the flight of the ball. When it dropped into his hands, somehow staying, he nearly fell. Then he careened back through the goalposts, nonchalantly flipping the ball over his shoulder like the cockiest halfback who ever lived.

Lord ran after him, laughing. "Where'd you learn *that*?" he called.

"Watching TV," Christopher said in triumph, and then his look became hopeful. "*Two* more, okay?"

"No," Lord answered finally. "It's good to end with something perfect."

They drove back to Marcia's, Christopher leaning against him. He grew quiet as they reached the street.

When Lord parked in the driveway, Fred was watching from the porch. Christopher turned to him.

" 'Member when we went to the beach," he asked, "and Mommy got cold and stayed in the car?"

"Sure. We pulled the blanket over our heads. It was like a tent—we couldn't see anyone, and nobody could see us."

"Can we do that again?"

"Uh-huh." Lord kissed his forehead. "Next weekend's *our* weekend, remember?"

His son hesitated. "Can I keep the football till then? For both of us?"

"I'd like that." Don't blow this now, Lord thought, and quickly hugged him close. "I'd better go, son."

" 'Bye," Christopher said, and scooted from the car.

Too quickly, Lord thought. Then his son flipped the football over his shoulder and ran onto the porch, turning for Lord's smile.

"Pick that up," Fred told him with paternal authority, then glanced at Lord.

You and I, Lord silently promised him, are going to have a talk.

His son came back for the ball.

He picked it up facing Lord. Through the glass, his lips formed the words "I love you."

"Me too," Lord answered.

Turning, Christopher tucked the ball under one arm and shoved both hands in his pockets. He walked that way past Fred, and disappeared inside.

They sat at the edge of the pines.

The ocean danced with afternoon light. A white speck of sail marked where water touched the sky, so distant that only time could make it move. Only Phoenix knew that on the sheer-looking cliff close to them, hidden by underbrush, was a rope ladder leading to the deserted shore below. The one he'd use to leave her there, tied up on the beach, to be rescued. Phoenix wished that he could tell her.

Silent, they waited for Lord's answer.

He had only beer left. She sipped hers with incongruous delicacy, bottle tilted to her lips, not knowing it was his favorite. He wondered if she could see his eyes smile at this, or tell their color. Or if she guessed that he was not smoking dope because she did not like it.

There was nothing he could say or do, except to help her wait.

Time passed so slowly, and he had forgotten his watch.

Hers was a Cartier. He saw how much she wished to read it, how frightened she still was of offending. It made him sad to watch what she tried.

Wrist slowly raising, to rest on her knee. Gaze sweeping the ocean, until it stopped above the watch. Lashes dropping to veil her downward glance.

She saw him out of the corner of her eye.

Her hand drew back, as if from a match. And then she turned, so vulnerable that she seemed naked in her fear.

Not daring to look up, he covered her hand with his.

She tried to smile.

He stood quickly, pulling her up. As she faced him, confused, part of him wanted to hold her.

Please, he told her husband silently, do what I ask. Lord can take her place.

He turned from her toward the cabin.

She trailed a few steps behind. Reaching the grave, obscured by what he thought of as Stacy's rain, they stepped around it. On the other side, her hand grazed his again. Seeking reassurance.

When he opened the door, they were drawn to the television. His own voice greeted them.

"If Mr. Lord does not, *both* hostages will die at 9:00 P.M. tomorrow, on SNI. . . ."

On the screen, Tony Lord hurried from the Federal Building in a covey of reporters. He hardly seemed to notice them.

"Though Lord already knows of it," the newswoman resumed, "the precise nature of Phoenix's request is being withheld. But coupled with the demand for money, it may entail certain risks—"

Pushing aside a microphone, Lord reached his car.

"The character of Lord's involvement is further complicated by his pre-dawn visit, disclosed by a reliable government source, to assassin Harry Carson inside the state mental facility at Atascadero—"

Phoenix stood abruptly.

"Whether Lord can reveal this conversation, and what bearing it may have on his decision, are not yet known."

Watching him drive away, Phoenix wondered in his anxiety how much Lord must know or guess, and whether he would agree to come.

Lord had to come now. Not only for Alexis's sake, but for Phoenix's own.

Instinctively, he turned to her.

As if she sensed his tension, she held out her wrist, showing the face of her gold Cartier.

Three hours.

Leaving his son began a kaleidoscope of Christopher disappearing; a stranger, recognizing him at a stoplight; cameras whirring as he drove in the garage; the unreal silence of his living room.

He felt as if he had traveled half a lifetime in a day. Christopher looked so much older than his picture.

Kilcannon.

There was a sadness that he did not have time to feel. Least of all for himself.

In two hours, he would drive to SNI.

Lord began to do that which would get him there. Showering. Picking a suit, then a tie. Wondering how the ordinary could seem imagined.

Asking himself, finally, why he should care about Alexis.

He began knotting his tie in the mirror.

Two nights before, he had found Stacy in the dressing room, wondering if she would see herself again. Now his own face looked different to him.

Damn Carson, he thought. Damn *you*.

Where was she, and what did she think?

The telephone rang. Quickly, he answered it.

"Mr. Lord?"

Lord sat down on the bed. "Hello, Mr. Parnell."

"I haven't heard from you." His tone became querulous. "This *waiting* . . ."

"I'm sorry." Lord tried to understand his reasons. "It's moral cowardice, really. I haven't wanted to feel any more than I already do. . . ."

"But he'll kill her in front of me. Please, you have to . . ."

"Dammit, I don't *have* to do anything."

"Please . . ." As if hearing himself, Parnell's insistence shattered. "Please, I'm begging you. . . ."

Lord forced himself to sound calm. "I would, too. I'm only trying to understand where my obligations lie . . ."

"What other obligations could there be?"

Lord paused between weariness and anger. "I have a son," he answered, "who's seven."

There was silence. "A son," Parnell repeated.

"Yes."

"I see." Parnell was quiet again. "What I've been asked to do—it's very hard. I was hoping you could tell me, before."

"I'm sorry, Mr. Parnell. I'm only hoping that I'll know what to do. . . ."

"Then you're considering it," Parnell put in quickly.

Lord's jaw tightened. "Yes."

"Thank you. For that much . . ."

"Good-bye," Lord said. It was a moment before Parnell hung up.

Picking up the telephone, Lord threw it against the wall.

It cracked on the floor. Lord was staring at it when the dial tone started to beep.

Don't just react. Think your way through this.

When someone knocked, the phone was still beeping.

Lord replaced it, then opened the door, keeping the chain latched. "Doorman let me up," Moore explained. "Your line's busy."

"Parnell called," Lord said tersely, and let him into the living room.

When Moore sat, Lord did not. "The liquor's next to the fridge," Lord told him. "Make yourself a drink."

"No. Thanks."

"Then what can I do for you?"

Moore gazed up at him. "Somehow, you're feeling responsible for this. If it's something you can tell me . . ."

"Nothing that could get you to Phoenix by tomorrow." Lord's tone sharpened. "How could four hours change that?"

Moore exhaled. "This afternoon, your friend Rachel reported the visit to Carson."

Lord sat down. "DiPalma?" he asked finally.

"I assume—his reasoning's not hard to follow. If Carson knows something, and Phoenix knows *you* know, it's more dangerous for you to face him." Moore watched for his reaction. "DiPalma's using that to break you first, get whatever it is, then nail Carson to the wall."

"And you?"

"I thought you should know. Before deciding."

Turning, Lord stared out the window. "Fuck you," he said tonelessly. "You invited him in."

He heard Moore walk to the kitchen, then return. Lord looked up to find him standing with a glass of bourbon.

"At the time," Moore told him, "I didn't quite appreciate how that would work out."

"You don't mind using it. . . ."

"Look, even before DiPalma leaked this to Rachel, those calls you told me about bothered me. I think Phoenix may have it in for you."

Standing, Lord drifted to the window. "When you interrupted," he said at length, "I was thinking about Alexis."

Moore waited a moment. With dispassion, he asked, "That she's close to sixty?"

"That she's becoming hostile to her husband. Last night's broadcast turned my stomach for Parnell."

"It's an old story. Captivity twists people until they identify with their captors, and *this* one's brought back the captivity of a son. For whom Parnell wouldn't pay."

Hands in pockets, Lord took a few aimless steps, until he stood facing the picture of Christopher.

"So what are you going to do, Tony?"

"I'm not sure." Lord kept staring. "I've tried to imagine watching her die. . . ."

The phrase ended in a shrug. Behind him, he felt Moore watching.

"What about Damone?" Moore finally asked.

Lord turned from the picture. Quietly, he answered, "What about him, Johnny?"

For some time, Moore studied him. Then he carefully put down the glass.

"I'll drive you to SNI," he said.

The face of her Cartier read 7:46.

On his television, Tony Lord pushed through the crowd which filled SNI Plaza.

"Moments ago," the newswoman was saying, "Anthony Lord passed through the enormous crowd gathered here to see the principals in what has become, quite simply, the most terrifying landmark in the history of television.

"The tension is extraordinary. To protect his hostages, Phoenix has forced SNI to broadcast transmissions which might include their death, triggering a national psychodrama. . . ."

As if fearing to face each other, they stared at the montage of stills which took Lord's place: Phoenix speaking to the camera; Stacy's first appearance with Lord; Parnell reading his tax returns; Stacy with her head bowed at the concert; Parnell's sick look toward Gustafson; Damone with a shotgun in his mouth. Rachel narrated.

"As Stacy Tarrant and Colby Parnell fought to save those they love, we have witnessed things almost too personal to watch: her struggle to overcome the trauma of James Kilcannon's death; the surprising help of Anthony Lord; the Parnells' shared yet divisive agony over their lost son, Robert. . . ."

Alexis's throat began working. Frozen in the tennis dress, the last still image was hers.

"And now the largest audience in history waits to save Alexis Parnell by voting, a vote Phoenix will consider only if Parnell and Lord meet his final demands. But the other possibility—her televised execution in little more than an hour—is beyond imagination. . . ."

Her watch read five minutes until eight.

On screen, her face dissolved, becoming Rachel's.

"Upstairs," she continued, "Parnell waits with his attorney in an office near the set. And though Lord and Special Agent John Moore are watching from the SNI control room, Lord has declined to speak with anyone but Phoenix. . . ."

Her fingers reached for his.

Feeling this, he turned to her. When he tried to smile, it hurt him that she could not see.

"As for Stacy Tarrant, she has not been seen." Rachel paused. "Whether this relates to some decision Lord has reached, or to Harry Carson, no one knows. . . ."

Alexis seemed to sense his sudden stillness. Gently, as if fearing to offend, she touched his shoulder.

"But within minutes," Rachel finished, "we will know Parnell's decision."

Her skin felt cold. As they turned back to the screen, her hand stiffened.

Parnell sat alone. There were circles beneath his eyes, and his round-bellied slouch seemed spiritless. His forehead glistened in the lights.

For a moment he did not speak. "Phoenix," he said dully.

Somehow, Phoenix thought, it made him more aware of her.

"How much—" Parnell choked, then repeated, "How much, how very much, you must hate me. . . ."

Save her, damn you.

"Please, do not hate *her*." His voice faltered. "I—I've prepared the five million dollars. . . ."

Phoenix felt himself slump, and then he touched the forehead of his hood.

As if to soothe him, her fingers grazed his shoulder. Only Parnell's silence made Phoenix look again.

Parnell was shaking his head in bewilderment. "You've asked me," he mumbled, "to explain something personal. . . ."

Phoenix tensed. With palpable effort, Parnell made himself stare fixedly at the camera.

"The only way I can do this . . . is talk to my wife. As if she were here, in front of me. . . ."

Her hand stopped moving.

"Lexie . . ."

Phoenix felt his flesh rise. He could not look at her.

"I wanted to protect you from this. Robert and I . . ."

What would he say? What would she think?

"You were so beautiful. . . ." As her nails dug into Phoenix's shoulder, Parnell blurted, "God help me, I thought he wasn't mine. . . ."

She stood, trembling.

It brought him to his feet. Suddenly, she shrieked at her husband's image, "God damn you, he was *yours*. . . ."

Parnell's face fell in his hands.

She turned from him, pale with shock. Her voice seemed to echo in the cabin.

"He was *ours*. . . ." she whispered, to Phoenix.

"Jesus," Lord said.

He stood with Moore behind two control consoles manned by technicians, sloping downward to a wall of television screens. Each showed Parnell at multiple angles and ranges.

"Forgive me—" he mumbled to his wife.

"Camera two," the producer said, "and hold."

A close-up of Parnell covering his face filled all but one screen. Lord turned away, brushing past Moore.

At the end of the hall, Danziger appeared, leading Parnell from the set. Lord walked toward them in the semidark.

It took a moment for Parnell to see him. When he looked away, reflexively touching his glasses, Lord remembered their cross-examination. It seemed longer ago than it had been.

"Will you do it *now*?" Parnell asked.

Lord hesitated. "We need to talk, alone."

"Please, he's waiting for your answer. . . ."

"It's nearly eight-thirty, Mr. Parnell. We're running out of time."

Danziger's shaken look moved from his client to Lord. "There's an office down the hall," he said.

It was a room with one table. When the two men sat, Lord saw that Parnell had cut himself shaving. He stared at Lord's watch as Danziger shut them inside.

The watch read 8:23.

"You ask a lot of me," Lord said softly. "To save a woman I don't know, from a terrorist I'm afraid of, when it seems that she's started to help him."

Parnell reddened. "She's a prisoner. . . ."

"She's also turning on you, and now I can't be certain what she'll do if I show up. She might even turn on *me*." Lord paused. "If you can't tell me exactly why this is happening, and what Phoenix has found to play on, I'm afraid you've asked too much."

Parnell's hand tremored. "Please, I've just explained. . . ."

"I've known my son for seven years now, Mr. Parnell. I've found better reasons for loving him than that he's mine."

Parnell watched the time become 8:27.

"He—" His throat sounded dry. "Robert was too close to Alexis. . . ."

Parnell stopped, embarrassed by tears that jarred Lord with their suddenness. His eyes shut against them.

" 'Close,' " Lord repeated quietly.

Parnell swallowed. "It came between us . . . even when he was small, he hated me. I'd come to his room, and he'd cover his eyes. For years, he'd just cover his eyes, and wait for her. . . ."

Lord watched his shudder of repressed emotion. Nothing followed.

Softly, he asked, "Then why did Robert leave her?"

Parnell touched his glasses. "There was an incident . . ." he began, and could not finish.

Tears were running down his face.

The watch read 8:29, Lord saw, but Parnell no longer knew.

His voice startled Lord. "She would dress at the window," he murmured. "Sometimes, her skin seemed to glow in the sun. So beautiful . . ." His speech became thick. "It was like that, the morning I went to Robert's room. . . ."

When Lord looked up, Parnell was pale.

"His clothes were on the bed. We both could see his mother, through the curtain where he stood." Parnell's eyes opened in remembered shock. "When he turned, I saw what she had become to him."

Lord stared at the table. "So you told him to leave. . . ."

"I offered him an arrangement." The word echoed with shame. "If Robert left that morning, she would never know. . . ."

Lord's eyes rose to his. "Does she?" he asked.

"Yes." Parnell raised his head, and then turned away abruptly. "She was sickened," he mumbled. "Sickened. . . ."

Lord felt a slow, appalling comprehension. "You told her," he said quietly, "*before* the kidnapping."

Parnell gave a convulsive nod. "Afterwards, we could never talk of it." His voice rose. "How could we, when I refused to ransom him, and she'd been too ashamed to stop me. . . ."

Lord could only stare. Turning, Parnell's face was ravaged.

"You see," he blurted, "part of me wanted him dead."

He was crying, Lord knew, from guilt.

Parnell's gaze broke. "This monster has opened it all up for her. Without him, it never would have happened. Never. . . ."

For a brief moment, Lord thought of Carson. He could feel his own silence.

"Please, Mr. Lord, it's not her fault. She doesn't deserve to die. . . ."

Lord touched his arm, to stop him.

Mute, Parnell stared at this, and then he saw Lord's watch.

It changed to 8:34.

Alexis's watch read 8:35.

They faced the television, Phoenix standing behind her. He could not bring himself to watch her face.

"At this moment," Rachel said, "Parnell is closeted with Anthony Lord. . . ."

To wait for them filled Phoenix with the angry dread of a child whose parents had locked the door. He could almost feel her heartbeat.

Please, you bastard. Let her live.

In his desire for this, he imagined leaving her on the deserted beach below, to be rescued once he called them. Perhaps still wanting to be with him, watching as he disappeared with Lord to make his final broadcast.

On SNI, he would announce to them that she was safe. But when he turned the camera, Lord would be sitting in her place.

As two hundred million people watched, he would gently place the Mauser to Lord's temple, and pull the trigger.

He would let the camera linger there, as his mind was now; the moment was so startling in its beauty that he could not imagine his movements following the blackout.

Burying Lord's body.

Suddenly, he would be alone. Tearing apart the control room, dumping its pieces in the Eel, leaving his van and cabin as remnants of another nameless isolate who had simply disappeared. Telephoning SNI where to find Alexis. Still missing her.

Escaping.

Two weeks in the wilderness of Humboldt as they hunted him. Then a nighttime flight through California to Mexico, along the secret route of dope smugglers.

Night again would cover his landing in the Cayman Islands. Then the hours until morning, with the Mauser for protection.

At nine the next day, he would enter a selected bank, with five million dollars on his back.

The bank would ask no questions. Through five different countries, they would transfer the money by wire to a numbered account in Switzerland. As they had for many others.

In the days and nights that followed he would pass as a beachcomber, watching their search cool as it spread across the world, wondering how she lived now. Waiting for the flight to Geneva that would settle his own fate.

There was a plastic surgeon there, and Phoenix had never liked his face.

Yet this, and most of all her life, depended on Lord coming.

His mind flashed once more to Lord, dying in her chair.

When the picture changed, Lord was sitting where Parnell had been, on SNI.

Instinctively, Phoenix touched Alexis's shoulder. Her shudder became his.

Lord's stare had a bleak directness. "I'll be brief," he said. "First, you've asked Stacy Tarrant to pledge her concert money to specific groups. She will. . . ."

As his eyes closed, Lord's words came through a fog. "Second, you've asked that I 'reclaim' the hostages." Lord paused. "I will."

Alexis collapsed against him.

He felt his heart pounding.

When at last she faced him, SNI was flashing telephone numbers for voters to call. They used photographs as background: Alexis the starlet; Alexis smiling, the day of her wedding to Parnell. Alexis with her husband and young son.

"Please," she whispered.

Gently, she placed one finger on the hood, tracing the angles of his face. He quivered as it crossed his cheek.

As she reached beneath his hood, he could not stop her.

On the screen, a computer printout appeared. Ninety percent of callers in the first three minutes wished for her to live.

Lightly, her index finger traced the curve of his mouth.

He did not move as she found the lines at the corner of his eyes, his eyelids as they shut again, the ridge of his nose. Her touch lingered there.

It stopped at the tears on his face.

His skin tingled. He could feel her head tilt, imagine her looking at him. He opened his eyes.

She was staring at the eye slits of his hood.

Her hand slipped from beneath it, fingers raising to touch beneath each slit, barely grazing the burlap. As if she felt his breathing stop.

Paralyzed, Phoenix saw them as two figures beneath a single bare light bulb, utterly still. Each waiting for the other to move.

Slowly, she pressed the burlap to his face.

Blood pounded in his temple. Lips parted, she saw the color of his eyes. Phoenix could no longer see or hear the television. Only Alexis.

Hand trembling, she began to slide the hood above his mouth.

"*No*," he cried out.

Her face turned white.

The sound of his voice froze him there. Her hand seemed to move on its own.

"No," he whispered, and then she looked into his face.

As she took one stunned step backward, his hood fell to the floor, between them.

When Lord walked from the set to the hallway, Stacy was there.

For a moment, they faced each other. The darkness lent a few feet of privacy.

"I tried to call." Her voice was quiet. "You were out, and then the line was busy. So I came."

He did not know what to say. "Did you ever have a day," he finally asked, "when it seems you've relived your entire life story, and some other people's."

"Yes. Except I put you there."

"No." He paused for emphasis. "I did."

Her head angled slightly, as if to hear what was not said. Finally, she murmured, "Carson told you something about John."

"That dream." He leaned against the wall, both hands in his pockets. "You've wondered about Damone, haven't you. All along."

"Not consciously—I haven't wanted to face it." When she flicked back her bangs, the gesture stopped at her temple. "I think now I wanted *you* to. Maybe, at first, I thought you knew something about him."

"I keep hearing that."

She looked away. "Whatever Carson said this morning, you didn't know, did you?"

"No."

"Oh, Tony—" she began, and then leaned on the wall across from him. "I'm so sorry. . . ."

"Don't be." He smiled a little. "Know what I wish, though?"

Her shoulders moved. "No."

He waited until she looked at him again. "That we'll be friends for a very long time, and never have to ask another question. Not like these."

As she studied his face, Moore appeared at the end of the corridor.

Lord nodded to him. Stacy turned, saw Moore, and turned again.

"I'm going back to Sea Ranch," she said in a lower voice. "I'd like you to come. You know, when you get free."

"Sure."

For another moment she just looked at him. Then he touched her lightly on the shoulder, and walked toward Moore.

Moore glanced at Stacy. "Ready?" he asked Lord.

"Uh-huh."

They walked to the elevator and got inside. When he turned, she watched them from the corridor, until the doors shut.

Day Seven: Sunday

"We'll try to follow," Moore said finally. "At a safe distance."

They sat in the shabby motel room Moore had found to hide him: a lamp, two chairs, traffic noise outside, SNI droning in the background. A telephone they both kept watching.

Lord turned from it. "Safe for whom."

"For you, and the hostages." Moore leaned forward. "We can plant a transmitter on you and your car, and track their signals. That way Phoenix doesn't see us, but we know where to find you. And if the drop's not too complex, we can cover it—especially in a populated area."

"Won't he know that?"

"Maybe." Moore paused. "We have helicopters, jeeps, even planes. There aren't many places we can't go."

The murmur of Rachel's voice came through Lord's silence. "Though the FBI has clamped a lid on details, it is known that Phoenix has chosen Anthony Lord as the only acceptable courier. On the eve of the final broadcast, during which the terrorist threatens to execute Alexis Parnell, Lord has disappeared. . . ."

"My own personal Greek chorus," Lord murmured.

Rising, Moore turned off the sound.

"I feel like I'm on a conveyor belt," Lord told him after a time. "All my life, the thing I've been most afraid of is having no control."

Moore only nodded. When Lord glanced at the telephone again, it was close to six.

This was their first discussion of Phoenix in several hours.

The time between had reminded Lord of being younger and away from home, in some strange place which held an uncertain future, and talking to hang on to what was known. They covered Lord's only wife and Moore's current one; the two years undercover with the Weathermen which had cost Moore his first marriage; what Lord thought Christopher might become; Moore's daughter, his greatest pride and astonishment, and her success at Wellesley. What they both might do differently.

"I don't know how you can stand this job," Lord ventured now. "The waiting."

"Oh, it's interesting work, if people interest you, and you get used to the drawbacks." Moore studied him. "I don't know how you can stand the moral ambiguity."

Their eyes met, and then Lord shrugged.

"Being undercover's ambiguous, Johnny. It all is."

"That's your rationale?"

"Part of what it was. If no one is completely moral, I told myself, then what's to keep them from railroading someone for reasons of their own." Lord paused. "Some days it felt as if I was all my clients had, and now that seems so strange. Except for Christopher, if something happens to me it would be like resigning. Someone else would take my place, that's all."

Moore glanced at the telephone. After a time, he asked, "Just Christopher?"

Staring past him, Lord saw dawn breaking at the edge of the curtains.

"It amazes me, Tony, considering how she *should* feel. I wasted half of Friday wondering if you were born with a horseshoe up your ass."

Lord felt himself smile. At this, and for Moore's efforts.

The telephone rang.

It made him start. Moore seemed slow to answer.

"Yes," he said, then became quite still. "I can remember."

The voice came to Lord as a reedy noise. Listening, Moore gazed at the wall, the television, his watch.

His eyes stopped moving.

Lord's stomach tightened. The room felt cold.

"I'll get back to you," Moore said, and hung up.

He examined the floor for some moments. Lord forced himself to keep silent.

"He called our Boston office." Moore's voice was without emotion. "At six-thirty this morning. You're to start in four hours."

"Where?"

"To a roadside clearing off 101." Moore looked up at him. "Four miles past the Eel River."

Lord touched the bridge of his nose. "Humboldt County."

"You're to wear shorts and a T-shirt," Moore went on, "to prevent concealed weapons. The money will be in a backpack in your trunk. When you reach the clearing, there's a john and a telephone. At four o'clock, you'll receive a call telling you where to go for more instructions. He'll be watching with a rifle and a Bearcat scanner—that's a box that picks up transmitter signals." Moore folded his hands. "If you call anyone, or he picks up a signal, you die. Then her."

Lord watched the hands. "In other words," he finally said, "you can't follow me."

"From the point of the call, Phoenix says he means you to disappear. Only after that do you get Alexis."

Lord looked up. "Not Damone?"

Moore's gaze was level. "He didn't specifically mention that."

Lord turned from him. On the television, Rachel's mouth moved, making no sound.

"Where do you think I'm going?"

"On foot, eventually, along a route he or his people could watch to make sure no one follows. Maybe until sometime between darkness and the broadcast, to cover his escape."

Lord stood, hands in his pockets.

"You'll have to keep alert, Tony. Remember the route. As soon as you get there, start thinking of a way out."

"What's to keep him from stopping me."

Moore hesitated. "It's much better for him to return Alexis. And you."

Lord walked to the television, and switched it off.

When he turned to Moore, the agent's eyes seemed larger than normal.

"I've never been a fatalist, Johnny."

"We can try to tap in from the phone company. Catch his instructions."

"Is that it?"

Moore studied his folded hands. "As long as you're driving," he said at length, "we can probably follow in a plane with a telescopic sight, from high enough so he can't see. At least we'll know when and where you've driven."

"What about at night?"

"Then we've lost you."

Lord sat on the edge of the bed.

Moore exhaled. "Once you get there, keep as far back as you're able—you've got no hope with him up close. Don't worry about getting a look at his face: if he means not to harm you, he'll be wearing the hood so you can't ID him later. The important thing is to make him show you Alexis."

"And if he won't?"

"Then something's wrong." Moore considered him. "Drop the money and run as far and as fast as you can."

Lord was quiet. "Without Alexis."

"You're supposed to help us bring her back. Get yourself killed, and you've been no help at all. . . ."

"He won't let me go far," Lord cut in softly, "and you'll never find me. Or her."

"We'll sew a transmitter in the band of your shorts—you can activate it by pinching." Moore kept his tone factual. "Its signal has a five-mile range. If we pick it up, we'll get there as soon as we can. At least that way there's a chance you'll lead us to Alexis."

Rubbing his temples, Lord could not imagine moving from the room.

"There is one other option," Moore said evenly. "I can take your place."

When Lord turned to him, Moore's gaze was without judgment.

"Listen to me, Tony. You're a civilian, and risk is in the nature of my work. I can try giving Phoenix the same choice we'll give Parnell. Me or no one." Pausing, Moore finished slowly. "Phoenix gave one reason for wanting you to come. I'm not sure there aren't others, are you?"

Lord found that he could not look at him.

"It's gone too far," he said finally. "When I get back, you can buy me a drink."

At eleven, Lord crossed the Golden Gate Bridge in a white government car, wearing a T-shirt and running shorts with a thin silver disk sewn in the band. Moore had retrieved his running shoes.

From San Francisco to the Eel River was close to three hundred miles, the last five hours Lord was sure of. He drove the first two as if in a dream; passing the turnoff for Sea Ranch, the familiar slipped behind him.

Far ahead, mountains began rising in green waves. They grew nearer on a level of consciousness that Lord did not quite accept; the last seventy-two hours had moved too fast, and he had slept for six of them. Four cups of black coffee shot through him like a second pulse.

Sunset would come at 7:10.

Somewhere overhead, Moore was in a light plane. But the time before dusk kept running as the traffic thinned around him.

Think of Alexis.

The concrete narrowed to two lanes. Mountain and shadow grew larger, foothills rose to surround him, civilization became scattered churches, ice sheds, gas stations, pickup trucks with gun racks. To pass them carrying five million dollars seemed surreal.

Abruptly, the road started a precipitous climb, tracing the contour of cliffsides which kept winding out of sight. Shadows began falling, and then the country closed around him.

To his left, the Mendocino River ran through a deepening gully. Mountains thrust from all sides; the pines became taller and mixed with redwoods; tumbled by spring torrents, boulders lay beside the road in broken chunks.

His watch moved toward two o'clock.

For an hour Lord climbed a twisting pattern of shadow and rock and white-water gully as its pieces changed shapes and colors. By three the Mendocino had become the Eel, deeper and wider, and the mountains rose so steeply they seemed to fall on him. The pines had vanished; the green and brown deepened in the permanent shadow of redwoods which came to the road in dense towering stands, blocking the light. The sky narrowed to a ribbon above the Eel.

The redwoods, Lord realized, might soon hide him from view. His palms grew damp in the constant rhythm of shifting and braking and accelerating.

Three-thirty. In one half-hour, he would hear Phoenix's voice.

The river twisted suddenly.

Lord saw the bridge first, then the redwood grove beyond it, a monolith without light. A few seconds later he could read the sign: Humboldt County.

Crossing the river, Lord looked east. The Eel swept from a trackless wilderness of mountain and forest that went to the Sierras; miles away, thin fog sat like smoke at the tops of trees. Then he left the bridge behind, and there was no more sky.

It was like entering a cathedral—vast, dark, still. Lord watched four miles start on his odometer. Driving slowly now, already tired. His stomach raw-feeling.

At ten minutes until four, he found the contact point.

It was a dirt path, almost hidden between the trunks of two redwoods. One turn, and the road vanished behind him.

His car was alone in a clearing. A rustic bathroom with a phone stuck on the wall, surrounded by redwoods so tall and close that there was still no sun.

Lord stopped a few feet from the telephone.

Cracking open the window, he smelled bark and needles decaying. He did not get out.

There was no sound. Through the windshield, he searched the grove for a glimpse of someone. Within five feet they became too dense to see.

Lord forced himself not to stare at his watch.

Let his instructions be simple, he thought, let Moore's people tap in to them. Let this be over quickly.

His eyes moved from windshield to mirror; the silence chafed his nerves for minutes he did not count. Finally, reluctantly, he looked at the time.

Two minutes after four.

When the telephone rang, it echoed in the trees.

Lord was still.

It rang twice more before he left the car open behind him, keys in his hand, Phoenix a sixth sense on the back of his neck. He could not make himself move faster.

The phone kept ringing.

As he reached it, Lord turned his back to the wall, facing the woods and the trees. His mouth was dry as he picked up the phone.

"Lord," he answered.

A tape clicked on.

"This is a recorded message," the slurred voice said, "sent by cordless telephone, sixty feet from where you stand. . . ."

Shock running through him, Lord touched the transmitter.

"Your death is that close. If someone had followed, by transmitter or otherwise, you would not have reached the telephone. But I do not wish to meet you here, or give instructions that might be overheard by wiretap."

As Phoenix paused, Lord felt the last words on his skin.

"Twenty paces beyond the redwood scarred by lightning, I have placed a cassette recorder with a tape. You will play it without moving."

By instinct, Lord held the telephone further from his ear, listening for a second voice.

He was still listening when he heard the dial tone.

Panicky, his eyes swept the trees for scars or a glimpse of something moving. Saw nothing but a hundred trunks as the telephone started beeping.

Lord put it down, trying to collect himself.

From left to right, he began to search each tree, peripheral vision straining.

Straight across the clearing was a redwood with a black scar in its bark.

Walking slowly toward it, Lord imagined Phoenix laughing.

Behind there was nothing but grove. Twenty paces, wondering if he watched.

He started counting them, back burning with anticipated gunshots.

At five paces, Lord began looking to his left and right, stopping to face behind him. The woods were damp and cool on his skin. Too thick to walk a straight line, so dark that little grew except toadstools and moss.

Turning, he could not tell the redwood he had started from. He turned again, disoriented, then sick to his stomach.

Fifteen paces, he remembered.

Redwoods surrounded him. They formed a chamber of half-light and shadow, where everything seemed larger or smaller or distorted in shape.

A red coffee can.

To the side of him, still covered by its plastic lid. Next to a broken branch where Phoenix had stepped.

Lord fumbled open the can.

Inside were a cassette recorder and a tape. Around the tape was a woman's Cartier watch.

Her wrist must be quite small, Lord thought. Sweat cooled on his face.

The Cartier showed 4:15.

Inserting the cassette, Lord pushed the "play" button.

"Only if you follow these directions," the voice began, "will I give you Alexis Parnell. . . ."

Lord's head snapped up, watching as he listened. Phoenix's voice seemed to filter through the trees.

"But not before dusk," the tape continued, "and not where cars or jeeps can follow. . . ."

The cold felt deeper than before.

"Upon playing this tape, return with it to your car. If you so much as move toward the telephone, you will not live to reach it. Nor will Alexis live beyond my final broadcast."

Lord stood, turning full circle.

"You will drive another two-tenths of a mile north to a dirt path on the left. Once you turn there, you can call no one, and no one else can see you.

"All that will be left you is to come for Alexis, or let her die."

He was still now. Listening.

"The path continues through the redwoods, to a ridge. For a few minutes thereafter, you will drive in the open.

"We can see you at every point.

"If you stop, she will die. If you do not reach our meeting place by sunset, she will die.

"Listen well."

Through a surge of anger, Lord forced himself to concentrate.

"From the ridge, the road descends to a valley, crossing a bridge. Six miles past the bridge, you will turn left on an abandoned logging trail. Just beyond its first curve is a small grove of oaks." Phoenix paused for emphasis. "Park beneath it, where your car cannot be seen from above. Then take the backpack from the trunk and put this tape inside.

"I will be watching. If you do not have the tape, you will not receive Alexis."

No evidence. Nothing for Moore to follow or find.

"Through the grove, you will find a path. Follow it left for five miles.

"At its end is an uprooted trunk which resembles a lion's head. I will meet you there.

"If you reach it by sunset, she will live."

Alexis's watch showed 4:30.

"Hurry," the voice finished softly. "You have far to go, and time is of the essence."

The silence was sudden and complete.

As the tape kept running, soundless, a second, cooler part of Lord saw how clever Phoenix was.

Bending back his head, he tried following the redwood trunks. He could not find where they ended.

Once he left here, no one could follow from the air.

He was still for some moments. Only his eyes moved.

Remember where you've been, Moore had said. His car was twenty yards away, and he was no longer sure in which direction.

Taking twenty careful steps, he looked to each side. Lost, feeling time vanish. Holding the cassette player and watch.

Something to his left, barely visible. A change in the quality of light.

Lord exhaled, and then walked to the clearing.

Facing the telephone, he stopped. Phoenix could have called from feet, he thought, or miles. Nothing moved or made a sound.

Her watch showed twenty minutes until five.

Lord tried to imagine how she must feel. How grateful she would be.

The telephone still froze him. Tempting him to try to use it, call for help. Too long.

He turned away, walking to the car. His fingers were awkward as he started it.

Looking in the rearview, he returned to the edge of the road. He stopped there for a moment, the tape beside him, then headed north.

When he turned again, the second path felt like a tunnel.

Heavy branches sagged above the car. A mist hung in the air, barely different from the thin half-darkness. Within feet, Lord was forced to use his headlights.

The temperature dropped, thickening the mist.

The car slowed to ten miles an hour, a barely moving target. He drove like this for endless minutes, through the giant trunks of redwoods, branches which leapt from the mist with startling suddenness. Drained and tired and half-expecting to be shot, Lord searched for odd shapes, sudden movements, armed men at the side of the road or in his rearview mirror.

He's wearing you down. You're tired, cold, so strung out from watching that when you finally meet, he'll take you like a child.

An arm.

Lord braked abruptly.

At the edge of the road, his headlights struck the gnarled roots of a redwood which had fallen among the others, leaving a wound in the earth. Nothing else.

Her watch showed 5:30.

When Lord started driving again, his face and hair were damp.

The mist became swirls.

The path was climbing. Moving again, he was caught in a few seconds' elation. He was still alive.

Surely that meant Alexis was.

Lord pushed the gas pedal, driving for the open valley.

For more miles upward, redwoods turned to pines on a path he took too fast. A dull ache on the back of his neck became a pounding at the temples.

His car had been lost to Moore for almost two hours, he figured, moving westward on a route they could not follow. When the path ended high on a ridge, Lord stopped.

Beneath him, a river flowed through a valley, gentler hills.

He had broken clear of cover.

For less than an hour now, the sun would cast this failing light, then vanish. The slower he drove, the better Moore's chance to find him from above, and Alexis's to die.

He had forgotten his directions.

Head throbbing, Lord played the cassette. It seemed to take longer than before.

A logging trail, six miles past the bridge. Then a five-mile path to an uprooted trunk in the shape of a lion's head.

When Lord turned, downward from the ridge, it was 6:20.

For the next ten minutes, he descended in nerve-racking slow motion to the bottom of the valley, hoping Moore's plane was circling the area, to spot his car again. He saw nothing in the sky ahead.

Past the wooden bridge were a gas station, a store, two houses. A telephone beside the road.

Lord slowed, staring.

Beyond the telephone was a mountain range; on the other side of the river, rolling hills. He was exposed.

As the telephone receded in his rearview, the road turned with the river, and it was gone.

Forty minutes until sunset.

Lord stepped on the accelerator. He had given Moore all the time he could.

Within minutes, he found the logging trail.

It quickly curved between madrone trees, hiding him from view. As he entered the grove of oaks, their branches met above his car, ending his hope that Moore could see it.

Lord felt skin pricks as he took the tape from its player.

Leaving the car, he unlocked the trunk, slid the tape in the cumbersome pack, and strapped it on. He did not stop to look inside.

Five miles from here, the outside range of his transmitter signal, with twenty-eight minutes left. He had never run that far that fast.

Pushing through the grove, he reached the edge of a hillside and saw that the river had suddenly curved from the road, below him. A path ran beside it.

Lord clambered down the hillside, sliding, grabbing branches, half-falling to the path.

From the hill he could be watched or shot. Opposite, through a thin line of birch trees, the river blocked his escape.

Along the path, following the river until it disappeared, the sun fell to meet it.

Lord started running toward the sun.

His calves were taut from not warming up. With each minute, the sun kept slipping, the river opening ahead of him. An endless line of birches moved at the corner of his eye.

His feet kept pounding.

If he made it, they would meet at dusk, giving Phoenix the hours of darkness to broadcast and then vanish. Perfect for returning Alexis, or killing an exhausted courier.

Twenty minutes until sunset, then fifteen. He imagined himself from above, a dot in fading light, too small for Moore to see.

Touching the horizon, river met sun.

Fresh wind braced his skin. So cold and strong and steady that it seemed to have nothing to stop it.

"Please, Mr. Lord. She doesn't deserve to die. . . ."

A first edge of sun vanished, and still more river appeared between the birches, specks of white at its end.

Lord ran faster. The wind which battered him now carried a sound, low and distant and steady.

The specks must be whitecaps.

As he ran, the pummeling sound grew deeper, the wind a bitter cold. He felt a twinge in one leg, a cramp starting. The sun was half gone.

"But you'll always be my dad, right . . . ?"

Larger, the whitecaps came from a pool of orange on the river. But the path rose to a dune, concealing the shore; only the beating sound told of its harshness.

Once he stopped, his calves would knot in the wind and cold.

"I'm going back to Sea Ranch," she had said. "I'd like you to come. You know, when you get free. . . ."

Think of Alexis.

The whitecaps were fifteen-foot waves where river met ocean. The dune he ran toward seemed thrown up by the pummeling of a shoreline he could not see.

The sun was a sliver.

One minute left. Phoenix haunted him now.

"Phoenix gave one reason for wanting you to come. I'm not sure there aren't others, are you . . . ?"

In an aching final sprint, Lord reached the top of the dune.

It was like nothing he had ever seen.

Miles of black sand strewn with the dead trunks of redwoods left by the punishing surf, then stripped and bleached by wind and sun and saltwater. Some lay piled across one another like the bones of mastodons; others were hewn by the elements into modernist sculpture. The bark of newer redwoods peeled in rotting strips.

Panting, Lord searched the debris.

It was desolate, endless. Waves crashed through jagged rocks with the sound of an explosion, rushing onto the beach to suck back the closest tree trunks in a savage undertow, to be met by more waves exploding. Two hundred feet from them, Lord felt spray. Wind stung his eyes.

Suddenly, he stopped searching.

To his left, the roots of an enormous redwood were torn open in a gaping jaw, beneath an eye hollowed by wind.

No one was there.

When Lord turned, he was alone.

On each side of the river, brush-covered cliffs rose steeply from the beach. The only way out was as he had come, or south along the shore. His legs began tightening in the cold.

He was to wait by the lion's head.

Remembering Moore's instructions, Lord moved stiffly away from it, toward the ocean, putting as much distance and as many logs as possible between himself and where Phoenix might appear. He stopped just short of the surf, its colors basic now: slate-gray rocks, a red haze on the water. Spray hit him that he could not see.

He turned from it.

The green mountains became a shadowed yellow-brown. The waves at his back half-deafened him; with each successive crash he imagined being caught and then swept out in a riptide. His heart raced.

A distant figure stood atop the dune.

It wore no hood. In the failing light, they watched each other.

The figure was alone.

There was something slung across his shoulder, a boxlike shape hanging from his belt. His hair seemed dark; he did not have a beard.

Lord could not see his face.

The figure raised one arm, and waved him forward.

Lord's skin crawled.

A wave struck his calves, pulling him back. When he caught his balance, looking up again, the figure was an outline.

Wind whined at his ears; his legs were turning numb. It was half-light now.

Cupping both hands, Lord called out, "I want to see her." His strained voice seemed to carry on the wind.

The figure remained still. Behind him, the full moon became clearer, larger.

Lord waited for some sign or motion.

There was nothing.

Lord shivered.

"Where is she?" he cried out.

The figure did not move or answer. And then the light changed, and his outline was part of it. Lord was no longer sure that he saw him.

His eyes strained.

Metal, glinting in first moonlight, where Phoenix had stood.

Lord unslung the backpack and held it by one strap. Not certain Phoenix was moving, yet sensing him grow larger.

His free hand touched the transmitter.

"Stop," he called out. "Show me Alexis."

The figure grew clearer. Coming.

"You've got no hope with him up close. . . ."

Split seconds to decide.

Perhaps she was hidden on the beach. Phoenix might take him there once he had the money.

"You're supposed to help us bring her back. Get yourself killed, and you've been no help at all. . . ."

Distance closing, the figure growing larger.

Activate the signal, Moore had said. Run and hope the FBI could find them with it, and then Alexis.

"*I have to see her—*"

There was no answer. Backlit by the moon, Phoenix seemed to step from darkness. An outline with a rifle aimed at Lord.

Sixty feet now. Moving closer.

"*Stop—*"

Fifty feet.

Lord pinched the transmitter.

The figure froze; the box it carried was a scanner.

Whirling to his left, Lord threw the backpack into the surf and ran in the opposite direction.

His steps were hobbling and painful. Twisting, he saw Phoenix dive after the money.

Lord fought to put distance between them, running where the surf erased his footprints. Surf swept to his knees, sucking him sideways.

An enormous wave crashed ahead, twice Lord's height. He stumbled forward through its undertow.

From his left, a log was rushing toward him, too fast to escape. He tried to jump.

The log struck his calves.

He fell sideways, tumbling on the sand, and then the following wave came down on him.

Cold blackness, swirling, caught in a vortex filling his lungs and sweeping him out to sea. Flailing, drowning, trying to get his head above water.

Something struck his ribs, knocking him sideways. Blindly he wrapped one arm around it.

The log swept him back to shore.

He fell off it to his hands and knees, ribs aching, coughing in the surf. Another wave broke behind him.

He staggered up as it struck his back.

It catapulted him forward, struggling for balance, falling in the last tame spill.

He lay there, gasping, lungs raw.

In the moonlight, Phoenix was a wraith emerging from the ocean with a bundle clutched above his head. Perhaps two hundred feet away.

Righting himself, Lord ran. Waves plummeted next to him; his footsteps were leaden; he shivered from cold and exposure.

A giant wave broke in front of him.

Lord zigged to avoid it. There were sudden slapping sounds, and then a straight line of jets split the path he had been running.

Bullets from a semiautomatic rifle aimed at knee level. Meant to wound, not kill.

Over his shoulder he saw Phoenix coming after him, closer.

Lord kicked off his shoes and veered across the beach, seeking the cover of darkness.

Ahead, a sheer cliffside merged with the sand; dead trunks lay across his path at every angle, silver and black. He careened among them, half-falling, steeling himself for bullets. The beach was cold and without color, a moonscape.

He heard no gunshots.

Forty feet in front of him was a pile of logs.

Turning as he ran, Lord saw nothing but dark; perhaps Phoenix had vanished with the money and Alexis. Perhaps he had failed.

Stay alive, Moore had said.

Lord lowered his head and ran for the pile.

His bare feet flung sand, calves so stiff they did not feel part of him. The logs grew nearer.

With a last effort, he lengthened his stride and hurtled in a headlong dive.

His head and chest cleared the pile, then he landed on his face, feet caught in the logs, wrenching them out. Feeling like an animal.

Sliding back, he peered over the log. Wondering if Alexis were close by. Looking for Phoenix.

Nothing.

Maybe Moore could find them, Lord prayed, and then his stomach wrenched.

If Phoenix still hunted him, the transmitter was his enemy.

Teeth chattering, he stripped off his shirt and shorts and wadded them beneath the logs.

Naked, Lord scrambled away from the transmitter. Half-crawling among more logs, looking back, then forward for cover.

There were no other piles. Only a thick trunk, straight ahead. Changing direction to avoid it, he saw nothing better.

Hurriedly, he crab-walked to the trunk, falling over and behind it, on his side.

Arms clasped for warmth, Lord looked at where he'd been.

The moon glinted on the surf and whitecaps. The trunks were half-lit wreckage, scattered across the darkness between Lord and the sea.

A black form moved among them.

He was framed by moonlight, against the ocean. His head turned from side to side.

The way Phoenix moved and held his weapon reminded Lord of Carson.

On the wind, beneath the pounding of the surf, he heard a faint beeping sound. The scanner.

Stopping, Phoenix stared at the pile where Lord had hidden.

He took a few steps toward it. As the beeping grew louder, he seemed to gaze beyond.

Lord pressed his face to the sand, body curled on itself.

Phoenix watched the pile, waiting for some sound or movement.

There was only beeping. He adjusted something on his rifle; Lord waited for him to shoot the quarry he thought hidden there.

There was no shot. The beeping seemed shriller than before.

Phoenix stood over the pile.

He bent to it, and then held the scrap of Lord's running shorts to the moonlight.

He began tearing them apart.

Finding something, he placed it on top of the log, just beneath his rifle barrel. Lord quivered at the gunshot. The scanner stopped beeping.

Lord's face was wet. Maybe Phoenix would turn, he thought, and leave. Perhaps he only wished to stop the signal; Lord had not seen his face, could not identify him.

The figure began moving again, slowly and carefully, a little to his left. Perhaps twenty feet.

Phoenix was still hunting him.

The trunk was angled between them. Lord slithered toward its far end, trying to hide.

One step at a time, Phoenix drew even with him, looking from side to side. Staring in Lord's direction.

Lord lay like a second log.

One more step, then another, and Phoenix was a few feet past.

He stopped, raising his left wrist to his face, to read his watch.

A hunter with a deadline.

Lord got to his knees.

Phoenix's stare swung to the ocean. Head cocked toward him, Lord began to circle. Cramps made him limp.

When Phoenix's gaze swung back, Lord was just beyond it, moving softly.

Phoenix's head kept swinging; Lord kept circling, at his back. Stopping straight behind him.

Between them was a log shaped like a club.

Lord hobbled forward, grasping it. The wind and ocean howling covered his steps.

Clamping his teeth, Lord rose again.

Phoenix stepped forward, broad-shouldered, graceful. Lord's legs were so stiff that the distance narrowed too slowly.

Eight feet more.

Lord started moving in a crouch. Soon Phoenix must look back.

Six feet.

Raising the club, Lord's eyes sought the back of his neck.

Four feet.

Phoenix's shoulders tensed. As he stopped, Lord drew back the club.

Phoenix spun on him.

In the split second he could not decide to kill him on the beach, Lord swung at his skull.

There was a thud, shock running through Lord's arm, the rifle firing. Then Phoenix was toppling in its echo, dropping his weapon.

Lord lunged at him.

His head cracked against the terrorist's rib cage, changing the direction of his fall. Backward, Lord on top of him, screaming, unable to see his face.

Phoenix chopped at his windpipe.

The scream became gagging. As Lord's throat constricted, an elbow smashed into his jaw, knocking him to the sand. Feeling ripped tissue in his mouth, tasting blood.

Phoenix crawled toward the rifle.

Pushing to his knees, Lord dove to grab the terrorist's feet, then pull himself up over his back as Phoenix grasped the rifle.

Lord clutched his throat with both hands.

Muscles straining, Phoenix twisted under him, trying to turn and fire. Lord pushed for the back of his throat.

With primal strength, Phoenix turned beneath him, grasping the rifle in one hand, finger reaching the trigger, as his other hand flailed at Lord. The only sound was the wind and roar of the ocean.

Lord's fingers dug for his larynx.

The rifle stopped moving. Then, slowly, it slid from Phoenix's hand.

In a final spasm, his fingernails scraped the back of Lord's wrists. A gurgling sound came from the darkness.

Choking with his last ounce of force, Lord bent his face to the terrorist's.

His eyes were John Damone's.

They were stretched open, like the mouth gaping for air. As Damone gazed up at him, Lord could feel the pulse in his throat, his own convulsive swallowing. Damone could no longer breathe.

Grasping the rifle, Lord held its barrel to his temple.

Damone shuddered beneath him as air rushed to his lungs. It came back as ragged panting in Lord's face, two inches away.

"*Where is she?*" Lord whispered.

Damone's eyes shut.

In the silent seconds while Lord waited for his answer, he felt their heartbeats link them like two animals.

Slowly, Damone's head moved from side to side, once.

For an instant, Lord was only aware of the trigger he still touched, his free hand clutching Damone's throat.

"*Why . . .*"

Damone opened his eyes to stare back at him. In a voice so low it became a curse, he answered, "Because she saw my face."

* * *

Parnell put down the telephone.

His father's standing clock showed five minutes until nine. Somehow, it was important that he remember the time.

Through their curtains he saw police holding back onlookers, TV lights, the black-haired woman who had badgered him for interviews, facing a camera. She spoke behind him from the television: "Within minutes, we should know the fate of John Damone and Alexis Parnell. . . ."

Turning off her voice, he heard instead what Moore had told him.

They had found Lord on a deserted beach, naked, a rifle jammed to the back of Damone's throat. Damone, the enemy he did not know.

His footsteps had come from a rope ladder on the sheer cliff beyond the beach. At its top, hidden by a stand of pines, was a cabin.

Inside was a single chair, spotlit by photographer's lights, waiting in front of a camera. But Alexis lay in a shallow grave, overlooking the water.

They would bring her body, and Damone, to San Francisco.

Parnell was still, imagining her final moments.

For once, he did not cry.

His hand was steady as he dialed. He felt disembodied, more mind than heart.

"Hello?" Danziger said.

"This is Colby," he began, then realized how foolish this was. "She's dead, John."

His voice surprised him with its flatness. Only Danziger's silence made him feel pain.

"Colby, I'll be right there. . . ."

"Just keep them away. Please." Pausing, a vision of the night to come formed in Parnell's mind. "I'm leaving the telephone off the hook. To have some privacy with this."

Danziger paused. With a quiet that underscored his meaning, he asked, "Will you be all right, alone?"

"Yes. Thank you."

"Then I understand," Danziger murmured. "I'm so very sorry—"

"I know you are," Parnell answered softly, and pressed the receiver down.

He placed the telephone on the blotter, next to his revolver.

Picking it up, his eyes closed.

He had loaded it this morning, he remembered, after calling Danziger. To protect her once Lord returned.

She would be changed, of course. But he had asked Danziger to find psychiatrists who specialized in such cases, rather than wait here with him. Tomorrow had not seemed too soon to start.

His grip tightened on the revolver.

Alexis had died before him, in agony and fear. This was the first hour of knowing that for as long as he lived.

With the same clarity, he knew he could not bear it.

He placed the revolver to his temple.

It remained there, until Parnell was satisfied.

When he stood again, two hours had passed.

Walking to his window, he saw more police, the crowd of press growing, the dark-haired woman still talking to a camera. On the screen, her lips moved silently; Parnell could sense her confusion. It made him feel more certain.

There were precautions to be taken first, he thought. Ways he must prepare.

He went back to his desk.

From the telephone directory, he wrote down the address for the Hall of Justice, then dialed a second number.

"Thank you for calling MUNI," the tape began. "If you are requesting route information, please tell the operator where you are located, and where you wish to go. . . ."

The tape reminded him of Phoenix.

"MUNI information," a man's voice broke in.

"Pardon me," Parnell answered politely. "I wonder if you might tell me the route from Broderick, near Broadway, to 850 Bryant Street."

"At what time, sir?"

"Night." Parnell glanced at the clock. "After midnight."

Hesitance. "Will this be daily?"

"No. Just this once."

"Weekdays, or weekend?"

"Weekend."

Hearing pages flip, Parnell tensed.

"Yeah, okay . . . you'll walk to Jackson at Divisadero. Take the three Jackson to Van Ness, and then transfer to the forty-two bus going south. It'll take you right along Bryant. . . ."

Parnell wrote this down. "Three Jackson," he repeated. "Forty-two south on Van Ness. . . ."

"That's right," the man said, and hung up.

Parnell stuffed the paper in his shirt pocket, and unhooked the telephone again.

Climbing the stairs to their room, he selected a tie and his oldest sport-coat, found a hat he seldom wore. Then he opened their coat closet.

Her furs and wool coats stopped him.

Sudden tears began welling. He pulled out his raincoat and closed the door.

When he hurried downstairs, the crowd outside had swollen. The woman was still waiting there.

Opening his desk, Parnell took the press pass his staff had given him at the annual party, and put it in one pocket of his coat. The other sagged with the weight of his revolver.

Pausing, he saw the woman on his screen, and turned up her voice.

It sounded strained. "We are still waiting for the final broadcast, or some word about the hostages. All we can promise is to maintain live coverage until this terrible drama comes to an end. . . ."

He slipped out their pantry, entering the rear grounds.

The wind was cool on his face. There were stars above the bay, and the lights of boats were like more stars. But the home separating theirs and Broderick was not lit. Only a stucco wall between them, with the cherry tree she'd planted next to it.

Grasping its branches, he put one foot in the crotch of the tree and pulled himself up. The street shoe nearly slipped; Parnell's arms shook as the tree buckled beneath his weight. Pushing with one leg, he hooked the other over the wall, pulling his body up. Lying on top now, already panting.

A dog barked inside his neighbor's home.

Pulse racing, Parnell dropped into their yard, falling on his hands and knees as the revolver slid from his pocket. Desperately, he began to pat the grass around him.

Floodlights bathed the yard.

Three feet in front of him, Parnell saw the revolver.

He shoved it in his pocket, running from floodlight to floodlight, a shadow holding its hat. Turning sideways to see the curtain open as he reached the steps to Broderick Street.

As he disappeared, the dog stopped barking.

Broderick Street was quiet. Its sidewalk ran along one curving private drive, heading downward toward the bay, away from Broadway.

He skittered down, knees straining, getting no traction from the flat soles of his shoes until he reached the bottom.

Pull yourself together, he thought. Don't look suspicious.

He wiped his forehead; suddenly he was a neatly dressed eccentric, calmly taking his late-night walk. A block right to Divisadero, a second steep one back up toward Broadway, looking for squad cars as his breathing became a wheeze. His glasses were steamed.

She had told him to exercise.

Cleaning his glasses, he looked one block down Broadway, at their home. Lights and sound trucks lined both sides of the street; the crowd filled their entire block and half the next. Above them was the steel web of an SNI satellite truck.

He turned away.

One more flat block, another downhill, still expecting the police. Then a bus was coming toward him with its sign illuminated. Three Jackson.

They would recognize him.

Quickly, Parnell took off his glasses. His palms were damp.

When the bus stopped, opening its door, he could not see the driver's face. Fumbling through his wallet, he found a bill.

"That's a five, sir."

"I know."

"We don't make change. Sixty cents, please."

"That's all right. Please, just take this."

As he took the bill, Parnell felt the man appraising him. He looked down. A hand appeared, holding something.

"It's a transfer."

"Oh, yes." Belatedly, Parnell took it. "Thank you."

A few vague shapes stirred to look at him. Hastily, he sat next to a black woman in a straight red wig.

The bus headed down Fillmore Street, past empty windows and blinking liquor signs Parnell could not read, then toward Van Ness or a street he did not recognize. Dark forms drifted from the liquor stores, aimless.

Parnell turned to the woman, holding out his transfer. "Pardon me," he asked, "but how does one use this?"

The woman stared at him, suspicious. Finally, she said, "Just give it to the driver on the next bus."

"Are we near Van Ness yet?"

"Is that where you're going?"

"Yes, to start." He hesitated. "I suppose I should tell our driver."

Glancing out, she pulled a strap above the window. There was a sound not unlike a department store chime, and then the bus was stopping.

"You're here," she told him.

Parnell stood, stuffing the transfer in with his revolver.

"Thank you," he said, reached for a pole beside the door, and stumbled from the bus.

Putting on his glasses, he oriented himself.

Alone again and colder, he watched waves of car lights pass. Without a bus, feeling outwitted by a city he had never known.

It was already half past one.

As more minutes crept by, Parnell waited, lonely and irresolute. The shock he could not think of turned to numbness.

Another sign, moving above the cars. Number forty-two.

He took off his glasses just before it stopped. Uncertainly, he offered up the transfer.

The driver took it.

Parnell slumped in the seat behind him, alone.

The bus crept forward, block by block, picking up drunks and strays who boarded in its bleak yellow light. Face to the window, Parnell knew with fleeting triumph that they would not recognize him, for he had come where he did not belong. Down through a district of warehouses, street after street without trees or people or any change at all, the image as alien and cold to him as the future John Damone had willed that he live out.

Damone would face him first.

The bus turned onto Bryant Street.

It was silent, barren as the others. Turning to the front, Parnell was suddenly sure they had taken Damone elsewhere, that he was performing one last feckless act. Then he put on his glasses.

Two blocks distant, the Hall of Justice was surrounded by the red flash of squad cars. For an instant, Parnell remembered films of the night they'd brought in Carson, and then he wondered if Moore had already arrived there with Damone.

Reaching for the cord, he could not bring himself to pull it.

The bus kept moving.

One block, then entering the second, Parnell's face pressed to the glass. Passing newsmen, handheld cameras, another satellite truck with the SNI logo.

It froze him.

When the bus stopped, he saw the dark-haired woman, standing across the street.

She was talking to her cameraman, Parnell saw. The man was facing the main doors of the building; as if agitated, she pointed toward a side street, to the exit of its underground garage.

Parnell jerked the cord.

It was 2:00 A.M. before Stacy saw Lord's headlights.

Since his call, she had tended the fire, unable to absorb what he had said. Her television remained on SNI; their films of Alexis, used as filler until they learned what had happened to her, made what Stacy knew but could not accept more eerie. And yet to turn off her living image seemed an act of disrespect; it was only John Damone she could not watch.

When she opened the door, Lord's mouth was swollen, and he seemed to look through her. He was white, as if he had been cold for hours.

Slowly, Stacy put her head against his chest.

His arms came tight around her.

For a moment, they stayed like that. Then she led him to the fire and brought a snifter of brandy. Next to them, Rachel reappeared on screen.

"There will be no televised execution," she said in a higher, rapid voice. "We now have confirmation that Phoenix *has* been captured, and is being brought to San Francisco. But the FBI has not revealed his identity, or the fate of Alexis Parnell, John Damone, or Anthony Lord. . . ."

Lord took a long swallow, staring at the flame.

"After you," he said at length, "I called my son.

"He thought I was in San Francisco. Were we still going to the beach, he asked me. I said yes, and that I had to get off now. I was just standing there in the phone booth. My voice hadn't changed at all, and I was crying. I didn't even know why."

She said nothing.

"I'm sorry, Stacy."

The words unloosed her horror and anger. "It's ten years of my life," she answered in a low voice, "and all I know is that I can't ever look back at that or him and feel the same. God, he must have hated me."

"It's more the opposite." Lord drank more brandy. "I think he wanted to know if you'd go through all this for him."

"But *Alexis* . . ."

"Something went wrong." His voice was flat. "I'm not sure what."

"Wrong," she repeated.

Lord still watched the fire dance. Almost as if he could not look away.

"He could have shot me right there," he said. "But he needed to do it on television."

Stacy was quiet. "John wanted to kill *you*," she said finally, "but Jamie was the first, wasn't he?"

He seemed to wince. In her confusing mix of hurt and horror and betrayal, Stacy felt both that this was right and that she had said something cruel. Reaching for his snifter, she took one sip, and put it next to him again.

"When I asked why he'd killed Alexis," Lord murmured, "all he said was, 'Because she saw my face.' "

It made her shiver. Then, in Lord's silence, she heard Rachel again.

"We are told that even at this late hour, millions across America are waiting in front of their televisions for their first glimpse of Phoenix, wondering who he really is. . . ."

Lord's eyes were still narrow.

"All those voices. . . ." When he turned from the fire, something in his face had changed. "When he said that, Stacy, he didn't have an accent."

"What do you mean . . ."

As he stood, turning to the screen, a streak of red split the night surrounding the Hall of Justice.

Red lights appeared in the distance, flashing without sirens. Moving toward him, they seemed to swirl on their own, suspended in a phalanx over Bryant Street.

Heart pounding, Parnell stopped at the corner, unsure of where to go.

As if to mirror this, the cameras and reporters hesitated across the street, torn between the front entrance and the underground garage. And then he saw the dark-haired woman start scrambling toward the alley.

Parnell clipped the press pass on his coat. The lights kept coming, too fast to stop in front.

He was running across Bryant, after the woman, when they swept past the main entrance.

A pack of the others bolted from the doors, scurrying between them. He ran at their backs through the alley, down the ramp to the mouth of the garage.

As the first lights swirled the corner, he was underground.

The garage was dim and enormous and dark at the corners, row upon row of cars facing sideways with drive-throughs between them. When the ramp ended, the mob veered sharply left toward a wall of elevators, footsteps echoing off cement. Parnell saw police lining the elevators and then a mop of dark curly hair already behind them with her cameraman, shoulder against the wall. Perfectly angled on the squad cars as they stopped.

At his back, the red lights flashed down the ramp.

The pack ahead kept pushing to the elevators, less people than bodies fighting for space, blocking his way.

Parnell broke from them and started running between two lines of cars, parallel to the wall they rushed toward. Sweating, chest constricted, legs feeling like lead. Torn between panic and elation.

Looking back, he saw the first squad car swing behind the mob, slowing as they pushed each other.

Parnell ran faster.

When he turned toward the woman, they were separated by four rows of cars. Sliding between them, he saw her mouth open, the man thrust his camera overhead with both hands. What she said was lost in shouted echoes.

He was one row from her now, a few feet at her back.

The first car stopped.

Parnell heard her voice above the tumult, speaking to her audience. "In seconds now, we will finally see the face of Phoenix. . . ."

As she raised to her toes, three sheriff's deputies burst from the car to the elevator. And then the second car was there.

Trembling, Parnell hurried through the final row, behind her. Heads kept moving in front of him: her, a deputy's, the cameraman's. No one saw him.

A line of vision opened between their shoulders.

In seeming slow motion, the rear door of the second car opened.

Moore got out, glancing behind him at the third car as it emptied two more deputies. There were shouts, flashbulbs.

With the woman, Parnell looked back to the second car.

Another man waited in the backseat. Only his legs and torso could be seen.

Moore reached inside to grasp his arm, and then the figure was bending through the door. Parnell saw the manacled hands first, then the muscled forearms and the top of his head. Dark, straight hair.

Grasping the revolver, Parnell could not take it from his pocket. The camera began to whine.

Then Damone stood, and Parnell saw his profile.

Parnell gaped in confusion. The woman thrust out her microphone, shouting to the murderer, "*Why* . . ."

Turning, he saw Parnell behind her.

Parnell felt himself raise the gun, still staring at his face, paralyzed by shock and disbelief. Then Moore and Rachel followed the killer's returning look of terrible recognition. As Rachel screamed, Moore started between them.

Instinctively, Robert Parnell raised cuffed hands, and covered his eyes. A shiver of horror and revulsion ran through Parnell to the trigger.

The gunshot echoed from her television.

In its reverberation, the man Stacy knew as John Damone fell back, blood coming from between his fingers.

"He's shot," Rachel cried out. "Oh my God, he's shot. . . ."

Moore was running toward her. Veering wildly to follow him, the camera found Parnell.

He stared at it, revolver to his temple. Almost shyly, he turned before he pulled the trigger.

Stacy and Rachel gasped together.

Facing Moore, Parnell's head snapped sideways. The agent caught him before he hit the cement, and then more cameras closed in around them.

There was blood on Rachel's blouse. "Colby Parnell has shot himself," she was chanting. "He shot Phoenix right in front of us. . . ."

The camera swung toward him.

Damone lay on his back, not moving. The dark stain beneath his head was like Jamie's.

Stacy turned, face pressed against Lord's chest. She was not sure which one of them was shaking.

CONSEQUENCES:
APRIL–SEPTEMBER

They stayed at Sea Ranch two more days.

Lord ran a fever, sleeping fitfully. Stacy did the things for him that friends do for each other; seeing what Colby Parnell had done, and knowing who Damone was, drained their desire to talk of it. Neither could turn on the television. They did not make love.

On the third morning, when Lord was better, they drank coffee in the window seat. He had talked to Moore; they were burying the Parnells that morning, and that Damone was their son had been confirmed from dental records. There was nothing more to do.

Stacy was quiet; the horror of what they had witnessed still showed in her eyes.

"It's not just John," she said finally. "It's that Colby and Alexis are dead, and what we did was meaningless."

For a while Lord gazed at the ocean. "All of it?" he asked.

She seemed almost to memorize his face. "There's such a lot to live with, Tony. One part, we can never really talk about, can we?"

Lord hesitated, searching for an answer. "That leaves a world of other subjects. I can see myself going through a day, and thinking of something, and then wanting to call you."

"Sometimes I'm really bad on the phone." She sipped her coffee, still watching him. "I guess it's that you have to fill it with words, and when I'm confused, they don't seem like what I'm thinking."

Lord felt awkward. "We can try mental telepathy, I suppose."

"Or letters." For the first time in days, Stacy smiled. "If I can read your writing."

When Lord returned to the office, Cass kissed him. Grinning, she said, "That'll have to hold you for fifty years or so."

"That's why I went to all that trouble."

Cameras and reporters still waited outside; his desk was covered with requests for interviews and calls about publishing deals.

"You're a hero, Tony."

"It didn't feel like that."

He put the phone slips aside, trying to do his normal work; his clients' demands started making him short-tempered. Then Cass came back to say that Rachel was on hold, requesting an exclusive interview.

"Now that I'm still alive," Lord said. "Hasn't she had enough?"

"What should I tell her?"

"Just ask her that. Even she'll understand."

As she closed the door, Lord knew that part of his anger was that Carson had left him feeling like a fraud.

Moments later, he dictated a brief statement, saying only that he had nothing to say.

The statement appeared the next morning, along with speculation that Lord was whetting the public appetite for a prospective book. That evening, at the beach, his son hung close to him; Lord wondered if he could ever hear the surf again and not think of Robert Parnell.

On Sunday he dropped Christopher with Marcia and Fred, went home, and wrote Stacy.

"Nothing's changed," he told her. "Except me.

"I want to look at what's happened, have more time with Christopher. But I'm behind on my cases, still see him every other weekend, and spent part of this last one at the office so I can keep up his support.

"I've finally figured out what my dad surely always knew: that most adults can change their lives only over time, even when they know what they should do.

"Guess I'm a slow learner.

"I don't envy what you must be feeling about Damone. But the success you've earned may help now—you're one of those rare people who's free to act, at least once you figure things out. In a while, I hope that makes this better.

"I'll be thinking of you, all along."

On the envelope, Stacy's headlong scrawl reminded him of her profile, hair falling across her eyes. It made him smile.

"Being glad you wrote," she said, "is the only thing I'm sure of. I wish I could send you and Christopher some of the time I have—Jamie's death remains this terrible blank, a question not quite answered.

"Because of John, I don't know if I can ever trust my sense of things or people as they appear to be.

"One of the things I hate him for is that I don't always remember to hate him.

"Another is how angry I am at myself. For ten years, while he was helping my career, it was too convenient not to look inside the person I thought I knew. So I helped bring down who he really was on the people who came close to me.

"I'm still not sure how many were hurt. Only that the price I paid is cheap.

"I can never accept that what we saw that night had to be.

"Sorry to burden you with this. But who else would I say it to?"

Thoughtful, Lord telephoned Moore.

"I need some information on Robert," he began.

"That depends." Moore sounded flat. "The money thing's alive again—how Robert financed the kidnapping. DiPalma's looking for Carson as an accessory, among other things."

Lord rubbed the bridge of his nose. "It's a favor I'm asking, Johnny. For Stacy's sake."

They talked for a while. Hanging up, Lord felt the hopelessness of his own situation, caught between Stacy and Carson.

"What strikes me about Robert Parnell," he finally wrote her, "is the care he took to hide himself.

"Moore says he started with the birth certificate of a dead infant—the real John Damone died in a Bronx orphanage—which got him in and out of the Army and then to Berkeley on the GI Bill. In the sixties that was easy enough to do: radicals and drug dealers had a network built on false ID, for anyone who wanted to disappear or simply beat the draft. Robert just reversed the process.

"Two weeks before he faked his own kidnapping, he enlisted in the Army as John Damone. Moore is certain that his plan was to hide the ransom money, enter the military on his enlistment date, and then pick up the hidden cash two years later—complete with new identity.

"When his father refused to ransom him, he followed the rest of the plan: Robert was nothing if not adaptable.

"He was also an actor, and a kind of genius.

"While they searched the country for him, Robert was in boot camp, a street kid with his hair shaved off. No one thought to look for him there. As far as the authorities were concerned, Robert had utterly vanished, murdered by his kidnappers. And the Army gave John Damone an identity completely his.

"By the time you met him, he'd been working on his role for seven years.

No sane twenty-one-year-old would expect all that. Neither did any cop or lawyer who dealt with him later, as important as he was to all of us.

"Especially me."

Lord put down the pen, wondering what to say about the trial.

"After James Kilcannon died," he finally wrote, "it was clear to me that Damone wanted to avoid publicity and, especially, testifying at the trial. I considered all the possible reasons for that except that he was someone else.

"When he finally did appear, the judge allowed no close-ups of witnesses. On SNI, he was a thirty-four-year-old man with a beard and a Bronx accent. Not even his own mother would have recognized him.

"I realize how haunting that last sentence is. But the larger point it makes is valid—especially applied to you, who knew him only as Damone, your manager and friend.

"I know you're looking at things pretty hard right now. I just hope you'll be fair to yourself, that's all."

For my sake, too, Lord thought. And then he realized that he could not yet bring himself to visit Harry Carson.

For several weeks, Lord heard nothing. He kept himself from writing until the evening he went to see Marcia and Fred.

"We were sitting in what had been our living room," he wrote later that night. "Christopher was in bed; Fred wasn't there. When Marcia brought out two glasses of wine, it was jarringly familiar.

"I'd come to ask for joint custody. What Marcia wanted to communicate was that she had broken up with Fred—that she 'just couldn't relate to his lack of ambition.' I hope I didn't look as stupefied as I felt.

"What I did was offer to ease her new burden by taking Christopher two weeks a month—perhaps she could pick up her education. I saw her face close: since the breakup, Marcia said flatly, she'd 'learned to value her nurturing side.'

"One of the unexplained effects of divorce is that it makes people talk funny.

"What was less funny is that she's been out three nights this week. But that makes me convenient; we finally worked out one week and unlimited babysitting privileges, to start. It was all very civil.

"I left before she changed her mind."

Lord stopped there. In Stacy's silence, he was talking to himself.

When her letter arrived, Lord ran upstairs to read it.

"I'm sorry not to have answered before this, but glad in a way.

"When I got to the part about John, I didn't know what to think, for many reasons. But every few days, I read it again.

"Yesterday, I realized how much it had helped.

"I've started fooling around with the piano. When I was young, my mom and dad loved Gershwin and Cole Porter, so I did, too. This morning I wondered how it would be to record some. Sure would whip the problem of *People* mag reading bullshit into my lyrics.

"But enough about me. I've stopped seeing your face on the tube. Does this mean you're unemployed, or spending all your time at playgrounds?

"How's Christopher?"

It was signed with a large script *S.*

Smiling, Lord sat to finish his letter.

"It means I don't film well," he answered, "and don't like some of the company I'd be keeping. But there's nothing wrong with Gershwin."

He stopped for a moment, thinking.

"I don't know how to say this, exactly, but I've missed the idea of you. I guess it's that I came away feeling there are better reasons for being friends than what we went through.

"I know the problems. But I liked you then. and miss you now."

Hastily, he mailed it, then started wondering if he had said too much, for this or any time. Looking at the calendar, he saw that she would get it a day or so before June second.

For the next two weeks of silence, Lord was certain he had lost her. Then Cass brought in a telegram:

> JUST REREAD YOUR LETTER STOP I GUESS YOU'RE NOT RECONCILING
> WITH MARCIA STOP OR RACHEL STOP SO MAYBE WE CAN GIVE THIS A
> WEEKEND
> HOW'S SEA RANCH STOP JULY TWELFTH

She stood in the door, smiling at him. For a moment, Lord didn't know what to do.

Stacy kissed him.

Her mouth was full and warm. When her body came against him, the way Lord felt went through them both. Her face fell to his shoulder; what followed was half-shudder, half-sigh.

Softly, he closed the door behind him.

Her head drew back with its click, eyes large and serious. "This is really going to happen, isn't it?"

They walked together to the window seat and sat in the afternoon sun, shoulders grazing.

"I don't know how to start with you, Tony."

The tightness in his chest stirred a memory. "Do you remember," he asked, "the first time you ever kissed someone?"

"Sure."

"I didn't know what to say or how to do it." Lord bent his face to hers. "Except like this."

He kissed her gently, lightly, with his mouth closed.

"That was all?" she asked.

"No," he said solemnly. "I gained confidence."

When he kissed her again, it was exactly the same, but longer.

Their foreheads touched.

"What happened next?" she inquired.

He smiled a little. After a moment, he said quietly, "I'm not sure I can wait that long."

The trace of an answering smile came to her eyes. They turned to the window; there was only sea grass, the ocean.

As they undressed, her look never moved from his.

When they were naked together, Lord held her. Gently, throat constricted, he stroked her hair and skin.

Her breasts touched his chest.

Beneath his fingers, he felt her skin change, then his own heartbeat. Her kiss was deeper. As they slid to the cushion, her hair fell beneath them.

Her arms went tight around him.

He felt their bodies meld together, moving slowly at first, without haste or thought or reservation, until he was lost in her. It was sweet and intense.

And then they were still, looking into each other's face. Lord could feel the difference in them; he could not bring himself to speak.

Smiling, she seemed to know this. "It's funny how faces change," she said softly. "You don't look arrogant to me, now."

"About you, I never was."

After a time, they lay beside each other, fingers touching.

"How was it really," she asked, "the first time you made love."

His face turned to hers, resting on the cushion. "Her name was Mary Jane Kulas," he answered, "and we were both Catholic and sixteen, and so ridden with guilt that I used two condoms."

Her eyes widened. "How was *that*?"

"Like making love to a radial tire."

Stacy's mouth turned up. "I meant for Mary Jane." ˌ

"Hard to say." Lord kissed her. "Given my finesse, her face never changed."

Stacy burst out laughing.

She was more drawn to him than she thought possible.

They made love in every soft or warm spot she could think of. Like their conversation after, this seemed to feed on itself.

For two days they talked of everything but Jamie or Harry Carson. They did not go near the television.

On the third morning, they drove up the coast and bought abalone at a place where no one seemed to recognize them. Their drive back was spent planning an elaborate cookout in a cove she knew, her favorite since childhood. When it was time for dinner, she led him along the cliffside until it cut sharply inland, to form a bay where surf pounded on a rocky beach. To the nearest side the small cove curled back toward them, sheltered from the wind and ocean. Its view was of the bay; a residue of deep aqua waves spilled across brown, fine sand. Ropes secured several flights of rickety wooden stairs which tumbled there from the cliff.

At twilight, between two logs, she started a fire as her father had taught her. Lord looked out at the bay. "Christopher would love this," he said. "He's nuts about water."

"How's he getting along now?"

He threw on another piece of wood. "Better, I think. He seems happy we're together more."

"I've never spent much time around children, really." Stacy finished her first glass of wine. "Since college, I've known I couldn't have any."

Lord reached for the chilled bottle. Watching him, she realized, foolishly, that she was hoping for some word or sign that this did not matter.

"I can always expose you to mine."

"A little *boy*," she said in mock horror. "With a loud voice and a penis and everything? What would I do with him?"

Looking up at her, Lord smiled. They ate the abalone, Stacy leaning against him, his down jacket around them both.

They were making Irish coffee when the telephone rang.

"It's for you," she told him. "Marty Shriver."

When Lord took the phone, she left the coffee half-made, and walked to the window.

"I'm sorry to call here," Shriver said slowly, "but Cass had the number, and I thought you might not know yet."

"What is it?"

"Harry Carson's dead."

Lord sat down. After a moment, he looked for Stacy; though it was dark, she was staring toward the ocean.

"How did it happen?"

"They're calling it an escape. Early this morning, Harry used a couple of old 'Nam tricks and got out the window with a rope made from bed sheets. Before anyone knew it, he'd knocked out the front guard and then hot-wired a Harley in the lot. They only heard him speeding out the gate."

"Was he shot?" Lord asked quietly.

Stacy became quite still.

"No—he got out onto Highway One and drove until the sun came up. It happened about seven, with the Highway Patrol after him. They were near San Luis Obispo, on some winding cliffs above the water, heading for a hairpin curve. Harry gunned the cycle to a hundred and just kept on going. Didn't even leave skidmarks." Shriver paused. "He meant to kill himself, Tony. A classic case, right to the bitter end."

In the last flat phrase, Lord heard how wasted Shriver was, and how sad. Then heard his doubt.

Finally, Lord said, "Is anything being done?"

There was silence. "There may be a service, if Beth and Harry's mother can get together on it."

"Then I'll be there." Lord hesitated. "Thanks for calling, Marty."

"Sure." A last, brief pause. "Talk to you later."

When Lord put down the telephone, she did not move.

At first, neither did he. In those moments he saw Carson shooting James Kilcannon, remembering that his mother smelled like strawberries, a thunderstorm breaking over the farm and Beth handing him a poem. The last time he and Carson had faced each other.

He could feel Stacy waiting.

For a final moment, Lord watched her straight, slim back. Then he walked behind her.

As gently and as clearly as he could, he explained that Carson was dead, why he had shot James Kilcannon, how Damone had used the concert money.

When she turned, tears ran down her face.

Lord felt helpless. "If I'd seen through Harry Carson, Stacy, the Parnells might still be alive. Right there, you can stop blaming yourself for Damone. . . ."

"So every time I look at you, I can remember that, like I can remember bringing Jamie to him." For a moment, the tears were the only part of her that seemed to move. "Oh, Tony, how did we think this could go anywhere?"

He gave a dispirited shrug. "This isn't the time. . . ."

She ran past him to the bedroom.

Lord passed the night in the window seat, too miserable to sleep, certain only that she had to be alone.

At dawn, sitting on the point overlooking the seals, he heard her come up behind him.

"Did you sleep?" she asked.

"Of course not."

For a moment, she was quiet. "Part of me always understood what you couldn't say. But *knowing* . . ." Her voice fell. "Tony, I never realized about the money."

He nodded, silent. After a time, he felt her watching him.

"When I found out, I wanted to quit." He shrugged at the hopelessness of that.

She sat beside him, a few feet away. There were circles beneath her eyes; she picked up pebbles and threw them in the water.

"It's so complicated, Tony."

He turned to her. "There was no way you ever could have understood Robert Parnell. He wouldn't have let you."

"I didn't mean just that." Her eyes closed. "Later, maybe at least we can talk about it. But I've got to be alone here now. Please."

* * *

Carson's service was in a white-frame Catholic church, a few miles from the farm. When Lord arrived, a handful of people were trickling between the photographers and television cameras Beth had barred from the inside.

She was waiting in the alcove. Nearby, Cathy peered out at the cameras; Lord saw that she had Carson's hair, but that her eyes were Beth's.

"She doesn't know what to think," Beth told him.

He nodded. "I'm sorry."

"I knew it would be like this. But she's old enough that I can explain a little. That her father was a good man, but the war did something to him."

Silent, Lord watched Cathy turn from the door, coming toward them. Then Beth squeezed his arm.

"Thank you for coming," she said.

As he entered, Rachel sat near the back, turning from his silent look of disbelief.

The mourners were sprinkled closer to the casket. Lord saw Carson's mother and Rob Bramley, Carson's friend from Vietnam, then Marty Shriver. When he sat next to him, Shriver raised an eyebrow; everyone else had the set, burdened look of those who know that whatever they say or do cannot be adequate.

The service was quiet and spare; Lord found that he still remembered it by rote. And then the casket was past him, borne by a few neighbors, outside.

Following, Lord saw Rachel hurry after it.

Rob Bramley was waiting on the front steps. They shook hands. "Give you a lift?" Bramley asked.

"Sure."

Cameras whirred around them. Then they got in a rented car and drove through the New Jersey countryside.

Bramley fidgeted with his tie. "I've been wanting to talk with you."

Lord turned to him, waiting.

"Look, I know how lousy you must feel. I mean, you wanted to help Harry. . . ." Bramley grimaced. "What you did is end up helping me."

"How, Rob?"

"The trial—it was the first I really looked at what happened. It's made all the difference in therapy, and everywhere. Sue—my wife—we're going to try again." He glanced across the wheel. "If you hadn't gotten me to testify, we never would have."

Lord gazed at him. "That's great," he finally murmured.

Bramley drove the rest of the way without talking.

As they parked, Lord touched his shoulder. "Good luck, okay? It'll mean something to me."

Bramley's face relaxed. They walked together to the cemetery.

The afternoon was bright and cool; a crisp breeze stirred the priest's robes as he spoke over the grave. Carson's mother sprinkled the first shovel of dirt, then handed the shovel to Beth. Beyond the white fence, on the grounds of an industrial park that had once been farmland, Lord saw cameras recording this.

When it was over, he told Bramley, "You go on, Rob. There's someone I need to talk with."

They shook hands again. As he said good-bye to Beth and walked from the graveside, Shriver was waiting by an entrance.

Both stood there for a while, leaning against the fence.

"I've always been curious, Tony. That morning, when you went to see Harry, what was it he wanted?"

For a moment, Lord looked back. Beth and Cathy stood alone, hands locked, beside Carson's grave. The moment had an odd, quiet beauty; then Lord caught the glint of a distant lens.

"It was strange," he said. "Harry didn't want me to go, because I might get killed. It was the one time I knew I'd gotten through to him."

Shriver was quiet for a moment, watching Beth. Then he put one hand to his eyes, and slowly shook his head.

A few weeks later, Johnny Moore bought Lord drinks.

He had chosen an Irish bar with dark wood, soft chairs, and all kinds of Celtic memorabilia hanging from the walls and ceilings. They both drank Bushmills.

"Until you caught him," Moore said over his second, "there was no way to know that Robert Parnell was still alive—he'd never been fingerprinted until the Army, as Damone. But after I'd read that file, it kept working on me that they'd never found his body.

"I wonder if that had occurred to Parnell. Before."

Moore looked up at him. "You wouldn't wonder," he said softly, "if you'd seen Parnell's face."

Lord nodded at his drink.

"The question is," Moore said after a time, "who'll play him in the movie? What with his recent windfall profits, Hart Taylor's formed a production company. To assure verisimilitude, he says, and the public's right to know. . . ."

"Oh, no—"

"In fact, he called the other day, wanting to hire me as a consultant. He even mentioned you."

Lord gave a short laugh.

Moore shrugged. "He figures what you must know would really juice up his story. He just doesn't know how true that is."

Lord watched his eyes. "You mean about the Parnells."

"That's one part," Moore said blandly. "Why Colby didn't ransom him, anyhow—the thing you told me about Robert and Alexis."

"Such a shame. Think what Taylor could do with it."

"The man would gag a maggot." Moore signaled for another round. "Considering all that's happened, how did it wind up with Stacy Tarrant?"

"Lonely, at the moment. Probably longer."

Quiet, Moore regarded him.

"Still, you're never going to say a word about Carson, are you. Not to me, or anyone. Not even for money."

Lord did not answer. When the drinks arrived, they sat untouched between them.

"Of course without you," Moore said finally, "DiPalma will never find the connection. Which is the only breakthrough that could keep him from going down the tube."

For another moment, Lord was quiet. Then he lifted his glass to Moore. "Absent friends, Johnny."

Moore smiled faintly. They drank together, in silence.

When Lord returned to his apartment, her note was waiting.

"Still don't like the phone," it began. "Especially now.

"But I do want to see you. I can't promise anything—even the minimum. I just don't feel right about how we left this.

"Is starting Labor Day all right, at Sea Ranch? I may even make sense by then."

Beneath there was a P.S.:

"If it's a Christopher week, that's okay."

Arriving with Christopher, Lord felt as edgy as she looked. After quick smiles and a few words, he shuttled Christopher's suitcase to an upstairs bedroom and his to another.

It was close to his son's birthday. The cake she brought out was covered with candles, the table with balloons.

"Lung power," Lord said.

With a fleeting smile, she turned to Christopher. "My mom always told me to make a wish. Then if I blew out the candles, it would come true."

"That's what *my* mom says, too."

Stacy angled her head toward the cake, still regarding him. "But can you do it?"

Dubiously counting the candles, Christopher then saw the red balloon nearest the cake. His eyes lit up. "Can I have that now?"

"Sure. It's yours."

He began to unknot it. "What about the cake?" Lord asked, and then Christopher triumphantly aimed his balloon at the candles and let go of the end.

Stuttering bursts of air blew out the candles and spattered a stream of frosting across the table. Moving from the frosting to Stacy, Christopher's look changed to horror and embarrassment.

For a moment, she watched his face.

"Damn," she said. "Why didn't *I* ever think of that?"

Christopher started laughing.

While he and his father washed the dishes, Stacy retreated to her piano. Lord recognized a few Cole Porter tunes.

"Sorry, Dad."

"Just be sure and tell Stacy that, okay?"

"Okay." Christopher handed him a dish. "Do you like her more than Mom?"

Lord turned to look down at him. "It's just that we're more alike, I think. Sometimes it's easier for us to understand each other."

His son considered this. "Can I listen to her play?"

"Wouldn't you rather wash dishes?"

Christopher ran to the living room.

After a while, the piano stopped. A couple of halting notes came that were clearly not Stacy's, then a few more. Once, Lord heard her laugh.

As he came in, they looked up at him with a half-smile of complicity. "Bedtime at the zoo," Lord told his son.

When he returned, Stacy was sitting in one corner of the window seat, reading a magazine. Delicate light and shadow were reflected in the glass; Lord saw himself sit across from her.

"How are you?" he asked.

She smiled a little. "Jumpy as a cat."

"Me, too." Lord glanced toward the upstairs. "It's a lot, all at once."

"He's a nice little boy, really. I think he senses I'm unsure of myself, even if he doesn't know all the reasons."

When Lord nodded, she was quiet for a moment.

"How is your work coming?"

"Better." He paused. "I've won a couple lately when I knew I should. That helps."

It seemed to make her thoughtful.

"I've decided not to do films," she said after a while.

Lord tilted his head. "Why?"

She turned to the window. "I just don't want to be that public, anymore."

He watched her, silent, watching his reflection.

"I've had some time with it, Tony. I finally remembered that you never would have known about Harry Carson if I hadn't come to you. We did this to each other, in a way."

She faced him then. Lord felt a look pass between them, filled with irony and knowledge.

Such a joke, he thought to himself, but what does it mean.

"What do you suppose," he asked softly, "Kilcannon would make of that?"

For a moment her eyes had a startled quality. Then they narrowed slightly, the trace of a smile that lingered when she spoke.

"That no one else but us will ever know the truth. I almost think he'd enjoy that."

* * *

They slept apart.

When he came down to breakfast, Stacy was in the window seat, watching the ocean. He gave her a tentative, querying look.

"I hate lima beans," she told him.

"What brought *that* to mind?"

"Christopher. Last night he was asking me to get some beets for lunch."

His face showed disappointment. "He's playing a trick on you, Stacy. I can't stand beets."

She grinned at him. "That's what *he* said," she answered, and then took them both to watch the seals.

What struck her was how Tony concentrated on what Christopher said or asked, so that his son knew at that moment that no one else was more important. She talked very little; it was enough to like him for reasons that had nothing to do with her.

When lunch was through, they went to the tide pools. The ocean had receded, leaving pockets of water on wet, shiny rock, filled with marine life. Christopher was drawn to small things—sea snails, mussels, miniature crabs. She dared him to stick a finger in the middle of a sea anemone; when it closed in harmless sucking, startling Christopher, she made the sudden slurping sound her father had used to trick her. Christopher laughed so hard he had to sit.

As they left the tide pool, Christopher ran ahead, kicking and throwing rocks.

"This must seem tame to him," she said.

"It's muscle memory—we usually play some kind of ball." Tony smiled after him. "Wait, though. He'll ask to come back tomorrow."

After dinner, Christopher led her to the piano, asking Tony to stay in the kitchen. When he had finished memorizing the notes to Brahms's Lullaby, he called his father in for a performance. She had a fleeting thought of Alexis; as Tony listened, pleased and careless, she remembered that he had not been there. The thought vanished.

When Christopher finished, Tony shooed him up for a story, and Stacy went off to shower.

She stretched it out, reflecting. Putting on a silk robe, she heard voices in the living room.

Tony had turned on the news, as she hadn't known him to do since the night they had learned who John Damone was. He watched intently, unaware of her behind him.

Softly, she walked upstairs.

Christopher was asleep, lineless, untroubled, yet so much like his father that Stacy smiled to herself. It was easy to love them, she thought wryly, as they slept.

Returning, she paused at the foot of the stairs.

Rachel Messer was an anchorwoman now.

"The major story from San Francisco's primary," she continued, "is the overwhelming defeat of District Attorney Ralph DiPalma.

"According to most analysts, the compelling factor was his failure to gain a conviction in the Harry Carson trial. Carson's recent death while attempting to escape seemed only to remind voters of their discontent. . . ."

Turning off the television, Tony saw her.

For a moment, they simply looked at each other.

After this, she suddenly knew, they would think in their own ways of Jamie or the Parnells, John Damone or Harry Carson. But she was somehow certain that this was the last time they might talk of that. It had all been said.

"Christopher's asleep," she told him. "Come to bed with me, all right?"

Lord awoke to find her gone.

When he got to the cove, Stacy and his son had rolled up their jeans and were shelling with a bucket. As the waves came in, she showed Christopher how to wait until the sand settled, leaving the water clear. They did not see him.

Lord decided to let them be.

Idly, he looked inside their picnic cooler. There was nothing but a single can of beets.

Opening the can, Lord commenced to eat the beets, imagining how crushed they'd be. And then he heard them turn, laughing from the water.

ABOUT THE AUTHOR

Richard North Patterson's first short story appeared in *The Atlantic Monthly* and his first novel, *The Lasko Tangent*, won an Edgar Allan Poe Award in 1980. Since then, he has written *The Outside Man* and *Escape the Night*.

Formerly a trial lawyer whose career included work with the Watergate special prosecutor, Patterson now lives in San Francisco with his wife, Lisa.

2